I'll Love You Tomorrow

I0543637

Book Three in the Trading Heartbeats Trilogy

Julie Navickas

The characters and events in this book are fictitious. Any similarity to real persons, living or dead, places, or events is coincidental and not intended by the author.

If you purchase this book without a cover you should be aware that this book may have been stolen property and reported as "unsold and destroyed" to the publisher. In such case the author has not received any payment for this "stripped book."

I'll Love You Tomorrow
Book Three in the Trading Heartbeats Trilogy
Copyright © 2023 Julie Navickas
All rights reserved.
2nd edition

ISBN: (ebook) 978-1-958136-45-4
(print) 978-1-958136-46-1

Inkspell Publishing
207 Moonglow Circle #101
Murrells Inlet, SC 29576

Edited By Toni Kelley
Cover art By Fantasia Frog Designs

This book, or parts thereof, may not be reproduced in any form without permission. The copying, scanning, uploading, and distribution of this book via the internet or via any other means without the permission of the publisher is illegal and punishable by law. Please purchase only authorized electronic or print editions, and do not participate in or encourage piracy of copyrighted materials. Your support of the author's rights is appreciated.

DEDICATION

I'll Love You Tomorrow is dedicated to my mother, Tracey, and my grandmother, Marlene.

From an early age, you both instilled in me a love for reading, an appreciation for storytelling, and a healthy fascination with scripted drama. Thank you for allowing me to watch *Days of Our Lives* when I was ten-years-old. I'm a romance novelist now because of it.

"Like sands through the hourglass, so are the days of our lives."
MacDonald Carey

JULIE NAVICKAS

CHAPTER ONE

Lauren

"I'm sorry, boss, I can't come in today." Miguel's sigh crackles through the phone before I can even respond, and it hits harder than it should—because when things fall apart, Miguel is the one who usually catches them. "You know I would if I could," he continues, voice heavy with regret. "But it's my niece's birthday dinner. It'll break her heart if I miss it."

I close my eyes and press the phone flat against my desk, bracing myself. For one reckless second, I want to ask him to come anyway. Want to say *please, I need you*, the way I've never had to before—because he's always shown up without being asked. "No. No—don't apologize," I say, forcing steadiness into my voice. "Family first. Always."

The words sound practiced. Automatic. I drag in a breath and open my planner, my fingers trembling as they skim the list of bartenders taped inside. The names blur, shrinking, vanishing one by one. No Miguel. Angela's on vacation. Tony's on medical leave. Carmen requested this weekend off.

My throat tightens. "Besides, you asked for this date off

way in advance. I'm just... grasping at straws."

"Did someone call in?" he asks. Because of course he does. He always sees the problem before I finish explaining it.

I scoff, a brittle sound. "Brandon called in sick thirty minutes ago. His shift starts in ten." My eyes flick to the clock on the wall. Ten minutes. Nine. Eight...

Miguel groans, long and low. "I'm really sorry, Lauren. You know I'd be there if I could."

And that's the thing—I do know. My mouth curves into a small, tired smile, even as everything inside me feels like it's cracking. Miguel has always been my favorite for a reason. He's the one who stays late without being asked. The one who fixes problems before they reach me. The one who treats this place like it matters—like *I* matter.

"I know you would," I say softly. "And I love you for it." I swallow. "But go. Enjoy the party. I've got it covered."

There's a pause. "What're you going to do?" he asks, and now the worry is unmistakable.

I let out a quiet laugh. "Pray nobody orders anything I can't Google."

"Wait," he starts. "You're not—"

"I am," I say, pushing to my feet so fast the backs of my legs slam into the chair, sending it rolling away. "It's me or we close the bar. And we really can't do that on a Saturday night."

Not after three straight months in the red. Not when every good night feels like borrowed time.

"Boss—"

"It's okay," I cut in, because if he keeps talking, I might break. "Please tell Izzy happy birthday for me."

"Wait, I can prob—"

"Nope! I've got it!" I say quickly, ending the call before he can offer the kind of help I know he doesn't actually have.

I shove my phone into my pocket and turn toward the window just as the lights of the new restaurant across the street—*Food for Thought*—flicker on, bright and smug. Because even the universe knows I'm hanging by a thread tonight. Then the intercom buzzes and I tap the blinking red light. "Yeah?"

"There's a Greg Owens on the line," the host says. "He says he's the newest rep with our vendor for plastic goods."

Of course he is. And of course today is the day everything decides to pile on with one more thing that costs money. I inhale through my nose—slow, measured—like I can breathe my way out of this. "Yep. Put him through."

The line clicks over, and I pull my shoulders back, smoothing my expression into something calm and capable. The version of me I sell to customers and vendors and anyone who might smell panic. "Greg?"

"Oh, hello there!"

"Hi, Greg. This is Lauren Templeton, owner of Pier Ninety-two. What can I help you with?"

"Just confirming your delivery on Thursday at four."

"Got it." I scribble it onto my calendar. "And feel free to use the east alley when you arrive—it's easier for deliveries."

"Will do, ma'am. See you Thursday."

The call ends, and the office goes quiet except for the hum of the overhead lights—too bright, too sterile, too unforgiving.

I stare at the note. Thursday. Four o'clock. Plastic goods.

How much is this shipment going to cost? And what happens if I can't pay it?

I rub my thumb over the ink like I can smudge the problem until it disappears. My eyes drift to the ledger on the corner of my desk—the one I've started avoiding. Three straight months in the red. Rent. Payroll. Repairs. Supplies. And now another delivery I can't cancel because cancellations have consequences, and consequences are the one thing I can't afford.

People are already leaving. Not in dramatic, fiery ways. In quiet, exhausted ways. One vacation that turns into a resignation. One "family emergency" that becomes "I found something more stable." One bartender calling in sick and never coming back. Pier Ninety-two is bleeding out in small cuts, and I'm standing here with my hands full, trying to plug holes with sheer willpower.

For a second, I let myself feel it—the fear that maybe I'm not going to fix this. That maybe I can't. Then the clock ticks again, and reality snaps its teeth. Brandon's shift starts in—

I don't look. I don't need to.

I head out of my office and march down the back hallway, heels striking the tile with more confidence than I actually possess. The freezer rattles loud enough to vibrate my bones as I pass, the kitchen humming with prep and heat and the faint scent of garlic and desperation.

I grab an apron from the hook and tie it around my waist with a sharp, angry tug—like if I cinch it tight enough, it'll hold the whole place together.

I built this. I'm not losing it.

"What're you doing?"

I turn and find Louis staring at me, eyebrows lifted, the kind of look that says he's trying to decide whether to stop me or call someone.

A laugh bubbles up—too bright, too wrong—and I let it out because if I don't joke, I'm going to crack. "Losing my virginity. Wish me luck."

His eyes widen just as I push through the double doors, weave around tables, and slide behind the bar like I belong there. Like I haven't spent the last year pretending everything is fine while my staff list shrinks and my expenses grow teeth.

Janine looks up from polishing a glass, a grin already forming. "Umm… where's Brandon?"

"Out sick." I plant my hands on my hips and force my stance into something solid while my stomach tries to cave in. The rows of liquor bottles stretch in front of me—endless, glittering, smug. Labels blur together in the dim lighting like they're written in a language I never learned.

And I think, *this is insane.* I think, *I'm insane.* I think, *but it has to work anyway.*

"You can go," I tell Janine, because sending her home is cheaper than paying her to stay. Because I can't keep bleeding over time. Because I can't keep asking my people to save what I'm supposed to be leading. "Your shift is over."

Her brow furrows. "Wait. Are you—"

I snatch the dishrag from her shoulder and laugh again, but this time it comes out edged. "Why does no one have any faith in me around here?"

She presses her lips together, unconvinced in a way that feels personal even though it isn't.

"Pour this, pour that," I mutter, nudging her toward the door. "I can't be that bad, can I?"

Janine backs out with her hands raised. "Whatever you say, boss." But the second she disappears through the double doors, my confidence evaporates like it never existed. The bar feels bigger without her. Colder. Like it knows I don't belong.

I stare at the bottles—a hundred of them, each one another way for tonight to go wrong. My stomach tightens so hard it almost hurts. I pull out my phone and fire off a group text to Mavis and Casey.

Me: SOS, girls. I need to cover the bar at Pier Ninety-two tonight and I have no idea what I'm doing. Experienced bartenders urgently needed. Also: if I die, tell everyone I tried.

"Lauren?"

I look up to find Ricky leaning over the counter, smirking like this is entertainment. "What're you doing back there… and in an apron?"

I blow out a breath, forcing a smile that tastes like metal. "Filling in. I'm officially out of bartenders."

His fingers tap the counter. "No offense, but do you even know what you're doing?"

I lift my phone like it's a weapon. Like it's the only lifeline I've got. "I've got experts on speed dial."

"Well then," he says, far too cheerful, "I'll start you off easy. Appletini. Scotch on the rocks with a twist. Two house reds. And a Moscow mule."

My cheeks heat as I grab a copper mug, praying I'm at least holding the right thing. "This one," I say, trying to sound like I'm in control, "right?"

He grins. "Phone a friend, girlfriend. I just wait tables."

I swallow hard and glance down. The first reply pops up—because Mavis doesn't wait for emergencies. She senses them.

Mavis: Former bartender at your service. And I have nothing better to do than watch your brother stare at his laptop like it's going to kiss him back.

Relief hits so fast it's almost dizzying. My chest loosens on a shaky exhale, like I've been holding my breath since I hung up on Miguel.

I don't even type back. I just hit FaceTime and the call connects on the second ring. I prop my phone against a dusty whiskey bottle and her face fills the screen—warm lighting, familiar eyes, hair pulled back. She looks tired in that pregnant way that's both soft and strong, but the second she sees me, her expression sharpens.

"Okay," she says, all business wrapped in sisterly sweetness. "How bad is it?"

I try for a joke, but my voice wobbles. "Define bad."

"Lauren." One word. Firm. Anchoring. "Talk to me."

My gut clenches. I hate that it's happening again—hate that my fear is showing, hate that I'm one more problem away from cracking right behind the bar where everyone can see.

"I'm out of bartenders," I admit. "Like... out out. And

there's a line. And Ricky just ordered things that sound like a prank."

Mavis's eyes widen—then she grins, the kind that says *I've got you* before she even speaks. "Okay. Breathe. I'm here. We're doing this together."

I blink, relieved all over again. "How do I make an appletini?"

She laughs and adjusts the camera like she's settling into her role. "God, it's been a minute." Her hand drifts over her baby bump—unconscious, protective—then she points with her other hand. "First, grab a shaker."

I scan the counter like I've never seen a bar in my life, snag a metal shaker from the sink, and rinse it out. "Okay," I say, holding it up to the phone like she can inspect it. "Now what?"

"Vodka," she says. "Pour until I say stop."

My hand shakes as I tip the bottle. Liquid glugs into metal, loud in my ears, like the sound is announcing my incompetence to the entire restaurant.

"Stop!" Mavis laughs, delighted and horrified at the same time. "Oh my, God, Lauren. That's gonna be a strong drink. But umm, apple schnapps next."

I switch bottles, my fingers a little steadier just from hearing her voice. Sweet apple hits the air and I exhale like that scent alone can keep me from spiraling.

"Now Cointreau," she adds.

I pour the orange liquor in and swallow. "Now what?"

"Shake it, sister."

I clamp the lid on and shake like my life depends on it— because in a way, it does. Because I can't afford another bad night. Because if customers stop coming, if word gets out that Pier Ninety-two is slipping, I don't know what I'm going to do.

"Okay, okay—that's good!" Mavis holds up her hands, laughing. "Chilled martini glass. Apple slice on the rim. Then you're done."

I blow out a breath and slide the drink across the bar like

I meant to do that the whole time. "You're a wizard," I whisper.

"Hardly," she says, eyes bright. "What's next?"

"Moscow mule." I groan and yank my hair into a low ponytail like I'm gearing up for battle. "Please tell me this one doesn't require an advanced degree."

"It requires ice," she says, dead serious. "Step one, breathe. Step two, ice—"

I glance at the growing list of orders, the clink of glass and low buzz of conversation rising like a tide. And my stomach drops. Because this is going to be a very long night.

And then it is. Because after an hour, Mavis begins to feel nauseous and Josh hangs up on me.

Time doesn't so much pass as it does blur—measured in ice scoops and shaker tins, in the rip of ticket paper and the constant slide of glass across wood. The crowd thickens one body at a time, the hum turning into a roar without anyone ever announcing the shift.

By the time I finally look up and try to orient myself, another hour has vanished. My shoulders ache from bracing against the counter. My ponytail slides loose, damp strands sticking to the back of my neck. I smile on autopilot, nod on autopilot, apologize on autopilot.

"Two old fashioneds!"

"Three lemon drops!"

"Can we get another round of—"

I reach for a rocks glass and nearly knock over the bitters. My hands permanently shake now. Just slightly. Just enough that I notice. Because it's too loud. Too hot. Too much.

But that's when the back door creaks open. I don't turn at first. I don't have time to turn. But I feel it—the shift in the air. The way the space behind the bar fills differently.

Miguel doesn't say anything. He just slips in beside me like he belongs here and grabs the stack of untouched tickets without comment. Scans them once. Twice. Then he moves. Confident. Efficient. Calm.

He clears the backlog like it's nothing. Shaker in one hand, pour spout steady, ice scooping in perfect rhythm. He doesn't rush—but he doesn't waste a second either. Drinks start sliding across the bar faster than the printer can spit them out.

"Thank you!" Ricky calls, but Miguel just nods.

I blink hard. And my throat tightens in a way that has nothing to do with the noise. Because the wall isn't gone—but it's smaller. Manageable. Shared.

He sets down a finished margarita and finally looks at me. Really looks at me. But my eyes are glassy and I hate that he can see it.

He pauses mid-reach. For half a second, the chaos continues around us—orders shouted, glasses clinking—but in the narrow space behind the bar, it goes quiet. He steps closer and his hands come up, warm and steady at my waist, and he pulls me in. Just enough that my forehead bumps lightly against his chest.

I exhale as his chin brushes the top of my head. Then he presses a soft kiss to my forehead—gentle, grounding, certain. I don't say thank you. I don't need to. Not with him.

He squeezes once, then releases me like we both understand there's still work to do. "I got you," he says quietly. And I know he does. He's the only one lately who ever does.

***

I twist the knob and shove the door open just as the garage seals behind me. Templeton Manor welcomes me home the same way it always has—too big, too silent, too aware of my presence.

The grandfather clock at the end of the hall strikes twelve. And each chime lands heavy in my chest, marking time the way it has my entire life.

I slip off my shoes and pad across the hardwood floors, every step creaking like the house sighs along with me. My feet ache with a deep, bone-level soreness—the kind that doesn't fade with rest. I dump my purse onto the kitchen counter and yank open the fridge, grabbing a bottle of water.

The cold rushes down my throat, but my jaw screams in protest. The muscles around my mouth ache from hours of smiling—forced, practiced, endless—like if I just smiled hard enough, no one would notice how close everything is to falling apart.

"So... fucking... tired," I mutter, pressing the cool plastic to my forehead like it might numb the ache behind my eyes. But that's when I hear it again.

Drip. Drip. Drip.

The faucet has been leaking for weeks—ever since the first time I noticed it and told myself I'd call someone tomorrow. Tomorrow turned into next week. Next week turned into when things calm down. And things never calm down.

In the quiet, it's a metronome. In the dark, it's a taunt. In my sleep, it worms its way into my dreams until I'm counting drops like they're seconds I'm losing.

Drip. Drip. Drip.

Each one lands with surgical precision, drilling straight into my skull, tapping on my nerves like a reminder I can't shut off. It's just one more thing I can't fix, one more small failure echoing through this house.

I squeeze my eyes closed, jaw tight, bottle still pressed to my forehead like I can hold myself together by force.

Drip. Drip. Drip.

Then a notification chimes from the depths of my purse, cutting through the steady rhythm. I dig through receipts and keys until my fingers close around my phone. But I quickly realize, I shouldn't have bothered once I see who it's from.

Mitch: `Why are you just getting home now? It's past midnight.`

I roll my eyes, but the motion does nothing to stop the

ache tightening my chest. Because his question lands like a blade—sharp, precise, and far too familiar.

"Why the fuck do you even care, Mitch?" I snap, ripping the hair tie from my ponytail and letting it snap against the counter. Then my thumbs fly over the screen.

Me: Are you actually home? Did I wake you or something?

I tilt sideways and peer up the dark staircase, squinting for any sign of light. But of course there's nothing there. Then my phone pings again.

Mitch: No. I'm at Josh's. The alarm went off when you opened the garage door. Are you okay?

A sound breaks loose from my chest before I can stop it—a small, broken sob. Months of swallowed hurt surge upward, burning my eyes and tightening my throat. I drop the phone onto the counter and fold forward, my cheek pressing against the cool granite as tears spill freely.

"Are you okay?" I repeat aloud, the words competing with the dripping faucet. A laugh bubbles up, sudden and unhinged, slipping out between tears. "No, Mitch," I spit. "I am *not* okay."

My phone lights up again, but this time, it's not a text. *Oh, God.*

I swipe to answer, already hollowed out. "I'm fine," I say, the lie tasting familiar.

His voice shakes, just enough to pull at something tender in my chest. "Then why are you getting home so late?"

I close my eyes. "I didn't have a bartender tonight."

The pause on the other end stretches—thin, brittle. "So...?" he presses.

And something in me snaps. "I had to pour drinks, Mitch!" I say, the words breaking loose before I can soften them. "I'm out of staff and I can't afford to lose another Saturday night." My voice cracks, and suddenly the fight drains out of it, leaving only the truth. "Why do you even care? None of this matters to you. I don't matter to you.

Remember?"

The silence that follows hurts worse than if he'd yelled. Then he exhales, tired and distant. "You know, Lauren, I'm really exhausted. I was just calling to check on you. God forbid I'm still allowed to do that." Then the line goes dead.

I stare at the phone like it might ring again. Like he might call back. Like he might say *wait*— or *I didn't mean that* or *I still care*. But it doesn't.

The tears return immediately, slipping down paths they know too well—quiet, relentless, and practiced. "Fuck you, Mitch," I whisper at first, then louder, the sound cracking open in the empty kitchen. "Just—fuck you."

I shove my phone into my purse and yank the whole bag off the counter like I'm ripping the moment away with it. I barrel out of the kitchen, the hardwood protesting under my feet. By the time I hit the top of the stairs, my thighs burn and my head pounds, fury and grief twisted so tight in my chest I can't tell where one ends and the other begins.

I shove my bedroom door open and collapse face-first onto the mattress. Instinctively, my hand finds his pillow— still fluffed, still unused, still waiting for someone who hasn't slept here in months. I press it to my face and inhale the faint traces of pine and cedar, already fading, already leaving me.

My phone buzzes near my feet and I jolt, heart leaping straight into my throat. For one stupid, traitorous second, hope flares—bright and painful.

Is that you, Mitch?

I snatch it up with shaking hands, thumb ready to swipe before I even look. But then I do. It's Casey's name that glows on the screen—not Mitch's. And hope collapses so fast it almost makes me dizzy. I squeeze my eyes shut and let out a tight, defeated breath. But I answer anyway, forcing my voice into something that won't give me away. "Hey, Case—"

"Lauren!" Her voice bursts through the speaker, bright and loud. "I just saw your text! We just got home!"

"Are you guys—"

"We've been out celebrating!" she interrupts.

And I can't help it. I bury my face deeper into Mitch's pillow. Because while I'm lying here mourning my marriage and my barely surviving restaurant... they're out *celebrating*. I swallow and clear my throat. "Celebrating what?"

"Austin's new job!"

The words land like a punch. Austin's. New. Job.

My eyes snap open as fresh tears spill over. I push myself upright, scrubbing my cheeks with the heel of my hand. "New job?" I choke out.

"Lauren!" Austin booms into the phone, drunk on joy. "You'll never believe it! I passed the Illinois Bar Exam— and Casey got me a new job!" He laughs. "You're talking to the new lead attorney for the Chicago mayor!"

Of course I am. Miraculous Templeton twin number two— collecting wins like they're inevitable.

"Oh," I manage. "Wow. That's... incredible. Congratulations." I hug the pillow tighter to my chest, like it might hold me together. "That's perfect for you."

"It is!" he shouts. "Wouldn't have happened without my Casey girl."

Static crackles as the phone clatters. "Oh, sorry!" Casey laughs. "Dropped it. But hey—did you survive tonight?"

I swallow hard. "Yeah. Mavis saved me. I owe her big time."

"I would've helped, too! I'm sorry!"

"It's fine," I say quietly. Too quietly. "You had something to celebrate." I pause, already too tired to pretend. "I'll talk to you tomorrow, okay?"

"Isn't it, like... really late?" she asks.

"It is." I close my eyes. "Go to bed. Tell Austin congrats again." I hang up before she can say anything else and toss the phone aside. I stare at the ceiling, the weight settling in fully now—heavy, immovable. "Why is everything always so easy for you, Austin?" I whisper. "You and Josh... you get everything."

I roll onto my side and yank open the nightstand drawer, pulling out my frayed purple dolphin. "Finn," I whisper, clutching him to my chest. And the memory floods in— Pacific Park, Mitch's teenage grin, the way his arm wrapped around me like I was already home.

"I love you, Mitch Benson," I cry into his pillow. "Please don't leave me."

I don't want a divorce. I just want you back.

CHAPTER TWO

Mitch

"It needs another layer," I say as I drop to my knees and dip the taping knife back into the tub of gray mud. I drag my knife across the drywall, pressing hard until the metal scrapes, the thick sludge spreading smooth beneath my hand.

"Dude, we're just adding to the timeline," Ryan says behind me. "Now it's gonna be at least two more days before we can sand again."

I shrug, lips pressed tight. "We can't do this half-assed, Ry."

"I'm not saying we should," he grumbles, sinking down beside me and dipping his own knife into the bucket. "But we're already chasing the clock on this flip."

I scrape the excess mud back into the tub. It clings to my fingers, drying fast in the creases of my knuckles and under my nails. A thick smear coats the bare skin where my wedding ring used to sit, like the job itself remembers something I'm pretending not to.

"We'll get there when we get there," I mutter as my pocket vibrates. "Hold that thought," I say, abandoning the

19

knife and pulling the device up to my ear. "Hello?"

"Mr. Benson, it's Dave Jensen. You got a minute?"

I straighten slowly, dread sliding up my spine like cold syrup. I catch Ryan's eye and mouth, *I've gotta take this*, then weave through the mess of sawhorses and drywall dust until I'm off the back porch and standing on the lawn. Only then do I lift the phone fully to my ear.

"Yeah," I say, forcing my voice steady. "What's up? I thought I filled out everything you asked for."

"Mostly. Mostly," he replies—too calm, too practiced, like he's reading from a script he's said a thousand times. "You completed the intent-to-file form, but you didn't sign it. No signature means we can't proceed."

My stomach drops.

I really didn't sign it?

"And," he continues, "while you *can* bring it in yourself and we'll contact your wife to get her signature, if you're going the 'part as friends' route, most clients just sign together. It's cleaner. Faster. It removes the back-and-forth."

My throat tightens around nothing.

"If you believe she's willing to proceed amicably," he adds, "then get her signature. It documents her choice to proceed and it speeds the process significantly."

There's a pause, just long enough for the words to sink in.

Get her signature.

Like it's a permission slip. Like it's a contractor approval. Like my marriage is a form that needs ink in the right place.

My chest constricts, breath catching hard. I stare out at the yard, at the bright grass and the quiet sky, and all I can think is—I haven't even said the word *divorce* out loud yet to Lauren. I haven't had the balls to string the right sentence together. And Dave is talking about us signing papers *together*.

My hand tightens around the phone until the plastic bites my palm. My jaw locks. And a hot pulse beats behind my eyes.

"Right," I manage, voice rougher than I want it to be. "So… I need to come in and sign. And if I think she'll agree to the 'part as friends' option, I should get her to sign, too."

"Exactly," Dave says, satisfied. "Can you swing by this afternoon?"

"I'll… swing by this afternoon," I say finally.

"Good. Belinda will be at the front desk until five. Stop by anytime and I'll move things forward next week. I'll be out of town until Sunday afternoon."

I nod even though he can't see me, the casual efficiency in his voice hollowing me out. Ending my marriage is just another checkbox on his list. I swallow hard, shoving my free hand into my pocket and curling it into a fist. "I'll be there soon," I choke out.

The call ends and I jam the phone back into my jeans, like shoving it away will shove the whole conversation away with it. But I can't move. I just stand here in the yard, boots planted in the dry grass, staring at nothing. The world tilts— subtle at first, then sharper—dizziness washing over me in a warm wave.

Get her signature.

The words loop in my head like a nail I can't stop tonguing.

"Benson!"

I flinch and look up. Ryan steps out onto the porch with his phone pressed to his ear, one hand braced on the doorframe like he's holding the whole jobsite together. Which—most days—he isn't. I am.

"The white shaker cabinets are on backorder for almost three months," he calls. "Can we just go with the farmhouse style on this one?"

My brain tries to process it. Cabinets. Backorder. Farmhouse. Words from a life that isn't currently imploding. But I couldn't give one flying fuck about cabinets right now.

Ryan lowers the phone and starts toward me, watching

my face with that careful look he usually reserves for when I'm about to tear something out because someone cut a corner.

"Can I place the order?" he asks, like he's asking permission to breathe.

His voice hits my ears as distant noise. Static. I squeeze my eyes shut and pinch the bridge of my nose, pain slicing clean through my skull.

Ryan ends the call and closes the distance. "Hey." He slugs my shoulder lightly—half brotherly, half *snap out of it*. "You okay?"

I open my mouth, but the truth is too big to fit through it. "Yeah," I manage, but even I can hear how thin it sounds. I swallow, forcing myself to stand straighter. Be the guy who leads. The guy who calls the shots. The guy who has the plan. "I just—forgot to do something kind of important."

Ryan's expression shifts—less joking, more alert. "Important like... *important?*"

I nod once. Sharp. Final. Like if I make it decisive, it'll feel decisive. "Can you handle things here this afternoon?" I ask.

Ryan nods. "Yeah. Yeah, man. I've got it." He tries to lighten it, play-punching my stomach like always. "Just— uh—the cabinets—"

"You pick," I cut in, already moving, because if I stop again I might not start. I yank my keys from my pocket and head for my truck. "Whatever you think will sell," I call over my shoulder.

"Wait—what? You never let me choose!"

I don't turn around. I can't. I grab the handle and haul myself into the driver's seat like it's an escape hatch. "First time for everything," I yell back, forcing the words out the window like a joke as the engine catches.

I throw the truck into reverse, gravel crunching beneath the tires while I back away—leaving behind wet drywall, unfinished walls, and a life I'm about to sign my name away from.

Within minutes, I merge onto the freeway and let the truck settle into a steady hum. I roll every window down and the cool breeze whips through my hair, sending the long strands dancing across my face.

By the time I take the exit ramp, my chest feels tight. Too tight. The Jensen Center for Family Law comes into view—a squat red-brick building with dark, reflective glass. I select a parking spot near the curb, kill the engine, and pull out my phone. My last exchange with Lauren stares back at me, frozen in black and white.

Lauren: Are you actually home?

My jaw tightens. "You don't even want me in our bed," I mutter as my fingers begin to tap out a new message. "Unless everything lines up just right. Why does it matter where I sleep?"

Me: Can we talk? Are you free tonight?

I send it before I can second-guess myself, then shove the phone into my pocket and climb out of the truck.

I have to get this over with. I'm sick of living in limbo.

Inside, the building smells faintly of lemon cleaner and paper—too clean, too orderly, like nothing messy has ever happened here. A woman with short brown hair and red-rimmed glasses looks up from behind the counter and smiles, bright and professional.

"Hello! Welcome to the Jensen Center for Family Law. How can I help you?"

"Uh—yeah." My gut clenches. "Mitch Benson. I forgot to sign a—"

"Oh! Mr. Benson." She lights up, already turning. "Dave left it right here for you." She reaches into a folder and slides a single page across the counter, spinning it so my handwriting faces me. Everything is filled in—careful, deliberate, unmistakably mine—except the last line.

"Just there at the bottom," she says gently, tapping the empty space. "You can sign it now."

I swallow and pull the paper closer, gripping the pen she

offers. But the room narrows. The words blur in and out, my vision tunneling until there's nothing left but that blank line waiting for my name—patient, inevitable. Because this is it. One stroke of ink and everything changes.

I brace my hand against the counter as my breath catches hard in my chest.

Lauren's smile flashes behind my eyes—easy and unguarded, the one she wore the day we met, like she already believed the world would meet her halfway. Then her laugh follows, warm and full, the sound that used to drag me out of my own head without even asking permission. And then her voice—soft, familiar—slides in close, like she's right behind me with her chin near my shoulder, saying my name the way she always has.

I've loved her since we were kids. Since the first second. That part of me never questioned it, never needed proof, never learned how to do anything else. Even now, with everything we've broken between us, I still know it—steady as a pulse. I love her. I always will. But love isn't enough to keep us from bleeding out. And we can't keep going like this.

"Are you okay, Mr. Benson?" Belinda asks. She squints at me, concern edging into her voice. "You look… sweaty."

I drag the back of my hand across my forehead and it comes away damp.

What the hell is happening to me?

I look back at the line. The pen. My name, hovering just out of reach.

I could sign it right now. Nothing is stopping me. Except… everything.

"Um," I say hoarsely, setting the pen down. It clacks too loudly against the counter. "Can I—can I take this with me? Drop it off in a few days?"

Belinda's smile softens, like she's seen this moment before. She nudges the paper toward me instead of pulling it back. "Of course. Take all the time you need. I'll let Mr. Jensen know you're having second thoughts."

Second thoughts?

The phrase lands wrong—too small for what's happening inside my chest. I *did* decide this. I spent months deciding it. I just didn't expect the decision to feel like standing on the edge of something I might not survive.

"It's not—" I shake my head, grabbing the form and stepping back until my hips bump the glass doors. "It's not second thoughts. Mr. Jensen said I should get her signature, too."

That sounds right. Reasonable. Clean. If this is really a *part as friends* thing… then she should sign. We should do it together. That's what people who end things the right way do. Right?

Outside, sunlight hits my face as I step into the breeze, still gripping the paper. I fold it carefully—too carefully—and open my truck door. Once inside, I shove the form into my wallet and snap it closed, like that might lock the decision in place. But my finger scrapes against something sharp.

"Shit," I mutter, touching the papercut to my tongue. Blood wells up, hot and metallic. I pull the culprit free—a folded piece of grid paper—and my breath leaves me all at once. Because it's my blueprint. Of a pencil-drawn rocking horse. Every line familiar. One I sketched late one night without planning to—without admitting what it meant.

My chest tightens as the image comes alive—dark hair, a pink bow, a little girl rocking back and forth in a future I want more than anything.

A drop of blood falls onto the paper, staining it red. And I smear it away with my thumb before stuffing it back into my wallet. My phone pings and Lauren's name lights up the screen.

Lauren: Sure, come on over. I'll make dinner.

I drop the phone into the cupholder. It lands with a sharp *clink*, like it's hit something small and solid. I glance over with a frown. But when I lean toward the passenger side to look, whatever it was has already slipped loose—skittering out of sight beneath the seat.

***

The salty bite of frying bacon hits me before my hand even reaches the doorknob.

"Lauren?" I call as I push my way inside Templeton Manor, already toeing my boots off on the mat without looking.

"In the kitchen!"

I follow the familiar path, each step pulling a tired creak from the old floors like they recognize me. When I round the corner, I spot her at the griddle, wrist flicking with practiced ease as she flips a pancake. The smile on her face hits me square in the chest—easy, unguarded, the same one she's worn since we were kids stealing glances across playground swings.

"Breakfast for dinner?" I ask, even though this is the kind of thing we've never needed to ask out loud.

"My favorite."

"Mine, too." The words come automatically, like a reflex. Like everything else between us. And that's what makes my stomach twist. Because the words I came here to say don't belong in this room. They sit heavy and wrong in my chest, poisoning the air. "Uh… how can I help?"

You'll ask me to warm the syrup. You always do.

"Maybe just… warm the syrup?" She gestures to the small white carafe behind her with the spatula.

"On it," I mumble, reaching for the bottle. The syrup pours out thick and slow, maple-sweet, folding itself into the scent of bacon and batter until the kitchen smells like years of Sunday mornings and lazy, rainy nights. Like a life I'm about to blow apart.

"I'm surprised you're here, Mitch," she whispers.

I turn as she slides the last pancake onto a plate. She tucks her hair behind her ears—another unconscious habit,

26

another knife to the ribs—and shrugs. "I'm kind of afraid to ask why, though."

Guilt presses down hard enough to make my shoulders sag. I set the carafe in the microwave and punch the start button, grateful for the hum filling the space while my words scatter instead of lining up.

I swallow. "Yeah, umm, I think we should talk."

She bites her bottom lip and drops her gaze to the plate, like she's bracing for what comes next. "Yeah. Okay. I get it. You want to make it official. Sign something…"

Her voice breaks and her shoulders cave forward. The sight of it—of her already folding in on herself for something I haven't even finished saying—hits me like a bruise from the inside out, so hard I almost miss the microwave's sharp beep slicing through the room.

She swipes beneath her eyes with the heel of her hand, quick and practiced. Like she's been rehearsing this moment without me. "Dinner first, though," she says softly. "Okay? Just one last time…"

The words *one last time* land hard—quiet, devastating. Like she's already saying goodbye. My throat tightens. My chest aches. I nod because if I open my mouth, I won't be able to stop what comes out.

I turn away too fast, yank the microwave open, and grab the syrup. The heat bites my skin, sharp and deserved. "Fuck," I mutter, shaking my hand—grateful for the sting, for something that hurts where I can name it.

She rolls her eyes—affectionate, automatic—and gathers the plates, carrying them into the dining room. I follow without thinking, dropping into my usual chair beside her like there's still a tomorrow.

"This looks really good," I say. "Thank you for dinner."

She shrugs, already cutting her pancake in half. "You know I never mind."

I scoot closer to the table, but the wallet in my back pocket digs in—right into my thoughts, my conscience. Because the form inside it is the whole reason I'm here.

Still, I pick up my fork and force the moment back into place, like I can postpone the collision if I don't look at it head-on. I shove the divorce train off the tracks for now, drown my pancake in syrup, and take a bite.

"Good?" she asks, chewing a piece of bacon.

"Perfection," I say, and mean it. "Like always."

The problem is, that's how it's always been—easy. Automatic. Like we still know the choreography even when the music's stopped. And that's exactly why staying for dinner is a mistake. I know it with the same quiet certainty I know where the spare batteries are kept, or that she takes her coffee with too much cream when she's stressed.

Her cheeks flush as she dabs her mouth with a napkin, eyes dropping to her lap. But as I spot the tears gathering in the corners of her eyes, they hit me harder than any fight ever has—quiet, contained, and somehow worse because she's trying so hard not to let me see.

Silence blooms between us, wedging itself into every bite, every breath. My pulse skitters. My throat tightens. And I can feel the moment tipping—one more second and I'll say the thing that ends us. Panic claws up my spine, so I do what I always do when I'm about to lose something. I grab for noise. For normal. For anything that isn't the truth. I reach for the first topic that comes to mind, even though it's a sore spot.

"Hey," I say, swallowing hard. "Umm, Mavs mentioned she helped you bartend the other night. What happened at the restaurant?"

Lauren lifts her water glass, but her eyes stay on mine. Like she heard the scramble in my voice and clocked it for what it was. For a second, I swear she knows I'm tossing out conversation like sandbags, trying to keep the flood from breaking through. Then she takes a slow sip and answers anyway, calm as ever. "Food for Thought."

I frown. "Huh?"

Lauren sets her glass down with a careful sort of steadiness—like she's placing a lid back on something that wants to spill. She draws in a slow breath, shoulders lifting and falling, her gaze dropping to her plate as she smooths her expression into something workable.

"The new place across from Pier Ninety-two," she says, voice even. "First they stole my customers. Now they're stealing my staff."

"Who?"

"Brandon." Her mouth tightens on the name. "He called in sick that night. This morning he emailed his two weeks' notice." She shoves a bite into her mouth, jaw clenched as she chews, forcing herself to swallow before she continues. "Took a job across the street."

"What a douchebag."

She snorts despite herself. "Definitely a douchebag." Then her smile completely fades. "But he's not the only one. Tammy and Christian quit, too. I'm short-staffed everywhere—bar, floor, kitchen." She pushes her empty plate away. "Reservations are down. The freezer's busted. No one can seem to fix it. Pier Ninety-two—"

"Will bounce back," I cut in, sliding my plate aside. The words come out too fast—too practiced—like we're still playing our old roles. Me steadying her. Me smoothing the edges. "It's a setback," I add, trying to keep my voice light. "That's all. The new place will lose its shine. You'll hire new staff." I hesitate, then push anyway, because I can't seem to stop myself. "And I can take a look at the freezer."

The offer hangs there between us, heavier than it should be—another instinctive reach toward normal when nothing about this is.

A small smile tugs at the corner of her mouth—the one that says she sees right through me. "How about you take a look at the kitchen sink first?"

I wrinkle my nose and glance back toward the kitchen. "What's wrong with the sink?"

"It leaks," she says, widening her eyes for emphasis, already stacking plates. No drama. No helplessness. Just problem-solving. She carries the dishes into the kitchen like this is simply the next thing on our to-do list.

I follow her, and then I hear it.

Drip. Drip. Drip.

I grip the faucet, turn the spray on, shut it off, and watch the water sneak where it shouldn't. "Old ass plumbing," I mutter, dropping to my knees and opening the cabinet.

I slide onto my back and shove my head inside, running my fingers along the pipes, cataloging the problem. But the cabinet door jabs me in the ass. I huff, tug my wallet free, and toss it aside so I can scoot inside farther. It's bone dry though.

"Probably just needs a new cartridge," I call out, already certain. "I think I've got a spare."

"Of course you do," she says, like this is the least surprising thing in the world.

I head to the garage, already feeling lighter. Useful. Needed. I yank open the third drawer of my tool chest and grin when I see it—replacement cartridge, adjustable wrench, exactly where I left them. "Bingo," I whisper, slamming the drawer shut. Then I call, "I need to shut the water off—hang on!"

The basement air slaps me cold and damp as I duck down the stairs just inside the door. Goosebumps rise on my arms the lower I go, but I don't hesitate. I twist the shutoff valve closed, listening for the change in pressure like it's second nature.

"Thanks, Mitch," Lauren says when I return, leaning against the kitchen entryway, arms folded tight, and eyes glassy—but she's steady. Always steady.

"You know I never mind," I say, and I mean it more than I probably should. I slide back under the sink and set the wrench, twisting hard. But nothing budges. Instead, the wrench slips, scraping skin from my hand. "Damn it."

"You okay?" she asks immediately.

"Yeah." I blow out a breath. "It's corroded. I need pliers."

"Channellock?" she calls, already moving toward the

garage.

"Perfect."

I slide back out and let my head rest against the cabinet, eyes falling shut for half a second.

"Eight or twelve inches?" she calls from the garage.

"Eight," I answer, a smile tugging at my mouth before I can stop it—because I've always loved this about her. That she knows the difference. That once upon a time, she let me teach her.

She comes back with a pair of yellow-handled pliers, and when she passes them to me, the words slip out on instinct. "Thanks, Peaches."

Her cheeks flush as her fingers brush mine. She grins, pointing toward the counter. "I did make a peach cobbler earlier…"

Straight. To. My. Heart.

With a twinge in my gut, I retreat beneath the sink, clamp the pliers tight, and wrench hard. The pipe gives with a satisfying snap and the corroded cartridge slides free. I swap it out, hands steady now, movements sure. Tighten. Seal. Done. "That should do it," I say, sliding out.

"I'll turn the water back on," she says, already halfway out of the room.

I stand and lean against the counter, watching her go, taking in the kitchen—the worn corners, the familiar light, the space that still feels like home no matter how badly we're breaking it.

"Did it work?" she calls as she heads back.

I turn the faucet on. Water sprays clean and funnels down the drain. I shut it off. No drip.

"Yep," I say. "Just needed a new cartridge."

She hops up onto the counter, relief softening her shoulders. "Thank you. It's been dripping for weeks. Been driving me crazy."

I frown. "Why didn't you call me?"

She shrugs. "I didn't think you'd come."

My chest tightens, the ache settling deep as I pull in a

breath that still doesn't feel like enough. When I finally find the nerve to look up, she watches me—eyes locked on mine, steady and unflinching.

"Just say it, Mitch," she whispers. "We both know you didn't come here for pancakes. Say what you came here to say."

The world tilts, and suddenly I'm eight-years-old again—Rosewood Elementary, the cracked blacktop, the swing set squealing under too much weight. Her small body collides with mine in line, her embarrassed laugh bursting out like it's a secret meant just for me. I've loved her before I knew what loving someone cost.

"Lauren..." But her name barely makes it past my throat.

Her tears spill over, unchecked. "Just say it," she whispers, dragging her hands through her hair, smearing tears across her cheeks. And something inside me gives. I step closer without thinking and my palms land on her thighs, memory taking over, gripping denim I've touched a thousand times. She inhales sharply, and my body responds like it always has—traitorous and hopeful.

My mouth finds hers—salt and tears and history—everything we've been, everything we're losing. My heart slams so hard it feels like it might crack my ribs.

"How did we get here?" she sobs, pulling me closer like proximity alone could undo the damage. But the truth hits like lightning—hot, blinding, unavoidable.

"We got here," I say, forcing each word out like it's cutting me open, "because we stopped putting *us* first."

Her breath stutters. My fingers slide into her hair, anchoring myself for half a second before I press a kiss to her forehead and pull back.

She grips my arms, desperate to hold on. "How can you think that, Mitch?"

"Come on, Lauren." I shake my head, exhaustion flooding through every inch of me. "You know how. It's... everything."

"Like what?" She wipes her nose with the back of her hand. "Please. Let's talk about it. There has to be a way to fix this."

Fix this? I almost laugh, except nothing about it is funny. Because where do I even start—at the beginning, when it was *us*, or somewhere in the middle when it became *everything else*? How do I summarize years of feeling like I've been slowly erased? Not in one blowout fight, not with a dramatic betrayal—just the quiet kind of disappearing. The kind that happens when your place gets smaller and smaller until you realize you're living in the margins of your own marriage, waiting for a turn that never comes.

"—the restaurant," I choke out, starting with the obvious time suck. "Let's start there."

She frowns, tilting her head, seemingly confused. "What about the restaurant?"

"Lauren." I scrub a hand over my face. "Pier Ninety-two has taken over our lives. It's twenty-four seven for you."

"Twenty-four seven?" Her eyes narrow.

"Yes. It's all the time." The words leave my mouth like a match striking—small, quick, and suddenly there's no taking it back. And once it's out, I can't stop myself. My pulse kicks hard, my hands go cold, but the truth has teeth now. If she wants to talk—if she's really asking—then I have to tell her. Not the watered-down version. Not the one I've been feeding myself so I can survive another week, another month, another year.

So, I allow the dam to break...

"We live and breathe your fucking restaurant," I say, the words coming faster, harder, like they've been waiting years for permission. "It's there when we wake up and when we go to sleep. It hijacks every conversation, every weekend plan, every night that was supposed to be ours." I shake my head, the pressure in my chest finally cracking open. "I kept telling myself it was temporary. That it would slow down. That eventually, I'd matter again."

"That's ridiculous," she snaps, folding her arms.

"You've always mattered."

Disbelief hits first—sharp and hollow. I just stare at her, waiting for it to flicker across her face. Recognition, shame, anything that says she's been living in the same marriage I have.

But there's nothing. And that hurts worse than the argument. Worse than the words I've already thrown. Because it means she isn't even choosing this consciously—she doesn't see what she's doing. She doesn't see what she prioritizes, and how often it hasn't been our relationship.

"You're blind, Peaches." But the nickname tastes wrong now—spoiled by everything underneath it. I shove my hands into my pockets so I don't reach for her, don't undo myself. "You really don't see it."

I take a breath, trying to steady the tremor in my voice, but the words keep coming—because they've been waiting.

"And it's not just Pier Ninety-two," I say, shaking my head. "Even when it's not the restaurant, it's the Templeton name. It's always about living up to it. Protecting it. Making damn sure you never fall short of what anyone expects."

I swallow, heat rising behind my eyes. "And where does that leave me? The guy who doesn't come with a legacy or a reputation or a last name people respect—just... me. Always trying to fit into a story that was written long before I showed up."

"Mitch," she says, exasperated. "You've been part of this family—"

"For far too fucking long, Mrs. Templeton." The words tear out of me, raw and ugly, years of resentment finally clawing free.

"It's Templeton-Ben—"

"It's not," I cut in. "It's not. And you know it." A hollow laugh slips out as I rake a hand through my hair, heat rising fast under my skin. "You never use my name—because what kind of clout does a fucking Benson have in this town, huh?"

It isn't the whole truth. I know that. But it's the truth my gut can't stop reaching for.

Mavis and I both came up the hard way—different versions of hard, but the same lesson carved into us early. Make do, keep your head down, don't ask for more than you've earned. We grew up in a foster home full of hand-me-downs and busted knuckles, with a last name nobody ever said with respect. And we grew up learning what people take from you the second they decide they've got you figured out.

So when the Templetons smile and gesture like we belong, my chest still tightens. They've handed us a seat at the table, sure—but some part of me can't shake the feeling it's conditional. That we're still being measured. Still being tolerated. Like we're the footnote they'll never quite stop reading as less-than. Like we don't belong on the invitation—even when we're standing in the same room, together.

Her voice drops to a whisper as she slides off the counter. "That's not fair. I can't help who my family is, Mitch. You know that's not fair."

"Do I?" I scoff, the sound bitter even to my own ears. "My God, Lauren." I shake my head slowly, like maybe if I move enough the truth will rearrange itself into something I can live with. "You really don't see it."

I step around her, because if I stay right in front of her—if I look at her too long—I'll start backpedaling. The truth is out now, raw and undeniable, and the expression on her face—confused, hurt, genuinely blindsided—snuffs out the last small part of me that hoped she'd finally understand.

"Where is this coming from?" she calls after me. "We've been married seven years! You've never—ever—said any of this!"

I shove my boots back on and grip the doorknob, my stomach rolling violently as she follows. "Then it's about fucking time I did." Bacon and pancakes churn in my throat as I turn back to her. "It's overdue, Lauren. Long overdue. I should have said all of this a long time ago."

The weight of it all crashes down at once—every missed night, every second-place finish, every time I swallowed what I needed because hers, or her family's, was louder. I drop my gaze to the floor like it might hold me up, squeeze my eyes shut, and when I finally speak, my voice splinters. "Even if we could... how were we ever supposed to bring a baby into this mess?"

Her breath catches. For a beat, the fight drains out of her, leaving only the hurt.

"Like that wasn't already breaking my heart," she says, voice thin and raw. Then she looks at me—really looks at me—and whatever softness is there hardens into something sharper. "But don't act like that was something you were still reaching for," she adds, each word measured and cruel in its precision. "You checked out long before tonight, Mitch. You don't get to grieve a future you already decided to walk away from."

I just stare at her. For a second, I don't move. I don't breathe. I can't. The disbelief is physical—like someone shoved their hand into my chest and squeezed. Because that wasn't just an argument. That wasn't just a line. That was proof. Proof that we've been standing on opposite sides of the same life, looking at completely different futures, and calling it a marriage.

Something in me goes cold and hollow all at once. I think about all the nights I let myself imagine it anyway—the weight of a baby against my shoulder, Lauren's laugh in the next room, a tiny pair of shoes by the door. I think about how I kept grieving it quietly, alone, like a secret I wasn't allowed to want too loudly. And now she's saying it like it meant nothing. Like it was never real.

"Maybe it could've been real," I snap, the words ripping out of me before I can soften them, before I can save either of us from it. I yank the door open hard enough the hinges complain. "If we didn't have to schedule sex on a fucking calendar!"

The words hit her like a slap. She freezes—breath

caught, eyes glassy—mouth parting like she's trying to find her footing in a room that's suddenly tilted. And I hate myself for saying it like that. I hate that it came out as rage when it's really grief. Grief for the baby we'll never share. For the version of us that used to feel inevitable.

"You know what—just forget it," I mutter, because if I stay one more second, I'll either fall apart or I'll fold. "It doesn't even matter anymore."

I bolt down the porch steps and cut around the side of the house toward the driveway, my chest burning like I've been running for miles, my hands shaking so hard I can't even make a fist.

Behind me, her voice slices through the night. "I didn't sign whatever the fuck you came here for!"

I stop for half a beat, swallowed by the dark, the cold, the ache.

Neither did I, Peaches. Neither did I.

CHAPTER THREE

Lauren

The water crashes over my hands, scalding hot, but I don't pull away. I stack the dirty plates in the sink and drown them in soap, watching the syrup slide and cling like it refuses to let go—sweet, stubborn, and impossible to rinse clean.

"How fucking clueless are you, Mitch?" I shout at the empty kitchen, slamming the sponge into the rising pool of steam. I dunk my hands back in and grab a plate, scrubbing until my wrist aches. "You might be able to fix a leaky sink," I mutter, anger vibrating through every word, "but you have no idea what it takes to keep a restaurant open." I drag the sponge in harsh circles, jaw clenched. "Staffing. Licenses. Payroll. Vendors. Insurance." I rinse the plate and shove it into the rack. "None of which can be fixed with a pair of fucking pliers."

My eyes flick to the abandoned wrench on the counter, then past it to the window. The Templeton grounds stretch endlessly—perfectly trimmed lawns, the ocean flashing in the distance as the sun sinks low, painting everything pink and gold. Beautiful. Untouchable. The same view I've stared at my entire life from this exact spot, washing dishes and carrying expectations I never asked for.

"And I do too, use your name," I mutter, grabbing another plate. "It's on my driver's license. My checkbook. My passport." I scoff, the sound brittle. "Lauren Templeton-Benson."

But the words catch in my throat. Because how do I introduce myself?

The answer comes too fast, too honest—and it makes my stomach drop. Because I *don't* say Benson. Not out loud. Not when it counts. Not when I'm shaking hands and smiling and being *Lauren Templeton* in rooms full of people who already know exactly who I am before I've even opened my mouth. I keep it clean and simple and familiar— my family's name sliding out like it belongs there, like it's the only one anyone expects to hear.

And Mitch's name... stays tucked away where it's required. On forms. On legal documents. In the places no one notices.

The realization lands like a punch. I freeze, sponge dripping in my hand, as the house seems to inhale around me—family history pressed into every wall, every staircase, every expectation that existed long before Mitch ever did.

Okay, maybe he has a point there...

I dry the dishes and slide the plates back into the cabinet. They clink together, the sound snapping my thoughts straight to Pier Ninety-two's kitchen—orders flying, pans clattering, controlled chaos barely holding together. The place I've bled for. The place I'm trying to save.

"What am I supposed to do?" I say aloud, setting the glasses back where they belong with hands that won't quite steady. "My restaurant is circling the drain, and you're mad at me for pouring every ounce of myself into keeping it open?" I shake my head, heat burning behind my eyes. "That's not fair."

The thought comes sharp and mean, like a blade I could turn on myself. Maybe I should just sell the fucking place.

List it. Hand over the keys. Let someone else inherit the stress and the schedules and the constant, gnawing fear that one more thing will break and I won't have the money—or the energy—to fix it. Let Pier Ninety-two become a memory instead of a fight. Let my dream get boxed up and priced out like it never mattered.

Would that make you happy, Mitch?

That's when my toe bumps into something soft. I look down and spot his wallet. Worn leather. Familiar. Open and spilled like it wants to be seen. I pick it up, my thumb brushing the edge, and my breath catches when I see his driver's license. His eyes stare back at me—steady, patient, the same eyes that used to look at me like I was enough.

"Damn you," I whisper, snapping it shut. "Why can't you see how hard I'm trying?"

My finger grazes a folded paper tucked inside. And curiosity sparks, sharp and unwelcome. I flip the wallet open again, guilt pounding as I spread its contents across the counter. "I shouldn't be doing this," I mutter, even as my hands keep moving. "I shouldn't be doing this."

I pull out cash first. Then a business card for a woman named Shawna Sweeting. I scowl and flick it aside, her perfect smile skidding across the granite like she has no right to be that calm in my kitchen. Then I unfold the crumpled paper beneath it. *Intent to file for divorce.*

My chest tightens as I skim the page, legal language blurring through the burn in my eyes. Boxes. Checkmarks. Clinical options laid out like menu items for the end of a marriage. *Contested. Uncontested.* And then—there it is. *Part as friends.*

I stare at that line a second too long, like if I blink it'll turn into something else. Like it'll explain itself. Like it'll make sense. But it doesn't.

My gaze drops to the section that's been marked. The choice he made. The one that tells me what he wants this to be. *Part as friends.*

A sound slips out of me—sharp and breathless, not quite

a laugh, not quite a sob. Because friends? Friends don't say the things he said. Friends don't take a kitchen argument and turn it into a legal document. Friends don't leave paperwork like this buried under cash like it's a receipt.

I drop the page like it scorched me. "Well," I choke out. "There it is." My voice sounds distant, hollow, like it's coming from the end of a long tunnel. My ears ring. Cold sweat beads along my hairline as my fingers find the name at the bottom—steady, printed, undeniable. *Attorney Dave Jensen.* Right there in black and white.

I brace my arms on the counter and fold over them, pressing my face into my hands like I can hold myself together by force. "What do I do?" I whisper.

Panic surges, but the strategist in me fights to the surface—cold, practical, already making a list. If Mitch has a lawyer and paperwork, then I need help. I need Austin.

I reach for my purse and drag it across the counter with shaking hands, but my elbow clips the spread-out contents of Mitch's wallet. Paper skitters across the granite, sliding like the truth tries to escape before I can look at it.

That's when another paper slips free. This one is thicker and blue-edged. I unfold it slowly, bracing for another legal form. But instead, the penciled sketch of a rocking horse stares back at me.

The air leaves my lungs in a sharp, broken gasp. My knees wobble as memories crash in—bathroom tiles cold under my feet, the endless plastic tests shaking in my hands, always one lonely line where there should've been two.

"Oh, Mitch," I sob, tracing the pencil lines with trembling fingertips—over the curved runners, the careful shading, the neat list of materials written in his steady handwriting. He planned this. He imagined it. He built it in his head.

Tears come hard and fast, smearing the graphite, blotting the paper until the drawing wavers like it can't hold its shape either. I remember the first version of us—the hopeful, ignorant, *it'll happen for us* version. The version before we were reduced to calendars and apps. Color-coded windows. Fertile days circled in red. Alarms set, not for romance, but for obligation. For timing. For probability.

I remember how I stopped asking *do you want me* and started stating *now is statistically optimal*. How every late-night internet search told me the same thing. Best chances, best positions, best frequency, best days. How hope slowly turned into math. How sex stopped being something we fell into and became something I scheduled—something I *managed*—because that's what you do when you're trying to keep a dream alive.

"We wanted the same thing," I whisper, the words cracking as they leave me. But wanting turned into tracking. Into checking boxes. Into chasing percentages instead of each other. And somewhere along the way, I lost sight of us—of why we wanted it in the first place.

My knees buckle and I sink to the floor, pressing the blueprint to my chest like it's the only solid thing left in the room, like if I hold it tight enough I can hold us. Because at some point, it wasn't that we stopped wanting. It's that we started wanting in different directions—until we were so far off course, we didn't even recognize the map anymore.

***

"Lauren?"

The sound of my name hooks under my ribs and yanks. I surface with a jolt, eyes snapping open, cheek stuck to the couch cushion. In the same breath, the front door swings wide open.

Josh steps inside, keys dangling from one finger, his gaze sweeping the room like he's bracing to find something broken. "Whoa." He stops short and his keys go still. "Are you okay?"

I squeeze my eyes shut. Because the burn rushes back instantly and I let my head fall against the couch. The last few hours slam into me all at once. Mitch in the kitchen.

The paper in my hands. That word—*divorce*—sitting in my throat like a stone.

"I've been calling you for like three hours," Josh says, closing the door behind him. His voice is careful, like loud sounds might crack me. "I even called the restaurant, but Miguel said you left around lunchtime." He kicks his shoes off without looking and drops onto the cushion beside me. Then he presses the back of his hand to my forehead. "Are you sick?"

I shake my head, too fast—too sharp—like the motion is the only thing keeping me from splintering open. "No."

"Then what's wrong?" His hand falls away. "Why aren't you answering your phone?"

I stare at my brother like I've forgotten how to translate pain into words. Because if I say it out loud, it's real. Permanent. Un-retractable. So, I don't. Instead, I reach beneath my hip and pull out the folded paper. Then drop it into his lap because I can't trust my voice to carry the weight of it.

Josh's eyes track the page. His jaw tightens as he reads, the muscles working like he's swallowing something bitter. "Oh," he mutters.

"Yeah." The word comes out thin. Bitter. Almost a whisper. "Oh."

I push myself upright and tap the paper once with my finger. The click of my nail on the page is small and stupidly loud. "I guess I knew it was coming," I say, forcing the sentence out piece by piece. "But Mitch came over tonight for my signature."

Josh's gaze snaps to the bottom. "You didn't sign." His head lifts, something hopeful flickering in his eyes before he can stop it. "Wait. Neither of you signed."

I snort, wiping at my face with the back of my hand like I can erase the whole night. "Don't get too excited."

"Why not?"

I roll my eyes and tug my hair into a low ponytail. "Because he ran out of here after we started arguing." I nod toward the page. "I found this in his wallet after he left."

Josh exhales slowly and props his elbow on the armrest, resting his chin in his palm. His voice softens. "Tell me what happened?"

I shrug, even though my neck aches from holding myself together for too long. "The usual," I say, but the words feel like not enough the second they leave my mouth. "We didn't see eye to eye. I got mad. I yelled. He yelled back. Then he left."

"But you didn't sign anything," he says quickly, trying to grab onto the bright spot like it's a lifeline. "That's good. Austin should—"

"Do you really think I'm that stupid, Josh?" The snap in my voice surprises even me—sharp enough to sting the air between us. I rub at the knot forming at the base of my neck, like I can physically unknot the rage and grief twisted there.

Josh flinches. "Lauren, I'm sorry," he says immediately, reaching for my shoulder. "I just came to check on you. I didn't mean—"

"You're fine," I cut in, because if we keep going, I'm going to start crying again, and I can't—*I can't* do that while he looks at me like this.

I push myself to my feet before the conversation can dig any deeper. And that's when the second paper slips loose. It flutters down in slow motion, like it has all the time in the world, and lands face-up on the carpet between us.

"What's that?" Josh asks, eyes flicking to the paper on the floor.

"It's nothing." But the lie comes out too quick. I scoop up the rocking horse blueprint, my fingers clumsy with panic, and fold it tight—too tight—like I can crease the memory out of it. I shove it into my pocket just as the clock chimes nine, the sound loud enough to make me flinch. "It's late. Shouldn't you be home with Mavis?"

It's a deflection I've used my whole life. Reroute the conversation, point the attention onto someone else, make the problem about logistics instead of pain.

Josh doesn't bite though. He leans forward, elbows on his knees, concern etched across his face. "Mavs is fine," he says. "It's you I'm worried about."

I drag in a breath because his worry is the only thing keeping me upright. I force my shoulders back like posture can pass for stability. "Josh... it's really sweet of you to come check on me, but I'm fine. I'll—"

"Lauren." My name is quiet on his tongue, not a warning—an anchor. He stands and takes my hand before I can retreat. His grip tightens, warm and steady, grounding me in a way my own body hasn't been all night. "Talk to me. Please?"

I try to pull my hand back. But Josh doesn't let me. He just... stays. Like he's making a choice to be here with me, even if I'm being difficult. Even if I'm sharp-edged. Even if I'm trying to push him out with both hands.

"Did you forget I've been through this, too?" he adds softly, and that's the thing—there's no judgment in it. Just empathy. Just a reminder that he knows what it's like to feel your life tilt on its axis and not recognize the room you're standing in. He gives me a crooked, understanding smile, the one that used to get me through middle school bullying and college finals and every moment I swore I didn't need anyone. "Come on. You don't have to carry it alone."

Something in my chest splits—not dramatic, not loud. Just a quiet break, like a seam finally giving way after you've been pulling on it for too long.

"I just..." My voice falters and I swallow hard. "I don't know what to think anymore." The words shake out of me, unsteady and honest. "And I don't know how to fix it. Or if I even can."

Josh nods like he understands exactly what that feels like. He gives my hand one gentle squeeze and tugs my arm toward the kitchen. "Come on," he says. "Let's get a drink and talk through it."

I follow because I can't not follow him. Because even in

the middle of everything, my brother's love is a lighthouse—steady, unflashy, impossible to ignore. I hop onto a barstool as he rummages through the cabinet and comes back with two wine glasses, setting them down with a soft clink.

"Red or white?" he asks, like he's giving me an easy choice because the rest of the night has been nothing but impossible ones.

"Red," I say quietly. Then, because my mouth is finally moving and I can't stop it, I add, "And a lot of it."

Josh smiles as he selects a pinot noir and reaches for the corkscrew. He pauses just long enough to glance at me— eyes gentle, voice even. "All right," he says. "I'm listening."

I press my palms against the cool granite and let out a breath. "I don't even know where to start," I say, my voice shaking. "This whole thing is a fucking mess." I take the glass Josh slides toward me and drink like I'm trying to quiet something. "Mitch thinks Pier Ninety-two matters more to me than our marriage." I shake my head, heat building behind my eyes. "Like he doesn't see what it takes to keep the doors open."

Josh doesn't jump in right away. He watches me the way he always has—like he's listening for what I'm not saying. Then he tips his glass slightly. "So," he says carefully, "you're saying he feels pushed aside because of the time you spend there?"

"Pushed aside?" I echo, then sag a little. "I guess. I don't know." I scrub a hand over my face. "The restaurant is failing, Josh. Badly. I have to be there right now if I want any shot at saving it."

"What's wrong with it?" he asks.

I bark out a hollow laugh. "You mean what's *not* wrong with it?" The list spills out before I can stop it. "Staff quitting. Customers disappearing to the place across the street. Equipment breaking. Bills stacking up. Every day feels like I'm plugging leaks with my hands."

Josh lifts a hand. "Okay, so, real problems."

I nod, frustration buzzing through me. "Problems I can handle if Mitch wasn't standing here looking at me like I'm choosing something else over him."

Josh leans back against the counter, swirling his wine. "He really believes that, you know."

"Yeah," I say quietly. "He told me tonight. That I prioritize Pier Ninety-two more than him. More than us."

Josh studies me over the rim of his glass. "Do you?"

But his question lands like a shove. I choke on my wine, coughing hard. "Josh! How can you even ask me that?"

He doesn't flinch. "It's not an accusation. It's a mirror." He shrugs. "You do spend a lot of time there."

"I own the damn place," I snap. "Of course, I do. Whose side are you on here?"

He stays calm. Always does. "I'm not on anyone's side," he says. "Which means I'm not here to tell you what you want to hear. I'm here to help you see what's underneath." He drains his glass and nudges mine. "More?"

I finish my wine and push the glass toward him. "I know I spend a lot of time there," I say, steadier now. "But I do *not* prioritize my restaurant over my marriage."

Josh refills our glasses, rinses the bottle, then tosses it into the recycling bin with a soft clatter. "Then you need to tell Mitch that—directly."

The defensiveness rushes up fast, hot, and familiar. I scowl before I can stop myself. "Wow. He's really been bending your ear, hasn't he?" I say, sharper than I mean to be. "Roommates now, right?"

Josh lifts his brows, the look pointed enough to make me hesitate. I feel the warning flare—*don't*—but the hurt keeps pushing.

"How's the newlywed bliss going," I add anyway, because apparently I'm committed to making this worse, "with your brother-in-law camped out in the guest room?"

"Lauren." He groans. "Come on. It's Mitch. He's been our best friend since we were kids."

"Two Bensons for the price of one," I mutter, crossing

my legs. "Hope he's paying you rent."

Josh exhales and leans forward, elbows on the counter, patient in that maddening way that tells me he's not going to rise to it. "Can I say something without you swinging?"

"That depends."

"Lauren."

I lift my glass in surrender. "Fine."

"I'm not going to pretend I haven't talked to Mitch," he says. "You know I have. And yeah—the restaurant is part of it. But it's not the whole thing." He reaches out and takes my hand, his thumb warm against my knuckles. "This is about more than menus and margins. There's also something deeper going on."

My shoulders tense immediately. Defensive reflex. "Okay," I say. "What else have I done wrong?"

He shakes his head. "This isn't about blame. It's about patterns." He hesitates, then adds, "Mavis had the same insecurities when she came back."

I sigh, already tired. "Josh, I love Mavis. But she came back with a lot of baggage. You're going to have to be more specific." But the second the words are out, guilt slams into me.

He lets go of my hand, and it feels like a punishment.

"God—Josh, I'm sorry," I say quickly, reaching for him again. "That was unfair. I didn't mean—"

"It's okay," he says softly with a shake of his head. "I know you're going through it."

"That's one way to put it." I swallow. "But still, I'm sorry. Mavis didn't deserve that jab."

He nods and I take that as a sign to continue.

"So... tell me." I pause as my phone vibrates in my hand. I glance down, my mouth twitching as a meme from Miguel fills the screen—perfectly timed, like he somehow knows when I'm in the middle of something heavy and need a break. I shake my head and lock the phone, setting it aside. "What pattern am I missing?"

He takes a breath, steady and careful. "Mitch doesn't feel

like he's enough," he says. "For you. Or for this family."

My fist comes down on the counter before I can stop it. "But we've been married for seven years! Why is this suddenly now a problem?"

"I don't think it started when you got married," he says gently. "I think it's just finally coming up for air—after a lifetime of being buried and told to stay there."

"This is ridiculous," I mutter—but Mitch's voice from earlier flickers through my mind, sharp and bitter.

"When Mavis and I reconnected," Josh continues, "she carried the same weight. They were things I never noticed or even thought about when we were younger."

"Look," I say, rubbing my temples, "I get that foster care wasn't easy on them, but—"

"It's not just that," he cuts in, not harsh, just firm. "You know Rosewood. You know how this town works. The Bensons were never invited into the inner circle."

"Mitch and Mavis came to *everything*," I argue. "All of Mom's dinners. All of Dad's fundraisers."

Josh nods once. "Yeah. As our plus-ones."

The words land heavy, rearranging something deep in my chest. "Oh."

"Yeah. Oh," he says quietly. "Mavis helped me see it."

And suddenly Mitch's voice is back, clear as day—*What clout does a fucking Benson have in this town?*

Josh watches me for a beat—really watches me, like he's reading the parts of my face I'm trying to keep neutral. His expression shifts, the edges softening, and when he speaks again his voice is lower, steadier. Like he's choosing every word on purpose.

"Lauren, there's more," he says, gently, "we both know this isn't just about the restaurant. Or our family's name."

I stiffen, instinctively bracing for the thing I don't want named.

"I know this is the part that feels… private," he continues. His gaze holds mine, calm and unflinching. "And I get it. It's personal. It's not something you want to unpack with your brother over a glass of wine."

A pulse of embarrassment flares hot in my chest, and I look away. He lets me. And for a second, he just gives me space to breathe.

"But it matters," he says quietly. "And pretending it's not in the room doesn't make it go away—it just makes you carry it by yourself." He taps the counter once, not impatient, just grounding. "You don't have to tell me every detail. I'm not asking you to. I'm just saying…" His words trail off, and I assume he's waiting for me to acknowledge the elephant in the room.

But my stomach twists at the thought of having this conversation—like saying it out loud to a third party makes it more real. More humiliating. I look down at my glass, at the dark red wine trembling with my grip, and I can feel my pulse in my fingertips.

Embarrassment crawls up my neck, heat and shame tangled together. Then Josh shifts closer—not crowding me, just *there*—and it hits me with a kind of stunned clarity. He isn't looking at me like I'm broken. He isn't cataloging me or judging me or filing this away as another patient problem to solve. He looks at me the way he always has, like I'm his sister first. Like my pain doesn't make me weak—it just makes me human.

"We can't get pregnant," I say, the words tumbling out before I can find another way to rearrange them into something more eloquent. "I mean, in theory, we *can*. We just… haven't been able to."

Josh's face softens instantly. No surprise. No judgment. Just understanding.

"Lauren," he says, "that's something I can help with. You know that, right?"

I nod, but the motion feels brittle—like it could crack if he pushes even an inch. My throat tightens until swallowing feels like work. "I know," I manage, and then the words snag. Because. God. Of all people—my brother. An OB-GYN. The guy who spends his days talking about bodies and babies and the things most people keep behind closed doors. The irony hits like a slap. This is literally his world. His expertise. And still, my skin wants to crawl right off my body.

Because he's Josh. He's my brother—with his calm, competent voice and his stupidly gentle eyes—and the idea of saying any of this out loud to him makes me feel twelve-years-old again, mortified for reasons I can't fully explain.

"I just—" I let out a shaky breath and stare at the counter like it can hold me up. Heat creeps up my neck. And my stomach churns with that horrible, adolescent kind of humiliation—like I've been caught with something too personal in my hands.

"I feel embarrassed," I admit, voice small. "And exposed." My fingers curl tighter around the stem of the glass. "Like I failed at something my body is supposed to just... do." The last word comes out thin, almost a whisper, and I hate it immediately—hate how desperate it sounds, how broken. I blink hard, willing the sting out of my eyes.

He reaches forward and wraps his hand around mine. "You didn't fail." Josh's voice is gentle. "And you don't have to be embarrassed with me."

I nod, even though the feeling doesn't go away. "I know. But knowing that and *feeling* it are two very different things."

He doesn't argue. He just stays there with me, steady and present.

"Mitch feels all of this, too," he says carefully. "He just doesn't know how to say it without turning it into something else."

I close my eyes, the weight of it settling in my chest. "Yeah," I whisper. "I guess, I—"

Josh's phone rings, slicing clean through my words. He glances at the screen, thumb hovering. "It's Austin. I can call him back."

"No," I say too quickly, part of me thankful for the interruption. "Answer it. I... probably need to talk to him, too." Because if Mitch has a lawyer, Austin's going to be part of this conversation whether I want him to be or not.

Josh taps the speaker and sets the phone on the counter. "Hey, man."

"When's the last time you were in Vegas?" Austin asks, all energy and a grin-you-can-hear.

Josh's face shifts instantly—lighter, curious. He glances at me. "Uh… no idea. Why?"

"I want the whole family to fly there next weekend."

"Because?" I ask, leaning forward before I can stop myself.

There's a beat of silence. "Lauren?" Austin says, surprised.

"Yeah," I answer. "Josh stopped by. We're talking."

"Well, perfect." Austin laughs. "Saves me a call. You guys free next weekend?"

Josh's eyes sparkle, already excited, already onboard. But I stare at the countertop, willing my face to cooperate. "Why are we flying to Vegas?" I ask again, because my brain needs something concrete to hold onto.

"I lost a bet to Casey," Austin says. "She picked Vegas as her win. But what she doesn't know is that I'm going to propose to her while we're there."

My heart stutters—not from surprise, not exactly, but from the collision of it all. Joy, yes. Austin deserves happiness. Casey does, too. But grief barrels in right behind it, heavy and sharp, turning sour in the back of my throat—because the universe has a cruel sense of timing, and it never checks to see if you're already bleeding before it hands someone else their forever.

I lock eyes with Josh—and I can see it happening in real time. The way he pieces it together, the way his expression shifts as the timing lands. His jaw tightens, then softens, empathy flickering across his face like a shadow passing over light. Not pity. Not shock. Just this quiet, painful understanding that says, *of course it had to be now.*

"Wow," I manage, forcing the words to sound like celebration instead of surrender.

"I want everyone there," Austin continues, voice warm and earnest. "I want her to feel like family the moment she says *yes*."

That does it. Something inside me aches so sharply it's almost physical. But I paste on a tight smile anyway, because I love him, and because he shouldn't have to carry my wreckage in the middle of his joy.

"We'll be there," I say softly. But internally... I scream.

CHAPTER FOUR

Austin

The diamond catches the light and fires it back at me—
sharp, bright, alive—like it's got its own pulse. "It's perfect,"
I say, and my voice drops, thick with something that feels
dangerously close to reverence.

I can't stop staring at it. The way the facets flash even
under the dim showroom bulbs, like it's trying to show off.
Like it knows what it means. The silver band sits in my
fingers with a surprising weight—solid, undeniable—and
my chest tightens around it. A milestone. A line in the sand.
Proof that the long, winding road I took to get here actually
led somewhere real.

Casey girl, I think, warmth blooming behind my ribs. I
can't wait to ask you to marry me. The thought hits so hard it
almost steals my breath. *You're my forever. My Cinderella.*

And for a second, I swear I can already see her face—
eyes wide, hand flying to her mouth, that laugh she does
when she's trying not to cry. My pulse doubles. My palms
dampen around the ring. And I realize I'm smiling so hard
my cheeks hurt.

"I'm glad you're pleased, sir," the white-haired salesman

says, but his voice feels miles away compared to the roar in my body. "Congratulations again. This is an absolutely stunning stone."

I extend the ring, reluctant to let it go, like I'm handing over my future. He takes it carefully, nests it back into its velvet box, and slips it into a small blue bag.

The finality of it—*this is real, this is happening*—hits me like a rush. Heat crawls up my neck. And my grin turns stupid and uncontrollable.

"Thank you," I say, a nervous laugh slipping out as I grip the bag handles and take a careful step back—like if I stay any closer I might do something ridiculous, like hug the guy. "Now I just have to hope she says yes."

He smiles. "I've been in this business a long time," he says. "Very few women turn down a ring like that." He disappears behind the counter, and I shake my head, still grinning—still buzzing.

"You haven't met my Casey girl," I say under my breath, affection cutting through the nerves. Because knowing her, she'd rather have a Cubs World Series ring on her finger than any diamond I give her.

I push open the door, and the cold air slaps my face. Michigan Avenue is all wind and snow-dusted sidewalks and moving bodies, and I step into it like I'm walking on air. I jog half a block, tucking the blue bag deep into my jacket pocket like it's the most precious secret I've ever carried. At the corner, I lift my arm and hail a cab.

"Where to?" the driver asks.

"121 South LaSalle," I say, slamming the door against the unseasonably cold mid-March wind. "Just a few blocks up."

As the cab pulls away, Chicago blurs past—white edges of snow, gray sky, headlights smeared in the glass—and I sit here with a ridiculous grin plastered on my face like I can't physically wipe it off.

My hand presses over the ring in my pocket, right where the nerves pool in my gut, right where my heart keeps trying to climb into my throat.

One week, I think, breath catching. *One week, and then you're mine forever.*

My phone vibrates, and I yank it out of my pocket.

Josh: Flights are booked. Mavs and I can't wait to celebrate with you guys!

A laugh slips out of me—quiet and breathless, like my body can't hold the feeling in. Warmth floods my chest so fast it almost hurts. Because of course Josh is already all-in. Of course he booked the flights, ready to show up and make this real in the way he always does—by putting his whole weight behind my happiness like it's his own.

The cab eases to the curb beside a sleek stone building, tires crunching against slush.

"Ten even," the driver says.

"Thanks," I manage, handing over the cash, still grinning like an idiot at my screen. But the second I open the door, the wind comes roaring back, slicing through my coat and stealing my breath.

I bolt up the concrete steps and slip inside just as the first snowflake of the day lands on the city behind me. The lobby's warmth hits like a hug. I hop into the elevator and stab the button marked twenty-one. My fingers brush the lump in my jacket pocket again—*still there*—and the nerves spike like electricity under my skin. It's absurd, how a small velvet box can feel like it weighs a thousand pounds.

When the doors open, sunlight floods the hallway, bright and clean. It glints off the Chicago River twenty-one floors below, still tinted green from St. Patrick's Day, and for a second everything looks unreal—like I stepped into a life I used to only picture.

"Mr. Templeton," the receptionist says with a nod as I pass, and my stomach flips at the sound of it—my name said like I belong here. "Office of the Chicago Mayor," she adds, already scooping up a ringing phone. "How may I direct your call?"

I grin without even trying and duck into my new office,

closing the door behind me like I'm sealing myself inside a dream. I shrug out of my jacket, pull the little blue bag free, and set it on my desk—right next to the new laptop that showed up over lunch. Two symbols, side by side. The job. The ring. My future.

"This is perfect," I whisper as I run my fingers over the laptop lid like a kid with a new toy before dropping into my chair. My pulse still races, my whole body buzzing, like I'm vibrating a half inch off the seat.

I grab my phone to text Josh back—but my thumb hits Facebook by accident. The screen loads, and there it is. Their pregnancy announcement, front and center. A photo of my twin with his hands wrapped around Mavis's belly, her smile radiant and unmistakable. The kind of happiness you can't fake. The kind that makes your chest ache with it.

My grin softens into something gentler. Something almost holy. "I'm happy for you, Princess," I whisper to the empty office. "You both deserve this second chance." Then I close the app before the emotion can swallow me whole and hit reply.

Me: Thanks, dude! Celebratory drinks are on me!

His answer comes back instantly, like he's been waiting with his phone in his hand.

Josh: Don't forget, I'm drinking for two now.

I snort, leaning back in my chair, the laughter shaking through me. Excitement hums under my skin—raw and bright and relentless. I open the new laptop, and the screen flickers to life just as another message pops in.

Josh: That bill could get out of hand pretty damn quick!

I glance around the office—unpacked boxes stacked against the wall, file folders waiting on the table, sun pouring through the glass like the city itself is watching. A future that suddenly feels wide open.

The machine hums to life as I lift the lid, and a note

blooms on the screen. *Welcome to the team.* My throat tightens. Not in a bad way. In a *holy shit, this is happening* way.

I grin and respond to Josh.

Me: You know I'm good for it. I'm employed again.

I spin once in my chair because I can't help it—because adrenaline tears through me and there's nowhere to put it.

"Josh. Mavis. Lauren," I say aloud, letting the names settle in the room like a promise. Then my smile shifts, sharper and more determined, as my gaze drops to the blue bag on the desk. "That just leaves you, Mitch."

I tap his name and lift the phone to my ear. Four rings later, I hear his voice.

"Hey."

"Hey yourself." I lean back in my chair, staring at the strip of sunlight cutting across my office floor, trying to keep my voice light. "You didn't respond to me the other night."

There's a pause. Long enough that I know he's weighing it. Then Mitch exhales, the sound crackling through the line like he's been carrying it around in his chest all day. "What am I supposed to say, Austin?"

"That you'll come." The words are out before I can soften them. My heart kicks hard, the full weight of the ask finally landing—Vegas. An engagement. Celebration stacked on top of wreckage.

"Dude," he says carefully, "you know I'm thrilled for you and Casey, but—"

I wince, guilt climbing my throat. "I know. I am asking a lot. I get that." I swallow, because what I *don't* say is worse. *Please don't let this moment happen without you. Please show up for me even if your world is imploding.*

"It's probably for the best that I'm not there," he continues. "You know. With Lauren. And—"

My sister's face flashes through my mind. Her admission last summer. The way she laughed things off until she couldn't. The word *divorce* lands heavy, cracking straight through my excitement.

I'm being selfish. Asking you both to celebrate when you're falling apart.

But the truth pushes past the guilt anyway. "But I want you there."

Silence. Then Mitch sighs again, deeper this time. "Why?" he asks. "I'm divorcing your sister, man. I don't even know what that does to us."

I drop my gaze to my lap, fingers curling against my thigh. "I don't know either," I admit quietly.

Next to Josh, you're my best friend.

"Mitch," I say, forcing steadiness into my voice. "I have to ask—where are you right now? In all of this."

He groans. "I had Dave Jensen draw up—"

"Are you kidding me?" I cut in, my chair spinning as irritation spikes. "You hired Dave *fucking* Jensen?"

God, I hate that guy.

"Well, it's not like I was going to ask *you* to do it!"

"Come on, man!"

"Like it even matters who my lawyer is—"

"It does," I snap. "If you're going through with this, at least let me help. I've been a divorce attorney longer than I want to admit." Images of the L.A. office flash through my head—too many broken marriages, too many nights that bled together. "I don't want either of you getting screwed." My fist comes down on the desk, rattling my laptop. "Are you really sure you want to do this?"

"No."

The single word hits me like electricity. "Wait—what?" I scrub a hand over my face, adrenaline surging. "Did I hear that right?"

He groans. "I don't know what the fuck I'm doing anymore."

Hope sparks—small but bright. "Do you still love my sister?" The question tumbles out before I can stop it.

"Of course, I do," he snaps. "It's Lauren, for God's sake."

"Then what the hell is happening?" I ask, frustration and something like relief tangling in my chest.

"I don't know," he says. "I don't even have the words for it."

I grip the back of my neck, working through the tension. *You're not done. You're just lost.* "Then don't sign anything," I say quickly. "Don't sign a damn thing Dave gives you."

"Austin, it's not about who files the form—"

"That's not what I mean." My pulse picks up as an idea takes shape. "Why don't you take a break? Come to Vegas with us next weekend. Give it one more shot. Just—pause. Breathe. Remember."

"Booze, gambling, and poker tables are not going to fix my marriage."

"No," I agree. "But time together might." I hesitate, then lean into it. "You don't know what you want right now. You said that yourself. So, go with Lauren. Give yourself the space to figure it out. It's Vegas."

"Yeah, we eloped there."

"Exactly." I sit forward now, heart pounding. "Go stand in front of that same chapel. Look at her in the place where you chose her. And if you still can't see a future together, then at least you'll *know*. But Mitch—give it one last shot. For her. For me."

He mutters under his breath. "I don't know…"

"What do you really have to lose?"

"My sanity. Time on the house flip. The cost of a flight—"

"You'll survive," I say quickly. "And drinks are on me all weekend."

"You're out of your goddamn mind." He laughs and the sound loosens something in my chest.

I glance down at the little blue bag on my desk—the ring, the promise, the future—and my excitement surges again, hopeful and fierce. "Mitch," I say quietly, "there's nothing in this world I wouldn't do for Casey. And I know—*I know*—at one point, you felt that way about Lauren."

"I still do," he mutters.

That's it. That's the opening.

"Then I'll see you in Vegas," I say, hope blooming full and reckless in my chest. "Just give it one last shot."

He snorts. "Let the chips fall," Mitch says. Then the line goes dead—but I'm already smiling.

CHAPTER FIVE

Mitch

I shove my backpack into the overhead bin as the cabin pressure shifts, the sudden squeeze sending a sharp, blinding pinch through the back of my skull. I wince and blow out a breath, my jaw tightening as regret slams into me.

I shouldn't be here. I can't believe I let Austin talk me into this.

"Do you want the window seat?" Lauren's voice is quiet—measured. Careful. Like she's already bracing for rejection.

I turn toward her and shake my head, reaching for her carry-on before she can argue. "No. You take it." The words come out rough, clipped, like if I soften them I'll lose my footing. I hoist the bag up beside mine and squeeze my eyes shut for half a second, pressure building behind them.

She nods and slides into the row without another word.

I grip the plastic edge of the bin and snap it shut, then drop into the seat beside her with a frustrated huff. My knee bounces on instinct, nerves skittering under my skin as I try—and fail—to shake the familiar tightening in my chest.

"I brought ibuprofen," she says softly. "If you need it."

She digs into her purse and pulls out a small baggie. It crinkles between her fingers as she holds it out.

Despite myself, a smirk tugs at my mouth. Muscle memory. Habit. I take the bag, dump the pills into my palm, and toss them back just as she hands me a bottle of water. The cold slides down my throat, grounding me just enough to keep it together.

"Thanks, Lauren," I mutter.

"At least it's a short flight," she says, leaning back. "I know you hate flying."

I nod. Because she's not wrong.

"Honestly," she adds after a beat, turning toward the window, "I'm surprised you agreed to come at all." Her voice drops, fragile. "I promise—I'll keep my distance."

"Lauren—"

But laughter cuts me off. I glance across the aisle and there's Josh, grinning like an idiot as he deliberately extends Mavis's seat belt longer than it needs to be.

"Josh! I'm not that big!" She laughs, swatting his hands away as she tugs the seat belt across her lap. After fastening it, she catches his hands again and guides them back—pressing his palms gently against the small curve of her stomach.

And something ugly coils up my spine. I roll my eyes, but the reaction is too sharp—anger and resentment flaring hot and immediate. Jealousy floods my veins before I can stop it. They look so easy. So whole. Everything we were supposed to be.

Beside me, Lauren clicks her seat belt into place. The sound is loud in the cramped cabin. And I catch her swipe beneath her eyes before she drops her purse to the floor between her feet.

Mavis laughs again—pure, unguarded happiness she has every right to feel—but it darkens something inside my chest until it aches.

"You okay?" I ask, my voice catching as I shift, subtly blocking Lauren's view of them.

"Oh—yeah." Too quick. "Dry air. You know."

The ache in her voice radiates outward, stealing the air from my lungs. Josh's laughter rings out again, relentless, and I steal another glance as his fingers trail across the baby bump, both of them glowing.

"Yeah," I mutter, swallowing hard. "One of the reasons I hate flying."

But a tiny sob slips past Lauren's control. She sucks in a sharp breath and swipes at the tears betraying her, angling toward the window like she can hide from me that way.

"Peach—"

She turns back, and the sorrow in her eyes guts me mid-word. My chest tightens. And my hand moves before my brain can stop it—instinct, muscle memory, years of loving her hardwired into my bones. I take her hand and squeeze.

Her breath stutters as her gaze drops to our interlaced fingers. "Mitch," she whispers.

Then the overhead speaker crackles to life, the pilot's voice filling the cabin. But Lauren's grip tightens, her red-rimmed eyes lifting to mine like she's searching for something—answers, reassurance, hope—I don't know how to give anymore.

What am I doing?

"Sorry," I whisper, yanking my hand back like it burned me. I rake my fingers through my hair as the plane pushes back from the gate, dizziness rolling in, unease gripping my gut.

"Please, Mitch?"

Her voice breaks me. But before I can stop her—or myself—she takes my hand again and rests our joined fingers in her lap. And the familiar weight of it wrecks me completely.

Her wedding ring—the one I slid onto her finger so many years ago—catches the light, its tiny diamond glinting like a blade. My gaze drops instinctively to my own bare hand.

Where did I leave my ring?

As if she thinks the same thing, her thumb brushes the empty space where it should be. Her grip tightens. She sniffles, then presses her face into my shoulder, her body shaking as silent sobs break against my chest.

I tip my head and rest it gently against hers as the plane lifts into the sky—her hair brushing my cheek, her body convulsing beside mine. I close my eyes, breathing her in like I'm trying to remember how to be steady for her.

Austin's voice comes back to me, annoyingly calm, annoyingly sure. *Give it one more shot. Just—pause. Breathe. Remember.*

I initially resisted the idea on principle—because Vegas can't fix what we broke. Because a change of scenery doesn't rewrite months of distance and disappointment and words you can't take back. But holding Lauren's hand while she quietly falls apart against my shoulder, I can't pretend this is just paperwork. Just logistics. Just a decision I can make cleanly.

What do I have to lose? I think, and the answer is immediate and brutal. Not much I haven't already lost. So, I make myself a promise in the dark behind my eyelids. Not a grand one. Not a cinematic one. Just an honest one.

I'll try. I'll make an effort. I'll give her this weekend—give *us* this weekend—and see where it takes us.

Her breath hitches, small and broken, her fingers gripping mine like I'm the last solid thing in the world. And despite everything—despite how confused and torn I am, despite how afraid I am of wanting something I can't fix—I can't help it. I pull her closer. Because whatever comes next, I still know this. I don't know how to stop loving her. And I'm not ready to watch her heart break alone.

***

Her stomach growls beside me—low, unmistakable, cutting through the din of the casino like a confession. "Anyone else hungry?" Lauren asks, flashing an embarrassed grin like her body didn't just betray her.

Across the table, Josh slides an arm around Mavis's shoulders. "Duchess, do you want dinner?"

But she yawns in reply, neon lights strobing behind her as another roar of drunken celebration erupts nearby. She rubs her eyes and shakes her head. "Actually… I'm really tired. Do you guys mind if I call it a night?"

Josh doesn't hesitate. He presses a kiss on the top of her head and stands, already scooping up her purse. "You're right. It's been a long day. You should rest." He pulls her chair back and offers his hand. "Raincheck?"

"Oh—yeah," Lauren says quickly, lifting her wine like she can drink her way through the sudden shift in the air.

"I'm sorry," Mavis adds as she rises, her eyes flicking between Lauren and me—quick, careful. She hesitates for half a beat, like she can already feel the awkwardness she's about to leave behind. Like she hates the idea of walking away and making us sit in it.

I point at her belly, trying to keep it light. "For being tired? Pretty sure that's officially allowed."

Mavis gives me a tight little grin. "You know what I mean," she says softly—*I'm sorry for leaving you two alone. I'm sorry this is weird. I'm sorry you're both hurting and I can't fix it.* Her gaze lingers on Lauren for an extra second, an unspoken check-in.

Lauren's smile wobbles around the rim of her glass. "It's fine," she agrees, even though nothing is.

Josh taps the table with his finger, stretching the moment. "I can come back down after Mavs falls asleep or—"

Lauren hiccups beside me, a drop of white wine slipping down her chin. "Josh," she says dryly, "as delightful as it sounds to have my big brother supervising us all night—"

"I'm not supervising!" He flushes. "I was just—"

She reaches for his hand. "I appreciate the offer." Then she glances at me—careful, searching. "But go. Mitch and I will be fine."

My heart kicks hard at the sound of my name, louder than it has any right to. I nod before I can second-guess it. "She's right." And then the image hits me without warning—the white arch of the chapel, the heat, the way her hand trembled in mine as she said *I do*...

Austin's voice echoes in my head like a dare I can't unhear. *Go stand in front of that same chapel. Look at her in the place where you chose her. And if you still can't see a future together, then at least you'll know.* "Seriously," I add, forcing the words out while I still can. "Go. We're good."

Josh studies me for a beat, suspicion flickering in his eyes. "You're sure?"

"Go, Josh," Lauren says, shooing him with a weak smile.

"Okay, okay." He laughs, wrapping an arm around Mavis. "If you say so."

They head toward the elevator alcove, swallowed by lights and noise and laughter. I watch them disappear, something tight and tangled twisting in my chest. Because the space they leave behind is... loud in its own way.

Lauren drains the rest of her wine and wipes her mouth with the sleeve of her sweatshirt. Her gaze drops to her lap, fingers immediately going to her cuticles—picking, worrying. An old habit. One I've known for years.

I finish my beer and shift toward her, heart thudding. "Hey, Lauren—"

But a blonde waitress swoops in like a wrecking ball. "Howdy y'all," she says, her exaggerated southern drawl wildly out of place in Vegas.

I look up—and nearly choke. Her eyelids are coated in a thick layer of glitter that catches every light in the room. And her lashes are so long they look dangerous, batting her cheeks like aggressive spiders with every blink. Then there's her sky-high hot-pink stilettos.

Without thinking, I grab Lauren's knee under the table and give it a squeeze.

"Huh?" she whispers. "What?"

I tilt my head toward the waitress as she collects our

empty glasses and struts away, heels clicking.

Lauren giggles. "She reminds me of Tess."

A laugh bursts out of me before I can stop it—real, unguarded. "Oh my, God. She kind of does."

Lauren drags her hands through her hair, laughing alongside me now. "I do not miss that girl. Not even a little."

"What happened to her, anyway?"

She shrugs. "I think she's still in town. Probably just screwing another one of Josh's neighbors."

I smirk. "I mean... she wasn't *that* bad, was she?" The lights flicker overhead, stars dancing at the edge of my vision as the noise swells around us.

"Not that bad?" Lauren rolls her eyes. "She cheated on Josh for, like, a year."

"Yeah, but..." I hesitate. "He didn't really love her, did he?"

Lauren gives me a look—flat and unimpressed. "Okay, whatever. You've hated her since high school. Why're you defending her now?"

But the second the words land, I realize what I'm doing—hiding behind Tess, hiding behind old drama and easy jokes because it's safer than talking about *us*. Safer than saying anything that might crack open the air between us.

"This is stupid," I mutter, more to myself than to her. I straighten in my chair, the words coming out before I can talk myself out of them. "I don't want to talk about Tess Browning. I want to get dinner. With you."

She squints at me, suspicious. "Really?"

"Yeah." I playfully poke her in the middle. "I can hear your stomach growling from here."

Her lips twitch and something eases in my chest. "You know you don't have to, right?" she says after a beat, hesitation flickering across her face. "I can—"

I reach for her hand before she can finish. Her fingers are warm. Familiar. And still fit perfectly in mine like they always have. "I know I don't have to," I say quietly. "I want to."

I'm following your advice, Austin. For better or worse.

She frowns and searches my face. "Since when—"

"Lauren." I sigh, because I'm sure I sound deranged. I know I'm doing a one-eighty. But like I promised myself on the plane, I'm going to give it my all this weekend. "Do you want to keep interrogating me, or do you want to go find some food?"

She snorts, then pushes to her feet, slinging her bag over her shoulder. "Food," she says decisively. "Definitely food."

I stand with her, heart pounding—not just with nerves, but with something fragile and reckless and *hopeful.* The kind of feeling I've been avoiding for months because hope is dangerous. Because hope asks for more than I'm sure I can give. And yet—for the first time since we landed in this city—I let myself believe that taking her back to where it all started isn't just a gamble. Maybe it's a chance.

I lace my fingers through hers, the way I used to without thinking, and tug her along. We weave through the hordes of gamblers until the stale, recycled casino air gives way to the cool night breeze of the Las Vegas Strip. The change is immediate—like stepping into another version of the world. Neon lights glitter against the inky sky. Music thumps from somewhere unseen. Laughter spills out in waves. The city hums—loud and alive and unapologetic.

Across the street, the Eiffel Tower replica rises into view, and just like that I'm seven years back. Red-eye flight. No sleep. Adrenaline and nerves and that wild, breathless certainty that this was the beginning of everything. Her laugh echoing off the chapel walls. The way she said *yes* like it was the easiest thing she'd ever done.

"What do you feel like having?" I ask, forcing my voice to stay steady even as my chest tightens.

"Um… I don't know." She tilts her head, the streetlights catching in her dark brown eyes. "Any ideas?" She steps closer to let a couple pass behind her, and my body reacts before my brain can catch up. The breeze lifts her hair, dark strands brushing her shoulders. She smiles—soft, unguarded—and the sight of it hurts in the best possible way. Like muscle memory. Like home.

"Hot dogs," I say, tightening my grip on her hand and steering us down the Strip before I can overthink it.

She laughs, warm and familiar. "Well. Tradition, I guess."

I slide an arm around her waist, instinctive as breathing, and point ahead. "Food trucks should be this way. At least they used to be."

She falls into step beside me, matching my stride with ease. We dodge tourists chasing the Vegas night, our shoulders brushing, close enough that I can feel the heat of her through her sweatshirt. To our right, the Bellagio fountains erupt—water swaying in perfect synchronization, golden lights dancing across the pool.

"I think that's where Austin is planning to propose tomorrow," she says, pointing. Crowds line the railing, phones raised, waiting for magic.

"Then why did he need us here?" I ask. "He'll have half of Vegas to watch."

"Oh, come on," she says, smiling. "I think it's sweet he wants to make it a big showy deal."

"And you think that's what Casey wants?" I ask. "A spectacle?"

She frowns and grips my arm as we cross the street, her fingers pressing into bare skin. The contact sends a small, involuntary jolt through me.

"I think what Casey wants most," she says carefully, "is just Austin. The rest doesn't matter."

Her words settle in my chest—quiet, steady—and then the ache follows right behind them. *Because why can't you look at us like that,* I think. *Just me and you. No spectacle. No scorecard. No proving anything to anyone.*

But I don't say it. I can't. The thought is too tender to hand her, too easy to drop and break. So, I swallow it and keep walking, focusing on the one thing I can do without making it worse. Keep us moving. Keep trying. Keep making the effort like I promised myself.

A row of white food trucks comes into view, the air thick with grease and salt and fried comfort. Picnic tables are packed with people laughing, talking, living—life loud and messy and real, unfolding around us.

I point to the second truck. "It's still here," I say, reading the words *Hot Dogs in a Hurry* splashed in bold yellow letters. "What do you want?" I ask, making my voice casual—lighter than my chest feels.

Lauren scrunches her nose, eyes flicking up to the menu board like she's studying it seriously. "Chicago-style," she decides.

"Of course," I say, and my grin comes easy—almost automatic.

Her lips twitch as I guide her toward the truck, still holding her hand. The desert wind kicks up, ruffling my hair and raising goosebumps along my arms, but I barely feel it. All I can feel is *her*—the familiar fit of her fingers in mine, the way she walks beside me like we haven't spent months tearing each other apart.

We step up to the counter, the fluorescent lights washing everything in harsh brightness. The guy inside looks bored in that Vegas way, like nothing on earth could surprise him anymore.

"What can I get you?" he asks.

I squeeze Lauren's hand once—an unconscious check-in—then lean in. "Two Chicago dogs," I say, nodding toward the toppings like I'm reciting a prayer. "Extra sport peppers." Then I glance at Lauren. "Fries, too?"

She hesitates like she's going to pretend she doesn't want them, and I beat her to it.

"And a large fry," I add, because I know her. Because I've always known her.

The guy grunts, then taps the screen. "Last name?"

"Benson," I say, but the sound of it feels strange here—like I'm somebody else in this city.

I pay and he hands me a receipt before we step aside to wait, shoulder to shoulder, our hands still linked like neither of us is ready to let go first. And for this moment—just this one—it feels like we're back in the same story again. Like the pages haven't been ripped out. Like the ending hasn't been decided.

"Will you hold my purse for a second?" Lauren asks, pressing it into my chest like always.

I take it automatically because some habits never die. And I watch as she gathers her hair and pulls it into a ponytail with the pink tie from her wrist—the same easy, practiced motion I've watched a thousand times. The streetlights catch her cheekbones, soft and familiar, and a flush of color blooms across her skin. She drops her gaze, smiling to herself, and something in my chest gives way.

The sight of her hits me all at once. Not sharp—deep. Like the echo of a life I used to live without thinking twice.

"What?" she asks, glancing up when she feels me staring.

And the words slip out before I can talk myself out of them. "You look really pretty tonight."

Her eyes widen, surprise flickering across her face like she's not sure she heard me right.

"Benson!" the guy at the counter calls, slapping a greasy paper bag onto the metal ledge. "Enjoy."

I grab it and peer inside. Steam rises. Fries. Two hot dogs. Salty. Perfect. I drop onto the nearest picnic table bench, the wood cold beneath me.

"I'm starving," Lauren says, reaching for a fry with a grin. "This is way better than room service." She laughs and tears into the hot dog wrapper next, biting in with unfiltered delight. Her eyes close as she chews, and suddenly I'm not here anymore.

I'm seven years back again. Plastic chairs in a tiny chapel. A wrinkled suit. Her hand in mine as we ended up exactly here. Her laughing with mustard on her lip because we were too giddy to care. Me thinking—*this is it. This is forever.* And my heart slams against my ribs like it's trying to break free.

Without thinking, I reach out and wipe a tiny smear of mustard from her upper lip with my thumb. The motion is instinctive. Familiar. Intimate in a way that takes my breath.

Her smile turns shy. Embarrassed. Warm. The kind she used to save just for me. And that's it. It's not a strategy. It's not a decision. It's just want.

I tilt her chin up, barely giving her time to register the surprise in her eyes before my lips meet hers. The kiss isn't careful. It isn't dramatic. It's soft and real and aching—like I've been holding my breath for months and just remembered how to breathe.

For a fleeting second, the world around us disappears. We're not standing in front of a tacky chapel in Vegas this time. No neon lights. No plastic flowers pinned to an arch. Just the cracked pavement outside *Hot Dogs in a Hurry*. But somehow it feels exactly the same.

Because the vows I spoke seven years ago come crashing back through me—raw and loud and devastating—as if I'd said them only seconds ago.

CHAPTER SIX

Lauren

Seven Years Before

"For four years," Mitch says, his voice steady even as his thumb trembles against my hand, "I lived on a ship with over three hundred men. From the moment the sun came up until it went down, there was always noise. Always voices. Always someone within arm's reach." His throat works as he swallows. "And still—there were nights I felt so alone it scared me."

The words hit me like they've been waiting for the exact right second to land. Tears spill down my cheeks before I can stop them, hot and stunned and wildly out of place in this tacky little chapel with plastic flowers and twinkle lights. The last four hours blur together—love and adrenaline and impulse and *are we really doing this?*—and I grip his hand tighter, terrified that if I loosen my hold even a fraction, this whole thing might vanish.

"I left Rosewood thinking I wouldn't miss it," he continues, softer now. "Thinking I didn't need home anymore. That maybe my life belonged somewhere else—

out there, on the open sea." His voice cracks, just slightly. "But every night, when I closed my eyes, the only thing I saw was you, Lauren."

My breath stutters as Mitch lifts my hand and presses it to his chest, right over his heart. It pounds—fast and frantic and unmistakably alive—each beat thudding against my palm like a promise he hasn't even put into words yet.

"You were the only constant," he says. "The only thing that felt true no matter how far away I went." His eyes lock on mine, fierce and certain. "Your heart was my compass. It kept turning me toward you. It kept pulling me back— back home, back to myself." His thumb strokes my knuckles. "Back to where I was always meant to be." He inhales, like he's steadying himself. "Right beside you."

My skin tingles from head to toe. His vows wrap around me like a lullaby—soft and steady and impossibly sure—and suddenly this tiny Vegas chapel feels too small to hold what's happening inside my chest. The air hums. The twinkle lights glow too bright. I clutch my cheap bouquet of red and pink carnations like it's something sacred as Mitch slides a silver band onto my finger. The tiny diamond flashes under the lights—bright and defiant—like it knows this moment matters even if the rest of the world never sees it.

"I love you, Peaches," he whispers, squeezing my palm. "And I don't just mean tonight. I mean on ordinary days. On the hard ones. In every version of our life that comes next." His voice turns rough with emotion. "I promise I will choose you—again and again—for the rest of my life."

Whatever nerves I had dissolve instantly. Melt away. Fold themselves up and tuck deep into my chest for safekeeping. I swipe at my tears and lift my gaze to his, smiling through the tremor racing through me.

"Mitch," I say, and my voice shakes even as the truth steadies it, "I've been in love with you for as long as I've known what love was." My laugh breaks free—half-sob, half-joy—as I squeeze his fingers. "You're my best friend. My home. My forever."

I take a breath, trying to keep my heart from spilling right out of my mouth. "When you were deployed, I used to stand outside at night and stare at the moon," I whisper. "I'd look at it until my eyes burned, because it was the only thing I could picture reaching you—this quiet, constant light we both belonged to. I'd wonder where you were in the world, and if you were looking at the same sky. And somehow… I always knew you'd find your way back." My throat tightens. "Like the ocean would carry you to shore when you were ready."

His grin spreads, boyish and stunned, cheeks flushing pink, and something in my chest aches with how much I love him. "You've held my heart since the day you let me cut in line for the swing set," I continue, emotion swelling until it nearly chokes me. "Not many people get to say they found their person at six-years-old. But I did." I blink hard, steadying myself. "I fell in love with you that day, and I never looked back. Even when life got complicated. Even when the world tried to pull us in different directions." My voice steadies as the truth settles into place. "You will always be the one I come back to."

I slide the band onto his finger, my hands trembling as if they understand the weight better than I do. "So, if you'll let me," I whisper. "I'll spend the rest of my life choosing you. Loving you with the same kindness and patience you've given me—over and over, in the big moments and the small ones." My eyes lock on his. "I love you, Mitch."

A fist pounds on the chapel door, rattling the cheap frame.

"Oh, hell—you kids still have three minutes!" the officiant calls, frowning toward the noise before turning back to us with a wink. "Best make this quick, though." He clasps our hands together. "By the power vested in me by the state of Nevada, I now pronounce you husband and wife."

The floor drops out from under me. And for one dizzy, weightless second, the only thing tethering me to the earth is Mitch's fingers locked in mine.

"You may now kiss the bride."

His brilliant green eyes burn into me as he pulls me close and kisses me—sure and deep and breathtaking. His hand cradles the back of my neck, grounding me as everything inside me ignites. My skin hums, buzzing with adrenaline and joy and the wild, rebellious thrill of choosing each other without permission.

But the pounding on the door returns, dragging us back to reality. "Congrats, kids," the officiant mutters, gently ushering us aside. "Go on—celebrate."

Laughter bursts out of me as Mitch grabs my hand and jogs down the aisle, joy pulling him forward like gravity. "Come on, Mrs. Benson!" he calls over his shoulder. And just like that, I follow him—heart racing, fingers locked in his—into whatever comes next.

The chapel door flies open as the next couple barrels in, laughter and nerves colliding behind us, and then we spill out into the night. The dry summer heat crashes over my skin, the sudden contrast making me dizzy. My wrinkled white sundress flutters in the breeze, cheap fabric and all, but I've never felt more beautiful.

Mitch lets out a triumphant whoop, pure and unfiltered, and fist-bumps the first stranger who happens to be close enough. "I just married this beautiful woman!" he shouts, like the entire Strip deserves to know.

Before I can even process it, he pulls me into his arms and holds me close. "Come here, Mrs. Benson," he says, kissing me again—quick, breathless, like he can't help himself.

My heart slams wildly against my ribs. My knees wobble, the adrenaline finally catching up to me, the reality of what we just did crashing down in the best, most terrifying way.

"Mitch—my family is going to *freak*," I blurt, laughter bubbling out of me before I can stop it. I press my hands to my cheeks, my skin still burning—from the chapel, from him, from the sheer gravity of what we just did. My gaze drops to my left hand and I actually gasp. The diamond flashes under the neon lights, bold and unapologetic, sitting there like it's always belonged. Like it was waiting for me all along. Butterflies erupt in my stomach, wild and unstoppable.

"They're never going to believe this," I continue, the words tumbling out as the weight of what we just did hits me in full force. "The country club. The catering. The deposit on the band. The flowers—oh God, the flowers. The music, the seating chart, the linens…" I let out a breathless laugh, half-joy, half-panic. "My mom is going to lose her mind."

Because we planned it all. The proper way. The Templeton way. The kind of wedding that looks good in photos and keeps everyone comfortable and impressed—but somehow never quite felt like us. And then, on a whim, with our hearts pounding and logic nowhere in sight, we hopped on a plane and ran toward something truer. Something lighter. Something that felt like laughter and midnight and choosing each other without an audience.

"We can worry about all of that tomorrow, Peaches," Mitch says easily, like tomorrow is a problem for another lifetime. "But tonight?" His eyes flick toward the Strip—lights flashing, horns blaring, drunken tourists screaming over competing casino music. His grin turns reckless and boyish, the one that always undoes me. "Tonight is for us." Then, louder, triumphant—"It's fucking Vegas!"

And suddenly I know, deep in my bones, that this is exactly how it was supposed to happen. Mitch swings me in a full circle. The breeze cools my overheated skin, the world blurring into color and sound and him. When my feet hit the pavement again, I laugh so hard my ribs ache, my chest tight with joy.

"What first, my wife?" he asks, and the word hits me like a live wire—thrilling and unreal and suddenly permanent. "Craps? Blackjack? Roulette?" He tugs my hand, already moving. "I'm feeling lucky tonight."

Before I can even pretend to weigh my options, my stomach betrays me with a loud growl—somehow louder than the trumpet player blasting three feet away. "Oh—um—" I manage.

Mitch bursts out laughing, pure and delighted, and kisses my forehead as he loosens his tie, yanking it free like he's shedding an old life. "And to think," he says, shaking his head, "we just saved ourselves from dry country club chicken and two-hundred-dollar plates of mushy vegetables."

I lose it. Completely. Laughter pours out of me, the absurdity of it all settling warm and electric in my chest. I feel alive—reckless and light and so far removed from seating charts and etiquette and everyone else's expectations that it feels like I might float off the sidewalk. And it's one hundred percent out of character for me.

"My parents will never forgive us," I say, half-laughing. "Do you know how much money they put down for that dry chicken?"

"I can do the math," he says cheerfully, pointing down a side street, "or we can celebrate with a hot dog."

I blink at him. "A… hot dog?"

"Yes!" He points again, genuinely thrilled. "*Hot Dogs in a Hurry*. Come on—it's perfect."

And the thing is—it is. Because nothing about tonight is about perfection. It's about us. About choosing joy over polish. Laughter over rules. Still laughing, I jog after him, my sandals rubbing my toe as we reach the truck, neon lights buzzing overhead.

"What do you want?" he asks, scanning the menu like this is the most important decision of our lives.

"Chicago-style," I say, gripping his arm, completely mesmerized by the way my ring keeps catching the light—like it's showing off. Like it's proud of itself.

He orders with a grin. "Let's grab two bottles of water. A chili dog for me—and my wife will have a Chicago dog and a large fry."

My wife.

The words land somewhere deep and permanent, settling into my bones like they've always belonged there.

"You're my husband," I say, dropping onto a picnic table bench. "I think I've wanted to call you that for... maybe twenty years."

"Me, too," he says, then immediately winces. "Wait. I mean—I've never wanted to call you my husband."

I laugh so hard my cheeks hurt, my stomach aching in the best possible way.

When the order's ready, he hands me the bag like it's a sacred offering. "For you, Mrs. Benson."

"Mrs. Benson," I repeat, grinning as I unwrap mine—only for the pickle to immediately slide free along with a glob of mustard. It lands in my lap, but not before splattering down the entire length of my chest. "My *dress!*"

Mitch pours water onto a napkin and hands it to me, eyes sparkling with mischief. "I've heard it's good luck to stain your wedding dress."

"Well," I sigh dramatically as I blot at the mess, "then we'll be married forever. This stain is committed."

He scoots closer, fingers brushing the fabric—then lingering just a second longer than necessary. My breath catches. "Mitch—"

"What?" he teases, kissing my cheek. "Just helping it dry."

I giggle as his arms wrap around me, warmth everywhere, the world shrinking down to this table, to this night, to this man. Neon lights. A mustard-stained wedding dress. And absolute, reckless bliss.

"Hey," he says when another order is called. "As romantic as this wiener adventure's been... hotel?"

I snort. "Did you just call our wedding night a *wiener adventure?*"

"I might have." He grins.

But I know that grin. That's the grin that convinced me to hop on a plane and bolt for the first wedding chapel we passed. The grin that's undone me for decades. The one I wake up to every morning—and the last thing I see before I fall asleep in his arms. It's the grin that will undo me for the rest of my life.

"What happened to craps, blackjack, and roulette?" I tease as he leans in, his lips brushing my neck—our wedding meal now completely forgotten.

He snickers. "I think a continuation of our *wiener adventure* sounds way more fun."

I laugh, realizing he's definitely no longer talking about hot dogs.

We practically sprint back to the hotel, his arm snug around me, my heart pounding with every step. At the door, he kisses me—slow, sure, anchoring—and whispers, "I want you, Mrs. Benson. For the rest of my life."

And I believe him.

CHAPTER SEVEN

Mitch

Present Day

The door to her room waits at the end of the hallway—dark mahogany against stark white walls. The thirteenth floor is silent. No footsteps. No voices. Just the echo of ours as we walk, every step sounding louder than it should, like the hotel holds its breath with us.

Vegas has always done that to me. Made everything feel heightened. Electric. Like one wrong—or right—choice could change everything.

"You didn't have to walk me up," Lauren says softly, digging through her purse. The tips of her ears flush pink. "Didn't you say your room's on the second floor?"

"Third," I say as my stomach dips.

She finds the plastic key and slides it into the slot. The green light flashes and the door unlocks, but she doesn't move right away. Instead, she turns back to me, her hand still resting on the handle, her cheeks warm with color. "Mitch, tonight was…"

Do you want me to stay? The thought hits me hard and fast, knocking the air out of my lungs. I step closer and her breath catches—just barely—but I hear it. And that tiny sound lands straight in my chest.

I lift my hand and trace my fingers along her cheek, my thumb brushing her jaw. She's warm. Real. Here. And adrenaline floods me, sharp and relentless—the same rush I used to feel when a ship slipped its lines and eased out of port, open water waiting ahead, full of the unknown and possibility.

Her eyes flutter closed as she leans into my palm. "I don't understand," she whispers. "Why—"

I kiss her. And the second my mouth meets hers, everything else falls away—the noise, the doubts, the months of silence and resentment and exhaustion that hollowed me out. Her lips part like they've been waiting for this, like they remember exactly how we fit. The kiss is dizzying and achingly familiar, yanking me backward through time—to neon lights, tangled sheets, and promises we thought were unbreakable.

"There's so many memories here," I say against her mouth. "So many ghosts."

She makes a soft sound and I nudge the door open with my foot, guiding her inside. It clicks shut behind us, sealing the world out.

Her purse slips from her shoulder and hits the floor. But she doesn't seem to notice. Instead, her hands slide up my neck and into my hair, confident and instinctive, like her body never forgot mine even when we did. She kisses the spot beneath my ear and heat detonates through me, my pulse roaring, my heart pounding so hard it feels like it might burst.

Happiness—sudden, reckless, overwhelming—swells in my chest. After months of gray, of waking up already tired, it feels like oxygen. Like I might drown in it if I'm not careful.

She stumbles back onto the mattress with a breathless laugh. And I follow, bracing my weight over her, the world narrowing to this moment—her beneath me, her hands on my back, the quiet hum of the room cocooning us. Her legs part without hesitation. Without fear. And second chances blaze in my chest, bright and dangerous.

I don't want this night to end. I don't want to go back to who we were before tonight.

"What happened to us?" I whisper, my hand tracing her neck, my thumb brushing her shoulder.

She arches into me, a low sound slipping from her throat. "I don't know. But there isn't anything I wouldn't do to fix it."

And those exact words hit me harder than anything else she's said. They split something open in me—something I've kept buried because wanting her hurt too much, because hope felt cruel. I kiss along her collarbone, slower now. Reverent. Letting myself feel it. Letting myself believe that maybe we aren't too broken to find our way back. "Peaches," I whisper, brushing her hair from her face.

Her breath shudders—then a shrill alarm explodes through the room.

"What the fuck?" I sputter and twist my head.

Lauren lunges for the clock, slamming her hand against it until the noise cuts off mid-scream. But the silence that rushes back in feels heavier than the sound—thick, electric, vibrating with everything we were about to lose ourselves in.

"Please don't stop, Mitch," she whispers. Her voice is rough and stripped bare. "I missed you so much."

And the way she says it—like a confession, like a wound—obliterates any restraint. I touch my forehead to hers, breathing her in like I've been starving. "I missed you, too," I admit.

Her fingers skim my ears and my hairline, lighting sparks I don't want to put out. "What changed?" she asks softly.

"You did," I say without thinking. Then I steady myself. "You said you want to fix this. I didn't think you did."

Before she can respond, the alarm blares again.

Lauren groans and drops her head back onto the pillow. "Why would anyone set an alarm for midnight?"

"No idea," I mutter, slamming my palm down on the clock. Silence again—but this time it doesn't settle. It hangs between us, fragile and waiting to be broken again.

I rest my forehead against her shoulder, my breathing uneven. "How do we start over?" I ask quietly. "Where do we even begin?"

She shifts beneath me, then reaches past my side, her fingers brushing my pocket. She tugs my wallet free and holds it up between us. "We start," she says, firm but trembling, "by ripping up the stupid form you're carrying around."

The alarm screams again.

"That's it," I growl. I roll off her and rip the plug completely free from the wall. The red numbers vanish instantly as I toss it aside.

She lets out a breathless laugh, pushing her hair back as she sits up and leans against the headboard. I climb back onto the bed beside her, but the heat drains from my body, replaced by something heavier. Truer.

My hand brushes the wallet where it landed on the bed. "You want me to tear it up?" I open it and unfold the *Intent to File for Divorce* form.

"I've never wanted anything more in my life," Lauren says quietly. She pulls the paper from my hand before I can stop her, her fingers tracing the crease down the center until they reach the blank signature lines.

The physical desire we shared moments ago fades completely, replaced by something older and aching. Sadness seeps back in, slow and suffocating, filling the space where hope just lived.

"I couldn't sign it anyway," I admit. I tap the empty line where my name should be. "I tried." My hand slides down her arm without thinking, grounding myself in her, gripping her hip through the fabric of her sweatshirt. "But I couldn't do it."

She turns toward me. Her gaze drops to my fingers where they toy with the hem of her shirt, slipping beneath it to brush her skin. "Tell me why, Mitch."

"Why I couldn't sign?" I ask.

"No." Her voice is gentle but unyielding. "Why did you fill it out in the first place?"

The question cuts clean through me. Splits something I've kept sealed shut. "I told you why," I mutter, pulling my hand back like the truth might burn us both.

She exhales slowly, then takes my fingers and deliberately places them back on her hip. Her palm covers mine—warm and steady.

"Mitch," she says softly, "we just shared the best night we've had together in years." Her smile is small but hopeful, color returning to her cheeks. "Please, let's talk. Without armor. Without defenses."

My throat tightens. I nod, unable to trust my voice. So, I take her hand and press it to my chest, right over my heart, letting her feel the chaos pounding beneath my ribs— everything I don't know how to say.

"We can fix this," she says. "I know we can."

"And you want to?" My voice cracks. "You want to fix us? Fix our marriage?" I press her hand harder into my heartbeat. "You still want me?"

Her eyes widen, emotion flashing sharp and bright. "Mitch Benson," she snaps. "I have wanted you—and only you—my entire life. Why do you think that has suddenly changed?" Her nails dig lightly into my chest. "Don't you feel it? Don't you see it?"

My lungs deflate. I stare at the space between us, the truth clawing its way up through years of silence and resentment.

"I'm not sure what you see anymore," I admit.

"What?" She shifts suddenly, straddling my legs before I can stop her, pinning me in place like she's afraid I'll bolt. Her hands frame my face, firm and unyielding, forcing my gaze to meet hers. "I see the boy I fell in love with. I see the man I married. I see a Navy veteran who served his country. I see—"

"Lauren, stop." The words scrape out of me. Guilt floods my chest, like I've been holding it there for years just waiting for the moment it finally spills.

"I won't," she says fiercely. "You asked me what I see." Her thumbs press into my jaw. "I see an honorable, incredible man—"

I drop my gaze. Because I can't look at her when she says things like that. Shame burns hot and immediate, crawling up my spine as my fingers trace the maroon pattern on the bedspread. But all I see are flecks of dried white paint around my nails—evidence of jobs finished, rooms fixed, things I can point to and say *I built that* even when I don't feel like I've built much else. I curl my hand into a fist.

"Say it," she demands, softer now but no less determined. She takes my hand and drags it to her chest, pressing my palm over her heartbeat. "Say whatever the hell is eating you alive. I know this isn't just about my fucking restaurant."

I inhale, lungs straining, searching for words that won't wreck us—and find only the ones I've swallowed for years.

"You should've married someone better," I force out. The truth lands heavy and ugly between us. "Someone who actually deserves you." My voice fractures despite my effort to keep it steady. "Not some washed-up handyman who peaked at twenty-five and has been scrambling to feel useful ever since."

Her face hardens. "Washed-up handyman?" she repeats. "What are you talking about?"

"There's a reason you don't use my last name, Lauren," I snap, pulling my hand free like the contact hurts. "It doesn't mean anything unless you need hardwood floors or countertops installed. Or a paint job. Or to build a—"

"Rocking horse?" she whispers.

My stomach drops out completely. The blueprint flashes through my mind—every careful measurement, every line drawn like a promise I wasn't sure I could keep. "You saw that?"

She nods toward my wallet on the bed. Her eyes soften—then fracture, like she's been holding herself together with sheer will. "You know I want that, too," she says, voice thin. Her hand slides to her stomach, not possessive—almost protective. Almost apologetic. "I just… never thought it would be this hard for us."

The sudden grief in her hits me like a wave. Not dramatic. Not loud. Just heavy and old, settled deep in her bones. I feel it in the way her shoulders cave, in the way she won't quite meet my eyes, like she's ashamed of wanting something so badly.

"I'm sorry," she whispers, and I know it's not about anything that happened tonight. It's about everything. "I'm sorry I turned our life into—" She lets out a shaky breath. "Into calendars and ovulation windows and plastic test sticks. I know it made our house feel like a clinic." Her mouth trembles. "I just… I didn't know another way. If I could control the timing, if I could track it, measure it, do it *right*… then maybe it would happen."

My chest tightens, the shame burning hotter now because I can see it—really see it—the loneliness inside her routines, the desperation behind the lists. I thought it was pressure. Control. Criticism. But it was grief. It was hope bleeding out in tiny, invisible cuts.

"And when it didn't happen," she says, her voice breaking, "I didn't just wonder if it was me—I knew. The tests, the numbers… they made it clear." Her hand presses to her stomach again. "It's me. I'm the reason we keep coming up empty."

The words land in my gut like lead, heavy with years I can suddenly feel the weight of—and I realize, with a sick twist of regret, that I should have been listening to her long before tonight.

I pull her into my arms and hold her as she collapses against me, her sobs shaking through my chest. I bury my face in her hair, breathing her in like it might anchor her— like I can make up for all the times I left her alone inside this.

"I'm so sorry," I whisper. For being blind. For doubting myself. For doubting her. For doubting us. For letting my fear turn into distance.

Her shoulders shake, then she goes still—just for a beat. Not calm. *Bracing.* She pulls back enough to look at me, eyes red and wet, searching my face like she's reading something there that scares her. Because I know what she sees. The way my jaw clenches. The way my gaze drops like I'm taking the blame and filing it away as proof I don't deserve her. Like I'm about to let her confession turn into my exit ramp.

"Hey." Her voice sharpens, cutting through the softness. "Don't do that."

"What—"

She huffs a broken little laugh, wipes her cheeks hard, and then—like she has to physically stop the spiral—she punches my shoulder.

"Ow." I rub the spot, stunned. "What was that for?"

"For this," she snaps, crossing her arms like she's holding herself together. "For the way you're looking at me like you're about to make *my* grief another reason to disappear." She swallows, breath hitching, then steadies. "Mitch, if I wanted a boring accountant or a fancy surgeon or a smug lawyer, I would've married one! But I chose *you.* I have always chosen you." She exhales sharply, frustration and love tangled together, her voice thick with both. "Damnit. Josh was right."

"Josh?" I blink, still trying to catch up. "You talked to your brother about us?"

She gives me a look—tired, fond, a little defensive. "Oh, like you haven't."

Okay. Fair.

"What did he say?" I ask quietly.

She hesitates, just for a beat, like she's deciding how much more she can carry. Then she slides off the bed and heads for the minibar. "I think we need a drink before we finish this conversation."

I nod, watching her move around the room, my chest still tight but lighter than it's been in a long time. Like something essential finally shifted and I don't want to spook it by moving too fast.

"Vodka, gin, tequila…" Bottles clink as she rummages. "Oh—or bourbon." She glances back at me, a small smile breaking through the emotion, and grabs two black coffee mugs. She pours bourbon over ice and hands one to me, our fingers brushing briefly.

"I did talk to Josh," she admits after a sip. "He… reminded me he's been where we are. He knows what it feels like to have legal papers shoved in front of you." A shiver runs through her. "And he said maybe we've both been a little blind—maybe we've both been avoiding what's actually hurting us."

I take a slow swallow of bourbon, the burn grounding me. Josh is a doctor—I know that. I just didn't realize he could also read a marriage like a chart. Like he could name the wound without even touching it.

"Yuck," she says after another sip. "That's definitely not Angel's Envy."

I choke on a laugh, the cheap bourbon blazing all the way down as I clink my mug against hers. "No, it's not. But cheers anyway."

She smiles—soft, real, a little unguarded. And then she moves back toward me, settling onto my lap, her legs draping along my sides like they remember exactly where they belong. The friction of her body against mine sends a jolt straight through me—adrenaline flaring, bourbon fogging my already exhausted brain.

I slide my hand to her thigh and squeeze, my chest tight again, but this time with something that feels dangerously close to hope. I press on because we've thrown the door wide open tonight. There's no point in stopping now. "You're too good for me, Lauren," I say quietly. "You settled. And you shouldn't have."

She swirls the bourbon in her mug, ice clicking softly against the ceramic, a small, thoughtful sound in the charged quiet between us. When she lifts her eyes to mine, there's no anger there. Just confusion. Hurt. "How can you think that?" she asks.

"I don't just think it," I say, the words heavy and certain. "I know it."

Her hand settles over my chest. The diamond on her finger catches the lamplight and flashes—bright and undeniable. A reminder of vows I've been measuring myself against for years and always coming up short.

"Can I try to tell you something," she asks carefully, "without you getting defensive?" Her fingers trail up my neck and I close my eyes, leaning into the familiar comfort of her touch as I nod.

"I know it's not the same," she says softly. "I know we came from different places. Had different childhoods. Different experiences."

I open my eyes and really look at her—at the way her mouth tightens, the way she's choosing every word like it matters.

"But if you want to talk about feeling unworthy," she continues, her fingers pressing harder now, nails biting just enough to make the point land, "about feeling like you don't really belong—like you're not actually part of the family…" Her voice wavers. "I understand more than you think."

The words hit somewhere deep. I wince and cover her hand with mine, easing the pressure, then bring her fingers to my mouth. I kiss them, slow and with intent. "How?" I ask, because I genuinely don't understand.

She lets out a short, humorless laugh and rolls her eyes. "Haven't you ever noticed? I joke about it, sure—but Mitch, can you imagine what it's been like living in my brothers' shadows?"

I frown, bourbon sliding hot and hazy through my veins, dulling my edges but sharpening my focus. "Help me understand."

A quiet sob slips past her before she can stop it. She looks down at her mug like it might hold the answer. "You really don't see it?"

"See what?" I shake my head, trying to line up the facts the way I always have. "You're a Templeton. Same as Josh. Same as Austin. You had the same childhood. The same opportunities. The same—"

"Did I?" She squints at me, then drains her cup and slides off my lap, crossing the room to the minibar. "Gin and tonic this time?"

"Sure," I say, sitting up. "But don't stop, Peaches. Tell me."

She twists the cap off the tiny bottle of gin, pours with steady hands that don't match the strain in her voice. "I'm not a doctor. I'm not a lawyer. I didn't go to Georgetown or Harvard." Tonic hisses as it fills the mugs. "I'm just me. A glorified waitress." She snorts. "Maybe bartender."

I snicker before I can stop myself. "A waitress? Bartender? Come on." I take the mug from her and sip. "You *own* a restaurant. You built it yourself. That's impressive as hell."

"Is it?" She drops back onto the mattress, the fight draining from her shoulders. "Pier Ninety-two is failing, Mitch. It's going under. Fast." Her voice cracks. "How am I supposed to tell my parents the money they fronted is gone? That I failed?"

The weight of her words settles heavy and unfamiliar in my chest.

So, you think you're a failure, too.

I rub my hand along her back, slower now, absorbing the truth I've been blind to. "We can fix it," I say automatically. "Bring in new customers. Adjust staffing—"

"That's not the point." She shakes her head, tears slipping free. "I let it get this bad. And Templetons don't fail." Her voice drops, stripped bare. "I can't live up to it." A tear slides down her cheek. "I'm not good enough."

Something inside me snaps into focus. Not painfully—but cleanly. Like a lens finally adjusted. I pull her back onto my lap and hold her there, my heart pounding with a new, unsettling clarity. This isn't just my shame. This isn't just her fear. This is the same wound, mirrored. I run my fingers through her hair and press my lips to the top of her head, breathing her in.

"So," I whisper, like I'm afraid to disturb what we've uncovered, "what you're saying is… we're a lot more alike than we've ever admitted."

She sniffles and wipes her cheeks with the back of her hand. "I guess so."

And for the first time, I don't feel alone inside my own insecurity. Despite the tears warming my skin, something inside me lifts—subtle but unmistakable. Like a weight I've been hauling for so long I forgot what breathing normally feels like, and suddenly it shifts just enough to let air back in.

Lauren's hands slide down my torso, slipping beneath my shirt. Heat flares instantly—sharp, instinctive—my body responding before my mind can catch up. She kisses my neck and tugs my shirt free, leaving me exposed to the cool air and the warmth of her want all at once.

"I want the rocking horse," she whispers. "I want all of it—even the messy, painful parts we've been avoiding." She exhales shakily, her forehead resting against mine. "I still choose you, Mitch. I choose us. I want our family. Please. Don't give up on us."

My chest tightens so hard it almost hurts. "I'm not going anywhere," I say, the words coming out rough, urgent, and undeniable. I slide my hands to her face, holding her there so she can't miss the truth in my eyes. "I want you. I want this. I want our marriage—and I'm not walking away again. Whatever it takes. I'm here."

The relief on her face is instant. She kisses me then—slow at first, like she's testing whether I mean it. I answer her without hesitation, pulling her closer, my hands firm at her waist. The heat builds fast, familiar and intoxicating, her body fitting against mine like muscle memory waking up after a long sleep.

My heart races. My head goes quiet. Too quiet. And that's when it hits me—clear and sharp beneath the desire. This matters too much to let it blur. Too much has finally been said between us. Too much truth finally on the table. I pull back just enough to breathe and catch her hand gently, grounding us both before momentum carries us somewhere we can't take back.

"Not tonight," I say softly, even though every part of me wants to keep going.

She looks up at me, breath unsteady, eyes searching mine. Not hurt. Just confusion.

"We're moving too fast," I add, forcing myself to hold the line. "Yesterday, we were ready to sign the papers. Let's just ease back into this, okay?"

Saying it out loud hurts. But pretending it didn't happen would hurt worse. I don't want stopping to feel like a rejection. I want it to feel like we're choosing the long way back—to something real.

She nods slowly, understanding settling in. Then she leans in and kisses me—soft and lingering, full of everything we're choosing not to rush. "I'm sorry," she whispers. "I just... missed you." She curls under the covers, exhaustion finally winning. Her voice is quieter now, stripped down to need. "Stay," she says. "Please don't go."

I don't hesitate. Because I know what this night is. A breakthrough. A conversation we should've had a long time ago. Proof that Austin was right to push me here—because I was *this close* to giving up. To walking away without ever really understanding what divided us.

Vegas didn't just bring back memories of our elopement. It brought us back to each other.

I reach for the divorce form, tear it cleanly in half, and let it fall to the floor. The sound is barely there—but the relief is immediate. Tangible. Like something deep inside my chest finally unknots.

I turn off the light, slide in beside her, and pull her close. And for the first time in a long time, I fall asleep believing we actually have a fighting chance to fix it all.

CHAPTER EIGHT

Lauren

Mitch's hand finds my knee beneath the table. I grin and peek at him just as he swallows a gulp of coffee and winks at me, casual and devastating all at once.

And for a split-second, my chest warms. Because—*do I really have my husband back?*

The question hits without warning. Because last night still feels unreal. Too fast. Too intimate. Too honest. Like I dreamed it in a moment of weakness and somehow woke up still inside it. It feels impossible. Like Vegas itself is playing a cruel, glittering trick on me.

Warmth spreads outward from my heart anyway, reckless and unstoppable, reaching my fingertips and toes as the scents of the brunch buffet drift through the air. Bacon. Coffee. Sugar. Ordinary things that suddenly feel sacred, like proof I'm awake and this is really happening.

I slide my hand beneath the table and grip Mitch's inner thigh, inching higher—not to be subtle, not even to be sexy. Just to make sure he's real. That he doesn't disappear if I blink.

A soft gasp slips from his lips. And something inside me

loosens. I grin into my orange juice and lift my gaze to his, and there it is—those familiar green eyes lit with something I haven't seen in so long it almost hurts to recognize it. Warmth. Amusement. Want. *Us.*

I missed you. I missed us, Mitch Benson.

My phone buzzes, rattling against my plate of pastries, and I jump a little, still wired and floaty.

"It's Austin," I say, already smiling as I open the text and read it aloud.

Austin: We just landed! See you at 7 p.m. on the south side of the Bellagio fountains. Don't let Casey see you guys. I want her to be completely surprised!

I laugh softly and send back three heart emojis without even thinking—because apparently I'm that person again. The one who believes in surprises. In love. In second chances that sneak up on you when you've already stopped hoping. And beneath the table, Mitch squeezes my knee again, like he's just as stunned to be here as I am.

"I can't believe they're getting engaged," Mavis says, her eyes shining as she reaches for her water. "Casey's like my little sister." Her voice trembles, caught between joy and disbelief. "And Austin—"

"Is your brother-in-law," Josh finishes gently, raising a brow and clearing his throat.

I press my lips together and glance down at my lap, warmth creeping into my cheeks as I think, *subtle, Josh. You're never going to be fully over their history, are you?*

He shakes his head like he heard me, then asks, "Do you think Casey has any idea?"

Mavis dabs at her cheeks with her napkin, blinking fast, then takes another bite of potatoes like she needs a distraction.

"No, I don't think she does," I say, setting my phone down and nudging at the soggy eggs on my plate. "I texted her a couple days ago and asked why they were heading to

Vegas. She said the Cubs beat the Dodgers in spring training and she won a bet. So no—I really don't think she has a clue. In her mind, this is just a celebratory weekend."

Mavis lets out a soft, hiccupping laugh. "That sounds like her."

"Are you okay?" Josh asks, leaning in to kiss her forehead.

She nods quickly, hands drifting instinctively to her belly. "Yeah. I'm just..." She swallows, emotion thickening her voice. "Casey's always been special to me. This is such a big moment for her." She forces a smile. "Sorry. I didn't mean to turn breakfast into a cry-fest."

Josh covers her hand with his. "You don't have to apologize." He toys with her wedding ring. "Want more potatoes?"

"Huh?" she asks, distracted.

"Potatoes," he repeats patiently.

"Po-ta-toes. Boil 'em, mash 'em, stick 'em in a stew," Mitch mutters.

Josh grins and fist-bumps him across the table.

Mavis groans, swiping at her eyes again, but she smiles now. "Can we please stop with the *Lord of the Rings* quotes before I start crying for an entirely different reason?"

"We're done," Josh says immediately, tucking a loose strand of hair behind her ear like it's second nature. "Sorry."

He keeps his hand there a beat, his thumb tracing a small, absent-minded circle near her temple. Then his palm drifts down, settling protectively over her belly—casual, unconscious, practiced.

Mavis leans into the touch without thinking and something in my chest begins to ache.

Mitch takes another sip of coffee and grimaces. But I barely register it. My focus stays across the table—on the way Josh watches Mavis like he's memorizing her, on the ease of it, the certainty. The way the future seems to have already chosen them.

A baby. A hand on a belly. A life moving forward

without hesitation.

The morning's warmth dims just enough to sting. Not jealousy exactly—something softer, sadder. A familiar twinge settling low in my gut. Because I'm genuinely happy for them. But I'm still grieving everything I don't have.

Mitch leans back and slips his arm around my shoulders, pressing a soft kiss to my cheek. When I turn toward him, his gaze meets mine—steady, knowing. No pity. No awkwardness. Just understanding. He squeezes my arm, a silent *I see you* passing between us.

Across the table, Mavis and Josh stare, momentarily confused.

Mitch scoots closer and snorts. "What? Never seen a man kiss his wife before?"

Heat rushes through me. Hearing him say *wife* again sends a shiver down my spine—disbelief layered over hope.

Josh squints, a slow grin spreading. "Wait. Are you guys—"

"Oh!" Mavis suddenly gasps. "The baby's kicking!" She grabs Josh's hand and presses it back on her belly. "Right there."

"I feel it!" Josh announces, wonder lighting his face.

I lean back, forcing a smile as something sharp and unwelcome pricks in my chest.

Mavis laughs softly, Josh's palm still pressed to the spot like he's afraid to miss the moment if he moves. They're glowing. And I love them for it. But sitting across from it— this ease, this certainty—it hurts in a quiet, persistent way.

Mitch leans in close, his breath warm against my neck. "Come upstairs with me?" he whispers—not rushed, not annoyed. Just gentle. Like he's asking if I need air.

An escape? Say less.

I nod and push my chair back, collecting my purse and phone.

"Wait, where are you guys going?" Mavis asks. Her gaze flicks between us, softening. "Oh my, God. I'm sorry. I interrupted you."

Josh straightens, suddenly more aware than he's been all morning.

But Mitch waves it off while slipping an arm around my waist. "It's fine," he says. "We'll catch up with you guys later."

Mavis's bottom lip trembles. "I didn't mean to—"

"You didn't," I say quickly, offering her a small smile. "I promise."

And before either of them can say another word, Mitch guides me toward the elevator alcove.

"Not that I'm complaining," I say as I tap the call button, glancing up at him when the doors slide open, "but why did we leave?"

He lets me step inside first, then follows and presses thirteen. The doors close, sealing us into the quiet.

"Well," he says carefully, "first... I don't think they realized how much that moment stung."

I lean into him, the solid warmth of his body grounding me. "The baby kicking *is* kind of a big deal."

He nods. "It is." A pause. "It's just... a lot to sit across from when we're still trying to figure things out."

The elevator opens on the thirteenth floor, and the quiet follows us down the hall. By the time we reach my room, my key card is already in Mitch's hand. We step inside and the brunch noise disappears like it never happened. The room goes still. And for the first time since breakfast, it feels like we're allowed to look exactly as hurt as we are. Because he's right. That moment stung.

Mitch collapses onto the mattress with a groan, stretching out like he belongs here. He grabs a pillow and presses it to his chest, his sweatshirt riding up just enough to reveal the familiar line of his lower torso.

My breath catches. And heat skates along my skin as my gaze drifts to the tattoo etched along his hip bone. My name. Permanent. Proof that at some point, we believed in *forever* without flinching.

He cracks one eye open and grins. "You like what you

see there, Peaches?"

I don't bother pretending otherwise. I sit beside him, adrenaline humming, and trace the ink with my fingertip. "Maybe," I whisper, laughing when he jerks away.

"You know that tickles," he teases.

I smirk and pull my legs up, wrapping my arms around my knees. "So," I say softly, "what's second?"

"Huh?"

"You said first it was because the moment stung. What else?"

He exhales and rolls onto his back, staring up at the ceiling like he's lining his thoughts into something honest. "Second..." He shrugs. "Even if Josh and my sister had tried—for five whole minutes—to think or talk about anything other than the baby, I still wouldn't have known what to say."

He reaches for my leg, his hand warm and steady. "We said a lot last night," he continues. "Important things. The kind you don't take back."

I nod, my chest tightening. "We did."

"We chose each other again," he says quietly. "That part's clear." He turns his head toward me. "We just didn't talk about what that actually looks like. How we *do* this differently."

The words land gently but solidly—true without being discouraging. I tip onto my side to face him, our noses nearly touching as he props himself up on one elbow. A strand of his hair falls forward and he tucks it behind his ear, the small, familiar motion squeezing my heart.

"We've got about eight hours before we have to stand around Austin and clap," he says. "Let's use this time to keep talking. Figure out our next steps."

A laugh slips out of me, soft and relieved. "You really don't have a lot of patience for my brothers right now, do you?"

"I don't have patience for my own sister either," he says, his hand trailing slowly down my arm. "All I want is to keep the conversation going—the one we finally started last night."

"Me, too." I toy with the drawstring of his sweatshirt, my voice softer now, more fragile than I mean it to be. "I still don't really believe this." I swallow. "I thought you didn't love me anymore."

He doesn't hesitate. Not even for a second. "I've never—not once—fallen out of love with you, Lauren. You can take that one to the grave."

I swallow hard. Because the certainty in his voice almost undoes me. "Then what happened?" I ask quietly. "What pulled us apart?"

He shrugs. "I can tell you what started it. At least for me."

I nod, encouraging him to continue.

His gaze drops, his fingers tightening around mine like he's bracing himself. "It's not that I didn't support Pier Ninety-two. I did. I still do." He exhales slowly. "But it took over your life, Lauren. And eventually… it took over us."

My stomach dips. The words sting because part of me already knows they're true.

"I'd cook dinner and it'd be cold before you got home," he continues, not accusing—just honest. "I'd wake up alone on Saturdays because you were already gone. And even when you were home, you were always still working. Texts about scheduling. Constant phone calls with Miguel. Fixing problems from the couch."

"Mitch," I start, instinctively reaching for defense.

"You *own* the restaurant," he says gently, cutting me off with kindness instead of anger. "But you *manage* it, too. All the time."

The memory hits me all at once—me saying the same thing to Josh over greasy diner pancakes, swearing it wouldn't always be like this.

"It wasn't supposed to be that way," I whisper, shaking my head. And for the first time, I don't try to explain it away. I just let the truth sit between us.

"But it has been."

"I know," I say quietly. "And I also know that I don't…" I trail off, already wincing.

"Relinquish control well," Mitch finishes for me with a crooked, familiar smirk. He squeezes my fingers and presses a kiss to my knuckles.

I huff out a breath. "You're not wrong. But Pier Ninety-two is my baby," I admit. "It's hard to trust someone else to do it right."

"I get that." He nods, then hesitates—like he's stepping onto thin ice. "I just… I wonder—"

I frown and pick at a fleck of dried paint on his finger out of habit. "Wonder what?"

He shakes his head and rolls onto his back. "Forget it."

"No." I crawl over him before he can shut down, straddling his hips and bracketing him in place. My finger traces slowly down his chest, stopping at the button of his jeans—not seductive so much as insistent. "You don't get to retreat. Say it. What's on your mind?"

He grips my wrists like he needs the contact to stay anchored, his eyes squeezing shut. "I just…" He exhales. "I wondered if maybe—if you weren't always so stressed, so stretched thin at the restaurant—we might have had more space." His voice falters. "More room to breathe. Together. That we might have…"

My heart stutters. Because the fear underneath his words is worse than any accusation. "We might have what?" I ask softly, even though I already feel the answer.

"Don't make me say it," he whispers. His hands slide to my waist, tentative now, grounding instead of demanding.

But the warmth of his touch collides with the weight of the moment, and something sharp flares in me. "You think it's all my fault?"

"No." He sits up immediately, arms circling me, holding me close before I can pull away. "No. I don't blame you." His forehead presses to mine. "I just think we've both been drowning. And stress changes things. It steals energy.

Patience. Intimacy."

A tear slips free despite my effort to hold it back. I press a kiss to the side of his neck, my voice barely audible. "I'm sorry."

He pulls back just enough to look at me, his gaze fierce and steady. "Don't apologize. I'm not here for apologies."

"Then what are you here for?" I whisper.

"I'm here to fix this," he says firmly. "With you." He gives me a gentle shake, forcing my eyes back to his. "We've been running ourselves into the ground. Maybe if we slow down—things will change for us." His fingers brush up against my stomach, but even though his touch is gentle and hopeful, it still stings like a papercut.

I slip off the bed and drop into the rolling chair, my face falling into my hands as my heart pounds. "You don't understand," I mutter, not angry now—just exhausted. "It feels like everything has been on a timer. Like if I stop moving, something will fall apart."

I hear him before I feel him. His hands settle on my shoulders, warm and sure, kneading into tension. I sigh, my resistance melting under the simple kindness of his touch.

"Your knots have knots, Lauren," he whispers, thumbs pressing deep.

"What can I say? It's been a rough few months," I answer softly, leaning back into him.

"No argument there."

The pressure of his hands begins to unwind me, peeling back layers of frustration and fear until all that's left is honesty.

"I know I work too much," I admit. "And I know it's hurt us. I just... I was terrified of failing. And now that I'm close to it, I can finally see how much it's cost us."

His breath warms the curve of my neck, his fingers threading gently through my hair like he's trying to soothe something deeper than skin.

"I'm not saying it's the cause of everything," he says carefully. "Trust me, I know I played my part in this, too."

And despite the ache I still feel, a smile tugs at my mouth. Because even though I know I'm at fault for the restaurant, he's still willing to share the blame.

My gaze drifts to the room-service menu on the desk. Eggs. Potatoes. Bacon. Clean lines of black ink promising something uncomplicated. Circle what you want. It arrives warm. It arrives whole. No history. No hurt.

Across the breakfast table this morning, Mavis glowed. Josh's hand on her belly. A baby on the way. The kind of ease that doesn't have to be performed. It's just as simple as ordering breakfast.

I want that, I think. Not the performance. The peace. A steady marriage. A baby on the way. A future that feels chosen instead of constantly negotiated.

"I have a proposal," I say suddenly, because if I don't shift this moment, it's going to swallow me whole.

He stills. "I'm listening."

I turn the chair to face him. "I cut back my hours. I hire a real full-time manager."

He cups my face and smiles. "Promising, Peaches."

"And I throw the calendar away," I add. "No more scheduled sex. No more turning us into a checklist."

He kisses me without hesitation, relief and want colliding between us. "Yes," he says.

"If—" I start, then hesitate.

His lips still against mine. "If…" Mitch echoes quietly.

"If you agree to see a doctor," I say carefully—slow enough that it lands as an invitation, not an ultimatum—"if we haven't conceived in four months."

A beat passes. Then he exhales, the tension in him flickering across his face. "I really don't want to."

I roll the chair closer to him. "Tell me why."

He drags a hand over his jaw, gathering his honesty before he gives it to me. "Because it's embarrassing," he says, quieter now. "Because it turns this into… an appointment. A chart. Like we've failed at something that's supposed to just happen."

"I know." My voice softens, but I don't let the moment slip away because it's been on my mind for far too long. "Believe me, I know. But listen."

He stills.

"I already know my egg count is low," I admit. The words still sting, but they don't take me down the way they used to. "The tests confirmed that. And I'm not pretending otherwise." I take a breath, steadying. "But that doesn't mean it's the whole story. There could be more—things we don't know yet. Things we can't address unless we look at them together."

His brow creases, not with anger—just thought.

"It should've happened by now," I say. "It's been years. Even with my condition."

His shoulders sag a fraction, as if the fight leaks out of him. "Four months?" he repeats, but this time it's not a stall. It's him stepping toward me.

"Four months," I confirm. "I cut back my hours. I hire a real manager at Pier Ninety-two. We protect our time. We reclaim our bedroom." I swallow, my thumb brushing his wrist. "And if we're not pregnant by then, we go. Together. No blame. No shame."

Something in his expression shifts—acceptance, and underneath it, relief. His eyes shine under the lamp, green and earnest, and suddenly he looks like the man I married instead of the man I've been fighting.

"Okay," he says finally, and a small, crooked smile tugs at his mouth. He holds out his hand. "All right, Mrs. Benson. You've got yourself a deal."

I take it—firm, real—because the word divorce, ripped cleanly in two, sits forgotten in the wastebasket beside us.

Not an ending. A second chance instead.

CHAPTER NINE

Mitch

The mist from the Bellagio fountains cools my skin as we round the south corner of the hotel, water arcing high against the neon wash of the Strip. Music swells from hidden speakers, the choreography of water and light rising and falling in perfect time while crowds press shoulder to shoulder along the railing. Across the boulevard, the facades of Paris and the Flamingo glow in artificial twilight, every surface blinking, shimmering, demanding to be seen. The air smells faintly of chlorine and perfume and late-night possibility—the kind of charged energy that makes the whole city feel awake, like it's daring you to do something reckless and unforgettable.

"Oh! I see them!" Lauren grabs a fistful of my shirt and points through the swarm of tourists.

I squint past a wall of matching, vibrant orange family-reunion t-shirts and spot Austin and Casey across the pool, their blond heads crammed together fifty yards away. "How the hell did you see them that fast?"

"Well, it's not like they're part of the reunion, Mitch." She rolls her eyes and leans against the railing just as Josh and Mavis arrive.

Before I can say anything else, my sister barrels into me, wrapping her arms around my middle and squeezing hard enough that her belly bumps my stomach.

"I'm so sorry about breakfast." Her voice catches, soft and breathy against my shirt. "You and Lauren were about to tell us something. I could feel it. And I just… I bulldozed right over it."

Over her shoulder, Josh shifts, a crease between his brows. He rubs the back of his neck like he's trying to rewind the morning with his hand. "Yeah," he says quietly. "We got excited, and we kind of took the whole table with us." His eyes flick to Lauren, then back to me. "We didn't mean to steal the moment. And we're sorry."

Mavis's arms tighten once more. "I'm sorry," she says again, soft enough that I'm confident I'm the only one who hears it.

My throat tightens because I can't stay mad at her. Or Josh. Not after that.

"Hey," I say, squeezing her shoulders, forcing steadiness into my voice. "It's okay. Really. I know you guys—"

"Oh! Look! He's doing it!" Lauren's voice slices through the moment. She launches off the railing like she's about to take flight.

I follow her gaze and see Austin drop to one knee in the middle of the orange-shirted chaos.

"Come on! We can talk later!" Lauren disappears into the crowd, already pulling her phone from her back pocket.

I gently hand Mavis back to Josh and take off after Lauren, weaving through bodies, muttering apologies as I search for the swing of her dark ponytail. I spot her ten paces ahead and push faster—only to trip over a giant red umbrella abandoned on the pavement.

I catch myself just as the fountains explode again, a heavy spray drenching my face and shirt. I wipe my eyes and finally see her—arm stretched high, phone in the air—snapping photos as Austin opens a small blue box in front of Casey.

That's when time starts to slow. The fountains hover midair. The crowd noise dulls to a hum. And Casey's scream pierces the night as Austin spins her in a dizzy circle while the Hodgkins clan loses their minds around them in a sea of orange.

And just like that, I'm somewhere else.

A quiet beach. A stretch of sand washed silver under a starlit sky. Lauren barefoot, wind tangling her hair. My hands shaking as I dropped to one knee—not because anyone was watching, but because everything I wanted stood right in front of me. The way her gasp caught in her throat. The way she laughed and cried at the same time. The way she said "yes" before I even finished the question. There hadn't been fountains. No crowd. No applause. Just certainty.

I look at Austin now—his face split open with hope—and I remember that feeling in my own chest. The reckless bravery of choosing someone forever. The wild, steady belief that we would build something unbreakable. When did I let that certainty blur into doubt?

I step forward and slide my hands around Lauren's waist, pulling her back against me. Her breath catches as she lowers her phone and melts into my chest like she's done a thousand times before—like she still fits there. Like she always has.

I promised to love you for the rest of my life. I meant it. I still mean it.

She turns in my arms, eyes bright from the mist and the moment. "Everything's the way it should be now, isn't it?"

I laugh softly as Austin and Casey finally notice us and start running our way, the crowd parting around them.

I tighten my hold on Lauren, my heart thudding—steady, certain, alive in a way it hasn't been in far too long. "Yeah," I whisper against her hair. "I think it is." But this time, I'm not just saying it. I really think it is.

***

"A toast!" Austin rises, champagne glass lifted high enough to catch the chandelier light. "To my fiancée. The woman who makes me laugh, calls me on my crap, and somehow makes everything feel like home." His voice catches, just slightly. "I'm the luckiest guy in this room. Casey girl, I can't wait to marry you." He clinks her glass and leans in with a grin that's pure relief. "I won the World Series."

The table erupts—cheers, whistles, the sharp music of crystal meeting crystal. And as the noise swells around us, I let the moment wash over me.

Three glasses of champagne in, I sink deeper into the velvet booth at Picasso's Lounge, the celebration carrying on above the low murmur of the restaurant. The whole place hums—gold light flickering against the walls, servers gliding past with polished ease, the soft clink of silver against porcelain. It feels indulgent. Suspended. Like we've stepped into a memory we'll talk about for years instead of just another Saturday night on the Strip.

I slide my arm around Lauren's waist beneath the table, my palm settling at her hip like it remembers the way without asking permission.

She smiles into her glass, cheeks flushed, eyes bright in a way I haven't seen in months. Her hand drifts to my thigh. The squeeze is subtle—almost absentminded—but it lights a slow fuse under my skin. For so long, everything between us has felt measured. Careful. One wrong word from splintering. And now she leans into me like it's instinct again.

"I'm just—" Casey hiccups, pressing a hand to her chest as she stares at the diamond on her finger. "I'm in shock. I had absolutely no clue!" She elbows Austin and then looks around at all of us, eyes glassy. "And you guys are all here! How is this real?"

Josh wraps an arm around Mavis and kisses the top of

her head. "Welcome to the family, Case. You're officially a Templeton now."

He tips his glass in her direction as I lean into Lauren's ear. "And... good luck with that," I whisper.

She giggles into her napkin, shoulders shaking, and the sound hits me square in the chest. I press a kiss to her cheek—not for show, not for anyone else—just because I want to feel her there.

But that's when Austin narrows his eyes at us, a slow grin tugging at the corner of his mouth. He taps the base of his champagne flute against the table once, like he's connecting the dots.

"Are we celebrating more than just an engagement tonight?" he asks, dragging the words out just enough to make the table go quiet. His gaze flicks from me to Lauren and back again, eyebrows lifting in exaggerated suspicion. Then he drains his glass in one confident tilt, like he already knows the answer.

The champagne in my bloodstream shifts from warm to electric. For a split-second, the old instinct flares—deflect, joke, dodge. Don't expose the fragile parts in front of an audience. But Lauren's tucked into my side. Not away from me. Not bracing. Just with me. And I tighten my arm around her and kiss her cheek again, buying myself a breath.

"Let's just say," I start, forcing a grin, "you don't always give terrible advice, Austin."

"Wait." Lauren's brow pinches as she looks between us, suspicion sharpening her voice. "What are you talking about?"

Austin barks out a laugh and reaches for the bottle. "All you, dude." Then he starts refilling glasses like he didn't just lob a grenade into the middle of the table.

Lauren doesn't laugh though. She turns fully toward me, her eyes searching mine—like she's trying to decide if this is a joke, a secret, or something that matters. Then she swats my arm, but it's half-playful, half-demand. "Tell me. Right now."

For a second, I consider dodging it. Making it a joke. Blaming Austin. Keeping the surface intact. That's what I've done for months—kept things light, kept things deflected, kept the real stuff tucked behind sarcasm and timing. It's easier to be charming than vulnerable. Easier to be the funny guy than the husband who admits he's been scared.

But she looks at me like she wants the real answer. And I'm tired of giving her anything less.

"Peaches, I didn't think you'd want me here this weekend," I admit, my eyes dropping to the table for half a second before I force myself to meet hers. "I wanted to celebrate. I just... didn't want to be in the way. It's not exactly a secret we weren't doing great." The words hang there, but they don't slice.

I lace my fingers through hers and lift her hand to my mouth. "But Vegas is kind of *our place*," I say. "So, Austin encouraged me to come. To relive some memories. To see what would happen if we gave ourselves some space to breathe."

Her eyes widen as the pieces click into place.

"He was right," I say, brushing my thumb over her knuckles.

Her smile spreads slow and bright—real, not forced. "So," she says, drawing it out like she's solving a case, "that's why you suggested we eat hot dogs last night?"

Austin sputters into his drink. "Hot dogs?" He coughs once, eyes wide. "What kind of wedding did you two have—county fair chic?"

Casey chokes on her champagne. "Austin—"

"What? I'm just trying to picture it." He wheezes. "Was there a veil? A bouquet? Or did you exchange vows over ketchup packets?"

Lauren laughs, then leans in close to my ear like she's about to share classified information. "*It was* a real wiener adventure," she teases.

I groan, but I smile so hard it hurts. "Yeah, well," I say, "that wiener adventure started—and kind of saved—our marriage."

Austin points at us with his glass. "I absolutely hate that sentence," he says, still laughing. "But also... I'm really happy for you guys. We all are."

Lauren leans into me without hesitation. No pause. No doubt. Just there. "So," she says, eyes bright as she tilts her head toward Austin, "what you're saying is I owe my brother a thank-you for interfering?"

Austin rolls up his sleeves like he's about to accept an award. "You may bow when ready, sis."

With a roll of my eyes, I tip my glass toward him, then turn to Josh. "*Both* brothers," I correct.

Josh lifts his brows, a small smile tugging at his mouth—quiet pride, but not the smug kind. "Hey," he says, holding up a hand. "All I did was share a spare bedroom."

But Lauren shakes her head. "No, you did more than that." She winks at him, but I can only guess at the way he must have helped her, too.

Josh gives her a quick, affectionate nod—a *we've got you* without making it a speech—just as two more bottles arrive. Austin pops the cork, foam spilling over his fingers as every glass lifts again.

And I look around the table—at Casey staring at her ring like it's a dream, at Austin watching her like he can't believe she's real, at Mavis glowing in a way that's equal parts joy and anticipation, at Josh pretending he's not emotional, at Lauren tucked into my side like she chose this seat beside me—and something in me unclenches.

For months, I've been living like we were already halfway gone. Like the ending was inevitable and I just hadn't signed the paper yet. But sitting here, her weight against me, her laugh in my ear... I feel hopeful.

"Refill?" Austin asks.

I raise my glass, meeting Lauren's eyes as I do. Because *yeah*. We've got a hell of a lot more to celebrate than I thought.

***

"Oh my, God, Mitch!" Lauren laughs, eyes wide, waving the payout ticket in the air. "I cannot believe how much money you just won!"

I pull her into me before she can say another word, the dark hotel room wrapping around us. The only light comes from the blinking red CVS sign bleeding through the curtains, flashing in slow rhythm across her skin.

"Oh, come on," I tease, grinning against her hair. "It was a Middle-earth slot machine. There was no way Tolkien's ghost wasn't going to come through for me."

She giggles and traces a finger over the tattoo on my forearm. "All that is gold does not glitter," she whispers, dropping the nine thousand-five-hundred-dollar ticket onto the dresser like it's nothing.

"Not all those who wander are lost," I answer automatically, because I've said it a hundred times before—but tonight it lands differently.

I lower my lips to hers and taste bourbon—oak and vanilla and warmth—and when she exhales against my mouth, something in my chest shifts. Not lust. But relief. Recognition. The feeling of finding my way back to something I thought I'd lost.

"I love you, Mrs. Benson," I whisper against her lips, my hands sliding down to her hips. "I never stopped. Not for one second."

Her breath stutters, and she grips my arms like she needs to anchor herself. "I love you, too," she answers as her hands slip beneath my shirt, fingers warm against my skin, moving slowly—relearning, remembering. "I want to show you how much."

I catch her wrists gently before she can pull back, pressing a kiss to the inside of one palm. "You don't have to prove anything to me," I say, my voice rough but steady. "Just being here. Choosing me. That's enough."

She pulls my shirt up and over my head just as the air-conditioning kicks on, a rush of cool air sweeping across my skin. I shiver despite myself, and she grins when goosebumps rise along my arms.

"Cold?" she teases, her fingers tracing lightly over them.

I step closer, brushing my knuckles down her side, letting my touch warm the path the air just claimed. "Trust me," I say, a crooked smile tugging at my mouth, "that's not what I'm feeling."

In the dim red light, her eyes shine—open and unguarded. No scorekeeping. No shadow of the things we've said or almost said. Just her, standing here with me. And the last of my restraint slips.

I slide my hands to the hem of her shirt and ease it up and over her head, my pulse thundering in my ears. But each layer that falls away feels like more than fabric—like we've been peeling back resentment, pride, and fear all weekend, stripping ourselves down to what's still solid underneath.

"Mitch…" she whispers, her hands sliding up my chest, palms warm and steady over my heartbeat. Her gaze holds mine—open, certain. "Don't stop," she pleads, a small smile curving at the corner of her mouth. "Not tonight." Her fingers trace the line of my jaw, then drift down, slow and deliberate, like she's memorizing instead of rushing. "I want this," she adds softly. "I want you."

And there's no world where I don't return that sentiment. I kiss along her shoulder, every confession we made since landing in Vegas humming under my skin. Every almost. Every what if.

A soft moan slips through her lips as I lift her, laying her back against the mattress, and I hover over her for a second just to look. To really look. At the woman who said yes to me once on a beach under a sky full of stars. At the woman I almost let slip through my hands because I forgot how to fight for us.

"You're my everything, Lauren," I say, but this time it doesn't feel like a line. It feels like the truth I had to earn my way back to.

We shed the last layers between us—her fingers tugging at my zipper, my hands tangling briefly in her hair as I work at the clasp of her bra. There's laughter in the friction, breathless and warm. It isn't clumsy. It's familiar. It's us—before everything got heavy, before we let silence do more damage than any argument ever could.

Her skin is smooth beneath my rough palms, and where I once felt the contrast like distance, tonight it feels like balance. We were never opposites. Just two stubborn people learning the same lessons at different speeds. Now, there's a shared knowing between us—hard-earned, but steady.

I want to slow it down. Memorize it. Let the reconnection stretch long and unhurried. But the way she moves against me—impatient, certain—the soft sounds she can't quite hold back, the rhythm of her touch pulling me closer—it's going to take everything I have not to lose myself too quickly in her again.

I line myself up and slip inside her, but when we move together, it isn't frantic. It isn't about proving anything. It's about closing distance. About pressing every doubt out of the space between us. Her nails dig into my shoulders and my name falls from her lips like a prayer I forgot I knew by heart.

I hold her face when she arches toward me. And I relish the sounds she makes, allowing myself to feel the way she meets me—not just physically, but fully. Present.

For months, I've lived like we were already done. Like the ending was inevitable. But here, in the dark, with the red neon blinking across her skin and her heartbeat racing against mine, the future doesn't feel fractured. It feels possible.

When we finally fall together, breathless and tangled in the sheets, I press my lips to her damp forehead and let out a quiet, almost stunned laugh. Because it feels like surfacing after being underwater too long.

I brush her hair back from her face, tracing the curve of her cheek with my thumb. "I forgot how right this feels," I whisper, my voice low. "How right you feel."

She shifts closer, her hand resting over my heart like she's reacquainting herself with its rhythm, her smile warm where her cheek presses to my chest. Her voice is husky with sleep and bourbon and something steadier than either. "I know," she whispers. "Me, too."

Then she draws the blanket up around us and curls into my side, her hair spilling across my skin. The room settles— the air conditioner clicking off, the hum of the Strip muffled behind the curtains, neon still blinking beyond the glass like the city refuses to rest.

"Vegas is..." she mutters, already drifting.

"One hell of a wiener adventure," I finish softly.

Her quiet laugh vibrates against me before her breathing evens out. And for the first time in a long time, sleep doesn't feel like escape. It feels like peace.

CHAPTER TEN

Lauren

The sun beats down like it has a personal vendetta, turning the cement patio into a skillet and my legs into something that's one shade away from identifying as a lobster. The air smells like chlorine, coconut sunscreen, and the sweet scent of overpriced frozen cocktails. Somewhere behind us, a DJ tries way too hard, and every few seconds someone shrieks from the pool like they've just discovered water for the first time.

My hotel-issued excuse for a beach towel slips through the slats of the lounge chair—again, and again, and again—until I finally sit up with a groan, wincing at the tight pull of sun-warmed skin across my thighs.

"More sunblock," I mutter, digging through my bag. I squirt a generous blob into my palm and toss the bottle onto Casey's lap. "You too, girlfriend. You are officially beet red."

My phone buzzes beside me. I glance down and laugh as I rub the last bit of lotion into my skin.

Miguel: New Friday special idea. Trust me. Call me.

I type back quickly, thumbs moving fast across the screen, smearing the sticky residue still clinging to me.

Me: I'm at a pool in Vegas. You're lucky I'm even answering.

A second passes before I text again with a smile. Because of course he's got me curious.

Me: Okay fine. What's your idea?

Then I toss the phone back onto the towel, already bracing myself for whatever idea Miguel has cooked up now.

Casey scowls and drags her hands down her arms. "It is so freaking hot here." She lifts her sunglasses and rubs beneath her eyes, the diamond on her finger catching the sunlight like it's showing off. "I'm going to go home looking like a raccoon." She squeezes a glob into her hand and smears it across her cheeks with zero dignity. "And I'm sweating like I ran a marathon," she adds, then lobs the bottle toward Mavis like we're in a relay race and sunblock is the baton.

"You think *you're* sweating?" Mavis fights her way upright, snapping the black maternity fabric away from her belly like it's trying to suffocate her. "Whoever designs maternity swimwear deserves to be tried for crimes against humanity."

I snort into my strawberry daiquiri—now more soup than slush. "Tell us how you really feel, Mavs."

She doesn't even blink. "Too. Much. Fabric." Each word gets its own little snap as a bead of sweat slides down her temple.

And even though I hate myself for it, a thought rises in me—sharp and automatic. But I swallow it before it can surface. *I'd trade you in a second.*

To my right, Casey pops up from her chair and adjusts the straps of her blue bikini. Her toe catches the edge of my lounge chair and she stumbles, laughing at herself as she reaches for Mavis's hand. "Come on. Let's cool off. Maybe the pool will stop your pregnant ass from complaining so much."

"I'm not complaining." Mavis huffs, tugging out her earbuds. "I'm just uncomfortable."

"Same thing," I say, pushing myself up and immediately regretting it as the cement sears the bottoms of my feet. I hop once and hiss. "Besides, I promised Josh I'd keep an eye on you, and I'm not getting blamed if you overheat while they're off on their dumb Pawn Stars tour."

Mavis rolls her eyes. "I'm so glad they didn't make us go."

"Oh my, God, same." I scoop up our drinks and fall in step behind them, weaving around chairs and pool bags and bodies slick with sunscreen. "I do not understand the appeal of watching grown men argue over antique junk."

"The show's fine," Mavis says, gripping the railing at the pool steps like she's about to descend into salvation. "I just can't stand for three hours anymore."

I smile, and for a moment the whole scene feels simple—three women, sun-drunk and slightly feral, doing what we've always done best—making each other laugh while the world spins loud and bright around us.

Casey lowers herself into the shallow end with a grateful sigh, water lapping at her hips. "How many weeks are you again?"

"Twenty-four," Mavis says, easing onto the top step and letting the cool water swallow her calves.

"Twenty-four?" I widen my eyes and drop down beside her, the shock of cold against my overheated skin stealing my breath. Goosebumps race up my arms. "That's more than halfway. I need to get serious about your baby shower."

Mavis blushes, waving a hand like she can deflect the attention. "You really don't have to—"

"Oh, please." I take a long sip of my daiquiri, buying myself half a second to steady the tightness in my chest. "Like I'm not going to throw you a baby shower. That's my niece or nephew in there." I gesture at the curve of her belly. "Baby Templeton deserves a party."

Her eyes gloss over almost instantly. More tears. Always more tears.

I soften my tone, because that's what good sisters-in-law do. "So, you're really not going to find out what you're having?"

"Wait, what?" Casey dunks her head beneath the water and pops back up, hair slicked to her shoulders. "You're not finding out if it's a boy or girl?"

Mavis smiles down at her stomach, fingers trailing along the surface of the water as she sits on the top step. "Josh wants to be surprised."

Casey flips onto her back and performs an ungraceful backstroke, splashing us both. "Why?" she sputters.

"I mean, it's kind of sweet, isn't it?" Mavis laughs. "He wants that moment in the delivery room. Josh wants to be the first to know."

I watch her as she talks—the way her whole face changes when she says his name. "That does not sound like my brother," I say, grinning. "He color-codes his Google calendar. Like, sub-categories, too."

"Exactly!" She laughs, tipping her face toward the sun. "But at the ultrasound he wouldn't even look at the screen. Just stared at me the whole time and interrogated the poor tech."

Outwardly, I smile. But something sharp coils low in my stomach. It's quiet and mean and I hate it instantly, that flicker of jealousy all over again. That whisper of *why not me?* I swallow it down, though. Because this is her moment. Not mine. So, I raise my hand toward the poolside waiter before my face has a chance to betray me. "Two more!" I call, flashing my fingers. "And another water, please!"

Because if I can't control biology, I can at least control the drink order.

I sink deeper onto the second step, letting the water climb to my shoulders, smoothing my expression into something bright and easy. "Okay, Mavs. Yellow and green it is. So, what are we thinking? Baby woodland animals?

Tiny foxes? Deer? Something Pinterest-worthy?"

"Woodland animals?" Casey doggy-paddles toward us like I've offended her. "Absolutely not. We'll go with a Cubs theme. If this kid is going to grow up in California, I am not losing them to the Dodgers. Auntie Casey cannot emotionally survive another Dodgers fan."

I laugh—because it's funny, because it's easy—and two fresh daiquiris arrive like they've been summoned by denial itself. I dip under the surface of the water for a second, just long enough for the noise to blur and the ache to dull. The coolness wraps around me, quiet and weightless.

When I resurface, I slick my hair back and aim a smile at Mavis. "I can't argue with her. You pick the theme," I say lightly. "I'll execute." Because that's what I do. I plan the party. I make it pretty. I keep the tone bright. I hold the sharp parts of myself underwater where no one else can see them.

But as I watch Mavis laugh—hand resting on her belly, eyes shining—I feel the sting anyway, quick and quiet. It flares, then I swallow it down with practiced ease, like a reflex.

I take another sip, let the sugar and cold hit my tongue, and force my shoulders to relax. Then, unprompted, last night slides back into my mind—Mitch's voice in the dark, the steadiness of his hands like he was reminding me where I belonged. Heat rises to my cheeks that has nothing to do with the sun. And while the ache doesn't disappear exactly, it does loosen.

"Hey." Mavis nudges my calf beneath the water, her grin suspiciously gentle. "So... you and Mitch are...?" She tilts her head like she already knows but wants the satisfaction of hearing it.

A laugh slips out of me before I can stop it. "I cannot believe I'm saying this," I admit, shaking my head. "But we're good."

Casey freezes mid-sip. "Define good."

"Like..." I press my lips together, trying not to smile too

hard. "More than good. Really good."

Casey slurps her cocktail through the straw. "Details, please."

"*Some* details," Mavis corrects, kicking her. "He's my brother."

Casey rolls her eyes. "Fine. PG-13. But answer the important question first." She leans forward dramatically. "Divorce off the table?"

My chest swells so fast it almost hurts. "No divorce," I say, but the words still feel surreal. "Mitch tore up the form. Threw it away two nights ago."

They both gasp like I've just announced a pregnancy of my own.

"I don't even fully understand how we got here," I admit, drawing in a deep breath as my cheeks flush. "There's just something about Vegas, I guess."

Casey lifts her ring and wiggles her fingers, the diamond scattering sunlight everywhere. "You're welcome," she says smugly, elbowing me. "But that is still not enough information."

Heat creeps up my neck—part sunburn, part memory. "It's hard to explain," I say. "One minute we were staring at divorce papers... and the next we were back in bed together."

Mavis scrunches her nose. "*Some* of the details, Lauren," she reminds me.

But I point at her belly and giggle. "Oh, please. Like I can't imagine what you did with my brother."

She groans and drops her face into her hands, laughing.

Casey looks between us. "What exactly am I marrying into here, ladies? You realize it's weird, right? Brother and sister marrying brother and sister?"

"Oh, stop." I splash her. "Mitch and I got married way before—"

"Excuse you," Mavis cuts in, sliding into the water deeper and splashing me back. "Joshua and I were together first."

"And then you took a light ten-year sabbatical," I shoot back, grabbing my new drink. "We were steady during your hiatus."

"Fine. Let's just call it even." She laughs and bumps her elbow into mine. Then she softens, her voice losing the tease. "I'm just glad you're working it out. Mitch has been miserable. Like… unbearably mopey."

My smile fades a notch. "Yeah," I say quietly. "Me, too." The humor settles into something heavier. "It's been a rough year," I admit. "Honestly, probably longer. I just didn't want to say it out loud."

"What do you think happened?" Casey asks, squinting against the glare off the water.

I lean back against the pool wall, arms resting along the edge. "It wasn't really one big thing," I say slowly. "It was a hundred tiny cracks. But a big one was the restaurant. Pier Ninety-two just… took over my life."

"The restaurant?" Mavis watches me carefully. "To me, Mitch always made it seem like it was—"

"What?" I prompt gently.

She hesitates. "Like it was…" She gulps. "More about who *you* were. Who *he* was."

I nod. "Yeah, it was that, too." Water ripples between us. "And I know he talked to you about that," I add. "I'm glad he did."

Her brows lift. "You are?"

"Yeah." I glance at her. "Because you two think alike. You always have. Even after all those years apart. Josh pointed it out to me and it gave me a new perspective."

Mavis goes still for a second, like that lands somewhere she didn't expect.

"He needed someone who understood him in a way I couldn't," I continue. "And you… you filled that role until I could see it."

Mavis looks down at the water, a little embarrassed. "I just told him to get over himself and go fight for you."

I laugh softly. "Well, it worked."

Casey waves her hand. "I have no idea what's happening here anymore, but I support it."

I grin. "I just couldn't picture my life without him," I say, and this time the truth doesn't wobble. "And apparently he couldn't either. It's kind of wild that it took a trip back to Vegas—and a meddling pack of siblings—to make us admit that."

Mavis nudges me. "This place is special to him. To you both."

I close my eyes for a second and feel Mitch's hands all over me again. His voice. The way he looked at me last night like he was choosing me.

"I should've dragged him here sooner," I say. "Maybe we could've skipped some of the heartache."

She bumps her shoulder into mine. "Still got the happy ending."

The word *divorce* flashes in my mind—sharp and ugly and final. "When I booked these tickets," I say quietly, "I thought they'd be the last ones I ever bought for us. I didn't think we'd fly home together as…"

"A happily married couple," Casey finishes, hauling herself up onto the edge of the pool, water dripping down her legs.

I let the words settle into my bones and nod. "Yeah. A happily married couple," I repeat. And this time, it feels real.

That's when a man cannonballs into the pool directly in front of us, sending a tidal wave over my head and drenching us all.

I sputter and laugh. And a second later, Austin's blond head breaks the surface with a grin so wide it looks painful. He wipes water from his face like he's on stage. "Where's my beautiful fiancée?" he bellows, turning in a slow circle like he's hunting for treasure. "Ohhh, Cinderellaaa?"

Casey shrieks with laughter and drops back into the pool, then swims straight for him. He catches her, they kiss, and the two of them disappear under the water in a tangle of limbs and ridiculous happiness.

And I can't help it—I smile. A real one. Then Mitch appears in the shallow end, all dark hair, tattoos, and smug amusement, and for half a second it's like the last year never happened. He dunks his head under, resurfaces with a dramatic gasp, and makes a show of slicking his hair back.

"Oh, to be young and in love," he says, fluttering his lashes in mockery.

I laugh, and it surprises me how easy it comes.

He wades over and plants a wet kiss on my cheek. "Miss me?"

Warmth spreads through me—quiet and immediate—because the answer is embarrassingly simple. *Yeah. I did.*

I nod, cheeks heating. "How was the tour, gentlemen?"

"Honestly? Awesome," Josh says, sliding into the pool beside Mavis. His hands find her belly like they belong there, and he kisses the top of her head. "You girls missed out."

Mavis rolls her eyes, but she smiles as he sits beside her. "I think our definitions of *missed out* differ."

"We tried calling you like five times," Austin says, hauling Casey behind him like she's a trophy. "Do none of you own phones anymore?"

I gesture toward our trio of lounge chairs. "We were swimming. Our phones are in our bags." I point. "Why? What's up?"

Mitch drifts to the edge of the pool and hooks a finger under one of my empty plastic cups. He nudges it like it's evidence. It tips, the last blush of pink sliding down the concrete in a slow, sticky ribbon.

His mouth quirks. "We were going to offer to bring you a late lunch," he says, all casual. "But it looks like you chose... the liquid route."

I snort and push the wet hair off my face. "Lunch is overrated."

"Spoken like a woman who's had three strawberry daiquiris and zero protein," he shoots back, and there's that familiar lightness in his voice—teasing, easy, like we're not careful around each other anymore.

I climb out of the pool, water streaming off my arms and down my sides, and brush past him on purpose. I run my fingers through his wet hair as I go, just because I can. Just because he lets me.

"You need sunscreen," I tell him, like it's a normal, domestic thing and not my way of keeping this moment anchored. Then I pad back toward our row of chairs, heat slapping my damp skin as soon as my feet dry. I reach into my bag for the bottle—but my phone screen flares to life against the lining, bright and abrupt, like a warning light in the middle of paradise.

Seventeen missed calls.

My pulse slams once, hard and violent, like my body already knows before my brain catches up. Because this is most certainly not about the new Friday special. I unlock the screen with fingers that suddenly don't feel steady. And the call log fills the display:

Miguel.

Miguel.

Miguel.

Miguel.

Over and over. Stacked minute by minute. Relentless. Like something urgent kept clawing at me while I was laughing, pretending the world couldn't reach me.

"What the hell..." I whisper, lowering myself onto the edge of the lounge chair. Water drips from my suit onto the towel that won't stay in place, soaking through like it's trying to disappear.

I tap his name. One ring. Two. Three—

"Lauren?" But his voice is all wrong. Thin. Shaking. Like it's barely holding together.

And my stomach drops so fast it feels like I've stepped off a ledge. "Miguel, what's wro—"

"It's gone." His breath crackles through the line, jagged and uneven. "The smoke... the flames..."

Behind him, a siren wails—close. Too close. It bleeds through the speaker and straight into my bloodstream.

"A grease fire," he says, the words tumbling over each other. "We tried—we tried to put it out—"

The air leaves my lungs in a quiet, stunned rush. My hand tightens around the phone until my knuckles ache. And I lift my head automatically, instinctively, scanning the pool for Mitch.

I don't even think about it. My eyes search through the glare of blue water and flashing sunlight and bodies splashing and laughing. The music still thumps. Someone cannonballs. Casey's laugh carries across the space. But it all sounds far away. Muffled. Like I'm underwater again.

"Miguel," I say, but my voice doesn't sound like mine.

"We tried to put it out," he repeats, and now he's crying. I can hear it. "But it spread so fast. The kitchen—Lauren, the whole kitchen—"

My vision blurs, but through the haze, I lock eyes with Mitch. He wades through the shallow end, water slick on his shoulders, hair dark against his forehead. He smiles because he hasn't caught up yet. Because he's still in the version of this afternoon where everything is light.

Then the smile drops from his face. Because he sees it. He sees that something is wrong before I can say it.

"I'm so sorry, Lauren," Miguel says again, but there's nothing left in his voice now but devastation. "It's gone. Pier Ninety-two is… gone."

But the words don't compute. Because the sun keeps shining. The water keeps sparkling. And the Strip keeps humming beyond the hotel walls. Something inside me fractures though. My lungs won't pull in air. My heart stutters, then pounds, then feels like it stops entirely.

Mitch reaches the edge of the pool and climbs out fast, water streaming everywhere as he moves in my direction. He drops to his knees in front of me, hands bracing on my thighs, his eyes searching my face like he's trying to decode a language he's never learned.

"Lauren?" he says.

I swallow, but it's like trying to swallow glass.

"It's gone," I manage, barely above a whisper.

But he still doesn't understand. Because how could he?

Miguel still talks—words about fire crews and damage and smoke—but they blur into static. Because all I can hear is the echo of that single word—*gone.*

The thing I poured myself into. The place that swallowed my time, my energy, my marriage. The place I defended. The place I chose over Mitch more times than I want to admit... *is gone.*

And the sick, hollow clarity hits me all at once. The thing I've been afraid to lose all year—the thing that nearly cost me my husband—has just been ripped away in a single phone call.

The pool water glitters. The sun beats down. But everything tilts.

CHAPTER ELEVEN

Mitch

Sleep finally wins. Lauren's head tips onto my left shoulder like her body has simply run out of places to hold all the pain. Her cheeks are still flushed, the skin around her eyes swollen and red-rimmed, and the sight of it hits me right in the sternum.

I slide my arm around her, pulling her closer until she's tucked against my chest. Like I can shelter her from the world with bone and breath alone.

The last four hours replay in jagged pieces—her sobs turning to anger, anger turning to raw, shaking grief. The way she screamed until her voice went hoarse. The way she stomped her feet like the hotel floor itself had betrayed her. The way I kept grabbing for solutions that didn't exist.

All I could do was get us out. Get her moving. Get her on a plane out of Vegas and headed back to L.A. Because staying there felt like it was allowing the wound to keep bleeding.

Overhead, the intercom pops and crackles. And the cabin's chatter dims.

"Ladies and gentlemen, this is your captain speaking. It

appears there's going to be a small delay taxiing out to the runway this evening. The aircraft scheduled for takeoff before us is experiencing a minor mechanical failure on the tarmac. I'm told it'll be no more than twenty minutes, so sit back and relax, and when I know more, I'll report back."

A wave of grumbles ripples through the passengers around us—annoyed sighs, impatient shifting, someone muttering about connections.

But Lauren doesn't move. She's sunk too deep, finally, into a sleep that looks less like rest and more like surrender. Her lips part slightly as she breathes, and then—like my heart needed one more reason to break—she licks them in her sleep, some small, unconscious motion that makes her look impossibly soft. Innocent. Like none of this ever touched her.

My chest flutters. And my grip on her tightens.

You're my forever, Lauren. You always have been. You always will be. No mistakes this time.

My hand drifts to my pocket and I pull out my phone, keeping my movements careful—slow enough not to jostle her. The screen glows dimly in the dark cabin, and I open my browser like I'm reaching for a lifeline.

My mind already races ahead, building something solid where everything else feels like it's falling apart.

Plywood.

Wood dowels.

Paint.

Screws.

Wood glue.

Nylon rope.

Sandpaper.

One by one, I tap each item and add it to my cart. The list grows until the makings of a homemade rocking horse stare back at me—ridiculous in this moment, maybe, but also… a promise. A future I can put my hands on.

I press a kiss on the top of her head, holding my lips there like I'm trying to transfer steadiness. Then I hit purchase and switch the phone to airplane mode before sliding it back into my pocket.

I settle deeper into my seat, keeping Lauren anchored against me, and close my eyes. In the dark behind my lids, I can already see it—smooth wood, curved runners, careful paint. I see her, too—our little girl riding it, laughing in a way that doesn't hurt.

And for the first time in over a year, the future doesn't feel like a threat. It feels like something I'm going to build.

***

Sixteen hours later, I turn onto Rainy Cloud Road and pull my truck into Josh and Mavis's driveway. The engine rumbles, then dies. And silence rushes in behind it—thick and startling after a day of airports, phone calls, and Lauren's grief still echoing in my head.

For a second, I just sit there with my hands on the wheel, like if I loosen my grip, the whole thing might slip away. *I'm back.* But this time I'm not visiting. Not crashing. Not hiding out in my sister's guest room.

"Thanks for picking me up," Mavis says, already working her seatbelt loose, trying to sound casual even though she looks wrecked.

"Hey, no worries." My voice comes out steadier than I feel. I glance at her belly—round, undeniable, proof that life keeps moving whether you're ready or not. "I needed to swing by anyway. Pack up my stuff." I nod toward her door. "Hang on—I'll come around."

I hop out and jog around the front of the truck, gravel biting into my boots. When I open her door, I brace it with one hand and offer her the other. "Sorry," I say, forcing a grin. "It's kind of a jump."

She grips my fingers and eases herself down, careful with every movement. "Thanks, Mitch."

"I'll grab your bag," I tell her. "Meet you on the porch."

She waddles toward the house, slow and steady, and I'm

about to reach for her things when something catches the light on the floorboard. A tiny flash. Silver. It's so small it shouldn't stop me. But my breath catches like I've been punched, and I lean back into the cab, heart hammering, fingers sweeping along the carpet until I feel it. *My wedding ring.*

For a beat, I just stare at it in my palm. The band is cool and unassuming, like it doesn't understand the chaos it's been through. Like it doesn't know how close I came to leaving it behind for good.

I slide it back onto my finger and the metal settles against my skin with a soft, final weight. But it feels different now—like it carries every mistake I made and every mile it took to get back here. It isn't just a ring anymore. It's a new promise.

I flex my hand once, watching it catch the light, and something in my chest unclenches. Because I have no intention of taking it off again.

The thought lands clean and certain, and a slow, almost disbelieving smirk tugs at my mouth. I reach into the backseat, grab Mavis's bag, and head up the walkway with the ring pressing a steady reminder into my finger with every step.

"When did Josh say he'd be back?" I ask as she taps the code into the keypad and pushes the front door open.

"Umm, not sure. The hospital called like four minutes after we landed." She yawns into her hand. "I'm sure he'll text me later. I just feel bad. He barely slept last night, and then traveling… He's exhausted. The last thing he needs is an unexpected shift."

I step over the threshold just behind her, the familiar smell hitting me—clean laundry, fresh flowers, faint citrus cleaner. It's weird how a house can feel like a chapter you never meant to live in.

I shrug. "Life of a doctor, right?"

"Yeah, I guess." She nods and rubs her eyes. "I gotta pee. I'll be right back."

The powder room door clicks shut. And there it is

again—that quiet. Not the painful kind from Vegas. Not the hollow kind from all those nights I pretended I didn't miss Lauren. A different quiet. A decision.

I take the stairs two at a time, pushing open the guest room door—the room I've called mine for months. Then I move. I yank open drawers and start shoving clothes into my duffel. T-shirts, jeans, socks—no folding, no careful stacks. I'm not trying to preserve a life I don't want anymore. I'm erasing evidence. Clearing space. Closing the loop.

I strip the closet bare, crank hangers aside, and cram everything into a suitcase with a reckless kind of purpose. My ring glints when I reach, when I shove, when I slam a dresser drawer shut, like it's watching me—holding me accountable.

Good. Let it.

I sweep through the adjoining bathroom next, tossing my toothbrush, razor, and shampoo into a backpack. The half-used bar of soap goes straight into the trash. No souvenirs. No lingering. No "just in case." Because there is no "just in case" anymore. There's only home.

Then I turn to the bed. I strip the sheets in one hard pull and ball them under my arm like I can't stand the idea of leaving my mess behind for someone else to handle. I jog downstairs and shove them into the washing machine.

Water thunders in a second later, loud and steady, and I stand there for a beat with my hands on the lid, listening to it fill. Like a reset. Like the house itself is helping me wash the last few months away.

"So, it's for real then?" Mavis leans against the laundry room doorway, chewing on a baby carrot, one eyebrow arched. "We're actually getting our guest room back?"

There's a teasing lilt to her voice, but I hear the question underneath it. *Are you really okay this time?*

Adrenaline hums through me. I pour in detergent and slam the lid closed like I'm sealing something permanent. "You know I appreciate the hospitality," I say, forcing a smirk as I hit start, "but when it comes down to it, the sheets are just too starchy here. I prefer satin."

She snorts. "So, it's the sheets that are making you leave, huh?"

"Superior thread count, Mavs." I scoop up my tennis shoes and work boots from the mudroom, then step close enough to press a quick kiss to her forehead, careful of the curve of her belly between us. "Yours just don't compare."

She studies me for a second—longer than the joke deserves—like she's measuring whether I'm deflecting or telling the truth. Then she follows me upstairs, carrot crunching with every step.

When we reach the guest room, I pause in the doorway. "I'm heading home," I say quietly. "For good this time." The word *home* leaves my mouth and spreads through my chest like warmth after standing in the cold too long.

"I'm glad," she says quickly. Then her face tightens. "Er—not that we didn't love having you here."

Heat creeps up my neck. "Subtle, Mavs."

She drops onto the now-bare mattress and runs her hand over the top, eyes soft. "You know that's not how I meant it."

I scan the empty room—blank walls, cleared dresser, no trace of me left behind. A few months ago, that sight would've felt like rejection. Like failure. Now it feels right. Like a reset button I finally had the courage to press.

I sit down beside her and stretch out, lacing my fingers behind my head. "Thanks for letting me crash here."

She mirrors me, staring at the ceiling. "My home is always your home."

At her words, my stomach dips and I turn my head toward her. "That's sweet. But I think you're going to need this space for someone else pretty soon."

Her hands fall instantly to her belly, palms spreading over the curve of it. Her expression shifts—soft, awed... then scared.

"I have absolutely no idea what I'm doing," she admits,

voice barely above a whisper. "You know that, right?"

The vulnerability in her tone slices right through me. I roll onto my side and prop myself up on one elbow, studying her face. "Oh, come on. Yes, you do."

She shakes her head.

I reach over and nudge her shoulder gently. "You and Josh have basically been parenting me for the last few months. Letting me live here. Calling me out when I was being an idiot. Telling me I was making the biggest mistake of my life." My voice softens. "Helping me—and Lauren—see it."

She covers her face with both hands, laughing through it. "Damn. That's a lot of interference."

"No penalty, though." I shake my head. "I needed it. Every bit of it." I reach for her hand and lace my fingers through hers. "You didn't judge me. You didn't give up on me. You just... loved me through it. That's motherhood, Mavs. That's the whole job."

She lowers her hands and looks at me, eyes glassy. "That's different," she says softly. "You're my brother. You can talk back."

I smile. "Trust me. That kid's going to talk back, too."

She lets out a shaky laugh.

"I'm serious though," I continue. "You already know how to protect someone without smothering them. How to push when they need pushing. How to sit beside them when they don't. You're going to be incredible."

Her chin wobbles just a little before she swallows it down. "Yeah, but you're a grown man. Not a tiny person I have to expel from my body."

I freeze. "Okay," I say slowly, sitting up and reaching for my duffel. "I'm going to let that visual stay right here in this room."

She bursts out laughing, and just like that, the tension breaks.

"And on that note," I say, slinging the strap over my shoulder, "I'm out. For good this time."

She rolls onto her side, giggling into the mattress. "Enjoy your satin sheets."

"I'll enjoy my wife more."

She scrunches her nose. "That's gross. But also… somehow really sweet."

I snort, but my throat tightens anyway. Because it is sweet. Because I almost lost that.

I tap the doorframe with my knuckles and pull up the handle of my suitcase. "Gross or sweet, I owe you one, Mavs. I don't know if I would've figured it out without you."

Her teasing expression fades, replaced by something steadier. Fiercer. "You would've," she says. "Eventually."

I step back toward her and wrap her in a careful hug, my arms circling both her and the baby. And for a second, I just hold on. "Thank you," I whisper into her hair.

"For what?"

"For not letting me quit."

She squeezes me back. "That's what sisters are for."

I pull away and clear my throat before I do something ridiculous like cry.

"Please hug Lauren for me—again," she says, blowing an exaggerated kiss into the air. It's dramatic and ridiculous. But it still lands square in my chest.

"I will," I promise. But as I head downstairs, suitcase wheels bumping behind me, straps cutting into my shoulder, a thought hits hard and humbling. I almost missed out on this, too. On her. On the relationship we get to share again.

I know I have Austin to thank for that as well. And I won't waste the second chance he gave me.

***

The garage door bangs shut behind me, the sound ricocheting through the Manor like an announcement.

I'm home.

The old floorboards creak as I step into the hallway, the

house settling around me like it recognizes my weight again. Like it's been waiting.

"Lauren?" I call, dropping my bags by the wall. "You home?"

The grandfather clock answers instead—six slow, deliberate chimes that roll down the corridor and wrap around me.

I move toward the kitchen, my boots softer now against the hardwood. "Lauren?" I try again, hopeful even though the silence feels pretty definitive. I exhale and brace my hands against the counter—but my fingertips brush a scrap of notebook paper, folded once.

Mitch,

Welcome home (officially)! I'm so sorry I'm not here. The insurance adjuster finally called back and was willing to meet with me this afternoon. Not sure what time you were planning to be home, but I don't think I'll be later than five—I'll make us dinner!

I'm so happy you're home! See you soon!

XOXO

Mrs. Benson

By the time I get to the bottom, I'm grinning like an idiot. *Mrs. Benson.* She's claiming it. Leaning into it. Choosing it again.

But even though my chest warms, I glance at the microwave and read 6:03 p.m. "Five o'clock, Peaches?" I mutter, but there's no bite in it—just affection. I pull my phone from my pocket and tap her name. And she answers on the first ring.

"I'm sorry!" she blurts, voice thick, like she's been holding herself together by a thread.

"Whoa—hey. You're okay. Your note said five, so I just—"

"I know, I know," she rushes. I can hear papers shuffling, traffic in the background, stress humming through the line. "I really wanted to be there when you got home. I did. But the insurance adjuster finally called, and now he's making me itemize everything. Estimate the loss of value. And Mitch, I don't even know where to start." Her voice cracks. "I can't do this without Miguel."

My chest aches. Because this is exactly what we talked about in Vegas. About boundaries. About not letting Pier Ninety-two swallow her whole. About choosing *us* first. And here she is—apologizing for handling a literal disaster because she doesn't want to break a promise to me.

"Did you call him?" I ask gently.

"Yes. He's on his way. But Mitch, I'm so sorry. I didn't want this interfering with our first real night back home."

"Lauren." I press my palm flat against the counter. "You're fine."

"But we agreed Pier Ninety-two wasn't going to—"

"Hey," I interrupt softly. "We agreed it wasn't going to come before us. That's different."

She goes quiet.

"This?" I continue. "This isn't you choosing the restaurant over me. This is you in crisis mode. And I understand that."

She exhales shakily, and I can picture her—head in her hands, shoulders curled in, fighting tears because she thinks she's failing me.

"You're trying," I say, voice low and steady. "Even with your whole world upside down, you're still trying to show up for us. I see that."

Silence. Then a small, broken breath. "I love you, Mitch," she whispers. "I just can't believe this is happening. My restaurant…"

"Can be rebuilt," I say, firmer now. Certain. "We'll rebuild it. Together. As a team." My fingers drift over the ink of Mrs. Benson again. "And hey," I add, forcing a little lightness into my voice, "perfect use of our Vegas winnings, right? That new freezer you wanted?"

She lets out a watery snort. "What would I do without you?"

"You'll never have to find out." Because I'm not going anywhere. "I'll see you soon," I tell her. "I'll make dinner."

"I love you."

"Love you, more."

The call ends and I stand there for a second, staring at the note in my hand. She tried to be here by five. Even with insurance adjusters and itemized losses and the rubble of her dream sitting in front of her. She tried.

I check the microwave again and read 6:07 p.m. And I know she won't be home for a while.

The adrenaline that carried me through the day finally starts to ebb, leaving exhaustion in its wake. My body feels heavy now that the emotional part is done. And I'm suddenly desperate for a quick nap.

I head upstairs, each step familiar and comforting. The master bedroom door opens with a soft creak, and I step inside like I'm crossing into something sacred. With a sigh, I fall back onto the king-sized bed with a grin, dragging my hands over the creamy satin sheets. "Oh, I missed you," I mutter, half joking, half serious.

I reach for Lauren's pillow, wanting to breathe her in— but something brushes the back of my hand. I frown and lift the pillow only to spot a flash of purple.

"No way…" I pull it free slowly. "Finn," I whisper.

The stuffed dolphin stares back at me with its crooked little stitched smile, and the air leaves my lungs in a long, steady exhale. Because I'm right back at Pacific Park. Back in the moment I first gave him to her.

The way she laughed. The way something shifted between us—subtle but undeniable. The moment the flirting stopped being harmless and started meaning something.

She kept Finn all these years. Through everything. Through the fights. Through the separation. Through the mess we made. She kept him tucked under her pillow.

I press Finn to my chest and fall back against the mattress, staring at the ceiling, emotion swelling thick and warm behind my ribs. Because it's not just a stuffed dolphin. It's proof. Proof that even when we cracked, the foundation held. Proof that she believed in us even when I doubted. Proof that the boy who gave her this toy—hopeful, certain, in love—is still here somewhere.

I close my eyes, Finn tucked against my heart, satin sheets cool beneath me, her note still echoing in my head. She's fighting for us. I'm fighting for us. We're not perfect. But we're choosing each other. And I know it's all going to work out. Because our love is forever.

CHAPTER TWELVE

Lauren

Alleged, accidental grease fire burns down failing L.A. restaurant while owner, Lauren Templeton-Benson parties in Vegas.

The headline feels like a slap. The words blur, sharpen, then blur again as a high-pitched ringing fills my ears. My pulse pounds so violently I can feel it in my gums, in my fingertips, and in the hollow at the base of my throat. I drag my eyes to the subheading and force the words out through clenched teeth. "But was it really an accident?"

The room tilts and heat detonates under my skin—thick, instant, volcanic. It starts in my chest and spreads outward, licking up my neck and down my arms. And I swear, I can smell smoke.

Mitch shifts beside me. "Nobody even reads the *Rosewood Register* anymore, Lauren. Hardly anyone is going to see this ridiculous story." Before I can react, he takes the paper from my hands, folds it once, and sets it aside like it's nothing more than junk mail.

But I scoff. "First off, I wasn't *partying* in Vegas. My brother got engaged." My fist slams down on the table before I can stop it, rattling the plates and silverware.

"I know," Mitch says evenly. "I was there, remember?"

I wrinkle my nose at him, batting away the sarcasm. "Like my travel plans had anything to do with a grease fire burning down my restaurant!" My voice cracks on the word *restaurant*, but I shove through it. "Which was a fucking accident!" But the word *accident* feels flimsy now. Weak. Questioned. Smudged with suspicion.

Mitch takes another slow sip of coffee. Then he sets the mug down and leans forward, covering my shaking fist with his hand. "I know it," he says quietly. "And you know it, Peaches. It's a completely unfair headline."

Unfair. That's polite language for character assassination.

"It's insinuating arson," I snap. "It's implying I burned down my own business for insurance money while I was off drinking champagne in Vegas."

My throat tightens because I'm not just reading a headline anymore—I'm back there. Back to the moment the plane touched down in L.A. Back to grabbing my bag before the seatbelt sign even chimed off. Back to racing through the terminal with my heart in my throat. Back to turning the corner onto the block where Pier Ninety-two has always stood—proud and gleaming and mine.

Only it wasn't. It was smoke. It was flashing lights. It was yellow caution tape snapping in the wind like a warning.

The brick façade—once warm and red—was blackened and blistered. Windows blown out. The front door hanging crooked on one hinge. The metal letters of the sign warped and sagging, as if the name itself couldn't withstand the heat.

Pier Ninety-two. I can still see it half-melted, barely legible.

The smell hit me first—burnt grease, scorched wiring, wet ash. It clung to my clothes. Crawled into my lungs. Even now, if I close my eyes, I taste it at the back of my throat.

Inside was worse. Tables collapsed. Chairs overturned. The stainless steel in the kitchen warped like tinfoil. My line—my beautiful, meticulously organized line—reduced to a charred skeleton. The spot by the prep sink where I'd leaned side by side with Miguel at two in the morning, calculating payroll. All of it soaked and black and silent.

I remember stepping over debris in heels I hadn't bothered to change out of. I remember reaching out and touching the brick, my fingertips coming away gray. I remember thinking, irrationally, that if I just stood there long enough, it would rewind. That the walls would inhale and straighten and the lights would flicker back on. Instead, a firefighter gently asked me to step back. Like I didn't belong there anymore.

So, when I look at this headline—when I see the word *alleged* next to my name—it doesn't just sting. It feels obscene. Because I was there minutes after landing. I saw what fire does. I saw what it took from me. And the idea that I would do that to myself? To my staff. To my dream. It makes my blood boil all over again.

"Who the hell wrote it?" I demand. "Because I'm calling Austin. He can file a lawsuit."

Mitch sighs and picks up the paper again, scanning the byline. "Some guy named Jerry Rowland."

I square my shoulders and fold my arms over my chest. "Well, Jerry is about to be in a shit storm of trouble. Because he can't print that," I say, my voice low and shaking. "He can't ruin my reputation over something I had no part in. It's slander, Mitch. It's a lie."

"He's a journalist," Mitch replies, maddeningly steady. "I know you don't like it, but he's allowed to pose questions. Even if we both know he's wrong," he quickly adds.

I push my chair back so hard it scrapes against the hardwood. "So, that's it? I just let him imply I'm some desperate business owner lighting matches to cash in?" I reach for the paper again, but Mitch gently swats my hand away.

"You're acting crazy," he says lightly.

"Far from it." My chest heaves and adrenaline hums through my fingertips, buzzing in my teeth. Because this isn't just about ink on paper. It's about future investors who might read it and hesitate. Lenders who might second-guess extending credit. Customers who might whisper.

Mitch tilts his head, studying me like I'm something remarkable instead of unraveling. "Have I ever told you how sexy you are when you're all fired up?"

The pivot throws me off balance. "I'm sorry, what?"

He smiles—soft, not dismissive. Not mocking. His palms slide over my hands, warm and deliberate. "You heard me," he whispers.

My pulse stutters. Because the anger is still there—but it's tangled now with something steadier. He isn't minimizing me. He's anchoring me. My gaze drops to his hands. To the way his thumbs press into my skin like he's trying to absorb the tremor.

"You built something real," he says quietly. "One headline doesn't erase that, Lauren."

His words slip past my defenses and settle somewhere tender. Because beneath the fury—beneath the fantasies of dragging Jerry Rowland into court—there's fear. What if the article sticks? What if the insurance company reads it and raises an eyebrow? What if failing becomes the narrative?

Mitch squeezes my hands once more. "You don't have to fight every battle with guns blazing," he says.

I swallow hard because deep down, I know he's right. He's being rational. And I'm most certainly *not*. "I just don't want anyone thinking I'd ever do that," I admit, my voice smaller now. "That I'd burn down my own restaurant."

"Anyone who knows you," he says, steady and certain, "knows you never would."

And for the first time since reading the headline, the fire inside me doesn't feel like it consumes me. It feels contained. Managed. Because his hands are warm. His voice is calm. And no matter what the paper says… Mitch has my back. Completely.

My gaze drops, tracking the slow, deliberate path of his fingertips as they glide from my wrist to the inside of my forearm. He doesn't rush it. He never does when he's trying to steady me.

His thumb lingers at my pulse point for a second longer, slow and deliberate, before he straightens. And without breaking eye contact, he pushes back and stands. He circles the table at an unhurried pace, gaze locked on mine the entire time. When he reaches me, he doesn't say a word. He just pulls out the chair beside mine and sits close—close enough that our thighs brush, close enough that the heat of him seeps through the thin fabric of my pajamas.

His hand finds my wrist again, thumb tracing that same slow circle at my pulse before drifting upward. He brushes over my elbow, then along the curve of my upper arm, fingertips light but purposeful.

I swallow as his hand slides to my waist and he turns toward me fully, knees angling in so I'm boxed in by him and the edge of the table. His palm spreads at my hip, firm and possessive, fingers splaying like he's claiming familiar territory. Like he's reminding me exactly where I belong.

Right here.

A shiver ripples through me. "You... can't distract me, Mitch," I warn, but the edge in my voice dulls as his other hand joins the first. His knuckles skim the underside of my jaw, tilting my chin up just slightly. His thumb drags slowly across my lower lip, catching the tremble there.

"It won't work," I insist, even as my breath shortens when his fingers slip beneath the hem of my shirt, brushing warm and deliberate against bare skin. "I'm too mad."

His hand at my waist tightens subtly, thumb stroking a lazy arc along my side. He leans closer—not kissing me yet—just close enough that I feel the heat of him, the steady rhythm of his breathing syncing with mine.

"Too mad?" he teases, fingertips gliding up my spine, sending a line of goosebumps in their wake.

My resolve wavers. My anger flickers, still hot—but tangled now with the slow, electric awareness of every place he touches me. And the worst part? He knows exactly what he's doing.

His mouth twitches like I just dared him. He stands slowly, pulling me with him. There's nothing rushed about him. No panic. No defensiveness. Just that grounded, confident calm that makes me feel like the world could be on fire and he'd still know where the exits are.

My body betrays me as his lips meet mine. And everything else dissolves. The article. The insinuation. Jerry-whatever-his-name-is. Gone. Instead, longing floods through me—sudden, sharp, undeniable. His mouth moves with confident familiarity, like he's reclaiming territory that was never truly lost. My heart pounds harder, chasing the rhythm of him.

"Can't distract me," I whisper against his lips, even as my hands slide up his chest and my leg hooks around his waist.

He laughs softly into my mouth. Scooping me up effortlessly, he grins. "Now who's distracting who?"

My back meets the dining room table, scattering plates and forks as his body presses into mine. The contact sparks through me like static catching flame.

His mouth trails from my lips to my jaw, down my neck, leaving heat in its wake. My breath stutters and my fingers tangle in his hair. "I guess I should get mad more often," I mutter, half-dazed, half-teasing, "if it leads to this."

He pauses just long enough to look at me, that wicked glint in his eyes making my stomach flip. "You can do anything you want," he says, voice low and steady, "if it leads to this, Peaches." And then he scoots my bottom right to the edge of the table.

My breath catches hard in my throat as he takes a seat, hooking a finger into the waistband of my pajama shorts. He tugs them away with unhurried confidence and the cool air hits my bare skin. I shiver, but not from the cold.

His hands trace the lace at my hips before sliding my panties down too, leaving me exposed and breathless. He leans forward and presses a kiss on my inner thigh—soft, reverent—and I nearly melt as he guides my legs until they fall open in front of him.

"I want to taste you, Mrs. Benson," he whispers. And the way he says it—possessive and proud—undoes me. His lips move closer, teasing, unhurried. Every brush of his mouth sends tingles skittering across my skin. My anger evaporates entirely, replaced by pure, aching want.

"Mitch…" I breathe, my back arching involuntarily as his tongue replaces the trail of kisses. Stars burst behind my eyelids. My fingers fist in his hair as pleasure builds, sharp and electric. His hands steady my hips as his mouth works with devastating precision. "Right there." I gasp. "Don't… stop…"

He doesn't. The pressure crests, unstoppable, and when he slips a finger inside me in perfect rhythm with his mouth, the dam shatters. My muscles tighten, toes curling as satisfaction floods every nerve ending. I cry out his name, the sound echoing faintly in the dining room. When the wave finally recedes, I sag against the surface of the table, breathless and stunned. He presses one last kiss to my thigh and looks up at me, smug and wicked. "Feel better?"

A laugh bursts out of me before I can stop it. I sit up and cup his cheeks before leaning over to kiss him. "Much better." Heat radiates through me as I reach for my pajamas and hop off the table.

He stands, swiping the back of his hand across his mouth like he didn't just dismantle me. "Always at your service, ma'am."

I narrow my eyes at him. "Perhaps I should repay the favor."

He winks. "You can repay that exact favor anytime you wish, Mrs. Benson."

I actually giggle—full, unrestrained—and collapse onto my chair. I glance around the room at the antique china cabinets and family heirlooms. "I can't believe we just did that on the dining room table."

He follows my gaze thoughtfully. "What year was this

house built again?"

"1908," I answer.

"Hate to break it to you, sweetheart, but there's no way that's the first action these walls have seen."

"Oh my, God, Mitch, stop!" I shove his shoulder, laughing. "I do not need those visuals."

He taps the table with a grin. "Like you, maybe Granny didn't just serve dinner here."

A roar of laughter escapes me. I lean forward—and knock my elbow into his coffee cup. The mug tips. And cold coffee spills across the front page of the *Rosewood Register*.

We both freeze. Then we watch as the brown liquid seeps into the bold, accusatory headline. The ink begins to blur. Smear. Dissolve.

I pick up the soggy newspaper, unable to stop smiling as the coffee drags the words down the page like they're melting under scrutiny. But then my eyes catch something at the bottom. I squint. Lean closer. "Oh. My. God."

Mitch frowns. "What? It's not like you wanted to frame it."

"You'll never believe this." I shove the damp page toward him and point. "Look who owns this paper."

He reads the fine print. Then barks out a laugh so loud it echoes. "No fucking way." He tips back in his chair, gripping his stomach. "You've got to be kidding me. Tess Browning owns the *Rosewood Register* now?"

I snort. "Well. That explains why I was painted as an incompetent, partying arsonist."

Tess Browning. Josh's ex-wife. The same Tess who once tried to dismantle my brother's life piece by piece—and apparently decided to expand her portfolio into sibling character assassination.

"Think she holds a grudge?" Mitch asks dryly.

I raise a brow. "Against our entire family? Apparently so."

He smirks. "Think it's time I hit her in the head with a volleyball again?"

"Permission granted."

We both laugh, but there's steel underneath it. Because of course it's Tess. Of course this wasn't random. I glance down at the ruined headline—ink bleeding, accusations dissolving into muddy streaks. But instead of feeling small, I feel... steady.

Let her write. Let her posture. I have the truth. And I have the man who just anchored me through the storm and then made me laugh about it.

CHAPTER THIRTEEN

Austin

"Lauren, it's not slander." I let the words out slowly, like they might shatter if I move too fast. The glow of the tablet reflects in the dark window across from me as I scroll through the full article on the *Rosewood Register*'s website for the third time. I already know she's not going to like my answer. But she didn't call me for comfort. She called me for my knowledge of the law.

"How can you say that?" she demands through FaceTime. Her face fills my screen—flushed, eyes blazing, jaw tight. "Tess is making all these false claims about me!"

I sink deeper into the sofa and rub my forehead with my palm. "I know it feels that way," I say carefully, scanning the phrasing again. Every adjective. Every clause. Every insinuation. "But semantically, she—and this Jerry Rowland guy—haven't actually said anything defamatory."

My heart stutters. *Jerry Rowland. Why does that name sound familiar?*

"This makes no sense," Lauren presses, desperation bleeding into her anger. "They accused me of arson!"

"No," I correct gently, even though I can hear the

tension creeping into my own voice. "They implied foul play. That's not the same as making a direct accusation."

"Oh, come on. It's the same thing!" she snaps, and for a second she looks less like a furious business owner and more like my little sister—cornered and overwhelmed.

I press my lips together and set the tablet aside, leaning closer to my phone. "In the eyes of the law, it's not," I say, softer now. "They never claimed the fire was arson. They posed a question. A loaded one. It's inflammatory. It's malicious. But it's framed as speculation. Which is exactly how you avoid a lawsuit."

Lauren exhales sharply. "They also made me look like I spend every weekend raging in Sin City—"

"Lauren," I interrupt gently. "You *were* in Vegas when Pier Ninety-two burned down."

Her eyes flash with hurt. "For one weekend. One. Their headline makes it sound like I'm some irresponsible party girl who torched her own restaurant." She drops her hands into her lap, and the smack echoes through my speaker. "And they said my restaurant was failing." Her face falters— just slightly—but I see it. And it punches straight through my chest.

"I mean..." I hesitate. "It wasn't exactly thriving." But the second the words leave my mouth, I want them back. Because they taste clinical. Cold. Like something I'd say in a courtroom, not to my sister.

A tear slips down her cheek. She wipes it away quickly, but it's too late. "I know," she says, voice breaking. "I know it wasn't perfect. But Austin, this feels so wrong. How can she get away with saying these terrible things about me?"

I sit up straighter. Because this isn't just about a headline anymore. It's about her reputation. Her investors. Her staff. Her future in the business.

"Look," I say, softening. "I don't like it either. You know that. And we both know Tess is doing this to be malicious." Because Tess doesn't do anything by accident. "But if there's one thing Tess is not," I continue, choosing my words carefully, "it's stupid. She's calculated. She knows exactly where the legal line is. And she stayed on the right side of it here." I rub my jaw, frustration simmering under my skin. "No provable false statements. No direct accusations. Just... strategically planted doubt."

That's the genius of it.

Lauren goes quiet, absorbing it. "So, there's nothing I can do?" she asks finally, her voice small now. Not furious. Just tired.

And I feel awful. Because I know she wants me to say that I'll file a lawsuit. Fight back. Protect her. Before I can answer though, the front door to our apartment opens. Casey walks in with grocery bags, kicks the door shut behind her, and immediately reads my face like a headline of its own. "*What's going on?*" she mouths from the doorway, bags dangling from her hands.

"Egg her house maybe?" I mutter into the phone.

Casey's eyebrows shoot up. "Whose house are we egging?" she whispers, tiptoeing toward the couch like we're plotting a felony in broad daylight.

"Tess Browning," I say, picking up the tablet and handing it to her.

Casey sets the groceries down on the floor, drops beside me, and starts reading. The crease between her brows deepens with every line. "Yikes," she mutters. "This is nasty, Lauren." She steals the phone from my hand so she can look at my sister directly. "But shouldn't we be egging this guy Jerry's house? He's the one who wrote it."

I shake my head. "He wrote it, but Tess owns the paper. She decides what runs. She's ultimately responsible." But that's what bothers me. Jerry might be the pen. But Tess is the architect.

Damn it. Why does Jerry Rowland ring a bell?

"Tess Browning..." Casey says slowly, tapping her finger against her chin. "Why do I know that name?"

Lauren sighs through the screen. "Among many things, she's Josh's ex-wife."

Casey's eyes widen. "Ohhh. Right. The ex-wife."

Heat creeps up my neck. Yeah. The ex-wife. The same one who outed me and Mavis with a single photo and detonated my life like it was a sport. The one who smiled while everything burned. "Yeah," I mutter. "That's her."

Casey's hand finds my thigh and squeezes gently. "So," she says carefully, turning to face me. "She's obviously not a fan of Josh. And I assume, probably not you either since you guys are basically attached at the hip. But what does she have against you, Lauren?"

Lauren shrugs helplessly. "I don't know. We weren't exactly close, but we got along fine when she was married to Josh. Maybe it's just… a grudge against the family. My restaurant going down in flames was an easy target."

I wrap my arm around Casey's shoulders and pull her closer, staring at Lauren's tiny image on the screen. "I think Tess knows," I say slowly, "that what hurts Lauren ultimately hurts Josh. And me."

Because that's how she operates. Strategic collateral damage.

Casey frowns. "Are you saying she's not over him? I thought Mavis told me Tess was the one who filed for divorce."

Lauren nods. "She did. But after Dalton—the guy she was having an affair with—dumped her, she apparently had a change of heart. It was right before she showed Josh the pho—"

I wince before she finishes the word. Heat floods my face. Because that memory still carries weight. I clear my throat awkwardly.

"Umm… I'm sorry. I mean—" Lauren stumbles.

I shake my head quickly and pull Casey tighter against me. "No. You're not wrong."

It's just humiliating reliving it out loud next to my fiancée.

Lauren continues carefully. "Tess showed up at Josh's house and begged him to take her back. But when he laughed and said no, I think she decided to find the one thing that would hurt him the most."

Casey lets out a low whistle. "Well, damn. She had smoking ammunition in her pocket, didn't she?"

I close my eyes and drag my hand down my face as she nudges me in the gut with her elbow.

"Not my proudest moment, Case," I mutter.

She presses a kiss to my cheek. "We all do stupid shit," she says like it's nothing. "You're forgiven, California boy."

My chest tightens, though. Because it suddenly all connects in a way I hadn't thought about before. If Tess hadn't exposed everything—if she hadn't blown my life open—I might never have confronted what I actually wanted. I might never have ended up here. In Chicago. With Casey.

Lauren clears her throat on the other end of the line, the fire drained out of her voice and replaced with something quieter. "So anyway... you're saying I can't sue her."

I hold her gaze through the screen for a second before answering. "Not successfully," I say gently. "Not with what she's published. If she crossed the line, I'd be the first one drafting the complaint. But she didn't. She danced right up to it and stopped."

Lauren nods slowly, lips pressed together. "Okay," she says after a beat. "Okay. That's what Mitch said you'd say. But I just... needed to hear it."

"He's right," I reply. "But hey—this doesn't mean we do nothing. It just means we're smart about how we respond."

She gives me a tired smile. "Smart. Right. That's your department."

"Always," I tease lightly.

There's a pause. Then she glances off-screen and back again. "I'm gonna let you guys go. I can practically feel Casey's eyes on you."

Casey grins and leans into frame. "For the record, I was absolutely not considering felony-level retaliation."

Lauren snorts. "Tempting. But I'll survive without a criminal record." She looks back at me. "Thanks, Austin."

"Anytime," I say. "Call me if anything else pops up."

"I will. Love you."

"Love you, too."

The screen goes black. But the quiet in the living room feels heavier without her face there.

Casey shifts slightly, studying me. "You don't think Tess is done, do you?" she asks.

I hesitate.

"Because the timing is weird," Casey continues. "Josh remarries. They announce a baby. And suddenly his ex torches Lauren in print?"

But the word *baby* snaps something into focus so sharply it almost hurts. I sit up straighter. Josh's Facebook post flashes through my mind—the sonogram photo. The caption about second chances. About full circles. "The baby," I say quietly.

Casey blinks. "What about the baby?"

"It's what brought them together in the first place," I explain slowly. "That first pregnancy. The loss. Mavs disappearing. It's what allowed Josh and Tess to even be together." I swallow. "If Tess wanted Josh back and he denied her... seeing him happy. Seeing him start over. Seeing him get the ending she didn't..." I shake my head. "That could've pushed her."

Casey nods thoughtfully. "Okay. But what does that have to do with Lauren?"

"I don't know yet," I admit. And that's what unsettles me most. Because Tess doesn't move randomly. She plans...

I stare at the tablet again and scan the article from the bottom to the top, landing once more on the headline. Then the byline. Jerry Rowland. And like a frickin' freight train, it hits me. "He was the one who snapped the photo at Java Jane's," I whisper.

Casey turns sharply toward me. "What?"

I replay it in my mind. The coffee house. My lips on Mavis's. The photo Jerry snapped and texted to Tess... I shake my head slowly. "He's not random."

Casey's expression shifts from confusion to concern. "You think Tess planted him?"

"I think Tess doesn't miss opportunities," I say, sitting in the hum of my thoughts.

I'm not sure how long I stay silent, but evidently too long. Because eventually Sloan Park flickers onto the television at Casey's prompting. The crack of a bat fills the room. And the announcer's voice drones on about spring training stats.

But I don't really hear any of it. My mind is miles away. Back in Rosewood. Back to Tess Browning. And the uneasy certainty settling in my gut.

She's not reacting. She's maneuvering. Moving pieces on her chessboard.

What's your endgame, Tess? Because I know you. And you never strike just once.

CHAPTER FOURTEEN

Mitch

The mower blades chatter beneath me, a steady *whack-whack-whack* that chews through the front lawn of Templeton Manor. I steer the tractor in clean, straight lines, the engine vibrating up through the seat and into my bones. The afternoon sun rides high and hot, and sweat slicks my bare chest, catching the light every time I shift.

It's the kind of work I can control. Precise. Predictable. A beginning and an end.

My earbuds are cranked to full volume, *The Funny Part* podcast blasting in my ears. I tug my cap lower, grinning at the hosts as they tear apart some ridiculous headline— something about a mayor, a goat, and a "misunderstood local ordinance." I'm mid-laugh when my attention catches movement at the edge of the driveway.

A car turns in. Small. Compact. And my stomach drops before my brain even confirms it. A Mini Cooper—familiar as a bad taste—parked beside my truck like it has every right to be there.

My grin vanishes. And my jaw tightens so hard it aches. I kill the engine and the sudden silence is almost violent—

only the tick of cooling metal and the distant hum of summer insects. I rip my earbuds out, shove them in my pocket, and swing down from the tractor with a burst of heat that has nothing to do with the sun.

I don't even wait to see her face. I simply storm toward the driveway, boots grinding onto the gravel path, and the first thing I catch is a flash of a Barbie-pink heel stepping onto the pavement.

"Uh-uh. No fucking way, Tess!" I yell, pointing back toward the road like I can physically direct her presence out of existence. "Are you out of your goddamn mind coming over here?"

She slams the car door with theatrical calm and clicks across the driveway like she's walking into a brunch reservation, not a confrontation. When she reaches the edge of the freshly mown grass, she stops and fans herself with a white envelope. Then she slides her sunglasses off her face and perches them on top of her blonde head like a crown.

"Oh, calm down, Mitch." She rolls her eyes and plants a hand on her hip, lips curling into a grin. "I'm just here to drop this off."

I drag the back of my hand over my forehead, wiping sweat and irritation in the same motion. A strand of hair sticks to my temple and I shove it back behind my ear. "Drop what off?" I ask, already hating the answer.

"This." She extends the envelope and presses it into my palms like we're exchanging cookie recipes.

I glance down. Josh's name sits beneath the clear address window.

"It was mailed to me by mistake," she says breezily, like that's a normal sentence for someone who no longer belongs anywhere near my brother-in-law. "It's just a W-4. But I'm sure he's probably freaking out because he can't file his taxes without it." Another eye roll. Another little performance. She drags a finger under her lower lip, adjusting the perfect line of pink gloss like she's on camera.

My nose wrinkles as I lift my gaze to her. "Why are you

bringing it here?"

"Well, I'm sure as shit not going over to *his* house," she snaps, tongue clicking once, arms folding tight across her chest like I just asked a stupid question.

"You couldn't... dump it in his mailbox?" I gesture toward the envelope, toward the *obvious solution*, trying not to let my temper boil over.

Her eyes narrow to slits. "Is it really that big of a deal? Like you won't see him anyway to give him a stupid tax form?"

"That's not the point," I bite out as my pulse thuds in my throat. "I can't believe you'd even show your face around here after printing that load of bullshit about Lauren."

Her eyebrows lift—slow, pleased. Like she's been waiting for me to say her name. "You saw that, huh?" she says, a smile cracking across her mouth.

I let out a sharp, humorless laugh. "You fucking know we saw it. You published it *knowing* we'd all see it."

She tilts her head, smile widening. "All right, maybe..." She shrugs, all faux innocence. "A little guilty."

My hands curl into fists at my sides. I can feel my heart pounding under my ribs, can feel the urge to shout, to throw the envelope back at her, to say every word I've been swallowing since that headline hit the table. Instead I force myself to breathe. "Why?" I ask, voice rough. "Why hurt her like that?"

Her grin softens—not into remorse, but into amusement. Like this is all just sport.

"Weren't you guys kinda friends?" I add, and the question surprises even me—because it's the one thing I still can't make sense of.

Tess's eyes flicker, just for a second. Then the mask settles back into place. And I know, with sick certainty, that she didn't come here just to deliver a tax form.

She adjusts her hands on her hips and drops her gaze to the freshly cut grass like she's contemplating something profound instead of stirring the pot. "It's nothing personal, Mitch," she says smoothly. "Just simple journalism. My readership has a right to know the tr—"

"Don't say it," I cut in, stepping closer. A crooked, dangerous smile pulls at my mouth. "Don't you dare say it. Because you and I both know the word *truth* doesn't belong anywhere near this."

She lifts her gaze to mine—icy, assessing, surgical. "That's for the reader to determine," she replies coolly. "All Jerry and I did was offer a possible new perspective on a questionable—" she pauses delicately, "—tragic event."

Before I can react, her hand darts forward. Her nails skim across my bare, sweat-slick chest. The contact is quick. Intentional. And I glance down automatically as her fingers drag over my skin and snag a stray blade of grass clinging to my pec. She plucks it free, rolls it between her fingertips, and gives me a slow wink before letting it flutter to the ground.

My stomach dips. And my breath catches for half a second—an involuntary, traitorous response to an unexpected touch. I swallow hard and step back, adjusting the brim of my cap like I need something to anchor me. But heat floods my cheeks, and I hate that she sees it.

She grins, clearly delighted by my reaction, and slides her sunglasses back over her eyes. "Why're you out here mowing the lawn anyway?" she asks lazily. "Can't you pay someone else to do it?"

I clear my throat, forcing my pulse to slow, forcing that unwelcome flicker in my gut to die where it started. "I-I-I like doing it," I stutter, folding Josh's envelope in half and jamming it into my back pocket. "Clears my head."

"From?" she presses.

I snort, regaining my composure. "What's it matter to you?"

She shrugs like she's bored. "Just curious. After all these years, I wondered if maybe..."

"If maybe what?" I challenge.

She bites her bottom lip, just enough to make it look thoughtful instead of manipulative. "Never mind."

"Yeah, well, shove it, Tess," I snap. "I'm not your next article. None of us are." I take two more steps back and lift my hands slightly—not in surrender, but in warning.

Her smile turns sharp. "No," she says softly. "You're not really my target, are you?" She winks and turns toward her car. But her last words land heavier than anything else she's said.

I watch as she opens the door and pauses, glancing back over her shoulder. "But I can't deny—a picture of those sweaty muscles on the front page might buy me a few new readers. Lookin' good, Benson." She gestures lazily at my chest, smirking as she slides into the driver's seat and slams the door.

The engine hums to life. But I just stand there, jaw tight, watching her taillights flare red as she backs out of the driveway and steers toward the road. Seconds later, her Mini Cooper disappears beneath the drooping branches of the weeping willows like it was never here.

My hand drifts over my chest, fingers dragging through the thin sheen of sweat where she touched me. "What the fuck was that?" I mutter before yanking the envelope from my pocket and staring down at Josh's name.

Because the tax form feels like an excuse. A prop. "Why'd you really come over here?" I whisper, knowing that Tess Browning doesn't make social calls. And she sure as shit doesn't drive across town just to deliver paperwork for her ex-husband.

***

I slam the knife down through a head of lettuce like it owes me money. The crisp crack echoes off the tile, satisfying in a way it shouldn't be. I chop again. And again. White core, green leaves—shredded into bite-sized pieces with more aggression than the salad deserves.

Behind me, the oven hums, heat rolling out in waves. The cheesy pasta I shoved in there earlier is almost done. I can smell it—rich and sharp, the top layer of cheddar bubbling and browning into a golden crust. Comfort food. Domestic. Normal. Except my head isn't normal. My head is still in the driveway with a Mini Cooper and Barbie-pink heels.

I scoop the lettuce into a bowl, toss in a handful of spinach, then yank the oven door open. Heat hits my face as the cheese on top sizzles. I turn the oven off and slide the pan to a cooler rack, forcing myself to focus on something tangible. Dinner. Lauren. Home.

I open the fridge and grab a tomato next. I chop it into chunky wedges and drop them into the bowl. But that's when Tess reappears in my mind again like she never left— her nails gliding over my chest, her grin, the way she said I wasn't her target.

"Tess Browning…" I whisper to the empty kitchen, like saying her name out loud will make her make sense. It doesn't though.

My eyes drift to my phone sitting at the edge of the counter. A sane man would ignore it. A sane man would let it go. But Tess doesn't show up for no reason. She doesn't deliver a tax form in person when mail exists. She doesn't touch me like that and then throw out that line about *targets* unless she's fishing for something. Or someone.

"What do you really want?" I mutter, jaw tight. My gaze drops to the phone again, pulse thudding. "Or maybe…" I add, voice lower, "*who* do you really want?"

I snag the phone with tomato-stained fingers and tap Josh's name. It rings once. Twice. Three times.

"Hey, man." Josh's voice comes through, steady but distracted. Hospital steady. "What's up? Everything okay?"

"Yeah," I say quickly. "Yeah, everything's fine. You got a second?"

"Sure. I'm at the hospital though—I've got like five minutes."

"Yeah. Five is fine." I lean my forearms on the cool counter, trying to keep my tone casual even as my stomach knots. "Take a guess who showed up here today."

"Give me a clue."

"Blonde," I say flatly. "Malicious. Kind of a bitch in pink heels."

Josh exhales a long, weary sigh. "Why was Tess over there?"

I snort, and the memory of her smile makes my gut turn. "She said she came to drop off a tax form, but—"

"Oh!" Josh cuts in. "Was it my W-4?"

"Yeah, but Josh—"

"I've been waiting for that stupid thing to show up for weeks. Are you telling me she had it?"

I squeeze the bridge of my nose. "Yeah. She dropped it off. But—"

"Awesome," he says, relief rushing into his voice like this is the only crisis in his day. "Thank you. It's been driving me crazy because I can't file without it."

"Sure," I say, trying not to grind my teeth. "But listen, dude—I'm not convinced that's the real reason she stopped by. I think—"

"Huh?" Josh interrupts, and I hear movement on his end. A door. Voices. "Hold on a second." The connection muffles like he's covering the speaker.

I push off the counter, irritation spiking. Then my phone buzzes, a text from Lauren flashing across the screen.

"Mitch?" Josh's voice returns, sharper this time. Urgent. "Sorry—can I call you back? I need to run to the ER."

I exhale, swallowing my frustration. "Yeah. For sure. No problem. Go."

"Thanks, man." And then he's gone—the call cutting off like a door shutting mid-sentence.

The kitchen falls quiet again, the kind of quiet that makes every small sound feel too loud. My phone buzzes in my hand again, a reminder that I have an unread text. I hesitate for half a beat, then open it.

Lauren: I have such good news! The insurance policy I had is going to cover a complete rebuild of Pier Ninety-two! Mitch! We can rebuild the whole thing!

For a second, I just blink. Because my first instinct is the one I want to have—the good husband instinct. The *thank God, we caught a break* instinct. The *this is what she's been praying for* instinct.

And it's there. It is.

A short laugh slips out of me because the idea of her not having to fight the insurance company for scraps feels like mercy. Like someone finally tossing her a rope instead of another brick.

I want to be happy for her. I want to grab her face when she walks in and tell her she's going to be okay. I want to believe this is the door opening. But my eyes drop back to one line in particular. *We can rebuild.* And something inside me goes cold. Because rebuilding doesn't mean a fresh start. Rebuilding means *more of the same*—just shinier.

More meetings with contractors. More permits. More decisions she'll obsess over because it has to be perfect. More late nights. More spreadsheets. More headaches. More Miguel. More emergencies. More of her phone lighting up at dinner. More weekends lost to "just one more thing." More of her showing up exhausted, smelling like stress, trying to pretend she still has room for us.

Pier Ninety-two didn't just burn. It burned our time together, too. It stole her sleep. It stole our plans. It stole whole evenings and weekends and mornings that were supposed to belong to us. At first, we survived it—barely—because she told me it was temporary. That once it was stable, once it was thriving, it would give back what it took. But it never did. And now she's saying the words like they're salvation, like we get to resurrect the dream exactly as it was—and all I can see is the strain. The distance. The same fire, just in a different shape.

I glance at the pasta. The salad. The small, ordinary dinner I made in our kitchen. This—*this*—is what I want. Home. A night in. The two of us in sweatpants. Watching a movie. But her text is bright and breathless and full of hope, and I can already hear how she's going to say it out loud— like she's daring the universe to try her again.

My throat tightens. Because I want to be the man who celebrates without hesitation. But instead, all I feel is the weight of it settling into my chest. Because rebuilding Pier Ninety-two doesn't feel like a door opening. It feels like a door locking.

I blow out a breath and force my thumbs to move.

Me: Wow. That's big news. Sounds like we should celebrate. I have cheesy pasta warming in the oven. I thought you'd be home by now.

The message sounds supportive. It is supportive. It's just... not the whole truth.

I set my phone on the counter and grab the fridge door a little harder than necessary. A beer sits on the top shelf like it's been waiting for me. I twist the cap and take a long swallow, the cold bite sliding down my throat.

I fumble past the milk for the avocados as my phone pings again.

Lauren: I'm so sorry! I was planning to be, but Mitch, this news is just incredible! I never expected a full rebuild. I'm on my way to tell Miguel right now. He has to know!

I drag my hand through my still-sweaty hair, frustration pressing at the back of my eyes. Because of course. Of course it's Miguel first.

It's petty, I know it is. He's her go-to guy. Her best friend at the restaurant. Her right-hand man. He's earned a place in her world. But the sting doesn't care what's reasonable. It's the same sting every time—this familiar little poke in my gut that says *you're home waiting, and she's running to him.*

"Peaches," I mutter under my breath, not angry exactly—just tired of feeling like I'm always bracing for second place.

My phone lights up again before I can even decide whether to reply.

Lauren: He's just down the street. I'll tell him the good news and then head home. Thirty minutes tops.

"Whatever you say, Lauren," I mutter, and I hate how flat it comes out.

I grab the salad bowl and the avocados and shove them back into the fridge like I'm putting my own expectations on a shelf. But that's when the doorbell rings. I freeze for half a beat, then pad barefoot across the hardwood toward the foyer. Through the front window, a delivery truck already rolls away at the end of the drive, easing between the line of weeping willows—following the same curve Tess's Mini Cooper took earlier—its brake lights flashing once before it disappears back onto the road.

My jaw tightens at the thought of her as I open the door and find a large cardboard box, stamped with the Ace Hardware logo.

"What's this?" I frown, crouching to lift it. It's heavier than it looks. And the cardboard digs into my forearms as I haul it inside. I carry it to the living room and drop it onto the sofa with a thud. Then I rip through the tape like I've been waiting all day for something to tear apart that isn't my own patience.

The flaps spring open. And I just... stare. Plywood. Dowels. A can of paint. Screws. Wood glue. Sandpaper. Nylon rope. Everything I ordered on the plane ride home from Vegas.

A grin spreads across my face before I can stop it. My chest warms, something steady unfurling beneath the irritation that's been sitting there all afternoon. "This'll be perfect," I whisper, lifting the spool of nylon rope. The edges tickle the back of my hand before I set it back carefully, like it's not just rope—it's the future.

I fish my wallet out of my pocket and pull out the folded grid paper I've carried for over a year. The blueprint. The one I drew when I didn't let myself believe I'd ever get the chance. I unfold it and my heart picks up speed.

A rocking horse. Not store-bought. Not generic. Mine. Handmade. Solid. Something that lasts.

I sink onto the couch and stare at my own pencil lines like they're a map back to a version of myself I thought I'd lost. I never thought I'd actually get the chance to build it. And for a second, I can almost hear it—the creak of wood, the little burst of laughter. A child rocking back and forth, fingers threading through the rope mane. Green eyes lifting to mine with awe that has nothing to do with headlines or restaurants or Tess Browning or any of the messy adult wreckage.

Just love. Just home.

My phone pings from the kitchen, the sound small but insistent in the quiet house. I fold the blueprint and tuck it back into my wallet, still smiling as I stand and return to the kitchen.

I reach for my phone. But my stomach immediately flip-flops as I see the name on the screen, glowing like a bad omen.

Tess: Do you still suck at volleyball?

I blink. Once. Twice. And the ancient memory hits—teenage Tess, the beach, my misguided serve landing square on her head. I snort, then type back without thinking.

Me: I think my shitty serve gave you permanent brain damage that day.

A laughing emoji pops up almost instantly and I stare at it, unsettled. "What the fuck is happening here?" I say as I toss my empty beer bottle into the recycle bin and grab another from the fridge. Then I pull down two plates and salad bowls from the cabinet and set them by the sink—automatic motions, domestic choreography—while my mind runs in circles.

Lauren's rebuilding. Tess is texting me. A box of rocking horse parts sits on my couch like a promise. And I can't decide which one makes my chest tighter.

My phone pings again, and my hand shoots out before I even think about it—curiosity sizzling under my skin like I'm sixteen and the twins just dared me to do something stupid.

Tess: I slept with a neurologist for over a year. Dalton assured me your shit-terrible aim had no lasting impact.

A grin tugs at my mouth in spite of myself. And I type back, fast and sharp.

Me: I'm no neurologist, but you might want to get a second opinion because there is absolutely no reason why you should be texting me.

I set the phone down like it might bite, then roll my shoulders back with a long stretch. The kitchen smells like melted cheddar and baked pasta and everything comforting I want my life to be right now. My mouth actually waters. And my stomach gives an impatient, hungry twist.

I glance at the clock and do the math against Lauren's last text. She should be home in about twenty minutes. "Just enough time to shower," I mutter, even though the truth is I'm trying not to stare at the driveway like a dog waiting for its person.

I tear my gaze away from the oven and head back into the living room. The Ace box sits on the couch like a secret. Like proof that I can build something that lasts. I scoop it up and carry it to the garage, setting it carefully on my workbench. The contents spill out beside the half-finished dollhouse I've been building for my niece. *Or nephew*, I remind myself. Little walls. Tiny windows. A miniature staircase that's taken me way too many tries to get right.

Then my eyes slide to the rocking-horse materials and

something warm swells in my chest. *For my daughter.*

It's a thought that still feels reckless, like saying it out loud might jinx it. But it's there anyway—steady and bright and stubborn. Excitement rushes through me, quick as adrenaline. I leave the garage and jog upstairs before I can overthink any of it.

Minutes later, cool water sheets over my skin, rinsing off sweat and sunscreen. I work the bar of soap over my shoulders—clean and fresh. My breathing steadies. And my head finally clears.

Then my hand slides across my chest and my body betrays me—skin remembering Tess's nails, that quick, calculated touch, the stupid dip in my stomach. A chill rips down my spine and I shake my head like I can fling the memory away.

I shut off the water, towel off fast, tug on gym shorts, but skip the shirt. One pass through my damp hair and I'm out the door.

The staircase creaks under my feet as I descend, each squeak echoing through the too-quiet house. Once I'm back in the kitchen, I check the clock again. "Thirty minutes, huh, Peaches?" I ask. Because it's been forty-five.

The worry tries to creep in—quiet at first, then insistent. My hand closes around my phone, wanting an *on my way!* text more than I want to admit. Instead though, there's another message.

Tess: I was serious about that front-page feature, Benson.

A GIF follows of some ridiculous bodybuilder flexing his pecs like a cartoon.

A bark of laughter bursts out of me, sharp and surprised. I drop my face into my palms, damp hair dripping onto the countertop as I shake my head. "You are something else, Tess Browning," I mutter, and it's half-amused, half-*what the hell is wrong with you?*

I pull on oven mitts and yank the pasta from the top rack. The cheese still bubbles and the smell hits me like a hug. I heap noodles onto one plate—one, because apparently I'm eating solo—and grab another beer. Phone tucked under my arm, dinner in hand, I head for the living room.

I sink into the corner of the couch and flip on the Lakers. My gaze catches on the *Lord of the Rings* DVDs lined up on the mantle—so much for our movie marathon.

I force down a forkful of pasta and try to follow the game—the squeak of sneakers, the announcer's cadence, the steady back-and-forth—but my focus keeps drifting. Every few minutes, I check the window like I can will her car into the driveway.

Halftime creeps closer. My plate empties. My beer lowers. Outside, nothing moves except the willows, swaying like they're in on the joke.

I stare at the bottle for a beat, then pull my phone back out. Tess's bodybuilder GIF is still on-screen, mid-flex, ridiculous and obnoxious. I snort, but the sound comes out wrong—more confused than amused. Because the only name I want to see lighting up my phone is Lauren's.

Not Tess's.

And definitely not silence.

CHAPTER FIFTEEN

Lauren

Miguel lifts one finger at me like he's presenting Exhibit A in a very compelling case. "Just one more. It's on me, boss."

Boss. The word sends a ridiculous spark of happiness through my chest. I'm not sure I'll ever get used to hearing it again—not after the fire. Not after standing in the ashes of Pier Ninety-two and thinking the story of that place—*my* place—had ended there.

But it didn't. The insurance money will cover more than we thought. The city isn't fighting me. Pier Ninety-two can be rebuilt. The thought is still so surreal I almost expect someone to tap me on the shoulder and tell me it was all a misunderstanding. That the dream I've been grieving isn't actually coming back.

Except it is. And suddenly every nerve in my body buzzes with the kind of hope I haven't let myself feel in a long time. I want to celebrate. I want to call everyone. I want to stand on the bar and announce to the entire restaurant that we're bringing it back.

I laugh into the rim of my nearly empty margarita, ice

clinking against my teeth as I tip the drink back and chase the last of the celebratory lime and tequila.

"I can't," I say, though the giddy feeling in my chest makes the words sound less convincing than they should. I set the glass down harder than I mean to. "I promised Mitch I would be home for dinner."

Miguel's forehead creases. "Why does that matter?" he asks, genuinely confused. "I thought things between you guys were... rocky."

He leans across the small patio table and settles his hand over mine. The touch is easy—natural, like it's always belonged there. Being around him has never required effort. With him, things have always simply felt... right. Safe.

As he shifts, his sleeve rides up just enough for me to catch a glimpse of the bandages wrapped along his forearms—white against tanned skin. The ones he keeps hidden beneath long sleeves. Injuries from the grease fire, still healing, still there. Proof of how much he's given to Pier Ninety-two... to me.

"I mean," he continues, eyes searching mine, "last you told me, you two were barely hanging on. So, why can't we celebrate tonight?" His voice stays gentle, but something flickers underneath it—hope, maybe. Or justification. "Doesn't he know tonight's a big deal?"

My pulse skips. I stare at his fingers over mine and feel that dangerous flicker low in my belly—the one I've been pretending doesn't exist. I slide my hand back and lean into my chair, putting space between us. Because how do I say it? How do I explain that things with Mitch aren't what Miguel thinks anymore?

The ocean air carries salt and grilled peppers and cilantro from the kitchen, and the sky above the patio deepens from pink to indigo. Everything feels slow and warm and hazy.

"Come on," he says, already lifting his hand to signal the waiter for another round. "If you go home to him right now, you're going to wind up watching a movie you don't want to see... or a basketball game you don't care about."

I giggle. "You know Mitch well, don't you?"

"No." His grin turns softer. Intent. "But I do know *you*. And I know you'd rather be here—celebrating, planning the future of Pier Ninety-two—than on a couch pretending to care about sweaty men running back and forth on a court."

I picture Mitch, freshly showered in gym shorts, probably in the kitchen grating a block of cheddar for that cheesy pasta he makes when he's trying to impress me. A movie or a game queued up on the living room TV. Ready. Waiting. And guilt presses into my ribs. "I mean, the Lakers are in playoff contention," I offer weakly.

"Lauren." He holds up a hand. "You and I both know neither of us cares about basketball. Text him. Tell him you're staying out with me for a bit longer to celebrate that big check you just got. He should be able to understand how important this is."

The waiter sets two fresh frozen margaritas in front of us, condensation already sliding down the sides. Miguel pushes one toward me with a slow smile. "I'll make sure you get home safely," he says quietly, like he can read my mind.

My heart pounds—too loud, too fast. A small voice in my head reminds me that I'm already late. That we made plans to spend time together. But the night hums around me—music, laughter, the lingering buzz of tequila—and I'm not ready for it to end. Not when everything finally feels worth celebrating.

Music shifts overhead, bass thumping through the patio speakers as the twinkle lights blink on, casting gold across Miguel's face. He starts moving in his seat, shoulders swaying, eyes bright with that infectious, boyish energy.

He looks at me like I'm his favorite person in the world, and something in my chest loosens. I pull my phone from my purse and start typing, already convincing myself it's harmless. Just a few more minutes. One more drink. Nothing that matters in the grand scheme of things. Not a big deal.

Me: I'm so sorry! I promise I'll be

home shortly! Looking forward to your
cheesy pasta, Mr. Benson!

My thumb hovers over *send*. The cursor blinks. Once. Twice. Then Miguel's chair scrapes against the concrete. He rises and steps in front of me, extending his hand, a crooked, irresistible grin tugging at the corner of his mouth.

"A dance with the most beautiful woman here tonight." But he doesn't wait for my answer. He simply pulls me up and his hand slides to my waist—confident, warm, steady— and the touch sends heat straight through me. A sultry samba replaces the mariachi, rhythm pulsing through my veins. "Just one dance," he whispers, tugging me closer.

And I let my phone fall to the table as I step into Miguel's arms. Because it's harmless. *He's* harmless. And I'm sure Mitch will understand.

***

I swing my legs out of the black sedan and stand, planting my heels on the Templeton Manor driveway. But the ground doesn't feel as solid as it should. It tilts like the whole estate has decided to suddenly start breathing.

I steady myself on the door and laugh. "Okay. Wow."

One margarita felt like permission—something cold and bright and harmless. Two turned into confidence, my laugh a little louder, my shoulders a little looser. By the time the third hit, responsibility started to fade into the background, and leaning into the moment felt a whole lot easier than thinking about what came next.

The alcohol hums through my bloodstream, warm and fizzy, blurring the edges of everything. From this distance, the house lights look softer. And my thoughts feel… slower. Like they have to wade through syrup before reaching my mouth.

"Hang on, let me walk you to the door," Miguel says with a grin just as I wobble again. He taps the driver's shoulder. "I'll be right back, buddy."

"I'm fine," I insist, waving him off. But the word stretches on my tongue. "I'm fiiiine." I take two confident steps forward, clutching my purse to my side like it might stabilize me. "See? Perfectly stable."

He rightfully ignores me and rounds the car in a second, his laughter low and familiar. A second later, his arm circles my waist.

"Oh my, God, Miguel," I say, trying to twist away but leaning into him instead. "I am f-i-n-e."

"You're drunk and adorable," he mutters, guiding me up the walkway.

Adorable. I snort under my breath. Because I'm not adorable. I'm a lightweight who makes very questionable decisions the minute tequila gets involved.

How late is it?

The porch steps loom in front of me. I reach for the railing, worn wood biting into my palm, and pause to let the world settle. Miguel stops at the bottom step and gently squeezes my hand.

"Congratulations, boss," he says softly. "I can't wait to watch you rebuild Pier Ninety-two." His voice drops— lower than it needs to be. Intimate. Familiar. And it brushes over me as my stomach flips, heat curling low and slow.

Tequila, I tell myself. *It's just the tequila.*

He steps closer, closing the small space between us like he's done a hundred times before. And in that split-second—before my thoughts can line up in a coherent row—he leans in and presses a quick, warm kiss on my lips. Light. Fast. Gone.

But I *feel it*. Every nanosecond of it.

Uh- oh.

My breath snags in my chest as if someone's tightened a string around my ribs. The porch light halos around him, soft gold against the dark, and everything tilts—not the dizzy sway from margaritas. The other kind. The kind that feels like you've stepped too close to a ledge and only just realized how far down it is.

That's when it fully hits me. The last conversation Miguel and I had about Mitch was weeks ago—months, maybe. Back when he found me crying in my office and let me word-vomit my marriage woes into his lap. Miguel doesn't know about the promises Mitch and I made in Vegas. About the late-night talks we shared. About him reaching for my hand again. About us trying—actually trying—to choose each other.

As far as he knows, my marriage is a cracked glass already falling from the counter. I never told him we caught it. With the chaos of the fire and the ensuing dance with my insurance carrier, I haven't had the chance to tell him we're trying to glue it back together.

My pulse pounds in my ears. Because from his perspective, this—us lingering too long, drinking, dancing, the way he looks at me—it isn't crossing a line. It's stepping into a space he thinks is empty. And that isn't fair to him. Because tonight, I let him believe it was. I never corrected the narrative. Never drew the boundary. Never said, *we're working it out. I'm still in this.*

I was having fun. I wanted to celebrate. And somewhere between the music and the tequila, it felt easier to lean into the moment than stop and set the record straight.

But the warmth of his mouth lingers like a brand, and guilt quickly floods in behind it, heavy and sobering. I swallow hard, the ledge suddenly feeling very, very real.

"Umm... thank you for taking me home," I manage, brushing damp strands of hair off my face. But my voice sounds floaty, like it belongs to someone else.

He nods. "I promised I'd get you home safely."

I turn toward the steps. One foot. Then the other. I focus on the simple mechanics of walking because if I don't, everything else will rush in at once.

Behind me, I hear him turn back toward the car. And panic flickers in my chest. Because I should stop him. I should say it—clearly, soberly, like it matters. *Miguel, Mitch and I are trying again. We're back on track. I'm in my marriage.* But the truth catches in my throat, tangled up with guilt and tequila and the terrible timing of it all.

Because standing here now, lips still tingling where his touched mine, the weight of that settles heavy in my chest. Miguel didn't imagine this out of nowhere. I let the night stretch longer than it should have. I laughed. I danced. I didn't correct the story forming in his head.

And that makes it worse. Because he isn't just some guy who misread a moment. I've leaned on him for years—for advice, for backup shifts, for steady hands when the bar was three-deep and I couldn't breathe. For the kind of loyalty that doesn't ask questions. He's been my sounding board. My safety net. My almost.

I blurred the lines. Whether I meant to or not, I let him hope. I never said the words, never promised anything—but I let my sadness sound permanent. I let my frustration feel final. I let him believe there was space for him to step into.

And I hate that. Because Miguel deserves something clean. Something chosen. Not something born from my confusion.

But the truth is just as ugly. I don't want to lose him. I don't want to lose the way he looks at me. The way he steps in without being asked. The way he makes me feel lighter when everything else feels like it's caving in. Miguel offers ease. The kind that feels like stepping into warm sunlight after months of gray.

My stomach twists, love and longing and shame braided so tight I can't separate them. I grip the doorknob, heart knocking against my ribs, but I find the strength to open my mouth. "Hey, Miguel?"

He turns, eyebrows lifting, hopeful without meaning to be. "Yeah?"

The right words rise up—honest, necessary. *I shouldn't have let you kiss me. I'm not leaving my husband. You can't wait for me.* They sit on my tongue, but go no further.

He takes a step back in my direction. "Lauren?"

And I panic. Because if I say the truth, I lose him.

The alcohol hums through my veins, softening the sharp edges of what I should do, making the easier choice feel like the kinder one. So, I reach for the one thing I know he wants—the one move that feels generous instead of cruel. The one move that lets me keep him close without promising him anything.

"When Pier Ninety-two reopens..." I say, the words tumbling out fast, urgent. "You're managing it."

He blinks. "What?"

"You've earned it," I rush on. "You've carried that place with me for years. I couldn't have kept it afloat without you. When we rebuild, you're running it. Salary bump. Full control of the floor. It's yours."

If I can give him this, maybe tonight becomes about business. About loyalty. About partnership. Not about the way his mouth felt on mine.

I square my shoulders like this is decisive. Responsible. Like I'm doing something noble instead of avoiding the truth. Because making him manager feels safer than breaking his heart. And right now, I don't trust myself to do anything harder than that.

His eyes widen. "What?"

"You heard me," I say, gesturing like I'm presenting a plan instead of a scramble. "Full-time. Scheduling, staff, vendors. Everything. No more bailing me out behind the bar. No more closing three nights a week. General manager." I hear myself keep talking, keep building the case. "It's a promotion," I add quickly. "Salary. Benefits. A real title."

And yes—part of it is for him. Miguel will be great. He already holds the place together in a hundred quiet ways. But another part of it—the part I don't want to look at too closely right now—is me trying to solve two problems at once. If Miguel runs the restaurant, Mitch gets more of me. Like I promised. Like we promised each other. And Miguel... Miguel stays close. Not beside me every night, not under twinkle lights with tequila blurring the lines—but still in my life. Still mine in some way.

It's selfish. I know it's selfish even as I say it. Because I'm trying to keep them both. I swallow, my throat tight. "I want you on my team," I finish, softer now. "Every step of the way."

Miguel rubs the back of his neck, a slow smile spreading across his face. "I'm always on your team, Lauren."

My chest tightens again—equal parts warmth and dread.

"But it sounds like we've got another reason to celebrate," he says, and then he steps away, sliding back into the sedan with a grin he can't hide.

I stand frozen on the porch, watching the taillights glow red and shrink into the dark. But my lips still tingle. My thoughts stay fuzzy. And the guilt—quiet, heavy, undeniable—settles deeper, because I know exactly what I just did. I didn't tell him the truth. And I found a way to keep him anyway.

With a groan, I turn the knob and step into the quiet house. But I barely make it two steps before I collide with Mitch. Because he's *right here*. Bare chest. Arms crossed. Jaw tight.

"Thirty minutes, huh?" His voice is low, controlled.

"Thirty minutes?" I blink, the foyer lights too bright, his face too close. "What?" I sidestep him and head for the living room, dropping my purse onto the couch before sinking down beside it. Then I press my spinning head into a throw pillow.

"You said you'd be home in thirty minutes." He follows, words sharp at my back. "That was two hours ago. What the hell happened, Lauren?"

Two hours? It's been two hours?

I wrinkle my nose and squeeze my eyes shut, trying to replay the night in the right order. The music. The drinks. The lights. The dancing. The—

"I texted you," I choke out, my lips still pressed against the pillow. "I decided to stay out a little bit longer to celebrate."

His silence stretches.

"You texted me?" He pulls his phone out of his pocket, taps the screen, but his frown only deepens. "The last thing you sent says you'd be home in thirty minutes. That was over two hours."

He tosses the phone into my lap and stomps away, but the screen swims as I lift my head. Icons wobble. I close one eye, trying to force the words to stay steady. But as I read, my stomach twists because he's right. The last message is exactly what he said. "No, that's—" I fumble for my purse and yank out my own phone, thumbing to find the last message I typed. But clearly... never sent...

Mitch comes back from the kitchen with a beer and drops into the chair across from me, the TV glowing with some post-game recap. "I'd offer you one," he says, tipping the bottle in my direction, "but it looks like you're way ahead of me." His lip curls. "What the hell, Lauren? I made us dinner. I waited. And then you just fucking blew me off!"

"I didn't blow you off," I say, holding my phone out toward him. "I typed it. I just—I didn't hit send."

He scoffs like my excuse changes anything. "How many drinks have you had?" His eyes rake over me, assessing.

"Two!" I shoot back, knowing full well it was three. "How many have you had?"

"Not nearly enough to forget how to send a fucking text." He drags a hand through his hair and leans back, frustration radiating off him.

The room begins to spin faster now—not just from the tequila. But from him. From the accusation in his voice. From the way guilt keeps creeping up my throat and tangles with defensiveness as I picture Miguel driving away.

How could I let him kiss me? What was I thinking?

"Mitch, I'm sorry," I say, but I know it comes out slurred and small. I drag my hands through my hair in frustration. "It was an accident. I really thought I sent it."

He shakes his head, but that hurts more than if he'd

yelled. "It's not even about the stupid text, Peaches." He blows out a heavy breath. "It's just more of the same thing over and over. It always comes back to the restaurant."

I lurch forward, elbows on my knees, alcohol-inspired angst flaring hot and reckless—momentarily overriding guilt. "We were celebrating! I got really good news today! I'm sorry if that's inconvenient for you!"

"That's not what I'm saying!"

"Then what are you saying?" I ask.

"It's no different than what I said in Vegas. Pier Ninety-two will always come first!" His voice cracks now, louder. "Every time! It gets the late nights. It gets the energy. It gets the celebrations. And I get the leftovers."

"That's not fair," I choke out.

"Isn't it?" he shoots back.

Silence slams into us as my head pounds. The tequila fog dulls my edges but sharpens his words, making them echo.

"I was excited," I say, weaker now. "I'm sorry. I wanted to celebrate."

"Yeah, with *him*."

My chest tightens—not from indignation, but from recognition. Because he isn't crazy. He isn't reaching. He just sees what I've been carefully refusing to name. But my pride won't let me admit it. Not right now. Not while we're fighting. So instead, I say, "With my *business partner*." But the words sound thinner now. Defensive. Incomplete.

"Yeah, with the man who gets more of you than I ever do."

I drop my face into my hands, elbows digging into my knees. Because it feels like we went right back to where we started. The same argument. The same fault lines. The restaurant. The time. The priorities. The feeling that I'm being pulled in two directions and disappointing someone either way.

"I'm sorry," I whisper into my palms. "Mitch, I'm so sorry."

Across from me, he exhales hard, beer bottle clinking

against the coffee table as he sets it down. "We can't keep doing this," he says, quieter now.

My voice begins to shake, but I push through it—grasping for anything that might make this better. "I asked Miguel to manage the restaurant when we reopen. Full time. He runs it. I step back. Like we said. Like we agreed to in Vegas." The words feel triumphant for half a second—proof that I tried—until my stomach churns when I see his face fall.

"Of course you asked *him*," Mitch mutters. He doesn't even look at me. He just stands and starts pacing, back and forth across the living room like he's wearing a groove into the carpet.

"What's that supposed to mean?" I ask, even though I already know.

He stops long enough to shoot me a look. "Don't insult me, Lauren."

"Oh my, God, you cannot be serious," I deflect with a laugh, but it comes out brittle. My pulse spikes, heat flashing through me as Miguel's hands on my waist replays in cruel, high-definition detail. The quick press of his mouth against mine. The way I didn't stop it. "Are you just looking for reasons to be mad at me tonight?"

"Looking for reasons…" He shakes his head as his voice trails off. "You know what? Just forget it." He waves a hand like he's batting away a fly. "I thought Vegas meant something. I thought we had a plan. I thought we had a chance again, but—"

A sharp ping cuts through the room and Mitch's phone lights up on the couch beside me. I glance at it in defeat. But that's when I see it.

"Why is Tess texting you?" I grab the phone before he can answer and open the message.

Tess: Have you been working out? What gym do you go to?

The words stare back at me, obvious and bright and humiliating. "Oh my, God." I look up at him. "She's flirting with you." I toss the phone at him, anger giving me something solid to stand on. "What—"

"Are you blind?" he yells, pointing toward the front porch like the night is still playing on a loop outside. "You think Tess Browning is the threat here? Your precious *Miguel* literally walks your drunk ass to the door with his hands all over you. You think I didn't see that? You think I don't know he's into you, Lauren?"

My breath catches so hard it hurts. Guilt floods my bloodstream all over again—hotter than the tequila ever had. And for one split-second, I'm almost grateful that's all Mitch saw. Just Miguel's hands. Just his presence.

I acted so stupid tonight. Selfish. I've been walking a tightrope and somehow managed to fall on both sides— leading Miguel on with my silence and my softness, while hurting Mitch at the same time, breaking promises I swore I'd keep. Promises about honesty. About boundaries. About choosing us.

"I—" My voice cracks on the first sound. My throat closes like it's trying to protect me from saying the words out loud. "I didn't know he—"

"Save it, Peaches. Just fucking save it. I can't do this anymore." He turns away from me and stomps toward the stairs. "There's cold pasta in the fridge if you get hungry," he calls back, voice echoing up the hallway. Then a door slams upstairs. And the sound reverberates through the house—and through me.

189

CHAPTER SIXTEEN

Mitch

Sunlight spears through the front window and stretches across the foyer as I head down the stairs, paint stiff on my jeans, dried primer cracking at my knees. Every step creaks louder than it should. I slow instinctively, like the house might call me out for trying to slip away unnoticed.

I slide my feet into my work boots by the front door. But that's when I hear it—Lauren's soft, uneven snores drifting in from the living room. I turn before I can stop myself.

She's curled on the couch right where I left her, long dark hair spilling over the armrest, lifting and falling in the lazy spin of the ceiling fan. Her knees are tucked tight to her chest. And her hands grip her bare arms like she's bracing against something colder than the room.

There's a blanket folded neatly over the chair across from her. I look at it. Then at her. And my chest tightens with that familiar, exhausting weight—the one that feels less like heartbreak and more like gravity. Like something that's always been there, just waiting for me to notice it.

Last night flickers through my mind all over again.

Because for the last week, I let myself believe we'd found something—some thread to pull us back together. I let myself believe the fire had burned away the worst of it. But here she is. On the couch. Hungover. Folded into herself.

And it's obvious. Pier Ninety-two still wins. Even burned to the ground, it still fucking wins.

I shake my head and turn away before I do something stupid—like carry that blanket over and drape it across her shoulders. Like pretend that covering her up would mean we're covered too. Like one small kindness could fix years of choosing something else—maybe *someone* else—first.

The garage door rattles open. Morning light floods in, too bright, too honest. I head straight for my workbench and start yanking open drawers—new brushes, blue painter's tape, a drop cloth. I shove everything into a ten-gallon bucket with more force than necessary.

Then I see it. The cardboard box, sitting beside the dollhouse like it belongs there. Like it's just another project, another harmless piece of our life stacked in the garage. But I don't have to open it to know what's inside.

"Damn it, Lauren," I mutter, the words scraping raw on the way out. Because last night didn't just crush something—it rerouted it. Like a hard detour sign planted right in the middle of everything I thought I understood. I'd told myself the fire would change things. That losing Pier Ninety-two might finally loosen its grip on her. On us.

But it didn't. She picked it again. Even in ashes, she picked it. And not just that—she celebrated it. *With him.*

Miguel's name flashes behind my eyes. The missed calls on her phone always stacked one after another. Relentless. Possessive. Like he has every right to keep reaching for her.

I've always known he was special to her. That he wasn't just an employee, or a friend, or whatever label made it easier for me to swallow. He's been woven into her life for so long I stopped asking questions I didn't want answered.

But last night... last night something shifted. Because there's "close," and then there's the way his hands wrapped around her. The way he pulled her in like he already knew where he fit. The way his mouth brushed hers—too familiar, too easy—like it was something he'd done before.

I saw it. And I didn't say a damn thing. I didn't have the courage, not really. I was too angry—too full of heat and pride and the urge to explode. If I'd opened my mouth, I would've said something that couldn't be taken back. I would've broken us in a way I couldn't repair. So, I swallowed it. I let it sit in my chest like a live wire. But today there's no heat left. Just the ache.

My vision blurs. I press the heels of my hands into my eyes hard enough to see stars because I will not cry in my own garage surrounded by sawdust and steel and all the proof that I'm supposed to be stronger than this.

You broke your promise to me, Peaches.

I grab the box before I can think. Before I can hesitate. Before I can do the pathetic thing—open it anyway, stare at the pieces, and pretend it's only about a stupid plan that got abandoned.

I carry it outside, across the freshly cut grass, to the side shed. I shove it into the back corner and throw a tarp over it like that'll suffocate whatever it represents. Like I can bury the image of her with him under plastic and dust.

Then I slam the metal door so hard it rattles on its hinges. The echo hangs in the air, metallic and final. I stand there for a beat with my hand still on the latch, chest heaving, staring at the dented siding like it might open back up and offer me something other than proof.

It doesn't.

So, I do what I always do when I'm about to feel too much—I move. I cross the yard on autopilot, boots cutting through the grass, keys already in my fist. I don't even remember opening the truck door. I just remember the solid thunk when it shuts, sealing me into something smaller than the life I'm failing at.

I start the engine, back out, and point the nose toward the road like distance might fix what I can't. Minutes later,

I'm on the highway with the window down and the wind clawing at my hair, the stretch of asphalt in front of me looking like an escape route I don't deserve.

"Fuck you, Lauren," I say under my breath as the chorus hits. "I really thought we were going to fix it. I thought we were finally going to fight for us." My grip tightens on the steering wheel. "But nothing's changed, has it?"

The Reynolds Street exit comes up too fast and I merge off the highway, snaking along the side streets until I arrive. The job site sits exactly where I left it—quiet, unfinished, waiting. I kill the engine and grab the bucket, climbing the steps like I'm reporting for punishment.

Inside, the sharp bite of drying primer hits my nose. The place feels hollow. Temporary. Like everything else lately. I set the bucket on the kitchen counter and spot a neon Post-it note in Ryan's barely legible scrawl.

Mitch—

We ran out of roller pads after priming the master bathroom. I'll bring more on Monday, but just in case you swing by this weekend, you won't get far. This house flip is a bitch. Can't wait to be done. Even the farmhouse cabinets are on backorder now.

Ry

"Why didn't you just text me, you dumbass?" I snap at the empty room. But the house doesn't answer. Nothing does.

I stare at the half-finished walls, at the non-existent cabinets on backorder, at the space that was supposed to become something better. And my jaw locks. Because I came here to fix something. To make progress. To feel useful. Instead, I stand in another stalled project.

I drop my head and let out a long, defeated breath. Then I turn around and head back to the truck—already rerouting to the hardware store. Because apparently nothing in my life gets finished on the first try.

As I angle back toward the highway, my phone pings

from the cup holder just as I roll up to a red light. I glance down and let out a tired breath when Tess's name flashes on the screen—again.

I scrub a hand over the back of my neck and rake my fingers through my hair, shoving it off my forehead. It snags in a knot, but I barely feel it. I'm too busy still spiraling.

The light turns green and I nudge the truck forward, then swing into the Ace Hardware lot, gravel crunching under my tires. I park, kill the engine, and grab my phone, unable to avoid her message any longer.

Tess: Well, if you don't want to talk about the gym, the least you can do is recommend the best brand of paint to buy, Benson. I'm out of my league here.

I stare at her text, thumb hovering over the screen. I could ignore it. Probably should. Let it sit there unanswered like every other complication in my life right now. Because Tess Browning does not need my help picking a paint brand. And I definitely don't need another distraction wrapped in blonde curls and pink high heels.

I blow out a slow breath and glance through the windshield at the hardware store, at the quiet morning like it's mocking me with how normal it looks. Meanwhile my life is a dumpster fire—marriage hanging by a thread, emotions ricocheting off the walls, and I'm one wrong sentence away from doing something I can't undo.

So, what's one more stupid decision? I drop my gaze back to the screen and type back.

Me: Interior or exterior?

I hit send and shove the door open, jogging toward the entrance. Cool air slams into me as I step inside. I hang a right and head straight for the paint aisle, letting Tess's ridiculous question crowd out everything else rattling around in my chest.

But my phone pings again.

Tess: Interior. I bought a house across from Highside. It has a purple

```
master   bathroom   and   it's   sickening
having   to   pee   every   morning   in   a
lavender bush.
```

A laugh slips out before I can stop it. I duck into the paint aisle, shaking my head as the image hits. Then I grab a six-pack of rollers and tuck them under my arm before typing back.

Me: I'd wager lavender smells better than the other bush in that bathroom.

I shove my phone in my pocket just as a woman's cackle echoes. I freeze, then edge forward and glance into the next aisle.

Tess Browning stands in front of the interior color display, shoulders trembling as she laughs at her phone. A blonde curl slips loose from her ponytail, and she absently tucks it behind her ear.

She looks up. Our eyes lock. And my stomach drops in a way that has absolutely no business happening. Before I can rethink it, I step into the aisle and nudge her elbow with mine.

She grins, cheeks pink from laughing. "You did not just make a joke about my pubic hair."

"I absolutely just made a joke about your pubic hair." I point up at the sale sign above her head. "And that brand's my favorite."

She tips her head back to read it, but another giggle slips through her lips. "You haven't changed at all, Mitch Benson. Still twelve. Sex jokes—"

"Hey, I'm versatile." I gesture toward the color wall. "So, if not lavender, what color are you trying to surround your bush with every morning?"

She snorts. "—and potty humor." But her finger taps a pink sample card. "I'll have you know I wax, but I think I could pee surrounded by this."

I pluck the card from the slot before she can and hold it up between us. It's soft. Warm. Just bold enough to make a statement. I flick my gaze from the card to her lips—glossed in a shade just a touch darker. "Yeah," I say, handing it back. "This fits you."

She slides it from my fingers. "So, what do I need? A gallon? A bucket? A barrel? How does one... buy paint?" Her eyes widen like she's asking me to defuse a bomb.

I grin. I can't help it. "Can't you just *pay someone* to do it?" I tease.

She rolls her eyes. "Believe it or not, Benson, running a local newspaper doesn't make me royalty. I'm going to paint the bathroom myself."

"You?" I bark out a laugh. "A Georgetown grad with a paintbrush?"

She elbows me in the gut. "Don't laugh! How hard can it be if *you* do it?"

I rub my stomach, still smirking. "Have you ever painted anything before?"

She hesitates. Just for a second. "Well... no."

The words come out quieter than the rest of her, and her shoulders dip like something heavy finally found a place to land. It's subtle—blink-and-you-miss-it—but I catch it. Her gaze drops to the tile, and she fusses with her purse strap like she can tighten it enough to pull herself back into control. Like she suddenly regrets asking me for anything.

And that hits me harder than it should. It's not pity. Never pity. Tess would spit in my coffee for that. But it is empathy. The kind that sneaks up on you when you're already off-balance. Because this morning I'm as uncertain as anyone gets—about my marriage, about what I'm doing, about why my chest feels bruised from the inside out.

Her flash of vulnerability is familiar in a way I don't want to admit. It looks a lot like mine probably did in the mirror before I left the house.

All we've ever done is needle each other. Compete. Clash. Tess is the girl I've been at odds with since high school—sharp edges, louder smile, always acting like she's got the room handled. But right now she doesn't. And neither do I.

My chest tightens, the frustration I've been hauling around all morning... then fizzing out, like it doesn't have enough fuel in here. The wreckage of my marriage still smolders somewhere behind my ribs, but standing in this paint aisle with Tess—laughing about bushes and bad color choices—it feels distant. Manageable. Like my brain can only hold one kind of mess at a time, and this one comes with a shopping list.

I exhale slowly and look at her again. "Alright," I say, grabbing a gallon of the brand I pointed to and setting it in her hands. "You need one of these. Two-inch angled brush. Drop cloth. Painter's tape—unless you want pink ceilings."

She blinks up at me. "You're helping me?"

"Don't make it weird," I mutter, reaching for a stir stick. "I can't let you commit a felony against interior design across from Highside. I have a reputation."

Her smile spreads slow and bright, and something in my chest lifts before I can stop it.

"How big is the bathroom?" I ask.

She shrugs like I've asked her the square root of pi. "I mean... like four walls."

I stare at her, then blink once. "Four walls," I repeat, deadpan.

Her mouth twitches, like she wants to be annoyed but can't quite commit.

I jerk my chin toward the counter where an employee waits, already bored out of his mind. "Come on. Let's mix your paint. We'll start with a gallon and come back if we need more."

She opens her mouth, but I keep going, because apparently I've lost every ounce of self-preservation I used to have. "Besides, I probably owe you after giving you brain damage a decade ago."

***

I stand in the doorway of Tess's master bathroom and

immediately regret every decision that led me here. The walls are aggressively purple. Not subtle. Not muted. Just… purple. The kind that makes your eyes water and your brain invent the scent of lavender whether you want it to or not.

She drags her hand over the wall above the pedestal sink and frowns. "See? Isn't it awful?"

I step farther inside, glancing around like I'm inspecting structural damage. "Yeah," I admit. "It's like peeing inside a craft store."

She giggles. "Exactly." Then she turns to me, arms folding over her chest, grin creeping in. "Why again are you helping me?"

I widen my eyes and shake my head. "I have no fucking clue."

Her pink lips twist into something smug. "I always knew you liked me, Benson."

"Let's not be too quick to rewrite history," I shoot back. "I *tolerated* you. Big difference." I shrug. "Especially when you were married to my best friend."

She rolls her eyes. "And how is my sweet Joshua these days?"

"Annoyingly happy," I mutter. "With my sister."

Her gaze instantly drops to the tile floor. She bites her bottom lip and nods once, toes dragging over the little accent rug like she's trying to ground herself. But I feel it. That quiet hit of shared wreckage hangs in the air.

I nudge her elbow. "Hey. Don't get all tragic on me. It's unsettling."

Her mouth twitches. "I'm not tragic."

"You're giving strong 'I might cry in a tiny bathroom' vibes."

She lifts her gaze to mine—sharp, blue, too close—then she scoffs, but it comes out softer than usual. "Fine. You're right." She squares her shoulders like she can bully her own feelings into submission. "So… what's first?" She nods at the paint like it's a plan. "I'm helping."

I swallow and point at her outfit—shimmery pink tank,

white jean shorts that have no business being within ten feet of a paint can. "First, you put on something you don't mind ruining."

She looks down at herself and toys with the fringe on her shirt. "I don't really have anything like that."

I shrug. "Then paint naked."

"You'd like that, wouldn't you?" Before I can respond, she yanks her top over her head and I freeze. Hot-pink strapless bra. No warning. No mercy.

"How's married life, Mitch?" she asks casually, like she didn't just detonate a bomb in my peripheral vision. "Still happy in love?"

I inhale wrong and clamp my eyes shut. Pressure builds low in my gut—equal parts adrenaline and aggravation. "Damn it, Tess. Come on."

She laughs and ducks past me toward her closet. "Okay, okay. Lauren must still do it for you, huh?"

"Of course she does," I snap automatically. "She's my wife." But the second the words leave my mouth, something inside me sinks. Because last night doesn't line up with that certainty. Last night was unsent text messages. Last night was Miguel's hands on her waist. Last night was me standing there, swallowing questions I didn't have the guts to ask.

The doubt creeps back in—quiet and steady. But I shove it down hard before it can spread and drop to my knees, fussing with the drop cloth like it's the most fascinating thing I've ever seen. I smooth the edges around the toilet, tug it straight, press it flat. Anything to keep my hands busy. Anything to keep from thinking about how fragile "she's my wife" sounded the second it left my mouth.

Tess reappears a second later in an oversized navy-blue Georgetown t-shirt that hangs past her knees. "Is this better?" she asks. Then, softer, "It was Josh's. So I don't care if I get paint on it."

"Yeah," I mutter, not looking at her too long. "It's fine."

She kneels beside me on the drop cloth and I glance sideways. "Please tell me you're wearing pants."

She hikes the shirt up just enough to reveal gray cotton shorts. "Relax." Then she studies me for a beat. "You know, just because you're married doesn't automatically make you happy."

I slap her knee lightly and force a grin. "Wow. Profound. Tell me more, little vixen."

She scowls. "Forget it. I just thought we might have something in common."

We do. You just don't get to know that.

I clear my throat, desperate to steer us away from anything that requires feelings. "You got a screwdriver?"

"Yeah. Hang on." Tess pops up and disappears down the hall.

The bathroom goes quiet—just the hum of the vent fan and the purple walls closing in on me like a dare. I stare at the pedestal sink, the rug, the ridiculous color, the fact that I'm here at all.

What the fuck am I doing?

I shake my head and do a quick mental inventory like I can reduce my life to a checklist. Repaint the bush. Leave. Go home. Simple.

Except nothing is.

For a second, my brain flashes to a different moment— Lauren kneeling beside me while I fixed the kitchen sink a few weeks back. Me elbow-deep in pipes, cursing under my breath. Her beside me, ponytail messy, already asking what kind of wrench I needed.

Channellock? she'd asked, like it was normal. Like we were a team. Like she knew my hands so well she could anticipate them. But Tess is not that. Tess is chaos in a cute package— something I will never admit out loud to.

She comes back carrying a pink plastic tool kit like she's five-years-old playing house. She drops to the floor beside me, flips it open with a flourish, and grins like she just solved world peace. Then she grabs a screwdriver and presses it into my palm. "Alright, Benson," she says. "Show me how to fix my bush."

I snort and hold up what she handed me. "This is a Phillips head."

She blinks, completely sincere. "Okay... is that bad?"

"It's not bad," I say, handing it back. "It's just not what you need right now."

She hovers over the open case, fingers skimming the tools like she's reading braille. "They all look the same."

"They absolutely do not." I point. "This one. See how it's flat?"

She nods slowly, concentrating. "Yes."

"And what's it called?" I ask, already bracing myself.

She pulls it out and offers it to me like she's presenting Excalibur. "A... flat Phillips?"

I stare at her for a beat, then take it with a straight face. "A screwdriver," I say. "Just... a screwdriver."

She groans and drops her head back dramatically. "Why are there so many kinds of the same thing?"

"Because God has a sense of humor," I deadpan, and the corner of her mouth twitches like she hates that she's amused.

I wedge the flat tip under the lid of the paint can. With a pop, the seal breaks and I lift the lid to reveal the color she picked—bright, shameless pink. The kind of pink that makes a statement. The kind of pink that definitely has feelings about itself.

Tess lets out a small, triumphant little hum behind me as I grab a wooden stir stick and start mixing. A few swirls later, I dip a brush, tap off the excess, and paint a small test square on the wall. Then I lean back and squint at it. It looks like the inside of a Victoria's Secret sale bag. "Is that... really what you wanted?"

"It's perfect!" she squeals, clapping her hands like I've just revealed the winning lottery numbers. "Yes. Keep going."

I gesture with my brush. "Then grab one. You said you were helping."

"Fine," she says, and snatches up a brush with the

determined energy of someone about to conquer a small nation. She dips it into the can, turns to the opposite wall, and slaps paint on with zero hesitation. Too much paint. Way too much paint. Thick pink liquid immediately starts to ooze downward in slow, tragic trails.

Tess beams anyway. "I'm doing it," she announces, brushing over the drips like that will somehow make them behave. "I'm doing it, Mitch!"

I watch the wall cry pink tears. "Yeah," I say dryly. "Sure thing."

She lowers her voice like it's a confession. "I've never painted anything in my life."

"That tracks," I mutter, then wince when she speeds up again, carving streaks into the wet paint. "Okay—slow down there, Picasso. You're gonna make it all streaky." I set my brush on the rim of the can and crawl over beside her. I wrap my hand around her wrist and guide the brush back over the wall.

"See?" I say, moving her arm in long, even passes. "Nice and slow. Spread it. Let the paint do the work."

She nods, focused. "Okay." Her face tilts toward mine as I guide her hand up and down, and her warm breath hits the side of my neck.

For a single second, my lungs forget how to function. I swallow, eyes fixed on the wall like it's suddenly the most important surface on earth. Because the pull between us is stupid and completely unwelcome.

"Thank you for teaching me," she whispers. Then she presses a quick kiss to my cheek—soft and light and entirely too real. Floral perfume flickers in my nose. And a blonde curl brushes my neck.

My fingers go numb. Because what is she doing? Heat rushes through me, sharp and immediate, and I drop her wrist like it burned. "Uh," I manage. "Yeah. No problem."

Tess smiles like she didn't just detonate a landmine. She dips her brush again and keeps painting, humming to herself while more pink spreads across the purple. "Can I ask you something?" she says casually.

I crawl back to the safer side of the bathroom and grab my brush again, turning my attention to the baseboards. I start cutting in along the trim with careful strokes. "Yeah," I say, keeping my voice even. "Sure."

"I heard a rumor you were divorcing Lauren."

My brush pauses mid-stroke. I exhale and roll my eyes, because if I don't act annoyed, I might crack. "That's not a question."

Tess drips paint onto the baseboard and curses under her breath. She grabs a wad of toilet paper to wipe it clean, then looks up at me, eyes too direct. "Are you getting a divorce?"

The words hit like a nail in the chest—small, sharp, and somehow right on target. I watch her toss the pink-stained toilet paper into the wastebasket.

"I don't know, Tess," I say finally. "One minute I think I am, and the next..."

She nods and turns back to the wall, laying down another coat of pink over the purple. This time her strokes are slow. Even. Careful, like I showed her. "Yeah," she says quietly. "Okay. I understand."

I drag my brush along the bottom edge of the wall, cutting a clean line against the white trim. It's steady. Controlled. Something in this room is. "I guess it is something we have in common," I admit, staring at the straight edge I just made. "Or... had in common." I tuck my hair behind my ears and glance at her. "Why're you asking?"

She shrugs without looking at me. "Because it's hard divorcing a Templeton." She dips her brush again. "I've got a divorce attorney I can recommend. If you need one."

I snort. "And why would you do that?"

She finally looks over. "I don't know, Mitch. We've known each other a long time."

"You mean we've despised each other for a long time," I correct, dragging my brush carefully around the chrome plumbing behind the toilet.

She laughs under her breath. "Maybe. But you're painting behind my toilet." Her eyes flick to the drop cloth like its evidence. "You can't hate me *that much*."

I glance at her again, and despite myself, a grin tugs at my mouth. It's stupid—this whole situation is stupid—but there's something disarming about her saying it out loud, like we're not pretending this is normal.

That's when the last twenty-four hours slams into me all over again—hard and sudden. Lauren on the couch. The box in the shed. Miguel's hands all over her. All of it balancing on a cracked foundation I've been pretending isn't there.

I drag a breath in through my nose and bite down on my lip, trying to swallow it back. It doesn't go though. "I don't know what I'm gonna do," I admit, the words rough like they've been scraping my throat all morning. "I want to stay married. I do. But I'm not sure Lauren really does."

My brush keeps moving along the trim—steady line, steady hand—while my chest tightens like I'm holding something too heavy in one place.

"She says she does," I continue, voice lower now. "She says all the right things. But then she…" I trail off and shake my head once. "We've had a rough year. We don't make each other happy anymore. Different priorities. Different… everything."

I should stop. I should shut up. Because why am I telling you this?

But Tess doesn't flinch. She doesn't make a joke or twist it into ammo. She just watches me over the rim of the paint can, the pink sitting between us like a line we're both pretending not to see. And for some reason—maybe because she's not *in* it, maybe because she can't call Lauren and pick a side, maybe because she's had her own heart broken and survived it—I feel okay telling her.

"I used to try to make Josh happy, too," she says softly. "The way you made Lauren happy."

My brush stills midair. "What?"

She nods, but she can't hold my gaze. Her eyes drop to the floor like the tile is safer than the truth.

"The first year we were married, I copied you," she says quietly. "I mimicked you. I watched how you treated Lauren and tried to do the same things for Josh." Her laugh is thin—more breath than humor. "Because it was obvious how much you loved her. And I loved him like that."

Something in my chest shifts, small and sharp. I keep my brush moving along the trim, but the line isn't the only thing I'm trying to keep steady.

She swallows, hard. "But he never looked at me the way Lauren looks at you." She dips her brush again, like she needs something to do with her hands. "So I gave up. And I found someone who did."

The words should land clean. Confident. A little vindicated. But they don't. Her voice drops on the last part, barely audible. "Until he didn't want me anymore either…"

For a second, the room goes too quiet. The vent hums. The bristles drag softly against the wall. My throat tightens like I'm the one trying not to break.

I stare at the baseboard like it might offer a way around what she just said. Like there's a trick to it. A fix. But all I see is paint and tile and the small wreckage people carry like it's normal.

"I'm not sure why I'm admitting this," I say slowly, because I can feel the loyalty to Josh pulsing in my veins, and still—still—I can't pretend I don't see it now. "Josh is my best friend. But…" I glance up at her. "He wasn't fair to you. Was he?"

She shakes her head once, quick and final. "No. He loved your sister. I never stood a chance." A humorless smile touches her mouth, like she's mocking the girl she used to be. "I was just too stupid to see it."

And it hits me then—not as gossip, not as some old drama I get to judge from the outside. As grief. As loneliness. As a person trying to survive being second choice and pretending it didn't bruise her.

My grip tightens on the brush. I don't know what to do with the ache in my chest, so I shift closer to her and smooth out a thick patch of paint she slopped on the wall, blending it evenly. "I'll never admit this to anyone," I mutter, keeping my voice low. "But I'm sorry you got hurt."

She snorts, and before I can react, she bumps her brush into mine. Pink flecks explode across the wall—and my shirt.

"Hey!" I bark a laugh, jerking back and shoving her brush away with mine. "Stop. You're gonna streak everything up."

She giggles, and it's lighter than I've ever heard her. Free. Unfiltered. The sound ricochets around the tiny bathroom and hits something soft inside me—something I've been keeping locked down. The weight on my chest loosens. Just a notch. Because where has this Tess been all our lives?

She laughs again, head tipped back, and I smile before I can stop myself. I should pull away. I should be the adult in the room. But then my mind flashes—too fast, too cruel—to last night. Lauren. Miguel. The way she didn't flinch from letting someone else hold her. The way I stood there swallowing rage and vows like they were my job to carry alone.

A bitter little thought slips in. *Apparently commitment is optional now.* And if she can cross lines and still come home like it didn't change anything… why the hell am I the only one bleeding for the rules?

The guilt tries to rise up—old instinct, old promises— but it's drowned out by something else. Something tired. Something lonely. Something that wants to feel wanted.

"Alright," I say, aiming for stern and landing somewhere near amused. "Hand it over before you redecorate me."

She lifts her chin, defiant. "I'm doing great."

"You're committing war crimes against drywall."

She opens her mouth to argue, but I don't wait. I wrap my hand around hers—steadying, guiding, pretending it's only about the paint—and take the brush from her fingers.

I set it on the rim of the can beside mine. Then I inch closer. Close enough to see the faint freckles dusting her nose. Close enough to catch that floral perfume again. Close enough to feel the heat of her laughter still clinging to her skin.

My hand rises like it belongs there. I cup her cheek. And my heart pounds hard enough to be stupid. *Lauren, if nothing's really changed between us… then why should I be the only one acting like it has?*

"Don't tell anyone what I'm about to do," I whisper, like I'm still trying to make this a joke. Like jokes can keep me safe.

Tess's smile turns soft, dangerous. Her breath warms my mouth. "Don't worry," she whispers back. "No one would ever believe me anyway."

Her fingers slide into my hair, nails grazing my scalp, and I suck in a breath through my teeth. "You got pink paint in my hair, didn't you?"

She laughs softly, eyes bright. "I got pink paint in your hair."

And for one reckless second, I let myself stop being the responsible one. The loyal one. The only one still trying to play by the rules.

I lean in—and I kiss her.

CHAPTER SEVENTEEN

Lauren

"I think it's really over this time." The words fall out of my mouth before I can dress them up into something smaller, something more reasonable. They hit the air and just... stay there. Heavy. Final.

I shove a fresh glue stick into the gun and prop it on the table to warm, then drag my palms down my cheeks like I can physically press the panic back inside. Like I can smooth my face into something calm enough to pretend this isn't my fault. But it is. Maybe not all of it. Maybe not the whole messy history between Mitch and me—but the last part? The part that tipped us into silence?

Yeah. That's mine.

The weight of what I did sits on my shoulders like a wet coat I can't peel off. I can still picture it too clearly. The decision to stay for one more drink, the sloppy confidence of thinking it didn't matter, the way the night blurred into something reckless and careless and *easy*—while Mitch was at home, waiting, trying.

My chest hurts. It's not dramatic—it's dull and constant, like someone is squeezing my heart from the inside out.

Three days. Three full days of silence from Mitch. No slammed doors. No sharp words. Just nothing.

And somehow that's worse. Because anger would mean he's still in it with me. Anger would mean he still wants a reaction. Still wants me to fight. But this—this quiet—feels like the sound of him letting go. And I can't stop thinking… if he's done, he'll have every right to be.

"Do you want to talk about it?" Mavis asks softly, pressing a paper bear cub onto a warm dot of glue. "Mitch hasn't said anything to me… but, um—"

"God! I'm such an idiot!" The words burst out of me, louder than I mean them to. I rake my fingers through my hair and grip at the roots. "I made a really dumb mistake. And for Mitch, I think it was the last one he was willing to let me make." I swallow the lump in my throat. "He hasn't spoken to me in days. And now we're right back to where we started."

"It can't be that bad, though, right?" Mavis leans back in her chair, one hand rubbing over the tight knit of fabric stretched across her belly. She winces and arches her back, trying to get comfortable. "I mean… he hasn't moved back in here." Her eyes flick to the second-floor guest bedroom.

I shake my head and let out a brittle laugh. "That's not exactly a victory."

Josh drops into the chair beside me with three bottles of water, setting them down like we're about to negotiate a treaty. "What happened?" he asks, picking up an envelope and a pen.

"The short version?"

He nods.

Probably for the best. The long version makes me look worse.

"I learned the insurance policy on Pier Ninety-two would pay out," I say, forcing myself to keep my voice steady. "The full restaurant can be rebuilt."

Mavis gasps and grabs my hand. "Lauren! That's incredible." Her smile blooms instantly. "That's amazing news. You must be so happy."

Josh tilts his head, studying me. "But…"

"But," I say, widening my eyes because there's no graceful way to land this, "I screwed up."

"How?" Josh asks, nose wrinkling.

Mavis dots another invite with glue, presses down a paper bear, then looks at me with matching confusion.

"When I got the news," I begin slowly—because this is the part where I know the story turns ugly—"the first person I wanted to tell was Miguel." But saying it out loud makes my stomach dip. "He's been with me since day one," I rush to explain. "Before we even opened. Before any of the problems. He's bled for that place with me. It felt… natural."

I twist the cap off a water bottle and take a long sip, buying myself a second to breathe. "I texted him from my insurance agent's office. He said he was right down the street, so I left to meet him. I wanted to tell him the good news in person."

"Okay…" Josh says carefully, sliding the other bottle toward Mavis.

"There's more," I admit as I grab an envelope and address it to Austin and Casey. I dot the I in Chicago with a tiny heart, because muscle memory doesn't care that my marriage might be imploding again.

"I met him at this Mexican place," I say. "We had a drink."

Mavis snorts. "Are you saying Mitch is jealous? Because if he is, that's ridiculous. I'll talk to him—"

"No!" I snap, sitting up straighter. "Don't talk to him. If you talk to him, he'll know I talked to you."

Josh frowns. "So? We talk all the time."

"Just—hang on," I mutter. "Let me finish." Because the drink wasn't the mistake. It was everything that happened after.

Mavis nudges my arm. "Sorry. Keep going." She shifts in her seat, hands braced under her belly like she's holding herself in place.

I nod and continue. "I texted Mitch," I say, staring at the half-finished invite like it might testify for me. "I told him I was going to tell Miguel in person and that I'd be home in thirty minutes."

Thirty minutes. I hate that number.

"He'd spent all afternoon mowing the lawn," I add quietly. "He was making dinner. We were supposed to have a quiet night in. Watch a game. Or start another stupid *Lord of the Rings* marathon."

"It's not stup—" Josh starts.

"It is," I cut in, because if I don't deflect I'll cry. "But that's not the point."

He mutters something about quests and keeps gluing.

"The point is…" I swallow. "One margarita turned into two. Then three. And before I knew it, we were dancing. And I was two hours late."

The silence that follows is thick.

"Oh, Lauren." Mavis's face hardens. "You left my brother waiting at home while you went out drinking and dancing with another guy?"

"It was just Miguel," Josh interjects quickly. "If there's anyone who'd be as happy about the rebuild as Lauren, it's him."

I glance at Josh, grateful for his support—even if it feels flimsy.

"Exactly," I say, leaning into it. "He understands what rebuilding means. I swear, Mavs, I wasn't sneaking around. I was just celebrating with him."

"Yeah, but Mitch…" she says, brows raised.

"I tried to text him," I insist. "I typed the whole thing out. I told him I would be home soon. But I was a little stupid and a little drunk and didn't actually hit send."

"Why'd you stay at all?" she presses, sliding a paper bear across the table. "If he was waiting for you—"

"Because I was happy!" I say, frustration bursting out. "Because I've been fighting for that restaurant for years and for once something went right. I didn't think sharing a drink with a friend was a federal crime."

But even as I say it, it feels hollow. Because I'm not sharing the full story. It wasn't just a drink. It was the way I didn't leave. It was the way I let the night stretch. It was the kiss we shared in the aftermath.

"But your husband was waiting for you," Mavis says, rubbing her lower back. "Lauren, all I'm saying is it was kind of crummy. Mitch has every right to be upset."

"I know," I say, quieter now. "It was wrong. But like I said, if there was anyone who understood what rebuilding meant to me, it's—"

"Your husband!" she explodes, hands flying up.

Josh leans forward, placing a calming hand over her belly. "Mavs, calm down. She didn't really do anything wrong."

"The hell she didn't!" She swats his hand away. "What about Mitch? Do his feelings not count in any of this?"

I drag in a shaky breath. "I *tried* to text him. I swear. I just... didn't hit send. It was an accident."

"After three drinks?" she presses.

"Duchess," Josh says gently. "Please, lay off her a little."

But it's not landing. Because deep down, beneath the justifications and the defensiveness and the technicalities, I know. I didn't mean to hurt Mitch. But I did. And that truth sits in my bones, heavy and unmovable.

Mavis's eyes fill with tears so fast it steals the rest of the air from the room. Her chair scrapes loudly against the floor as she pushes herself up, a sob catching in her throat as she waddles toward the staircase, swiping at her cheeks.

A door swings shut upstairs, and the sound echoes longer than it should. I slump forward, pressing my forehead against the cool wood of the table. "Great," I mutter. "Now I'm driving a wedge between you two, too."

Josh exhales and rubs the back of his neck. "You're not." His voice is tired, not defensive. "She's just... emotional lately. Please don't take it personally. She's just defending her brother. Same way I'm defending you."

He drags both hands down his face, and I see it then—the exhaustion. The deep, bone-tired kind that sits behind his eyes and dulls the edges of everything. "She cried for three straight hours the other night after watching *Grey's Anatomy*," he adds with a weak huff. "I know it's normal. Hormones. But I'm wiped. She's usually so level-headed."

I lift my head slowly. "Wait. Did you say *Grey's Anatomy*?"

He shrugs. "I think that's what she said. I don't know though, I didn't watch it."

My stomach drops. "Josh... if it was the most recent episode, that's really bad."

He frowns. "Why?"

I swallow. "One of the surgeons had a miscarriage last week."

The words settle between us, heavy. And suddenly this conversation isn't about me and Mitch anymore.

Josh's face twists like someone punched the air from his lungs. He slumps forward so fast his forearm clips the neat stack of finished baby shower invites, scattering them across the table like paper confetti.

"I actually meant to text her," I admit quietly. I tuck my hair behind my ear, stalling. "I was going to warn her. Tell her not to watch it." My throat tightens. "But... I forgot."

The shame is instant and suffocating. Because when did I become someone who forgets things like that?

Josh stares at the mess of envelopes, blinking like he's trying to stitch the last few days together. "Well, shit," he whispers. "No wonder she's been so..."

"God." I press my palm to my chest. "I'm sorry, Josh. I should've warned her. I can't even imagine what she felt watching that."

And I can't. Not really. Because it isn't just "pregnancy hormones" or an emotional TV episode—it's her. Seventeen-years-old, terrified, suffering the same fate. A secret she carried like a bruise. The miscarriage she survived as a teen and never really got to grieve out loud.

For a second, my own mess fades. Because this is a woman growing a human and trying not to fall apart every time the world reminds her how fragile that is.

Josh's eyes flick upstairs like he can hear her crying through the ceiling. He straightens, runs a hand through his hair, then shoves both hands into his pockets. "I should go talk to her," he says, already moving.

"Go," I tell him quickly, sitting up. "Please. I can finish these." I gesture toward the scattered bear cubs. "Seriously. Go." He hesitates, and I shake my head. "She needs you."

And she does. Not my drama. Not my guilt. Not my marriage imploding at the dining room table. She needs her husband.

Tears sting my eyes, but this time they aren't just for me. "I'm sorry," I say again, softer.

Josh pauses on the first step and looks back at me, gentler than I deserve. "I'll call you later."

I nod.

"Hang in there," he adds, then jogs up the stairs. But just before he disappears, his voice floats back down, louder now, half-brotherly command, half-desperate hope. "Call Mitch, Lauren! You won't solve anything unless you talk to him!" His footsteps fade into the carpet. And the house goes quiet.

I sit there, alone at the table, tracing the edge of a paper bear until it bends under my fingers. My breath catches, and something inside me curls tight—small and scared and so tired of hurting the people I love.

I want to argue. I want to say I'm trying. But the truth is simple and brutal. I'm at rock bottom.

***

I roll over for what feels like the tenth time and bury my face in Mitch's pillow. It still smells like him—pine, cedar, sawdust. Clean and warm and steady. The scent drags a memory into my head before I can stop it. Him in the garage, sanding down tiny, intricate pieces of wood for the dollhouse he's been working on for months.

What did I do? Did my selfish, dumb mistake really cost us our second chance at forever?

A tear slips out and disappears into the pillowcase as quickly as it falls, swallowed by the fabric like it never existed. "I'm so sorry, Mitch," I whisper into the dark. But my voice sounds small and pathetic. "I never meant for any of this to happen."

My heart hammers against my ribs, each thud louder than the last as the truth settles heavier. This isn't just about a missed text. This is about trust. This is about me choosing wrong in a moment that mattered.

I stare into the dark, mind racing. What if I rebuild Pier Ninety-two... and then sell it? Would that change anything? Would choosing him—finally, fully—fix this? Or is it already too late?

The bedside clock glows red. 12:02 a.m.

"Where are you?" I whisper, grabbing my phone off the nightstand. "Why haven't you come home?"

I open our text thread and type.

Me: Mitch, I'm so sorry. You have to believe me when I say that all I want is a chance to apologize to you. I was so wrong for what I did. And we have to fix this. I love you. Where are you? Please come home.

I hit send and stare at the message like I can will it to pull him back here. My chest tightens as I wait for the three little dots to appear. But nothing happens. The silence stretches, cold and unforgiving.

The bitter taste of defeat pools beneath my tongue, and I shiver even though the room isn't cold. "It's over, isn't it?" I whisper as I reach for Finn and drag him against my chest, my fingers smoothing over the matted purple fur. Because the stupid stuffed animal feels like the only thing that hasn't changed.

"A lifetime of love," I mutter, my voice breaking, "and it ends with the lime on a margarita."

The words sting. I close my eyes, and just as I start to drift into that hazy, miserable place between awake and asleep, my phone pings. "Mitch?" I gasp, lifting my head so fast it makes me dizzy.

But it's not him. It's Austin. And disappointment sinks deep and heavy as I read his message.

Austin: Are you awake?

I blow out a breath into the pillow before tapping his name and putting the call on speaker.

"Hey," he says, exhaustion thick in his voice. "Why're you up?"

"Why do you think?" I roll onto my back and stare at the ceiling fan spinning slow circles above me. "Why are you?"

"I've got a report due in the morning."

"Then why are you on the phone with me?" I ask.

A pause. "Because I just got off the phone with Mitch."

I let out a humorless laugh. "So, he'll talk to you. Just not me."

"Something like that." Austin sighs. "Lauren, he's really pissed. What the hell happened? I thought you two worked everything out?"

I pinch the bridge of my nose, trying to head off the migraine building behind my eyes. "We did. And then I made a stupid mistake. And now he won't even speak to me about it."

"What happened?"

"He didn't tell you?"

"He wouldn't give me details. Just how things feel. And it didn't sound good. So, I texted you."

"Isn't it like two in the morning for you?"

"I was up. He's up. You're up. What's the difference?"

I clutch Finn tighter against my chest. "I think it's over, Austin. For real this time."

"What makes you say that?"

"It's been three days," I say, my voice cracking. "He won't talk to me. He hasn't come home. He won't let me try to apologize. And I don't even know where he is. He's just... gone."

My brother exhales into the phone, static crackling between us. "He's at the house flip project. Sleeping on a blow-up bed in the living room."

I sit up slightly, staring at the clock now reading 12:14 a.m. "So, he'd rather sleep on a shitty blow-up bed in the middle of a construction site than come home and talk to me," I say flatly.

"What happened?" Austin presses again.

"I made a mistake!" The words burst out of me. "I should've come home. I should've put him first. I should've put our relationship first. I should've—" But I stop. Because what I don't say is louder. I shouldn't have stayed. I shouldn't have led Miguel on. And I really shouldn't have let him kiss me.

The tears burn behind my eyes, choking off the rest of the sentence. And for the first time, I let myself admit it. This isn't just a mistake. This is me breaking something fragile—and not knowing if it can ever be repaired.

"Then fix it," Austin snaps. "For fuck's sake, Lauren— fix it. Go over there and say the same things you just said to me to *him*."

The force of his voice hits me in the gut. Because Austin doesn't yell. Not like this. Not unless he's scared.

"I wish it were that simple," I whisper, throat tight.

"Make it that simple," he shoots back. "Go over there tomorrow. Apologize. Talk it out. Again."

I roll my eyes, staring at Mitch's pillow like it's going to give me permission to keep hiding. "It's not that easy."

Austin exhales hard. "If you did something wrong, own it."

I clutch Finn tighter, like the extra pressure might keep my insides from spilling out. For days, despair has been a dead weight on my chest—heavy, stubborn, familiar. But his words don't bounce off me the way everything else has. They sink in. They shift something.

Own it. Not defend it. Not explain it until it sounds prettier. Not wrap it in exhaustion and fear. Just... own it.

I stare at the wall like it might offer a loophole. Like it might whisper a way to fix this without walking straight into the mess I made. But there isn't one. There hasn't been one. I've already lost so much—my pride, my footing, my sense of control. I've already spent days drowning in worst-case scenarios like they were penance.

And now I know where he is.

That knowledge is a strange kind of relief. It doesn't erase what happened, but it takes away the helplessness—the pacing, the guessing, the imagining him somewhere unreachable. He's not a ghost. He's not gone. He's at that stupid flip house, stubborn and wounded. So, what do I have to lose by going over there tomorrow?

My stomach turns at the answer. My dignity. My pride. The last thin layer of armor I've been clinging to because it's easier to be angry than terrified. But I'm already scraped raw.

I let out a slow breath, and the despair loosens—just slightly—making room for something else. Not joy. Not certainty. Just... a direction. A path. A plan. My brain grabs onto it like a life raft because it's either this or keep sinking.

I'll bring him lunch. Something warm. Something familiar. Peach cobbler—his favorite, the one he eats straight from the pan like the rules don't apply to him. I'll show up at that house with flour on my shirt and an apology I don't try to soften or spin.

I won't beg. I'll just tell the truth. And I'll make him look at me. I'll make him hear me. Not because I can force forgiveness, but because he deserves to know how I feel. How much I regret my actions.

A stupid, reckless thought trails in behind the practical ones—my cheeks warming as it lands. *And then I'll show him how much I love him on that blow-up bed.*

The image flashes bright and desperate and intimate, and I hate that it sparks hope like I haven't earned the right to feel it.

I swallow hard, embarrassed by my own heart. Because Mitch isn't the only person I've been avoiding. I've been so consumed by the crater in my marriage that I've let myself pretend the other damage doesn't count. Like if I fix Mitch, the rest of it will magically fall back into place.

But Miguel is part of this, whether I like it or not. Miguel, with his steady hands and his easy presence. Miguel, who thinks he knows where he stands with me because I've let him believe a version of the truth that hurts less than the real one. I've taken his kindness and called it comfort. I've taken his loyalty and tucked it into my pocket like it didn't cost him anything.

I owe him a conversation. Not a flirty half-confession. Not a carefully edited story. A real conversation—the kind where I don't get to keep the parts that make me look better.

My arms tighten around Finn again, and for a second I feel the full weight of it—the web I've spun, the people I've pulled into it, the way I've been trying to survive by slicing the truth into manageable pieces.

Austin's words echo in my skull. *Own it.*

I nod once, small and shaky, like I'm agreeing to jump off a cliff I've been standing beside for weeks.

Tomorrow, I'll go find him. Tomorrow, I'll tell Mitch the truth. And then—because I'm done hiding behind panic and pretending silence is the same thing as innocence—I'll find Miguel, too. Because if I'm going to stop losing everything, I have to stop lying to the people who are still here.

I don't remember ending the call with Austin. All I know is that he was the voice of reason I needed tonight.

CHAPTER EIGHTEEN

Austin

"I lied to my sister." The confession scrapes up my throat and lands heavy between us. It tastes metallic. Wrong.

Casey frowns and reaches for the glowing orange button on the coffee maker. She presses it, and the machine coughs to life, rattling against the cheap laminate countertop of our apartment. "About what?" she asks.

I drag my fists over my bloodshot eyes and grind my knuckles in hard, like I can physically erase the last twenty-four hours. The burn behind my lids pulses in time with the dull throb in my temples. Because an all-nighter is no longer something I can power through—it's something my body now openly rebels against. My brain feels packed with cotton. And every thought takes effort.

"I gave Lauren hope," I say hoarsely. "When I don't think I should have."

Casey's nose wrinkles. "What's that supposed to mean?" She plucks a piece of lint off her royal-blue suit jacket with surgical precision, then points at me. "Have you slept?"

I shake my head and shove my laptop onto the cushion beside me. The screen flashes my report before going dark.

"I had to finish something."

She pours steaming coffee into her favorite Chicago Cubs mug and turns toward me. "Austin Templeton, you could teach a master class in time management. What happened? This isn't like you."

She takes a sip and nearly trips over the edge of the rug crossing the room. When she drops beside me, the couch dips. Her palm lands on my thigh and squeezes—steady, warm, real. "Talk to me."

I exhale through my nose and press the pads of my thumbs into my temples, trying to contain the splitting ache there. "It's Lauren and Mitch." But even saying their names makes something in my chest tighten. "They're headed for the cliff again." I swallow. "And I think Mitch has really had enough this time."

Casey's brows knit together. "And that's what you lied about?"

I shake my head. The room tilts for half a second before righting itself. "I told Lauren she needs to go see him—and apologize."

She lifts one shoulder. "What's so wrong with that?"

I tip my head back against the sofa and close my eyes. But the cushion feels too firm. My pulse pounds in my ears. I haven't felt this kind of mental fog since studying for the Bar the first time—right out of law school.

"Mitch isn't interested in an apology," I say. The words come out flat. Final. "He's done."

Her breath catches. "No. That can't be true. I mean… I haven't known you guys that long, but there's no way he's walking away from Lauren. They're too good together. They were so happy in Vegas."

I scrub my hands down my face, dragging my exhaustion with them. "I hope you're right, Casey girl. I really do." My voice cracks at the edges. "But I don't know. Something in his voice last night—it was different." Not angry. Not confused. Not hurt in that reactive, volatile way I've heard before. "Like he'd already made peace with it," I finish.

"Like he wasn't fighting anymore."

And that's what scares me.

"So," she says quietly, "you sent Lauren into the lion's den."

I shrug, but guilt coils tighter in my gut. It sits there, heavy and acidic. "I didn't know what else to tell her." Because what was I supposed to say? *Don't go. He's already gone.*

"What exactly did you say?" She cups my cheeks, her thumbs brushing the stubble along my jaw, and presses a soft kiss to my forehead. The tenderness nearly undoes me. Even through the exhaustion, tired butterflies stir low in my stomach.

"I told her she needed to go find him," I say. "Stop making excuses. Face what happened and own whatever she did. And to do it as soon as possible."

Casey nods slowly. "That's not bad advice."

"No," I admit. "It's not bad advice. But it's not honest either. I gave her hope." I open my eyes and stare at the ceiling. "And I think Mitch is just going to shatter it."

The image hits me hard—Lauren standing there, hopeful, vulnerable... and Mitch looking at her like he already let go.

"Well," Casey says gently, "you're not Mitch. You don't actually know what he's thinking. Or feeling."

I let my head fall forward again, eyes closing because it's easier than meeting hers. Because I have a pretty damn good guess.

"No," I say quietly. "I don't know exactly what he's thinking." My voice drops. "But Case... next to Josh, he's my best friend. I've known him my entire life. I know the difference between pissed off Mitch and done Mitch." My jaw tightens. "And last night? He sounded done."

She studies me for a beat. "How?"

I shake my head, but even that feels like too much movement. "I don't know. The confusion I'm used to hearing in his voice—it wasn't there." I swallow, my throat dry and raw from too much coffee and not enough sleep. I've been trying not to name the thing that's been sitting in my chest since midnight. "It was almost like he'd been... set free."

The word hangs there. Final. Irrevocable.

But Casey snorts and tilts her head at me. "A tad dramatic, California boy?"

Normally I'd shoot something back. A smirk. A lazy grin. But I'm running on fumes and dread. I don't even have the energy to roll my eyes properly. My chin drops to my chest instead.

"I wish I was being dramatic," I mutter. "That would mean I'm wrong." I drag a hand through my hair and let it fall uselessly back onto my lap. "But Case, he really did sound different. I'm not even sure he's interested in an apology at this point."

And that's the part that won't let me breathe. Because I told Lauren to go.

"Then you need to text Lauren," Casey says gently, like she's handling something fragile. "Tell her what you just told me. Give her a fair warning."

"How?" I lift my head, and my vision swims for half a second before I lock onto her icy blue eyes. Steady. Clear. Annoyingly rational. "What the hell do I say to her?" I drop my voice into a mock whisper, because humor is easier than panic. "Hey kid, so... forget what I said last night. Don't bother apologizing anymore. Your husband of seven years has emotionally detached and may have spiritually ascended."

Casey stares at me.

I sigh. "Too much?"

She rolls her eyes. "No. Duh." She snorts. "But you can warn her that what she's walking into won't be as easy as saying, *I'm sorry*."

I scrub a hand over my face because my skin feels too tight. My brain feels like it lags three seconds behind every thought. "Maybe you should text her," I mutter.

"Austin Templeton."

I let out a tired breath. Because it was worth a shot.

"I've never once known you to be a coward," she says.

"There's a first time for everything, Cinderella."

She grins at that, because she knows I'm deflecting and she loves me anyway. She stands, and coffee sloshes over the rim of her mug, streaking down the side. "I'm giving you a pass on that one, sir," she says, pointing the mug at me, "because you haven't slept. But Austin?"

I squeeze my eyes shut. And the burn behind them flares so sharply it rings in my ears. "Yeah?"

"You need to hand out a warning here."

I nod and lean forward, catching her hand before she can pull it away. I squeeze it—once, tight. Grateful. A little desperate. "You're a wise lady, Casey McDaniels."

Her smile turns smug in half a second. "Casey McDaniels-Templeton."

I crack one eye open. "You're gonna hyphenate?"

She nods like I've just asked if water is wet.

"Mavs didn't hyphenate."

She gags dramatically and threads her fingers through my short blond hair, tugging lightly at the ends. "And again—you get one more pass because you haven't slept," she teases. Her lips press to my forehead, warm and grounding. I breathe her in for a second longer than I mean to. "But I'm done," she says softly. "Go get some sleep. I'll see you tonight, okay?"

I nod because forming actual words feels like drafting a legal brief right now.

She grabs her purse from the dining room table and opens the front door, letting in a wave of early summer humidity. She blows me a kiss, and I pretend to catch it before she steps out and pulls the door shut behind her.

The apartment goes quiet. But Casey's words start echoing. *You need to hand out a warning here.* They bounce around my skull, wrestling with the last thread of rational thought I've got left.

"You said I need to hand out a warning, Casey girl," I whisper to the empty room, my voice rough, "but you didn't specify who that warning had to be for." Because I can't call Lauren back and rip the hope out from under her. I won't be the one to break my sister's heart before it even happens.

But Mitch? Mitch can handle a warning.

I reach for my phone on the side table and type.

Me: You need to know Lauren is going to come see you today. She's sorry. She's sad. She just wants to talk. Please, Mitch—hear her out.

I stare at the message for half a breath. Then I hit send before I can overthink it. Because the whoosh of it leaving my phone feels irreversible.

I pull my feet up onto the couch and wedge my head against a Chicago Cubs throw pillow. My body finally gives up the fight. The adrenaline drains out, leaving nothing but bone-deep exhaustion and a knot of fear lodged under my ribs.

Curling into the loveseat like it might hold me together, I close my eyes. And sleep takes me fast—but it doesn't take the dread with it.

CHAPTER NINETEEN

Mitch

I step outside for a quick break and drop onto the porch steps. The heat hits me like a wall—dry and relentless. Within seconds, sweat beads across my forehead and slides down my temples. I drag the back of my hand over my brow and squint down at my phone.

Austin: Lauren is going to come see you today. She's sorry. She's sad. She just wants to talk. Please, Mitch—hear her out.

"You can't be serious right now, man..." I mutter, stretching my arms over my head until my shoulders pop. Every muscle in my back protests. Three nights on that damn air bed and my spine feels like it's been folded in half and stored wrong.

"Why'd you tell her to come over here?" I huff out a humorless snort, then skim the message again, thumb hovering like I might throw the phone into the dirt. But the door behind me creaks open before I can spiral any further.

"Benson, I just got the call that the cabinets are finally in."

I twist on the top step and look up at Ryan. "About fucking time," I mutter, shoving the phone into my pocket. For half a second, Lauren—and the fact that she might actually walk onto this job site today—slips to the back of my mind.

Ryan nods, but doesn't smile. "Yeah, but here's the catch. The cabinets are in, but they can't work us into the delivery schedule for at least two weeks. Three's more likely."

I stare at him. "Three weeks?" I drag both hands through my hair and let out a sharp breath. "That's insane. We can't wait that long. We're already behind on this one." I glance over his shoulder, peering inside at the house. At the exposed beams. At the half-painted trim. At the plastic sheeting taped to tile that should've been done days ago. This flip's been a flop since day one.

"Yeah, I know," Ryan says. "But they're at a warehouse in Bakersfield—"

"Bakersfield?" I whine.

"Mmm-hmm. We can pick 'em up ourselves but it'll cost us a day of paint—"

"It's worth it," I cut in, already standing. Anything to claw back time. Anything to stop this project from bleeding money. "Take Dom and Billy. If you drive separately, you can probably haul the full set back in one trip."

Ryan pulls his keys from his pocket. "What about you?"

"I'll stay and paint." I roll my shoulders, trying to work the stiffness out. "If I get the master done today, we can start installation first thing tomorrow. Maybe we can buy back some time."

And maybe if I keep my hands busy long enough, I won't drown in my own sorrow.

Ryan grins and steps back inside. "Oy! Bill! Dom! Change of plans!" His boots crunch over the plastic drop cloth.

I follow, tugging my wallet from my back pocket. I slide my fingers into the billfold for my credit card—and my fingertips catch on worn paper.

The blueprint.

The rocking horse.

And my stomach drops like I stepped off the roof.

"Come on, boys," Ryan calls from the hallway. "Spontaneous trip to Bakersfield."

Dom emerges from the master bedroom with a wrinkled nose. "Why? I thought we had to finish painting today." He jerks a paint-stained thumb over his shoulder as Billy pokes his head out, too.

I step forward before Ryan answers. "I'll get it done— even if it takes me all night." My voice comes out sharper than I mean it to. I drop my credit card into Ryan's outstretched hand and point toward the kitchen. "But we need those cabinets if we want any shot at hitting the original timeline," I add as my phone vibrates against my hip.

"They're in?" Billy asks, already twirling his keys around his finger.

"Fucking finally," Ryan says. "But no delivery. So, gas— and lunch—is on Mitch."

I force a tight nod. "Fine. Thanks, dude. I owe you one."

The front door slams, and a minute later I watch through the dusty front window as three trucks pull out of the driveway. The squeal of tires fades down the street. And another buzz rattles against my thigh.

"Damn it, Austin," I mutter. "Stop intervening." I yank my phone out, fully prepared to ignore whatever follow-up guilt trip he's sent. But the name on the screen isn't Austin.

Tess: What're you up to today, handsome?

"Handsome?" I huff out a laugh, running a hand over my three-day stubble. My thumbs move before I think too hard.

Me: What everyone else in the world does on a Wednesday, Tess. I'm working.

I hit send and shove my phone back into my pocket, but

the house is too quiet to ignore. I head down the hallway toward the master bedroom, where one lavender-painted wall punches through the stark white around it—bold, clean, deliberate.

A slow smile tugs at my mouth as Tess's "lavender bush" joke drifts back to me—her exaggerated horror, the way she scrunched up her nose like the color had personally offended her.

But the smile fades. And a shiver skates down my spine, goosebumps rising along my arms. Because the guilt comes right on its heels.

I drop to my knees and snatch up the abandoned brush from the drop cloth. The bristles are stiff with half-dried paint, but I dip it into the tray and press it to the wall, dragging thick lavender across fresh drywall.

Stroke after stroke. Cover. Distract. Don't think. Except I can't stop it—the thought that keeps circling, persistent and unwelcome. If Lauren walks through that front door today... am I strong enough to tell her it's already too late?

I focus on the cut-in, hands steady—steadier than my head feels. The bristles glide up to the white trim without bleeding over. Precision I can control. Clean lines. No surprises. Then my phone buzzes again in my pocket. I blow out a sharp breath and yank it free.

Tess: Working where?

I stare at the screen in disbelief, then type back, pausing to wonder why I'm even responding.

Me: Wouldn't you like to know.

I add a laughing emoji like that makes it harmless. Like that makes it casual. Then I shove the phone back into my pocket because what am I even doing? Flirting with Tess Browning?

I dip my brush and bring it back to the wall. The paint glides on smooth and thick, lavender swallowing primer. I focus on the rhythm—dip, drag, feather the edge. But when I move to reload the brush, my stomach lurches—guilt rising fast, sharp and invasive, like it's been waiting for the next quiet moment to strike.

"What the hell was I thinking, kissing you?" I mutter. But the question just sinks into the drywall like the room already knows the answer.

I press my brush to the wall again. "You let a shitty situation cloud your judgment," I tell myself, laying down a long, even stroke. "You were pissed. You were hurt. It was one kiss." I swallow the lump in my throat. "One reckless, selfish, heat-of-the-moment kiss. And it won't happen again." I bear down harder, grinding lavender over white like I can suffocate the evidence beneath a fresh coat.

It won't happen again.

But my pulse refuses to cooperate, thudding heavy and uneven against my ribs. My chest tightens as the memory slams into me—Tess's hand at my jaw, the warmth of her mouth, the split-second where I knew I should pull away... but didn't. Heat and anger and validation all tangled together.

I exhale hard. "God, I'm an idiot."

Disappointment doesn't even begin to cover it. I'm disappointed in Lauren—for the half-truths, for the way everything between us feels cracked and fragile again. But I'm just as disappointed in myself. I didn't fix anything. I didn't prove a point. I just added another fracture. And betrayed my wife in the process.

But didn't she do the same to me?

I dunk the brush back into the can and slap more paint onto the wall. Stroke after stroke, I paint like I can outrun it—guilt over Tess, confusion over Lauren, the hollow disappointment of it all.

I don't know if I even want Lauren to walk through that door so we can fight it out... or if I'm terrified she will. I don't know what I'm supposed to do next. Apologize? Confess? Pretend? Walk away? I just know I don't recognize the guy staring back at me in the reflection of the window.

I keep going until my knees throb against the hardwood and my shoulders burn. When I finally shove myself upright, my legs wobble, stiff and unsteady. I stretch, my back popping in sharp cracks—and then the doorbell rings.

I freeze. But the sound slices clean through the house. I drop the brush into the tray and head down the hallway, wiping my hands on my jeans. My pulse ticks up, sudden and sharp. Because I'm sure it's Lauren...

But when I yank the door open, it's Tess.

Her smile hits me first—bright, white, effortless. That mischievous glint in her eyes scrambles my brain for a beat, like my body remembers her before my conscience can catch up.

"How—" is all I get out before she slips past me into the house like she belongs here. The scent of coffee follows her in, rich and warm, cutting straight through paint fumes and my three nights of garbage sleep.

"Don't look so shocked," she says over her shoulder. "If you recall, I can be very resourceful when I need to be." She turns and holds out a small Starbucks cup to me. "Tall, black roast. Right?"

I take it on instinct and the heat seeps into my palm. The smell alone wakes something in me—something human. I hate how quickly my throat tightens, how close relief sits to gratitude.

"I don't understand. Why did you—" My mouth trips over itself, because there are too many questions and none of them feel safe. "Actually... how did you find me?"

Tess rolls her eyes like I'm cute for even asking. "I looked up recent real estate purchases with your name. Took a gamble this was one of your flips and drove by. Your truck gave you away."

I huff a short breath, but it comes out familiar—easy. Like the last few days haven't been a slow-motion disaster. I glance at the cup again, like it might explain her. "Okay," I say, forcing my brain back online. "Next question." My gaze lifts to hers. "Why are you here?"

She shrugs and takes a sip, then winces when it burns her tongue. "I figured you'd refuse to see me after..."

My jaw locks. Because there it is. *The after.* The thing I've been trying to paint over, scrub out, pretend didn't happen.

I nod once, stiff. "That was a mistake, Tess. I wasn't thinking clearly when I—" I cut myself off before the image of her mouth on mine can finish the sentence for me. "Look, I'm sorry."

She lifts her free hand, stopping me with a grin that's too bright for how dark I feel. "I expected nothing less from you, Mitch Benson." She winks. "And no worries. Your secret's safe with me."

My stomach drops. Because she's the last person I want holding one of my secrets—and the worst part is, I can't tell if she's joking or claiming leverage.

I meet her eyes. All warmth and mischief on the surface, and something sharper underneath, like she's always a half-step ahead. "No offense," I say carefully, "but I don't believe that for a second."

I take a step back, putting space between us. Not because I don't want her close—because I do, and that fact makes me sick. My grip tightens around the cup until the cardboard creaks. "Why are you really here?"

Instead of answering, Tess turns slowly, surveying the space like she's appraising it for resale. Her pink heels crackle against the plastic drop cloth with every shift of her weight—sharp, decisive clicks that echo through the half-empty house and land in my chest like punctuation.

"I like this place," she says, almost thoughtful. "It has good bones."

I stare at her. "Well, thank you, Joanna Gaines, but the question still stands."

She snorts. "Wrong show." Then she smiles again as she pivots toward the hallway, already moving like the house is hers to explore. "How many bedrooms?" she calls over her shoulder.

I blink, thrown—because this is suddenly *us*. The banter. The ease. The way she can walk in and reset the air in a room like she owns the oxygen. And that only makes everything worse.

I follow the sound of her heels down the hall, coffee still warm in my hand, confusion crawling up my throat. I shouldn't want her here. I shouldn't feel steadier just because she is.

A second later, her voice floats back, laced with dramatic disgust. "You're *choosing* to paint this room lavender?"

I step into the master bedroom and find her planted in the center, hands on her hips, hot-pink nails digging into her skin. And I hate the way my mouth twitches—like I'm about to laugh—when all I've been doing for days is try not to fall apart.

I take a slow sip of coffee and, God help me, enjoy her scowl more than I should. "What can I say?" I shrug. "It's calming."

Tess makes a noise like *calming* is an insult.

I bend, grab my brush, and stir the thick paint with deliberate focus—something to do with my hands besides react to her being here. "And if you don't mind," I add as I drag the brush down the wall in a clean, even stroke, "this room has to be finished by tonight." I glance at the patch I've covered and blow out a breath.

"By tonight, huh?" she says, light and almost amused. "Sounds like you could use an extra hand."

Before my brain can catch up, she kicks off her heels. They thud softly against the plastic. Then she tugs her white knit sweater over her head and drops it to the floor like shedding layers in front of me is normal.

"I mean," she continues, already lowering herself to her knees with a wink, "I *am* an experienced painter now." She snatches an abandoned brush and lifts it like she's about to negotiate a contract. "What do you pay?" she asks sweetly.

"Tess," I say slowly—careful—watching her like she's a bomb ready to detonate, "what are you doing?" But butterflies riot in my gut as I speak. Unwelcome. Reckless. Colombian roast colliding with curiosity and something hotter I don't have the energy to name.

"Painting, boss," she replies, dipping into the lavender. The paint clings thick and sticky to the bristles before dripping back into the can. She wrinkles her nose. "Although this color makes me feel bad for the future homeowners."

I snort.

"You can't seriously think this is a good choice." She looks at the lavender like it offended her ancestors. "No woman wants her bedroom this color."

"Didn't realize you had a degree in interior design."

She splashes paint onto the wall—less precise than mine, but not sloppy. "I don't."

"Well then," I say, keeping my strokes tight along the edge, "what *did* you go to school for? I don't remember."

She huffs like I'm the one being ridiculous. "International relations and global affairs."

My brush pauses mid-stroke. A fat glob of lavender gathers at the bottom of the bristles and starts to slide. "But you run a newspaper."

Tess shoots me a look that could sand a floor. "Don't you think I know that, Mitch Benson?" She leans in and, with a quick flick, smooths out the drip before it can betray me on the wall.

I exhale, heat climbing my neck. "Sorry. I just—"

"Everyone was always so quick to side with Joshua," she mutters, not quite to me—more like she says it to the room.

My brows knit. "Josh?" I dip my brush again, forcing myself to keep working, but my attention stays on her. On the way her strokes turn slower. More careful. Like she didn't mean to say that out loud. "I don't follow."

She hesitates, then shakes her head once. "No one knows this," she says quietly, and the slightest flush creeps into her cheeks, "but I turned down an incredible internship with the White House."

I go still. "The White House?" I repeat, because my brain refuses to accept it on the first pass. "You're serious?"

Tess nods once, eyes on the wall like it's safer than

looking at me, then reloads her brush. "The Council of Economic Advisers offered me a position right after graduation."

My mouth opens, then closes. I try again. "And you didn't take it?"

She keeps painting—steady, controlled, like if she stops she'll have to deal with whatever's behind the confession. "I didn't," she says, softer now.

I stare at her profile, the curve of her jaw, the way she's suddenly not joking. Not performing. Just… telling me something real. And that's the most disorienting part of all.

She snorts softly. "I couldn't. If I accepted, it would've kept me in D.C." She presses paint into the drywall like she can anchor herself there. "Josh and I had already spent a year apart during his first year of med school."

The air in the room changes—subtle, but real. And the weight of what she says settles between us.

"You turned it down," I say slowly, "to be with Josh."

She nods once and for a long moment, I just watch her. The way her fingers tighten around the wooden handle. The way she drags a color she hates across the wall because I implied I needed help. A thin blonde strand of hair falls across her face and she blows it away without thinking, like she's trying to keep this casual when it isn't. And the lifelong picture I've carried of Tess Browning—sharp, selfish, untouchable—tilts on its axis.

"You don't believe me, do you?" she asks quietly, eyes fixed on the wall.

I hesitate, because the truth is I don't know what to believe anymore—from anyone. I shake my head and drag my brush slowly through the paint, buying time. "No," I say after a beat. "I do believe you." I glance at her from the corner of my eye. "Surprisingly… that actually tracks."

Her smile blooms—small and soft, almost shy. The pink in her cheeks deepens, matching her nails. "I never told Josh about it," she whispers.

I nod, because yeah. I get it. You don't touch a

Templeton's career trajectory. Not if you want to live through the fallout. "I understand," I say quietly. And I hate how much I mean it.

She turns back to the wall and lays down another stroke, a faint grin tugging at her mouth. "Knew you would."

I watch her for a beat longer than I should. "Why are you telling me this?"

Her smile stays, but her eyes slide away instead of meeting mine.

I move closer and nudge her elbow—barely there. But the flicker of surprise on her face sends something low in my stomach twisting, and I ignore it like I ignore everything else I don't want to deal with. "Why are you really here?" I press.

Tess exhales and shoves a curl off her face. "The truth?"

"It's preferred."

She bends to reload her brush, dragging it through the lavender with slow, deliberate care. "The truth is…" She pauses like she's deciding how honest she can afford to be. Then she looks at the wall again and says, "The truth is, Mitch, I didn't really stop by Templeton Manor the other day because of a tax form."

I snort under my breath. "Shocking."

"I wanted my next story," she continues, matter-of-fact now. "And the Templeton name is a guaranteed moneymaker."

"So, that's why you went after Lauren," I say, keeping my tone even.

Tess shrugs, but her gaze drops this time, and that— somehow—that feels like the bigger tell. "It wasn't personal." A small frown tugs at her mouth. "But we both know what hurts Lauren… hurts Josh, too."

I huff out a breath because she isn't even spinning it. She's just stating the ugly truth.

"Still spiteful then, are we, little vixen?" I tease, nudging her elbow with mine again as I shift closer.

"Maybe," she answers—then she pokes me in the

stomach, her nail dragging just enough to tickle.

A line of goosebumps erupts across my skin. I jerk back on instinct—and knock her brush clean out of her hand. It hits the floor with a wet slap and lavender explodes across my right side.

I squeeze my eyes shut and start laughing as I crouch to retrieve it. "You got paint in my hair again, didn't you?"

She laughs too, the sound bright and unguarded. Then she lowers her body, crawls toward me, slow and deliberate, until I can feel the warmth radiating off her.

"I got paint in your hair again," she whispers. Her fingers slide into my hair, gentle as she tucks dark strands behind my ears and plucks flecks of purple from the ends. I turn my head slightly—and suddenly her face is right there.

Blue eyes. Pink lips. That slow, knowing smile…

My heart slams against my ribs as her breath ghosts over my cheek. "You know," she whispers, her nail dragging lightly from my ear down to my neck, "I think you should cut your hair. You still look like the guy I hated in high school."

A shiver tears through me. "Well," I say carefully, forcing air back into my lungs, "you're definitely not the girl I hated in high school, Tess Browning."

And that's the problem.

I pull back and stand abruptly, grabbing an empty paint can before I do something monumentally stupid again.

Don't be an idiot, Mitch. Don't do this again. Keep your distance.

Her eyes follow me as I carry the can to the door and swap it for a fresh gallon. I drop back to my knees, putting a safe distance between us.

"Hand me that screwdriver, will you?" I say, pointing behind her.

She twists around, grabs the nearest tool, and turns back with a grin. She taps the flathead against her palm. "Not a Patrick's head."

My brain stalls for a second. Then it clicks. And a laugh slips out of me—short, surprised, more of a huff than anything. I shake my head, a reluctant smile tugging at my mouth.

She tilts her head and swats my shoulder. "What?" she says, dropping the screwdriver into my lap. She leans forward and grabs my knee. "Come on. It's not a Patrick's head, right?"

I fall back onto one hand, still smiling despite myself. "A Patrick's head," I repeat under my breath, rubbing at my jaw. "You're unbelievable."

"What?" she says lightly.

I roll my eyes, the grin lingering as I look up at her. And then she swings her leg over me.

Tess settles onto my hips, and the shift in weight steals the air from my lungs. Heat surges low and immediate, white-hot and reckless, dragging whatever restraint I had left straight down with it. My hands flatten against the plastic behind me, bracing, as if that will keep me grounded.

It doesn't.

She trails the handle of the screwdriver down my chest—slow, deliberate—over my sternum, along the ridges of muscle, down my stomach. The metal leaves a faint, cool path against overheated skin before stopping just above the button of my shorts.

My body reacts before my brain can catch up. I swallow hard. "Phillips head," I manage, voice rough, as I close my fingers around the tool and ease it from her grip.

"Phillips head," she corrects with a teasing grin, like she enjoys watching me unravel.

She leans down and presses a kiss to my cheek. It's barely there, but her breath is warm against my neck, and my eyes close on instinct. Her perfume wraps around me—floral, soft, intoxicating. Familiar in a way that feels dangerous.

When I open my eyes, a blonde curl brushes my cheek. My pulse pounds in my ears. Because she looks at me like I'm something she wants. And God, it's been a long time since I've felt genuinely wanted.

Not needed. Not expected. Not tolerated.

Just wanted.

"You can't be here for a story, Tess," I whisper, though my hand slides to her waist without permission, fingers hooking into the hem of her shirt. My thumb grazes warm skin, and she inhales softly. "My last name isn't Templeton."

She exhales near my ear, her voice losing its sharp edges. "It's shitty," she says, quieter now. "Watching the person you love find happiness with someone else, isn't it?" Her lips hover near my skin, not quite touching. "And I think," she adds, barely audible, "that's something else we have in common."

For a second, her words knock the wind out of me. And then I don't see Tess. I see Miguel's mouth pressed to Lauren's lips.

The heat in my veins flickers—but it doesn't disappear. It twists, tangles with jealousy and ego and hurt until I can't tell what drives me anymore.

Her hands slip beneath my shirt, fingertips brushing across my chest. The contact is electric. And my back arches slightly before I can stop it. Her hips shift, slow and intentional, and a strained breath escapes me.

I grab her wrists—not harsh, but firm—holding her there because if I don't, I'm not sure where this goes. "Tess," I rasp, fighting for oxygen.

The house creaks around us, old wood settling. But the sound feels too loud. Too aware.

"I did want another article," she whispers, her eyes locking onto mine. And there's no joke there now. No smirk. "But now…" She tips her head, exposing her throat. "Now, Mitch Benson, I think I just want *you* instead."

My pulse roars. The world narrows to her. To the pressure of her thighs around my hips. To the way my body responds despite every warning bell screaming in my head.

She shifts again, slow and deliberate, and whatever fragile grip I had on my thoughts shatters completely. "We shouldn't be doing this," I choke out, the words thin and unconvincing. "*I* shouldn't be doing this."

But my hands fall back to her waist. Holding her there. Pulling her closer instead of pushing her away.

Her eyes search mine—no teasing now, no smirk—just heat and something almost pleading beneath it. "Then tell me to stop," she whispers.

I open my mouth. But nothing comes out. Instead, I slide one hand up her spine, fingers tangling briefly in her curls. She inhales sharply, and that sound—God—that sound undoes me.

Our mouths meet hard, not tentative, not questioning. It's messy and urgent and fueled by every unsaid thing sitting between us. My grip tightens on her hips as I kiss her back, deeper than I should, like I'm trying to drown in it.

Her hand cups my jaw. Mine slides into her hair. And for a split-second, there's nothing else. No lavender walls. No wedding ring digging into my finger. No image of Lauren burned into the back of my mind.

Just this. Just being wanted.

She presses closer, and I feel it everywhere—her weight, her warmth, the undeniable pull of it. A low sound escapes my throat before I can swallow it down.

This is a mistake. I know it. But I don't stop. And then—

The front door slams. The sharp metallic crack slices straight through the haze like a gunshot.

We break apart instantly, breathless, eyes wide.

"I thought we were alone," Tess mutters, scrambling off me, breathing uneven.

"We are." I push myself up, heart hammering for an entirely different reason now.

She tugs her tank top down, smooths her lipstick with her fingertip, composure snapping back into place like armor.

"Stay here," I tell her, already moving. I pull the bedroom door closed behind me and stomp down the hallway, boots crinkling over plastic. My pulse hasn't slowed. It's just changed tempo.

"Hello?" I call as I reach the living room. "Someone

here?"

It's silent though. The house stands still.

But then I see it. On the kitchen counter sits a peach cobbler, steam curling lazily toward the ceiling fan. And just like that, the heat in my veins turns to ice.

CHAPTER TWENTY

Lauren

I press the thumbtack into the drywall and stretch up on the stepstool, straightening the banner above my head. The thick paper cards sway as I adjust the spacing, sliding the bear cub a little farther from the fawn, making sure each baby woodland critter hangs at perfectly measured intervals along the white ribbon.

"Does that look straight to you?" I ask.

Casey steps back, closes one eye, and tilts her head. "I think so?"

"Close enough," I mutter, climbing down and taking it in. It's cute. It's sweet. It's not enough, though. "Let's put three balloons on each side." I turn and point at Austin on the sofa as he forces his last breath into a light-green balloon, his cheeks pink with the effort.

"What colors?" Casey asks, grabbing a yellow one and bonking him on the head with it.

He rolls his eyes, knots the end, then swats her on the butt in retaliation.

"Green, yellow, and white," I say. "Hand me that ribbon, too. I'll tie them together."

Casey drops the spool into my palm and bends to scoop up the balloons from the floor. "Hey, Lauren? Are you okay?"

I scoff before I can stop myself. "I'm fine. Just—please—hand me those balloons."

She places a green and a white one in my hands, but her frown lingers. "Are you really, though?"

I loop the two together and pull the ribbon tight. "We do not have time to do a deep dive into my failed marriage right now," I say, keeping my voice steady. "Josh and Mavis will be here in less than twenty minutes and—"

"They'll survive if the party doesn't start at exactly two," Austin cuts in, standing and stretching his arms overhead.

I snatch the yellow balloon from Casey and secure it to the other two with a neat bow. But my chest aches as I climb back onto the stepstool. The air catches in my throat, thick and uncooperative. I swallow hard, forcing it down.

Hold it together. You do not get to fall apart today.

"Can I have a pushpin?" I ask, my voice thinner than I'd like. I keep my eyes on the wall.

Casey's warm fingers brush my palm as she passes it over and I jam the pin into the drywall before hopping down to inspect the finished cluster. It's symmetrical. Balanced. Controlled.

"Looks good," Austin says, grabbing three more balloons. He hands me a yellow and a white. "But, hey, Lauren?"

I focus on tying the ribbon, blinking hard against the sting building behind my eyes.

Don't. Do not cry.

"Lauren?" he presses, his hand settling on my shoulder.

"Austin, please." I jerk away, faster than I mean to. "We can't do this right now." Nausea churns low in my stomach and I swipe at the tear that escapes anyway. "Please, don't."

He nods, quiet, and takes the balloon bouquet from my hands to tack it up himself. And that's all it takes. A sob cracks loose before I can catch it. I cover my face with both hands, but the tears slip through my fingers, tracing a path they know too well.

Casey wraps her arms around me, smoothing my hair back. "Come on. Austin can finish. Let's take a minute."

But I shake my head and scrub at my cheeks, smearing mascara. Because taking a minute will do no good. I bend down, grab another balloon, and busy my hands. "No," I insist. "I'm fine. Today isn't about me."

"That doesn't mean—"

"Yes, it does." My voice hardens before I can soften it. I tuck my hair behind my ears and lift my chin. "Today is about Mavis, Josh, and their baby. And I will not let Mitch ruin anything else—for any of us." The words taste bitter and final.

"Is he coming?" Casey asks quietly.

I shrug. "I have no idea. I haven't seen or spoken to him in weeks."

Austin's face drains. "Weeks?"

I nod and plant my hands on my hips, bracing myself. "Not one word since I caught Josh's ex-wife dry-humping him."

The words land in the room like a grenade. And then the absurdity of them hits me. A laugh bursts out—too sharp, too loud. I bend forward, gripping my knees as it spills out of me. "Those," I say with a gasp between jagged giggles, "are not words I ever thought I'd say."

Casey's hand flies to her mouth. "Oh my, God."

"W—what?" Austin stammers, blinking at me like I've started speaking another language. "Huh?"

I straighten slowly, wiping beneath my eyes, mascara smearing at the corners. "You heard me."

"Lauren," Casey chokes out, her voice cracking. "Oh my, God," she repeats.

"No." Austin shakes his head hard, like he can physically dislodge the image. "No. Mitch *hates* Tess. We *all* hate Tess." He drags a hand through his hair, pacing once in a tight line. "That doesn't even make sense."

But it does. It makes terrible, humiliating sense. And all I can do is stand here, surrounded by pastel balloons and cartoon woodland animals and perfectly tied ribbons, and wonder how my life became the cruelest punchline imaginable.

A final, shaky giggle slips out of me, fading fast. "Yeah, well," I mutter, swiping under my eyes again, "I'd say his feelings for her have… evolved. Most people don't let someone they supposedly despise grind all over them."

The image flashes again—sharp, invasive, impossible to mute. Revulsion rolls through me and I shiver, remembering the way his hands cinched around her waist, fingers splayed possessively against her skin, paint still drying in the creases of his knuckles. The same hands that used to frame my face. Steady me. Claim me.

And her—straddling him like she belonged there. Like she hadn't trespassed into something sacred. Those stupid pink, glossy lips pressed against what was supposed to be mine, leaving a shine where my name used to live.

My stomach twists. It isn't just the betrayal. It's the familiarity of it. The way his body moved like muscle memory, like none of it was new. Like I was the only one who didn't know the scene had already changed.

I swallow hard, but the bitterness clings to the back of my throat, thick and unforgiving as Casey grips my arm—gentle but steady. "What happened?" she asks, guiding me toward the couch like I might tip over.

I sink onto it and fold over the armrest, pressing my cheek into the fabric, wishing I could disappear into the cushions. When I look up, Austin and Casey hover in front of me. Horror. Confusion. Anger. And something else, too. Protectiveness.

I lift a brow and force the words out. "I went to see Mitch. To apologize for my…" I sneer at myself. "Lapse in judgment."

"The Miguel thing?" Austin asks carefully.

"The Miguel thing," I echo, knowing full well I have

done nothing to address that problem, either. "I baked his favorite peach cobbler. I had this whole apology ready." My throat tightens. "But when I got to the job site, Tess's car was in the driveway." I swallow hard. "And when I went inside…" The memory flashes again, sharp and cruel. "I found them in the bedroom."

Bile climbs my throat. Because the image is branded into my brain—the curve of her body over his, the way his hands were on her like they belonged there. But worse than that? It was the look on his face. Pleasure. Excitement. Enjoyment.

I drop my head into my hands as nausea swirls low and vicious.

"I can't believe Mitch would do that," Casey whispers, running her fingers through my hair.

"Stupid motherfucker," Austin mutters, shoving his hands into his pockets. "I *told* him you were coming. Point blank. What the hell was he thinking?" He yanks his phone from his pocket.

But my head snaps up. "What are you doing?"

"What do you think I'm doing?" he spits.

"Austin. Please. Do *not* call him." I scramble upright, panic slicing through the fog.

"Why?" He holds the phone in front of him, Mitch's name glowing on the screen.

Tears surge again, hot and relentless. And each breath burns on the way in. "Not today," I whisper. "Please. Just—not today." I swipe at my cheeks and point toward the window. "Josh and Mavis are here. It's their day. I cannot ruin it with this."

Casey glances toward the driveway. Austin hesitates.

"Please," I beg, my voice cracking. "Just keep it quiet. For now." I push to my feet too fast and move toward the stairs. "I need a minute."

Austin sighs and slips his phone back into his pocket. "Fine. But when they leave, we're talking about this," he says firmly.

I nod without looking at him and take the stairs two at a time. Josh's voice echoes through the foyer—warm, familiar, excited—and it follows me like a taunt as I round the corner.

I barely make it to the bathroom before my legs threaten to give out. I grip the porcelain countertop like it's the only solid thing left in my world and crank the tap on full blast, splashing icy water onto my face.

But the tears keep coming anyway—hot and humiliating, spilling faster than I can wipe them away. I lift my head and meet my reflection. Pink cheeks. Swollen eyes. Mascara a smudged disaster. I look like a stranger. Like someone who lost a fight.

Breathe. Steady. This isn't about you today.

I try. I really try. I draw in air, hold it, release it like I'm forcing my body to remember how to function. But another wave hits anyway, bigger than the first, and it folds me in half. Tears soak into the cotton of my sundress as my shoulders shake. The sound escaping me is small— broken—like my throat can't even manage a full sob.

Downstairs, the doorbell rings and the sound of happy laughter floats up the staircase—bright, celebratory, innocent—and it scrapes against something raw inside me, like sandpaper on an open wound.

I fold over the sink and press my forehead to the cool porcelain. Hurt isn't enough. It's a whole-body ache—an emptiness spreading behind my ribs until even breathing feels like work. And then anger comes, hot and electric, surging up fast—until it crashes into something else.

Me.

Because I'm not innocent in this. I didn't let someone pin me against the floor and run their hands all over me— but I still betrayed what we had. I still let another man step into spaces that were supposed to belong to Mitch. I crossed a line I swore I never would, even if mine looked cleaner. Even if it came wrapped in celebration and justification instead of lust.

And that's what makes it worse.

I can be furious at him. I *am* furious at him. But beneath it, coiled tight and ugly, is the truth that I fractured us first. Maybe not the same way. Maybe not as roughly. But damage doesn't care about technicalities.

I lift my head, tears clinging to my lashes, vision blurred and burning as rage surges through me, desperate for somewhere to land. At him. At her. At myself. A broken sound rips out of my throat and I swipe my arm across the counter.

Bottles clatter against the tile. Toiletries explode across the floor in a scatter of plastic and glass. Mitch's electric razor smacks the wall and drops with a sharp crack that rings through the bathroom like punctuation—like the period at the end of something I don't know how to fix.

The room spins. And I don't know who I'm angrier at anymore.

I stare at the wreckage, chest heaving, and realize I feel exactly the same as before—shattered, scattered, irreparable. But just as quickly as the anger came, it drains, leaving me hollowed out. I take a step back until my spine meets the wall. The bathroom is a mess—drawers half-open, bottles on the floor, my breath ragged in the sudden silence.

I drag a trembling hand down my face and sink to my knees. One by one, I start picking things up. Soap. Toothpaste. Cotton pads. His stupid cologne—dark glass and sharp scent, like he still belongs here. I set each item back on the counter with careful precision, lining them up like if I can restore order here, maybe the inside of me will follow.

It doesn't.

With a final, broken exhale, I reach for Mitch's razor. I hold it in my palms longer than I mean to, thumb dragging slowly over the smooth plastic. Sorrow burns low and steady in my gut, the kind that doesn't spike and pass—it settles in. Heavy. Permanent. Because I think this is really it.

"You're not coming home this time, are you?" I whisper to the empty bathroom, to the hum of the fan, to the life we used to have. But the realization doesn't crash. It doesn't explode. It just… clicks into place. Quiet. Irreversible.

I open the lower cabinet and toss the razor inside. It knocks against the neatly stacked boxes and sends a white one tumbling out. It hits the tile at my knees and bursts open. Individually wrapped ovulation tests spill across the floor, skittering over the tile, bumping softly against my bare feet.

I go completely still. The air leaves my lungs in a slow, painful exhale, like my body finally remembers how deep this wound actually goes. My gaze drops to the tiny white sticks scattered around me, and something inside me splinters clean in two.

All those months of tracking. Hoping. Planning. All those quiet prayers I never said out loud because saying them made them real. All those times I told myself it would happen *soon*—as long as we were okay. As long as we held on.

My throat closes around a sob before I can stop it. I slide down fully onto the floor, my back against the cabinet, knees pulled tight to my chest like I'm trying to hold myself together with sheer force.

The tears come hard and relentless again, the kind that steal your breath and leave you shaking. I press my forehead to my knees, surrounded by little white plastic dreams scattered across cold tile.

And it hits me. I was wrong before. That wasn't rock bottom. This is.

***

"Awww!"

The chorus rises again as Mavis holds up a tiny yellow onesie with a duck stitched across the front. The living room is a sea of smiles and pastel wrapping paper, of folding chairs and half-empty mimosa glasses, of women leaning in like they're witnessing a miracle instead of the fiftieth piece of cotton.

From my folding chair near the foyer, I paste on a smile and clap lightly with everyone else, keeping my hands busy so no one notices mine shaking.

"It's absolutely precious!" Mavis beams, draping it over her belly like the duck might waddle right into her future. "Thank you so much, Sandra!"

Sandra—the nurse from Josh's office—waves off the praise with a proud little grin. "There's more in there for you too, sweetie!"

Josh obliges, digging deeper into the gift bag. He pulls out a jar of nipple cream, lactation pads, and a package of spare parts for a breast pump. The color drains from his face, then comes roaring back as his cheeks flare bright red. He holds the items up like they might bite him. "Umm…" He clears his throat, eyes darting anywhere but the room full of women. "These are… for you," he mutters, handing them to Mavis like he's disarming a bomb.

The room erupts. Women cackle. Someone whistles. A few people clap just to make it worse. And Josh scratches the back of his neck and grins like he wants the floor to split open and swallow him whole.

I cross and recross my legs, the motion restless and automatic. The grandfather clock ticks behind me, then chimes four o'clock with a bright, cheerful clang that makes my teeth grit.

How many times can we ooh and ahh over a damn onesie?

"All right, this looks like the last one!" Casey announces, crawling across the carpet toward the final gift bag like she's in a relay race. "And it's from Austin." She lifts her brows at the room, then rolls her eyes dramatically. "*Just* Austin," she adds, winking at Mavis.

Josh tears through the tissue paper and pulls out a dark-green onesie. He reads it aloud, already laughing. "One does not simply crawl into Mordor."

Austin, seated beside me, calls out like he's presenting a business case. "It's gender neutral! Practical!"

Josh digs again and bursts into a louder laugh. "The Lord of the Rings," he reads, holding up a second onesie decorated with stacked plastic baby rings. He grins and drapes it over Mavis's belly like a victory flag. "This is the going-home-from-the-hospital outfit."

"It absolutely is *not*." Mavis laughs, yanking it off and tossing it at him, effectively concluding the party.

The guests stretch and start rising, their polite goodbyes bubbling up in waves—chairs scraping, tissue paper rustling.

"Just get out of my house already," I mutter under my breath, checking the clock again like time is something I can control if I glare at it hard enough.

Austin leans in, voice low. "You're almost done. Hang in there, kid." He gives my knee a quick squeeze—silent, steady support—then stands to greet Aunt Millie as she shuffles toward us.

"My sweet boy!" Aunt Millie roars, cupping his face with both hands and planting a loud, lipstick-stained kiss on his cheek. The red smear is immediate and dramatic. "Congratulations on your engagement," she booms. "Casey is a delight!"

"Yeah." Austin laughs awkwardly, wiping at the mark with his thumb like it's contagious. "I think so, too."

"Another wedding. And a baby on the way. You boys are busy!" Aunt Millie cackles, squeezing him again. Then her gaze slides past him and locks onto me. "And what about you, dear?"

I paste on a smile that feels like it could crack my face. "What about me, Aunt Millie?"

She hobbles closer and wraps me in a hug. Powdery perfume hits my nose—sweet and stale—and her grip is stronger than it should be for someone holding a cane. My lungs tighten as she squeezes like she can wring the answer out of me.

"Oh, you know…" She pulls back, taps her cane against the floor, and points upstairs like she owns the place. "When are you and Mitch going to fill all those empty bedrooms?"

A cold shiver snakes down my spine. My stomach drops straight through the floor, taking my breath with it. I fold my arms across my chest, holding myself together in the most literal way possible. Because embarrassment hits first—hot and immediate. Then hurt. Then something darker that tastes like rage and grief in the same swallow.

"I—I…" My voice trips. Heat surges through my body, sweat breaking across my forehead. I swipe the back of my hand over my skin and clear my throat like I can scrape the question out of the air. "I don't think that's an appropriate question."

Aunt Millie blinks, offended. "Excuse me, dear?"

"That's just not something you ask someone." My voice sharpens despite everything in me begging it not to. "It's unbelievably hurtful and—"

Austin steps in fast, like he's been waiting for the moment to intercept the blast. He drapes an arm around Aunt Millie's shoulders and pivots her away with a bright, practiced smile. "Aunt Mill, have you seen Casey's ring? Custom design. Come here, I'll show you."

He steers her toward the crowd, then shoots me an apologetic look over his shoulder—an *I'm so sorry* that doesn't even begin to cover it. And I stand there in the aftermath, smiling at nothing, arms still wrapped around myself, trying to swallow the tremor in my throat before it becomes a sob in front of everyone.

The room begins to blur at the edges. Laughter swells again—bright and buoyant and harmless. Someone clinks a glass. Someone squeals about how "tiny" the socks are. It should sound joyful. Instead, it sounds far away. Like I'm underwater.

Every congratulations. Every well-wish. Every comment about babies and nurseries and sleepless nights presses against the bruise blooming inside my chest. I blink hard, trying to clear my vision, but the tears don't care about timing or guests or pastel décor.

I swallow. The pit in my stomach deepens. And standing here—surrounded by half-deflated balloons and smiling women with glowing skin and full lives—something inside me caves in. Not dramatically. Quietly. Like a ceiling giving way under too much weight.

Defeat wraps around my ribs and tightens. Because it's not just Aunt Millie's question. It's the empty bedrooms upstairs. It's the ovulation tests scattered across cold tile. It's the months of hoping. It's the way my marriage already feels like a ghost.

I force another brittle smile at a departing guest, nodding like I'm fine, like I'm stable, like I'm not seconds away from shattering. And I feel the last thin thread holding me upright begin to fray.

Everyone in the room smiles—radiant, effortless—celebrating the baby, the gifts, the glowing parents-to-be. The air hums with happiness like it's the only emotion allowed in this house today.

And then there's me. The girl with the burned-down restaurant. The girl with the husband who can't keep his hands to himself. The girl who can't get pregnant. The labels stack so fast I can barely breathe under them.

I edge away from the crowd on silent feet, keeping my face angled down. If I don't make eye contact, maybe no one will notice the crack spreading through me. I slip along the outskirts of the living room. Past the gift table. Past the pastel ribbons. Past plates of finger food that make my stomach churn.

The ache inside me swells until it's all I am.

I grab the knob to the garage door, twist, and shove it open. Warm air rushes at my face. I stumble down the short set of steps onto the concrete as bright afternoon sunlight floods the space—too sharp, too cheerful—like it's exposing something I'm trying to hide.

My lungs refuse to cooperate. I try to inhale. Nothing. Like someone vacuumed the oxygen straight out of my chest. A sob punches out of me—violent and involuntary. I grip the railing, knuckles white, as my body convulses.

This is what it feels like to break. Not gracefully. Not quietly. Just splintering. Pieces of me scattering across a garage floor while a baby shower carries on ten feet away.

I squeeze my eyes shut and try to breathe. Try to pull myself together. Try to remember the promise I made to myself that I wouldn't do this today—

"Peaches?"

His voice cuts through the chaos like a blade. For a second, I think I imagined it. Because that can't be him. It can't.

I open my eyes. And where anger should rise—where disgust should armor me—something else surges first. *Need.* Raw. Humiliating. And desperate. The starving urge to be held. To be anchored. To not be alone inside my own collapsing body.

"Mitch," I choke, his name breaking out of me like a confession I swore I wouldn't make.

He crosses the garage in two strides. And then his arms are around me. Tight. Sure. Familiar. He pulls my shaking body against his chest like it's instinct. Like it's still his job. Like we haven't detonated everything we built.

His heartbeat hammers against my ear. And the scent of him wraps around me—pine and sawdust and something achingly known. His fingers slide into my hair, threading through the strands the way they've done a thousand times. Smoothing. Holding. Grounding.

And my body betrays me. My muscles melt. Because it feels so good to be caught. So good to not have to hold myself up for one more second.

"I'm so sorry, Peaches," he whispers into my hair. "I'm so sorry."

For one suspended, fragile moment, I let myself believe him. I breathe him in. I let my forehead rest against his chest. I let my body remember what it feels like to belong somewhere.

And then—reality surges back. Hard. Cold. Unforgiving. The bedroom. Tess. The way his hands looked on her.

And just like that, his comfort turns to glass in my lungs.

CHAPTER TWENTY-ONE

Mitch

The second her body stiffens in my arms, I feel it. The shift. Like a door slamming shut from the inside. I tighten my hold without thinking, pulling her closer to my chest, desperate and selfish enough to believe that if I can just keep her here long enough, she'll remember *us* instead of what I did.

"Let go of me."

The venom in her voice cuts clean through bone and I freeze. "Peaches," I whisper, my arms already loosening even though every part of me wants to fight it. "Lauren, please—"

She shoves at my chest and I let her go. But it feels like dropping something fragile and watching it shatter in slow motion. Like the other half of me just slipped through my fingers and I'm too damn late to catch it.

"How?" she demands, stumbling back. "Why?" Her hands fly to her temples, pressing hard like she's trying to contain the explosion inside her skull. "Tess?" she spits. "You threw me away for Tess Browning?"

Every word hits exactly where it should.

She sinks onto the steps, shoulders folding inward, head tipping against the railing like she doesn't have the strength to hold herself upright anymore.

And I know—*I know*—I did that to her. The second I saw that peach cobbler on the counter, steam curling up like some cruel metaphor, it hit me.

Clarity.

Like Austin told me she would, she came to fix it. She came to fight for us. And I was with Tess. The truth sits in my chest like a stone. I've regretted it every damn day since—every hour, every minute I've lain awake replaying that split-second where I could've pulled away—and didn't.

Lauren's face tightens as if she's trying to hold herself together by force. Her breath catches. A sound slips out of her—small, broken—before she can swallow it back. She presses her fist to her mouth, but the sob still shakes her shoulders.

And it wrecks me.

"I regret every second," I choke out, bile burning the back of my throat. My heart hammers so hard it hurts. "Every second."

Her eyes squeeze shut. Tears spill fast, tracking down her cheeks in hot lines. She shakes her head once—as if the motion can undo what she saw.

I drag in a ragged breath, because the truth is uglier than weakness. "It's not an excuse," I say, forcing the words through. "But I need you to understand where my head was—because I wasn't thinking. I was spiraling."

A sharp, involuntary sound tears out of her—pure disbelief. She wipes at her face with the back of her hand and stares at the railing.

My hands curl into fists at my sides. "I thought we were already broken, Lauren. I thought Miguel was proof of it. Proof you were done. Proof I'd already lost you and I was just the last idiot still trying to pretend we were salvageable."

Her throat bobs. Another sob breaks free—this one rawer, uglier. She turns her face away like she can't stand to let me see it.

My voice cracks. "All I could see was him." I swallow hard, the confession scraping on the way out. "I saw it. I saw him kiss you." My stomach twists like it's happening all over again. "I saw his mouth on yours, and it… it gutted me. It rewrote everything in my head."

Lauren's breath stutters. She lets out a strangled sound and presses her palm to her chest, as if the words are physically too heavy to carry.

I blow out a heavy breath, shame flooding in hot. "So yeah—what I did was stupid. Selfish. Pathetic. But in that moment, it felt like you'd already walked away, and I was drowning in it." My gaze flicks up, then away, because I can't stand the way she flinches. "I wanted to hurt something back. I wanted to feel wanted by someone— anyone—because I couldn't stand the idea that you wanted him."

My gaze drops. "Tess was there, and she made it easy. She pushed. I let it happen." I lift my eyes again, voice wrecked. "And I hate myself for it. Because none of that changes the truth."

I step closer, careful, not touching—like my hands are the last thing she can handle. "You're my wife," I say quietly. "You're the person I love. And I took what I was feeling about Miguel and I turned it into the worst decision of my life."

I take another step toward her before I can stop myself, reaching for her hand like that muscle memory alone might save us. "She means nothing to me," I say, my voice cracking under the weight of it. "Nothing. You're the only woman I care about. The only woman I love."

But she jerks back like I've burned her. Her eyes lift to mine—red, swollen, blazing with betrayal—and it hits harder than anything she's said.

"Please, Lauren," I whisper.

She doesn't answer. Rather, her fingers tighten around the railing until her knuckles bleach white. Her throat works, like she's swallowing words she doesn't want to give me. She stares past me—at the workbench, at the dollhouse, at the floor—anywhere but my face. A long beat stretches out, thick with everything we're not saying.

When she finally inhales, it sounds like it hurts. "I was wrong," she says at last, voice shaking but steady enough to land. "What I did with Miguel was wrong. It's been wrong for a long time." She presses a hand to her chest like she has to push the truth out through her ribs. "I let him get too close. I liked having him there, especially when you and I were so distant." Her eyes flick up to mine for half a second, then drop again. "I liked the attention. I liked not feeling invisible." Her jaw trembles. "That was selfish. And I know that. I'm sorry I betrayed what we were building."

The admission lands heavy between us.

"But I never—" Her voice breaks and she swallows hard. "I never expected to walk into that house and see Tess Browning on top of you."

She says Tess's name like it tastes poisonous.

"The same Tess who lied about me in her newspaper. The same Tess who cheated on my brother. The same Tess who has hated our family for years." Her chest rises sharply. "I opened that bedroom door and she was straddling you, Mitch! Her lips were on yours. And you..." Her face crumples. "You looked like you wanted her there."

The accusation rips through me.

"That was the worst pain of my life," she whispers. "Worse than the restaurant burning down. Worse than every negative pregnancy test. Worse than anything." Her hand presses against her chest. "It felt like my heart got ripped out and I had to stand there and watch you stomp on it."

I can't breathe.

"I know what I did was wrong," she continues, tears spilling freely now. "But I was there to try and fix it. I baked you that cobbler. I came there ready to apologize. To fight for us. And instead..." She shakes her head, letting her words fall away.

"I hate you for what you did, Mitch," she says—and this time it isn't sharp. It's shattered. "I can't believe that after everything we've been through—after everything we promised each other—you chose *her*."

The words hang between us, heavy and final. Her chest rises in a shaky breath. She wipes at her face, but it doesn't stop the tears from spilling.

For a long moment, she can't look at me. Her gaze drifts past my shoulder instead, unfocused, as if her eyes need somewhere else to land before she breaks completely.

Then they catch on the workbench. On the dollhouse. And her expression tightens again, like the sight of it hurts in a different way—like it's proof of how hard we tried and how badly we failed.

She swallows. Hard. "...It's beautiful," she finally manages, voice ragged, like the compliment is being torn out of her against her will. And it is. Because saying it means admitting any part of me still matters.

"I'll make the rocking horse," I start automatically, desperate to offer something solid, something good.

But her scowl slices through me. "Don't you even—"

The door behind her opens hard enough to rattle the frame. Austin fills the doorway, eyes blazing, jaw locked so tight I can see the muscle ticking. And he doesn't hesitate. "You fucking asshole." His shoes pound down the steps, each step fueled by pure fury. The door crashes shut behind him. "How dare you show your face here after what you did!"

He lunges, but Lauren moves on instinct. She grabs a fistful of his t-shirt and yanks him back with more strength than I expect. "Austin! Stop!"

He fights against her grip, his entire body vibrating with the need to hit something—me. "How could you?" he roars, twisting toward me anyway. "How could you do this to her? And with fucking Tess Browning?"

Lauren plants herself between us, shoving at his chest.

"Austin, no!" Her voice cracks but she doesn't let go. "Don't. Not today."

"She doesn't need to protect you," he snaps, still trying to push past her. "You don't get to stand here and—"

"Austin!" she shouts, louder now. It echoes off the concrete walls. "I said *stop!*"

That does it. He stills, but barely. His arm wraps protectively around her middle instead, pulling her back against him like he's shielding her from a bullet. But his glare never leaves me.

Every accusation lands exactly where it should. I step back, hands raised slightly—not to defend myself, just to show I'm not fighting back. "I know!" I say, hating how wrecked I sound. "I know, okay? I fucking hate myself for what I did!"

"Good," Austin shoots back. "You should," he adds, taking a step toward me again. "Fuck, Mitch, of all people? Of all the women in this town?"

I drag my hands down my face and stare at the concrete. I deserve whatever he wants to throw at me. His fists included.

"Lauren," I say instead, my voice dropping, cutting through the noise. "I can't tell you how sorry I am. If I could take it back, I would. In a heartbeat."

She clings to her brother. And the look on her face— *God*—the hurt in her eyes burns straight through me.

I take one cautious step forward—but headlights sweep across the driveway. Voices rise. Car doors slam. Guests spill toward their vehicles as Josh rounds the corner with his arm wrapped around Mavis's waist, waving at departing guests.

"No one else but Casey knows," Lauren whispers urgently, her eyes snapping to mine. "Please, Mitch. Play along."

Even now. Even after everything. I nod. Because I'd crawl through glass if she asked.

"There you are!" Josh calls. "Where've you been, dude?"

Mavis waddles beside him, smiling—until her gaze lands on the workbench. "Oh. My. God." She points and then her hand flies to her mouth.

Josh follows her line of sight. "No way," he chokes out, guiding her closer. "This is insane, Mitch. You made this?"

I force a grin onto my face even as something inside me collapses in on itself. "Yeah," I say, steady enough. "I'm betting it's a girl."

Mavis's eyes fill instantly. "It's absolutely incredible," she whispers, tracing her fingers along the tiny chimney. "I can't believe you built this."

"Nothing but the best for my niece," I say and pull her into a hug before I can think too hard about it. She presses her face into my chest, her belly bumping against me. I close my eyes for half a second. Because will she ever let me hold her like this again? After she learns what I did?

"Damn, Mitch," Josh says, circling the workbench. "I'm blown away."

Mavis pulls back, still smiling at the dollhouse like it's magic.

"I'm sorry I missed the party," I say, the lie thin and brittle on my tongue. "I hope you guys had a great time."

The garage door creaks open again, hinges whining in the thick humidity like the house itself is exhausted. Casey pokes her head out and tosses a bag of garbage into the bin, as if this is just another ordinary moment in an ordinary day—as if my entire life isn't imploding in the same square footage where she's taking out the trash.

"Oh." Casey's brows lift as she takes in the scene—the tension, the red eyes, the way Austin's shoulders are still coiled like he's seconds from swinging again. "So, this is where you all disappeared to."

She hops down the steps and slides an arm around Austin's waist, grounding him with easy affection. Then she reaches for Lauren's hand and squeezes, her expression softening.

"Your mom can't get Aunt Millie to leave," Casey says

with a tired sigh. "She won't go until she sees you." She pauses. Her gaze flicks toward me—brief, measured. Not warm. Not hostile. Just... aware. "Hi-ya, Mitch."

The casual greeting lands like a test. I lift my hand in a small wave, like I deserve the normalcy. "Hey, Case." But my voice sounds wrong in my own ears. Too even. Too controlled.

She wrinkles her nose and shifts subtly closer to Lauren, a quiet protective move that would be invisible to anyone not looking for it.

Yeah, you hate me.

The garage door groans open again, the rusty hinges protesting the weight of everything happening beneath them. "Lauren?" Susan Templeton's voice floats out first—warm, concerned. She scans the space—and then her eyes land on the workbench. "Oh!" Her hand flies to her mouth. "Mitch! Did you—"

Her excitement punches me square in the gut. Because Susan has always loved me. Loudly. Fiercely. Like I'm the son she got to choose.

And you're going to hate me soon, too.

I nod once, but I can't hold her gaze. My eyes drop to the floor—paint flecks, sawdust, the dark oil stain by my boot. Anywhere but their faces.

"Oh, it's absolutely breathtaking," Susan gushes, stepping closer to the dollhouse like it's a museum piece. "My gosh, you're so talented, sweetheart." She tilts her head at me, smiling like she doesn't know I've detonated her daughter's heart. "We missed you this afternoon."

Heat burns behind my eyes. I clear my throat, forcing my voice to cooperate. "I'm sorry," I say. "I didn't mean to miss it."

But that's a lie. I meant to miss every second. I meant to avoid the smiles and the congratulations and the way everyone would look at me if they knew the truth. I only meant to stop by and silently put the dollhouse in Josh's Jeep.

Lauren inhales sharply beside me and grips the railing like she might tip over. She climbs the steps with uneven movements. "Aunt Millie?" she calls, her voice thin.

Susan's smile falters. "Honey... are you okay? What did she say to you?" She lowers her voice. "She insists on apologizing before she leaves."

Lauren shakes her head once—tight, controlled—and slips past her without answering. Austin follows, taking the stairs in a single leap. "Lauren, hang on. I'll come with you," he calls, disappearing into the house like he can physically stand between her and the rest of the world.

Susan claps her hands lightly, but her attention settles on Mavis. The look she gives her is different now—soft, maternal, touched with a protectiveness that's replaced the sharp edges from before, no longer bruised by the way she came roaring back into her sons' lives. "Well, come on." She gestures toward the door. "Mavs, let's get you back into the air conditioning with your feet up. It's been a long afternoon."

Josh guides Mavis toward the steps, murmuring something soft and reassuring. But the normalcy of it is suffocating. The way we're pretending nothing is wrong— like we're just a family gathering to celebrate a baby shower—makes my skin crawl.

Casey's fingers close around my wrist for half a second. Not warm. Not friendly. Just directive. "Come on," she says quietly. But her eyes never leave the doorway where Lauren disappeared.

I follow, but each step into Templeton Manor feels heavier than the last. The familiar scent of polished wood and lemon cleaner hits me, but instead of comfort, I feel exposed.

***

I slide the ottoman carefully under Mavis's swollen feet as she eases down into the center cushion of the sofa.

"How's that?" I ask, dropping down right beside her.

Her head tips back, eyes fluttering closed, exhaling like she just ran a marathon. "Perfect," she mutters, a tired smile tugging at her mouth. "That was exhausting."

The living room looks like a pastel tornado hit it—gift bags slumped against table legs, ribbons tangled in the rug, tissue paper draped over lamps like streamers after a parade.

"Quite the haul," I say, nudging a neon-green plastic frog with my toe. The stupid thing lights up instantly and starts belting out "Five Little Speckled Frogs" in a high-pitched, childish voice that pierces straight through my skull. I grimace and smack it on the head until it stops.

Mavis laughs softly and drags both hands over the curve of her belly, slow and protective. "She's so loved already."

The word *she* hooks in my chest. "So, you think it's a girl, too?" I ask, leaning back into the cushions.

She glances over her shoulder, scanning the room like she's about to leak classified information. "Can I tell you a secret?"

I lean closer automatically. "Always."

"I may have peeked at the ultrasound," she whispers, winking.

A grin spreads across my face before I can stop it. I take her hand and press a quick kiss to her knuckles. "Good," I say under my breath. "Then I didn't just waste several weeks of my life building a dollhouse."

Her laugh spills into the foyer just as Casey rounds the corner and drops dramatically into the seat beside us. She cracks open a beer with a sharp hiss and takes a long swallow, a little foam slipping down her chin.

Mavis snorts. "Have one for me, will ya?"

Casey freezes mid-sip. "Oh—shit. Mavs, I'm sorry!" She wipes her mouth with the back of her hand and sets the can down like it's radioactive. "I totally forgot. I'm being so rude."

"You're fine." Mavis huffs, shifting with a tiny wince as she readjusts. "You're owed one—or eight—after crawling around on the floor handing us presents all afternoon."

Casey drops to her knees and starts rifling through the pile again like a raccoon in a trash bin. She lifts a small jar and squints at the label. "What even is this?"

Mavis leans forward, lowering her voice. "Nipple cream."

Casey yelps and drops it like it burned her. The jar rolls across the room and bumps into Josh's shoe just as he and Austin wander in and flop onto the opposite couch in eerie twin-like unison.

Josh picks it up and reads the label with a skeptical frown. "I don't like what's in this stuff. We'll get something better." Then he tosses it toward me.

I catch it reflexively, but immediately drop it onto Mavis's lap like it's a live grenade. "Why are you giving it to me?"

Josh grins. "Because you're the only one in the room who looked more uncomfortable than Casey." He cracks his beer and points at the jar. "Try opening that in front of forty women."

Austin's face drains of color. "*And* Mom."

"Oh my, God." Mavis groans, covering her face. "Can we please stop talking about what I'm going to rub on my nipples?"

I gag dramatically into my elbow. "Thanks for that visual."

She smacks my shoulder, and the room erupts—real laughter, loud and unfiltered. It's easy. So damn easy. The kind of normal that settles into your bones—beer cans cracking open, harmless teasing, a baby on the way, a handmade dollhouse waiting on the workbench. From the outside, it looks like nothing in this room could possibly fracture.

I lean back into the couch, smiling along with them. But underneath the laughter, there's a hum I can't shake. A pressure. Because everything simmers just below the surface.

I look up as Lauren appears in the foyer beside Susan, one hand hovering at Aunt Millie's elbow as she guides her toward the front door.

"I'm just so sorry, Lauren," Aunt Millie repeats, her cane tapping sharply against the hardwood.

"It's okay, Aunt Mill," Lauren says, her voice thin. Controlled. "It's been a hard day. I overreacted."

Aunt Millie leans in to hug Susan, then turns her head and looks straight at me. She blows me a kiss, tilting her head with syrupy sympathy. "It'll happen when you kids least expect it," she calls brightly. "Just relax and don't think about it so much!"

The sentence floats there, light and careless. And I force a polite smile out of reflex—but my eyes drift to Lauren. Because she stares at the floor, arms wrapped tight around herself. And I can only imagine the depth of it—the kind of pain that doesn't stay in one place, but spreads. The kind that settles behind your ribs and makes every breath feel heavier than it should.

Susan hustles Aunt Millie out the door, murmuring something under her breath before practically ushering her off the porch. "God, I need a cocktail," she chokes out the second the door closes, already pivoting toward the kitchen. Her red heels strike the old hardwood with impatient clicks. "John!" she calls.

Then the house goes quiet. But Lauren doesn't move. She just stands there alone in the foyer, shoulders slightly hunched. Her head lowers slowly, hair falling forward to curtain her face. It's not dramatic. It's not explosive. It's small. Like something inside her just folded in on itself.

"Lauren, are you okay?" Josh pushes off the couch immediately. "What the hell was she talking about?" He crosses the room in three strides and wraps his arm around her shoulders.

She doesn't pull away—but she doesn't melt into him, either. She just goes still and lets him guide her back to the couch. When she settles between him and Austin, she doesn't ease down so much as collapse, her weight hitting the cushion heavy and final. She drags the heel of her hand beneath her eyes, smearing tears across flushed skin.

"Lauren?" Josh presses gently.

Her face reddens further. Then her breathing goes shallow—too fast. She presses her lips together like she's trying to hold something back. Then a sound escapes her. It's not laughter exactly. It's more like disbelief cracking open.

"Believe it or not, Josh," she says quietly, the corners of her mouth twitching in something that isn't a smile, "that was her attempt at encouragement."

Josh blinks. "Encouragement?"

Lauren exhales through her nose, shaking her head once. But there's no humor in it. "Please tell me, Dr. Templeton," she says, voice thinning, "that when a woman comes to you with fertility concerns, you don't recommend relaxation and *not thinking about it so much.*"

Her words break on the way out and she drops her face into her hands—not dramatically. Just... defeated.

And my stomach drops straight to the floor. Because I've seen her cry. I've seen her furious. I've seen her devastated. But this is different. This is her unraveling quietly, in front of everyone.

Helplessness floods me—thick and suffocating. My chest tightens like someone's cinched a strap around it. And my fingers go numb at the tips. Because her pain radiates outward, and it hits me in full force.

A sharp click of heels cuts through the moment.

Lauren inhales and drags her hands down her face, scrubbing away tears as if she can erase them. She straightens her back just as Susan sweeps in with a half-empty brandy snifter, John trailing behind her with his phone in one hand and a drink in the other. And just like that—the room shifts back into performance mode.

"I didn't take nearly enough pictures today!" Susan announces, her voice bright and buoyant, as if nothing in this house is splintering under the surface. "Let's get a group shot of all six of you." She waves us into position like we're centerpieces. "Come on, you three. Let's go."

Josh stands and slides down beside Mavis. He wraps an arm around her shoulders, palm settling instinctively over her belly. Austin follows and sits on the floor beside Casey, knees touching, fingers laced. But Lauren freezes in the middle of the room.

"Lauren, let's go!" Susan instructs, already lifting her phone. "Stop dilly-dallying and sit by your husband."

But that word lands heavy. *Husband.*

Lauren inhales so sharply I see her ribs strain beneath her dress. She doesn't look at me, but she does walk forward—slow, deliberate—like she's crossing a line she's not sure she wants to cross.

When she reaches me, she hesitates. Just a flicker. Then she lowers herself onto my lap. But it's not natural. Not fluid. It's a controlled descent, like she's placing herself somewhere uncomfortable on purpose.

The second her weight settles against me, her entire body goes rigid. Every muscle goes tight. Her hands drop to her own thighs, fingers curling into the fabric of her dress so she doesn't accidentally brush mine.

She smells like her shampoo. Like home. But she feels like a stranger.

I wrap my arms around her waist because that's what I'm supposed to do. Because it's what I've done a thousand times before—at weddings, holidays, lazy Sunday mornings. But this time it feels rehearsed. Careful. Like I'm holding something that no longer belongs to me.

Susan snaps the first photo and my heart pounds so hard it feels visible. Blood roars in my ears. My palms press against her hips—familiar curves, muscle memory—and the contrast between what this looks like and what it is makes the room tilt.

"Look at all our children," Susan coos, tapping the screen repeatedly. She elbows John. "Our children, John!"

"Susan," he mutters, eyes glued to his phone. "I've got like ten grand on this game." He stalks off, finishing his brandy, but Susan continues to snap photos.

Then a sing-song ringtone cuts through the tension. "Oh, it's Christina!" she says, already answering as she clacks away across the foyer again.

The performance pauses, but Lauren still sits on me. And I can feel exactly how much it cost her to do it. My hand moves before my brain catches up. I squeeze her hips and let my palm drift down her thigh like we're still the couple in the photo.

But she goes rigid. "Don't," she says quietly at first. Then sharper, "Mitch. Stop." She stands—not explosive, not theatrical. Just done. She steps away from me like she needs air.

And the room stills.

Mavis frowns. "Lauren, what's going on?"

But she doesn't answer right away. She just stands there. And I watch it happen in real time—the way her jaw tightens, the way she draws in a slow breath through her nose like she's trying to steady herself. Her eyes move around the room—Josh, Mavis, Austin, Casey, me—like she's taking inventory of who's here. Who's watching. Who's about to hear it.

She presses her lips together so hard they blanch white. And for a second, I think she's going to swallow it down. Smile. Apologize. Blame stress. Keep the peace. But then her shoulders drop. Not dramatically. Just… surrender.

Uh-oh.

"You want to know what's going on, Mavs?" she asks softly. Her voice isn't sharp. It isn't hysterical. It's just exhausted.

And I feel it in my gut. She's done performing. Done smoothing it over. Done pretending we're fine when we're so obviously not.

"My restaurant burned down," she says, the words careful and measured. "Then I got accused of arson." Her gaze shifts to Josh—not cruel, just factual. "By *your* ex-wife." A tiny, humorless snort leaves her. Not quite a laugh. "And that really sucked."

Josh shifts. "Lauren—"

"And somewhere in there," she continues, her voice steady but thin, "my marriage fell apart. Again."

Every eye in the room shifts to me. Including hers. And I nod once. Because that part is true.

"Mitch, *I'm sorry* I leaned on Miguel more than I should have," she says like we're continuing the conversation we started in the garage. "I liked having someone tell me I wasn't a failure. I liked not feeling invisible." Her voice fractures on the last word. "But kissing him was wrong," she says, softer now. "And I'm so sorry."

The admission hangs in the air and my chest tightens. Because while I've been desperate to talk to her—to hear those exact words spill from her lips—I wasn't prepared to do it in front of an audience.

"Lauren—" I start.

"But then I walked onto a job site, Mavs," she says, turning to meet my sister's eyes, her voice hollow and raw, "and found Tess Browning draped all over my husband. Her hands on him. Her mouth on his."

And… there it is. No screaming. No theatrics. Just the truth. Out in the open.

Josh's head snaps toward me. "Tess?"

I exhale as my face burns. Because part of me wants the earth to open and swallow me whole. Another part is relieved. Because we're finally saying it.

"It's true," I admit, my voice rough. "I kissed her."

Josh stares at me like I just confessed to murder. "You cheated on my sister," he says slowly, "with *my Tess?*" He taps his chest as if claiming ownership.

Mavis whips her head in his direction. "I'm sorry—*your Tess?*"

He scoffs. "This isn't about semantics, Mavs!" Josh snaps, hands flying out. "He kissed my ex-wife!"

"And Lauren kissed Miguel," Mavis fires back immediately. "Or are we skipping that part?"

Casey's head jerks between them. "Wait—what?"

Lauren closes her eyes for half a second, then opens them. "He saw Miguel kiss me," she says.

Every head swivels in my direction again and I nod. "I did." Then I point at the front door, to the porch, where the ghost of betrayal haunts each step.

"And?" Austin demands.

"And instead of addressing it," I say tightly, "I assumed the worst. I let jealousy eat me alive."

Lauren laughs once—short, hollow. "Jealousy?" She shakes her head. "You were already halfway out the door, Mitch. You just needed an excuse."

"That's not fair," I shoot back. "You were spending every second dealing with that fucking restaurant again. Just like always, Pier Ninety-two took priority over me! Over *us*!"

"Because it was my dream!" she shouts. "Because I built it from nothing! And it fucking burned to the ground!"

"Yeah, but it still built a wall between us, didn't it?" I say.

Josh moves first. He stands and steps forward, planting himself at Lauren's side like a guard dog, shoulders squared, jaw tight. "Don't you dare make this about the restaurant," he says, pointing at me. "You kissed Tess. That's on you."

"And Miguel isn't?" Mavis spits back from the couch, her voice sharper than I've ever heard it. She braces one hand against the cushion and leans forward. "Lauren didn't exactly slam that door shut, did she?"

Lauren stiffens beside me. "I didn't sleep with him."

"And I didn't sleep with Tess!" I snap, the words ripping out of me.

Austin's eyes go glacial. "Did you want to?" he asks, each word clipped and lethal.

"No. Fuck no. I—"

"It doesn't matter!" Mavis cuts across me, her voice rising. "The point is, none of this would have happened if Lauren had set a boundary with Miguel. This isn't just

Mitch's fault!" Her palm slaps against her thigh, emotion flashing hot in her eyes.

"The hell it isn't," Austin shoots back, stepping forward so fast Casey flinches. "Nothing—and I mean nothing—excuses what Mitch did with Tess." He actually shudders, disgust crawling all over his face.

"Guys," Casey cries, pushing to her feet slowly, hands out like she's approaching a pack of wild animals. "Maybe we should just take a breath—"

"No," I bark, cutting her off. Because we're already bleeding. Might as well finish the cut.

I close the space between Lauren and me in three strides and grip her hips. Not hard. Not violent. But desperate. I need her to look at me. To see me. To see that this isn't some game.

"Mitch—" she warns.

"I'm sorry," I choke out, my thumbs pressing into the curve of her waist. "I'm sorry for what I did. Peaches, you have to know that. Tess is—"

"Off limits, man!" Josh roars. He shoves me in the shoulder. It's not a punch—but it's not light either. And my hands fall from Lauren as I stumble back half a step.

"Josh, stop!" Lauren cries, moving instinctively between us. And even now—even wrecked and furious and exhausted—she shields me. Just like she shoved Austin back in the garage.

"He kissed my ex-wife!" Josh yells, chest heaving.

"Yeah, I know!" Lauren shouts back at him, her voice cracking.

The room vibrates with it. But then—a sound cuts through everything. A sharp, broken inhale.

We all turn.

Mavis cries. Not loud. Not hysterical. Silent tears slide down her cheeks as she folds forward slightly, one hand pressed to the swell of her belly.

"Mavs?" Casey drops to her knees in front of her so fast the coffee table rattles. "Are you okay?"

"Cramp," Mavis chokes out, face scrunched tight. Her other hand grips the couch cushion like she's trying to transfer the pain.

Josh is at her side instantly. "Where? Where does it hurt?" His hand hovers over her stomach, afraid to press too hard.

But she slaps it away. "Are you fucking kidding me right now, Joshua?" she roars, tears streaking her face. "You're standing here focusing on your ex-wife while I'm sitting here—"

"I'm not focusing on Tess!" he says, voice breaking. "I'm defending my sister!"

She winces again, folding in on herself, breath hitching.

Casey rubs her back in slow circles. "It's okay. Just breathe. Can I get you water? Ice? Anything?"

But Mavis shakes her head. "No. I'm fine. It's just—" Another shaky breath. "It's just stress."

Josh tries again, softer now. "Mavs, please. Tell me what you need."

"I need you to *go away*," she snaps. "Just… give me some space."

He stands, but wobbles. Like the ground shifted under him and he didn't see it coming.

And it hits me. This was their baby shower. Their day. And I detonated it. My marriage. My jealousy. My mistakes. All of it spilled out across pastel wrapping paper and half-eaten cake.

"Come on," Austin mutters, yanking the front door open so hard it slams against the stopper. "Let's get some air." He jerks his chin toward Josh. Then toward Lauren. The Templeton trio… while the rest of us certainly didn't get an invite.

But Lauren doesn't move right away. Rather, she turns to me. And for a second, the noise fades. Her eyes linger on mine—hurt, exhausted, furious, devastated. All of it layered together.

Everything in me wants to grab her. To pull her into my

chest. To beg her not to walk away. But I don't. I just stand here. And watch as she follows her brothers out the door.

CHAPTER TWENTY-TWO

Lauren

"Can I come stay with you for a few days?" I ask, staring down into the amber swirl of my beer. The booth at Highside feels the same as it always does—scarred wood, sticky tabletop, low hum of conversation—but tonight it presses in on me. "I just… I need space. Time to think."

Austin doesn't hesitate. "Yeah. Come to Chicago," he says, leaning in like this is the easiest decision in the world. Then he glances at Josh and adds dryly, "Hell, maybe you should, too. We've got an airbed. You two can commiserate together."

Josh groans and sinks further into the booth, rubbing both hands over his face. "Mavs has never told me to leave her alone before," he mutters. "Not once. She's really pissed."

Austin huffs out a laugh and Josh peeks at him through his fingers. "What did I do that was that bad?"

"You hit the Tess thing a little hard, man." Austin lifts his brows. "You said '*my Tess*' like six times. In under a minute."

"I did not."

"You did," I say, absently tracing the rim of my mug with my index finger. "It was… pointed."

Austin slips into a dramatic imitation. "'You kissed *my Tess?*'" he says, clutching his chest. "You made it sound like she was a signed Ernie Banks baseball."

Josh shoves him lightly. "Shut up. No, I didn't."

"I'm just saying," Austin replies with a smirk, "Mavs has a little wiggle room to be mad… and a little jealous."

Josh drops his head back against the booth and groans. And I take a slow swallow of beer, the bitterness settling heavy on my tongue. "Yeah, well," I say quietly, "her jealousy is nothing compared to the mess I'm in with Mitch."

Josh winces as he watches my finger slowly circle the lip of the glass. "Please don't drink from that again."

I hold his gaze and deliberately take another sip.

He shudders. "The germs, Lauren."

"You're ridiculous." I set the mug down and let my eyes drop to the table. The alcohol softens the edges, but it doesn't erase the ache. Mitch's voice keeps replaying in my head—his apology, the way he said he spiraled, the way he looked at me as I walked out the door, pleading for me to stay.

I know I blurred the line first. I let Miguel get too close. That's on me. But does that mean I'm wrong now? Thinking this is the end of us?

I look up at them. "What do I even do, you guys?" I ask. "I know I messed up with Miguel. I know that I started all of this. But I feel like Mitch crossed a line. Like, what would have happened if I hadn't shown up there?" A heavy breath slips through my lips. "I mean, can we even come back from this?"

Josh exhales slowly, chewing over his words before speaking. "Look, I'm not giving Mitch a pass here," he says, "but when Tess cheated on me, she *really* cheated on me. Lies. Secrets. Sex. Months of it. Mitch didn't do that. He made a mistake and then he owned it immediately. No hiding. No trickle truth. No sex."

"Yeah, but again, what would have happened if I hadn't shown up?" I ask, though the words don't land as solid as I want them to. Because deep down I know he would never have gone that far.

"Mitch isn't a liar, Lauren," Austin says gently. "You know that. And he told you back at the Manor, that's not something he wanted."

I let out a humorless laugh. "Three hours ago I was physically restraining you from punching him in the face. And now you're defending him."

"I'm not defending him," Austin replies. "What he did was shitty. But it didn't happen in a vacuum. You two have been bleeding out for months."

And that lands because it's true. I poured my heart out to Austin last summer—the wheels came off my marriage long before Josh and Mavis even said 'I do'. But before I can respond, Austin goes still. His eyes shift past me toward the bar and his jaw tightens. "There is absolutely no fucking way," he mutters.

Josh turns first. Then I follow.

Blonde curls catch the neon light like a spotlight found her on purpose. Tess Browning swings onto a barstool, crossing one long leg over the other like she owns the room. Pink nails flash as she pulls a menu toward her. She laughs at something the bartender says—light, careless, unaffected.

And my stomach drops so fast the room tilts.

"How?" Josh chokes out.

"And why?" Austin finishes, grabbing my elbow as I shove forward.

Jealousy hits first—hot and ugly. Then humiliation. Then something reckless that's been simmering under my skin since the job site. "Let go," I say, yanking my arm free. Because maybe I blurred a line with Miguel. Maybe I let him get too close. But she's the one who straddled my husband. And I am done sitting still.

Austin catches Josh's eye. "Uh-uh," he says under his

breath, tapping the table once. "You stay here."

Before I can argue, the twins rise in sync and move through the crowd. They flank Tess at the bar—one on each side. Casual. Confident. Blocking every easy exit.

She glances left. Then right. And her smile tightens.

Good.

A minute later they guide her back toward our booth. She slides into the red vinyl across from me, smoothing her skirt like she's settling into a board meeting instead of a confrontation. Josh drops in beside her, effectively sealing her in.

"Lovely to see you, Lauren," she says sweetly.

My pulse hammers so loud I can hear it in my ears. "I can't say the same."

Austin sits beside me, thigh pressing against mine in silent solidarity.

"That's too bad. I thought I was invited to the family reunion." Tess's fingers drift toward Josh's forearm, grazing him. "Although… we're missing someone it looks like."

Josh stiffens and brushes her hand away without looking at her. Then he grabs his beer and drains it in one swallow.

"Where's your beautiful bride, Joshua?" Tess continues, tucking a curl behind her ear. "And Mitch? I don't see him either." Her gaze flicks to Austin. "Oh, and congratulations. What's her name again?"

"Casey," Austin says through clenched teeth.

"Oh, that's right. Casey from Chicago." Tess smiles lazily. "It's good to see you've finally stopped pining for Mavis after all these years."

"Knock it off, Tess," Josh says, low and tight.

But her smile doesn't falter. It simply sharpens at the edges—like she enjoys that he still reacts.

Before anyone can say more, the waiter weaves through the crowd toward our booth, balancing a creamy drink on a tray. He slows when he spots Tess sitting with us. "Oh— hey," he says, half-amused, half-confused. "You moved."

Tess tilts her head up at him, all innocence. "Did I?"

He gives a quick, awkward laugh and sets the glass down in front of her. "White Russian," he says, then glances around the table at our nearly empty glasses. "I'll be back with refills."

"Thank you," Tess purrs, but it's too much. Too practiced. She wraps both hands around the cold glass like it's a prize and takes a slow sip as the waiter walks away. "Now," she says lightly, "why exactly was I summoned?"

I don't hesitate. "Why are you fucking around with my husband?"

Tess lifts a perfectly sculpted brow. "Ah. There it is." She stirs her drink with her straw slowly. "I wondered what happened to him. He hasn't answered me in weeks. Not since—"

"Leave Mitch alone," Josh cuts in sharply. "Don't fuck with him."

She turns in his direction, something flashing in her eyes that's no longer playful. "I'm not fucking him," Tess continues, turning back to me. "Though I can't deny I tried."

Austin shifts beside me. "Careful."

But Tess laughs quietly. "Relax. I'm complimenting him." She studies me. "You're a lucky woman, Lauren. That man worships you. I had to work my ass off just to get him to kiss me."

Heat floods my face. "You don't get to kiss my husband. And you really don't get to talk about my marriage," I snap.

She leans forward slightly. "Oh, I think I do."

My fingers curl around the edge of the table and I feel Austin stiffen beside me, preparing to intervene when I inevitably launch myself at her from across this table.

"You don't appreciate him," she adds.

Josh flinches. "Tess, don't—"

"No, let's do this," she says, her composure cracking just a bit. "You want to know why I'm 'fucking' with Mitch?" She looks at me again. "Because I know what it feels like to be married to someone who doesn't love you the way you love them."

Josh's head jerks toward her. "This is about *us*?"

She doesn't answer him. Rather, her eyes stay locked on mine. "You're about to throw him away," she says quietly. "And if you do? I won't hesitate to pick up the pieces."

I lean forward, bracing my forearms on the table. The vinyl sticks slightly to my skin, the bar loud around us, but the booth feels sealed off—like the four of us are sitting inside a pressure chamber.

"Why are you doing this?" I ask and my throat tightens despite myself. "We used to be friends, didn't we?"

Tess rolls her eyes like the word *friends* is naïve. "Oh, please, Lauren. Don't flatter yourself. You do realize this is absolutely not about you, right?"

I bark out a humorless laugh. "Not about me? Tess, you publicly accused me of arson and then climbed on top of my husband at a construction site." I tip my head. "Feels pretty personal."

Her gaze sharpens. "Yeah, well, you don't appreciate him," she says coolly. "And he likes that I do."

"Excuse me?"

"You don't see what you have," she continues, completely unfazed. "Mitch worships the ground you walk on. Always has."

Heat floods my face, running hot straight down my neck. "You are in no position to comment on my marriage," I snap, my voice rising before I can stop it. A few heads turn from nearby tables. I lower my tone, but not the bite in it. "I don't need you," I say slowly, carefully, "to tell me how my husband feels about me."

"Well, apparently I do." The snap in her voice cracks through the booth. She blinks fast, like something inside her just broke loose. Then she twists toward Josh, her knee bumping his. "Because let me tell you something, Lauren," she says, but she looks at him now. "It fucking sucks being married to someone who doesn't love you the way you love them."

The words land heavy. Not sharp. Not playful. Just heavy.

Josh goes still beside her. "So, this *is* about us," he says slowly, pointing between them. "That's what this is? You're still mad at me?"

Tess laughs, but there's no humor in it. "You think this is about me being *mad* at you? Joshua, you never loved me. That's what this is about."

The booth seems to shrink.

"The hell I didn't!" Josh fires back, color climbing up his neck. "We had good years. A lot of them. The day I married you was—"

"Don't." She shuts her eyes and shakes her head. "Don't rewrite it now because it's convenient." She takes a slow breath and opens her eyes again, glassy now. "I gave up so much to be with you," she says. "And you never gave any of it back."

Josh leans forward, disbelief written all over his face. "What exactly did you give up?"

She lets out a soft, broken laugh. Then her fingers tighten around her glass. "It doesn't even matter anymore. It's long gone."

For a second, the air changes. The sharp edges disappear. The smug smile is gone. And the woman sitting across from me looks... wounded.

Josh exhales and scrubs a hand through his hair, the fight draining out of him. "Okay," he says. "Maybe there were things you never told me. Maybe there were things we never dealt with. Didn't fully resolve." He glances between her and me. "But what I don't understand is why you dragged them into it." His hand flicks in my direction. "Why pull Lauren and Mitch into whatever this is?"

Tess swallows. "Because I didn't want what happened to me to happen to him." Her eyes shift to mine. "Mitch is actually a really decent guy," she says quietly. "And I can see—"

"Don't," I cut in sharply, setting my beer down harder

than I mean to. The glass thumps against the table. "Don't you think I know what kind of man I married?" I snap.

"No," Tess says calmly. "I don't think you do." The words sit there between us before she continues. "Because you're about to kick him to the curb," she continues, her voice steady now. "And when you do…" She lifts her glass and drains the last of it. "I'll be the first one there to pick him up."

The audacity of it knocks the breath out of my lungs. I watch, dumbfounded, as she sets the empty glass down with a soft clink, then nudges Josh's arm.

"Move. I'm leaving."

Josh slides out of the booth automatically, then reaches out a hand to help her up, but she swats it away.

"Congrats on the baby," she mutters, swiping at her cheek before she can stop the tear. Then she's gone. Her heels click across the floor, swallowed by the sudden roar of the bar as the Dodgers close out the seventh inning.

Josh drops back into the booth and drags both hands over his face. "What the hell just happened?"

Austin exhales low and long, draining the rest of his beer. "Man," he mutters. "You are not winning any husband—or ex-husband—awards tonight."

But while he jokes, I stare at the empty space where Tess sat. "I can't believe I'm about to say this," I mutter. "But I kind of feel bad for her."

Both of them look at me.

"I was ready to rip her apart twenty minutes ago," I admit, lifting my mug for another swallow. The alcohol hums through my veins now, warm and dulling. "Now I just… don't know what to think."

Josh stares at the table. "She really thought I didn't love her," he says quietly.

Austin's gaze drifts toward the TV, though I'm not sure he even sees it. "I guess she gave you both something to think about," he says.

Because yeah. She did. And now that she's gone, her

words loop in my head. *You're about to kick him to the curb. And if you do, I'll be the first one to pick him up.*

My hand slips into my purse without thinking. I pull out my phone and unlock it. But there are no missed calls. No texts. No voicemails. Just silence.

The bar erupts again as the game on TV shifts into another inning, glasses clinking and people shouting. But it feels distant, like the sound is coming through water.

I stare at my phone until my stomach twists. Because before any of this happened, Mitch was always the guy who called. Always checked in. Always tried to fix things. And now I don't know if the silence means he's giving me space... or if he's finally done trying.

My chest tightens at the thought. Because that's the part I haven't said out loud yet. The part I'm almost afraid to look at too closely. If Mitch still wants me—if he's still willing to fight for us even after everything we just tore open—is that still what I want?

I used to know the answer to that without hesitation. It lived in my bones. Mitch was my constant. My partner. My future. But right now? Right now everything feels cracked down the middle. I don't know if what we broke is something we can glue back together anymore. I don't know if love is enough when trust bleeds out on the floor.

CHAPTER TWENTY-THREE

Mitch

I push open the nursery door and flick on the light. A warm glow spills across the room that used to be mine. The queen bed is gone. In its place sits a white crib, perfectly centered beneath the window, and a rocking chair waits in the corner where my dresser used to stand.

I step inside slowly, like I've wandered into someone else's life. My fingers slide along the smooth railing of the crib.

"Do you like it?" Mavis asks.

I glance up. She stands by the bookcase, straightening a copy of *The Wonky Donkey* on the top shelf. The ridiculous cartoon donkey grins up at us from the cover.

I tap my fingers lightly on the crib rail and take the room in again—the pale yellow walls, the folded blankets, the tiny socks tucked in a basket. A whole future waiting to start.

"Did Josh build this?" I ask, giving the crib rail a light tap with my fingertips.

Mavis nods. "Four hours of our lives we'll never get back," she says, smiling softly. "But yeah. He built it."

I glance down at the crib like it's a suspect and give it a

careful, gentle wobble—just enough to test it. But the thing doesn't budge. "Okay," I tease, nodding once like I'm impressed. "Sturdy. Approved."

Mavis snorts. "Don't you start."

"I'm just saying," I add, giving it one more tiny shake. "If this thing collapses, I don't want it on my conscience."

"It's not going to collapse," she says, rolling her eyes. "Josh followed the instructions. Twice."

A laugh slips out of me before I can stop it. "He did a good job. But for the record," I say, looking at her, "I would've helped. Gladly."

Her expression softens in that way that always gets me—like she knows exactly what I mean, even when I don't say the rest. "I know you would have," she says quietly.

And for a second, it almost feels normal. I step forward and pull her into a hug.

Her arms wrap tight around my back immediately—like she knew I needed it before I did. The familiar scent of coconut shampoo drifts from her hair, and I close my eyes, breathing it in. But the knot in my stomach only tightens. Because even with the fresh paint and the baby clothes and the promise of a new life filling this room, I still remember what it was before.

The same four walls I slept between for months. The same quiet that followed every fight with Lauren. Except now it's worse. Now it feels like defeat.

"This room is beautiful," I manage, but my voice sounds rough even to me. "You guys did a great job."

"Thank you." Mavis exhales softly against my chest. Then she leans back and looks up at me. Her green eyes shine in the soft nursery light—identical to mine, but steadier somehow. "The new guest room is down the hall," she says gently. Then she sniffles. "I'm so sorry this is happening to you, Mitch."

I shrug, but it feels less like a shrug and more like my shoulders collapsing under the weight of everything. "Me, too," I say quietly. "A lot of it's my own fault, though."

The words hang between us as I step out of the nursery and walk down the hallway. The guest room door creaks when I push it open. I flip on the light. And there it is. My old queen bed. Waiting for me like nothing ever changed. Like the last few weeks didn't just blow apart.

"Sorry," Mavis says. "They're the same sheets you don't like." She sits on the edge of the mattress and pats the space beside her. "Sit."

I drop down beside her, the mattress bouncing under my weight as I scoot back. For a moment neither of us says anything. She studies me the way she always has—like she's looking past the surface and straight into whatever mess I'm trying to hide. And finally, she exhales.

"Look," she says carefully. "I know I'm probably the last person who should be asking you this." Her eyes widen a little, like she's bracing herself. "But Mitch... if you love Lauren as much as you say you do..." She wrinkles her nose. "...why'd you do what you did with Tess?"

Heat floods my face instantly. I stare down at my hands, rubbing my palms together like that might somehow wipe the memory away. "It's hard to explain," I mutter.

"Try anyway," she says softly. No judgment. No edge. Just... Mavis.

I drag a hand through my hair and shove the mess behind my ears. "I don't know, Mavs," I say with a frustrated breath. "I honestly don't have the right words."

I lean forward, bracing my elbows on my knees. "I was pissed at Lauren after she blew me off for Miguel," I say. "Then the next day I ran into Tess at the hardware store." I shrug helplessly. "We started laughing about some stupid joke. Next thing I knew I was helping her paint her bathroom."

I slap my palms against the mattress. "I swear, I don't even know how it happened. One minute we were arguing and splattering paint everywhere." I shake my head. "And the next minute we were kissing."

"Mitch." Mavis groans, shooting me a look.

"I know," I say quickly. "Trust me, I know. I'm not defending it. It was stupid. It was wrong." I rub the back of my neck, the memory making my skin burn. "She just... caught me off guard," I admit quietly. "She showed me this side of herself I never expected." I shrug again. "And suddenly we were talking about things we actually had in common."

Mavis stares at me like I've grown another head. "You've spent your entire life hating her," she says. "I just don't understand."

I let out a dry, humorless laugh. "And you think I do?"

She bites her lip, thinking. Really thinking. Then something shifts behind her eyes. "I'm not saying what you did was right," she says quickly, rolling her eyes. "And I'm definitely not giving you a pass..." She leans over and grabs my hand, squeezing it hard. "But... I kinda do understand."

She taps a finger lightly against her chest. "Because I've had feelings for more than one person at the same time, too."

Something clicks quietly in my head. A small, uncomfortable realization. Because yeah, she probably understands more than anyone else would. I watched her struggle play out between what she felt for Josh and Austin.

"Mavs," I say softly, shaking my head. "I know you loved Austin. And Josh. But I don't love Tess. I never have. And I never will." The words come out firm. Certain. "But..." I swallow. "I did feel *something* for her."

That's the part that still twists my gut.

"And that scares the hell out of me," I admit and stare down at the carpet. "Because I don't want anyone else but Lauren. I know that in my bones. In my soul. But Tess kind of filled this... hole in my chest," I say quietly. "Ever since Lauren and I started drifting." I shake my head slowly. "It just felt good to be wanted again."

Mavis nods slowly. "I get it," she says as her voice softens. "I know what it's like to feel torn in two..." Her words trail off, her eyes widening slightly like a realization just landed in her brain.

I drag in a slow breath, filling my lungs until my chest aches. A small, tired smile tugs at my mouth as I look at her. "Well... you got through it," I say. "Any advice?"

Because I sure as hell have no idea what to do.

She tilts her head, studying me with those deep green eyes we share. The same stubbornness. The same heart. But somehow she always sees clearer than I do.

"I had to admit some things to myself first," she says quietly. "Things I fought for a long time. Things I denied." She shrugs a little. "But once I finally did that..." She holds my gaze. "...the truth was easy to follow."

Before I can say anything, she leans forward and presses a soft kiss to my forehead. But it catches me off guard—the familiarity of it. Because it's the same way she did on the night we lost our parents. Back when everything was breaking and she pulled me close, anchoring me with that one small, steady gesture. Back when I didn't have to pretend I was okay.

For a second, I'm right back there—grief thick in my chest, her hand warm against my skin, reminding me I wasn't alone. And somehow, sitting here now, it feels exactly the same.

"Goodnight, Mitch." She stands and walks toward the door.

"Josh is going to be mad that I came back here with you when he gets home," I mutter.

She glances back over her shoulder and smiles. "Let me handle Joshua. You've got your own problems to sort through, big brother." She winks, then slips into the hallway.

The door clicks shut behind her, and the quiet sound sends a strange shiver down my spine as her footsteps echo down the stairs. But her words stay with me. *Admit some stuff to myself first.*

I fall back onto the bed, the mattress bouncing beneath me as my head sinks into the pillow. I stare at the ceiling for a long moment before closing my eyes and letting out a slow breath. "Admit some stuff to myself first," I whisper, testing the words.

My mind drifts immediately back to Vegas. To the hotel room. To the heat of Lauren's skin beneath my hands. To the way the truth spilled out of us like a dam had finally broken. No filters. No pride. Just two people admitting everything they were afraid to say out loud.

We made so many promises that night. And neither one of us lived up to any of them. "What the hell went wrong so fast?" I ask the scratchy pillowcase. And for a moment there's nothing but silence. Then something quiet inside me starts whispering back.

We agreed to change. To grow up. To build something better than the two stupid kids who got married there seven years ago.

I sigh into the pillow as my heart starts thudding harder in my chest. "But what did I actually change?" I whisper.

The answer lands immediately.

Nothing.

My eyes snap open and I push myself upright on the edge of the bed. "All I did was ask you to change…"

My pulse jumps, thudding harder with every second. Blood rushes through my ears as the truth keeps pushing its way forward whether I want it to or not.

I stand and start pacing the small room, dragging my bare feet across the carpet. "I asked you to give up your restaurant," I say out loud. But the words sound worse when they're spoken. "Your dream. Your livelihood. The thing you built from nothing."

I stop in front of the full-length mirror on the back of the door. The man staring back at me looks like he finally understands something he should've figured out a long time ago. "And what did I give you in return?"

My reflection doesn't answer. Because we both know. "All I did was say I'd maybe see a doctor."

The words hit harder the second time. *Maybe.* Not even full. Just the idea of one.

I drop my hands to my hips and shake my head slowly, embarrassed by the guy looking back.

"That's... not a trade," I mutter. "That's not even close."

Vegas flashes through my mind again—Lauren's voice thick with emotion, her eyes glassy but hopeful as she talked about changes. About what we needed to fix. About what she was willing to sacrifice to make it work.

And me? I swallow hard. Because I let her carry almost all of it.

"All I want is you, Peaches," I whisper into the quiet room. "All I want is us."

The words feel heavier now. More honest.

"And I mean it this time." I press my palms against the dresser and lower my head. "I'll do whatever it takes to find the future we talked about."

Downstairs, the front door opens. Josh's voice drifts up through the floorboards. "Mavs?" A second later his familiar nickname for her follows. "Duchess?"

I hear Mavis answer him, her voice softer now, and a small smile touches my mouth despite everything. "You guys figured it out," I whisper. "You found your second chance."

I exhale slowly. "Now it's my turn." *You're right, Mavs.* The truth *is* easy to follow once you admit where you screwed up.

My phone buzzes suddenly against my leg. I reach into my pocket and pull it out. But my stomach tightens as I open the message.

Tess: I gave your wife something to think about tonight... and it may have just saved your marriage. You're welcome.

I wrinkle my nose, completely thrown. Then I toss the phone onto the bed and collapse face-first into the mattress. "What did you do, Tess?" I mutter into the pillow.

Downstairs, Josh and Mavis's voices fade as they move

deeper into the house. A few moments later, everything goes quiet. The whole place settles into silence. Except for the steady pounding of my heart.

I stare at the wall in the dark. "How could you—of all people—save my marriage?" I whisper. The thought lingers there, uncomfortable and complicated. Because for all the ways Tess helped me screw things up... she also forced me to see something I'd been too stubborn—and too proud—to look at before.

And for the first time in weeks, I feel something close to gratitude for the woman who helped me make the biggest mess of my life.

***

I drag my hand over the top of my head out of habit—and come up with nothing. For a second my fingers keep searching, like they expect to find the familiar weight of my long hair. Instead there's only short, bristly fuzz. I glance up at the rearview mirror and widen my eyes at the stranger staring back at me.

Eight inches of hair. Gone. Left on the barbershop floor like some kind of symbolic offering.

The truck's air-conditioning hums, and a cool draft slips across the back of my newly bare neck. I shiver. Turns out my hair did more work than I gave it credit for.

My phone pings in the cup holder and my sister's name lights up the screen.

Mavis: I'm at a picnic table right outside Sandy's Surf and I put our order in. Where are you?

"Running late," I say under my breath, typing back one-handed.

Me: Be there in ten.

I pull onto the highway and head toward the beach, the truck rattling softly around me. For a few miles it's just the road, the hum of the tires, and the quiet in my cab. But quiet has a way of letting things in. And Mavis's voice from last night creeps back into my head. *I had to admit some stuff to myself first. But once I did that, the truth was easy to follow.*

I sigh and flick on my turn signal, easing off the highway. Right turn. Then another left. The ocean air sneaks in through the vents as I roll into the lot near Sandy's Surf.

I shift into park and glance at the mirror one more time. The haircut still looks weird. But maybe that's the point. I push the door open, hop down, and head toward the beach.

Mavis sits under a striped umbrella with baskets of food spread out in front of her. When I drop into the seat across from her, her arm freezes midair—a cheese fry suspended halfway to her mouth. The cheese slowly drips off the end and lands on her sandwich, but her eyes stay locked on my head.

My cheeks heat as I reach up and adjust the umbrella, tilting it so the shade falls across her shoulders. "You can stop staring," I say.

"Mitch..." She leans forward, eyes wide, and then a grin spreads across her face. "Your hair is *gone*." She bursts into giggles, shoving the cheese fry into her mouth. "I've never seen you with short hair before!"

I drop my gaze to the sand and grin. "Neither have I," I admit. "At least not since I left the Navy." I rub the back of my neck again, suddenly self-conscious. "Does it look stupid?"

She laughs and shakes her head. "No! I think it looks great." She nudges a basket toward me. "You're a new man. What made you do it?" she asks.

I shrug. "Tess suggested it."

The shift in her expression is immediate. The smile slips right off her face as she grabs her water bottle and twists the cap. "Oh."

I roll my eyes and pull the burger basket closer, peeling the tomato off the top. "Hey." I drop the tomato onto her plate and nudge her hand with mine. "I didn't do it because she asked me to. I did it because you got me thinking last night."

"Oh?" She pops the tomato into her mouth like a challenge.

I nod slowly, the words still settling into place in my own head. "You said you had to admit some stuff to yourself before you could move on. Remember?"

A small smirk tugs at the corner of her mouth. "I did."

"Yeah." I exhale through my nose. "Well… it made me realize something."

"What's that?"

I stare at the table for a moment before the words finally come. "That…" I drag a hand over my scalp and shake my head. "All I've really done is ask Lauren to change. Change how she acts. Change what matters to her." I let out a short breath that almost sounds like a laugh. "Hell—I basically asked her to change who she was." I grimace and pick at a fry. "And the worst part?" I glance back up at her. "I've been making those demands while not being willing to change a damn thing about myself."

Mavis tilts her head, studying me like she's deciding whether I've finally lost my mind. "Mitch," she says slowly, "that's… actually really self-aware."

I snort as she takes a bite of her burger, chewing thoughtfully before pointing it at me. "No, seriously," she says. "That's big."

I drop my gaze to the table. "Yeah," I mutter. "I mean… it's just a haircut," I say with a small shrug. "But it's also kind of not." I drag my hand over my scalp again, still getting used to the feeling. "It felt like… I don't know. A place to start."

Mavis inhales sharply and straightens. She slides her sunglasses up onto her head and reaches across the table, squeezing my hand. "I'm really proud of you, Mitch."

I snicker. "You're the one dropping wisdom bombs, kid."

Her eyes suddenly well with tears, the golden flecks in them catching the sunlight. She shakes her head and laughs through it. "I'm sorry! I can't do anything without crying anymore!" She wipes at her cheeks and sniffles.

I grin and grab my burger, taking a bite as the salty grease hits my tongue in the best possible way. I lean back and let my gaze wander toward the beach. Thirty feet away, the old volleyball courts stretch across the sand, the net swaying gently in the breeze. We spent half our childhood out here. Endless summers. Sunburned shoulders. I shake my head at the memories.

"Mavs," I say, gesturing toward the courts with my burger. "We've come a long way, you and me."

But the words feel heavier than they sound. Because two years ago, we weren't sitting at the same table like this. We weren't laughing over burgers and cheese fries. We weren't trading advice like we actually trusted each other. We were apart for so many years...

I smile a little wider. "Feels kind of full circle, doesn't it?"

Her breath catches. Mavis drops her chin into her palms as tears spill through her fingers, her shoulders shaking.

"Especially you," I add softly.

"Mitch, stop." She groans, sucking in a breath as she fans her face with both hands. "Are you trying to make me sob like a fool right now?"

I grin, but something in my chest loosens at the same time—like a knot finally slipping free. A weight lifts and drifts off with the breeze toward the ocean.

Just then a volleyball rolls past our table, bouncing across the sand. One of the teenagers from the court chases after it toward the water's edge. And suddenly a single memory slams into me.

"Hey," I say, pointing toward the courts. "Do you remember the day I hit Tess in the head with a volleyball?"

Mavis presses a hand to the side of her belly and winces and I lean forward immediately. "Hey—are you okay?"

She nods quickly. "Cramp." She exhales and shifts in her seat, then glances back toward the courts with a small snort.

"That's actually the same day I found out I was pregnant."

My burger freezes halfway to my mouth. A drop of ketchup falls back onto the plate.

"Talk about full circle," she mutters, dragging her hand slowly across the curve of her belly.

I set the burger down and let out a long breath. "If I haven't said it before," I say, pointing toward her stomach, "I'm really proud of you." My voice softens. "This can't be easy after... everything."

Her sunglasses slide off her head and land on the table as another sob escapes her. She wipes at her cheeks with both hands, shaking her head. "I try not to think about it. But I can't help but wonder what the first one would've—"

I lean across the table and grab her hands before she can finish. "You were dealt a really shitty hand," I say firmly. "And you fought your way back anyway." I nod toward her belly. "This sweet little girl—my niece—is going to be loved more than she'll ever understand. And she's going to have two incredible parents who were meant to bring more love into this world."

Her breath catches again as she nods, head tipping forward. She wipes her cheeks against her shoulders and sniffs. "I love you, Mitch," she mumbles, dragging the back of her hand under her nose.

My chest tightens a little. "Love you, too." I grab a cheese fry and toss it into my mouth, chewing as I drop my hand to the bench beside me. My fingers trace the deep gouge carved into the wood before I glance back up at my sister.

She shifts in her seat, and the change is immediate. Her shoulders stiffen, her mouth tightening like she's trying to breathe through something sharp.

I lean forward. "You, okay?"

"Yeah... I think so." She presses a hand to the small of her back and exhales slowly. "I just keep getting these really sharp cramps."

"Did you tell Josh?"

"Yeah," she says quickly. "He says it's normal. Just the baby moving around and running out of real estate."

I snort and take another bite of my burger. "How many weeks are you now?"

"Thirty-five." She pauses, thinking. "Wait—no. Thirty-six tomorrow."

"Getting close."

Mavis inhales and settles both palms over the curve of her belly. "I can't believe I actually have to birth a ba—" But the sentence shatters. The air rips out of her lungs like someone punched her in the stomach. Her back snaps rigid and her eyes go wide.

"What?"

She pushes herself to her feet so fast the bench scrapes across the sand. Then I see it. The wood beneath her is soaked.

"Oh my, God, Mitch!" Her voice cracks, panic slicing through every word as her breaths come short and frantic. "My water just broke!"

Everything around me goes still. The breeze off the ocean disappears. The volleyball game in the distance fades into silence. The entire beach freezes like someone hit pause. But my brain refuses to catch up. I blink at her. "I'm sorry—what?"

"My water broke, Mitch!"

Adrenaline detonates in my chest and I jump to my feet. "Uh—what do I do?" I choke out, my hands hovering uselessly in the air. "What do I do, Mavs?"

"Take me to the hospital!" she cries, yanking her purse off the table and launching it at my chest. "And call Josh!"

"Okay. Okay." My body finally remembers how to function. I rush around the table and wrap an arm around her waist. But my brain is still a full step behind my legs as we stumble toward my truck. I yank open the passenger door and she climbs in awkwardly, breathing fast as she fumbles with the seatbelt.

Her eyes meet mine. And all I see is pure terror. "It's too

early," she whispers, voice shaking. "It's too early." Tears spill down her cheeks as her hands move instinctively across her stomach.

I grab her fingers and squeeze them hard. "You have the best doctor in the entire state of California," I tell her, forcing confidence into my voice even though my heart pounds like a drum. I slam the door shut and sprint around the front of the truck. "And the fastest driver you've ever known," I add as I throw myself into the driver's seat.

The engine roars to life. I grab her hand, and with the other, slam the truck into gear—and the tires squeal as we tear out of the parking lot.

CHAPTER TWENTY-FOUR

Lauren

I slide into the aisle seat beside Casey and Austin and shove my bag beneath the seat in front of me. The cabin buzzes with the low hum of boarding passengers as flight attendants swing the overhead bins shut one by one.

I power off my phone and drop it into my purse with a tired sigh. "Thanks again for letting me crash at your place for a few days," I mumble.

Casey squeezes my hand. "You and Mitch just need a little space."

Do we, though?

The question lands like a stone in my stomach. Because what if Tess is right? What if I'm considering throwing away the best thing that ever happened to me? Maybe I should be home trying to fix things. Maybe I should be standing in our kitchen right now, forcing Mitch to talk to me until we figure out what the hell went wrong again. Maybe I should be fighting for my marriage instead of climbing onto a plane and pretending distance will magically solve anything.

And yet here I am. Running away.

The memory from yesterday's nightmare of a baby

shower hits before I can stop it. Mitch standing in the living room. The way his shoulders sagged when I followed my brothers out the door. The way his eyes tracked me across the room—like he was watching something fragile slip through his fingers and knew he couldn't catch it.

Lauren, please... He hadn't said the words out loud. But the plea was there. Sitting silent in his eyes. Raw and unguarded.

For a second I almost stayed. For a second I almost walked back to him. But I didn't. Instead, I walked out the door and told myself space was the responsible thing to do.

Overhead, the intercom crackles. "Hey there, folks, this is your captain speaking. Welcome aboard flight seven-eighty-nine en route to Chicago..."

But the rest of his announcement dissolves into a low, distant hum. I don't catch a single word. Because the truth settles deeper in my chest with every passing second. I really shouldn't be here.

My head throbs, the dull ache of last night's beer still sloshing behind my eyes. The recycled cabin air presses in on me, tightening my temples and turning my stomach sour. Tess's voice floats through my memory. *You're about to throw him away. And if you do? I won't hesitate to pick up the pieces.*

At first, I brushed her off. But sitting here now, trapped in this narrow seat with nowhere to run from my own thoughts, the words echo louder. Because do I really want to leave Mitch? Even after what he did. Even after what *I* did. Do I still want out?

My thoughts turn to Pier Ninety-two next. To the endless hours. To the way Mitch's face fell every time I stayed late. To the way our life slowly shrank around the restaurant until there was barely any room left for *us*.

I press my palms into my thighs as I come to the conclusion that something has to give. Because this—this constant spinning, this constant pushing—it's not working.

With a long breath, I sink deeper into the seat. Outside the window the ground crew moves like ants beneath the wing. The plane shudders slightly as the engines wake up.

I stare at the aisle in front of me as Pier Ninety-two flashes through my mind again. The first cocktail served. The first dinner rush. The first night a table of strangers left smiling with full bellies.

For years that place was everything. My dream. My pride. Proof that I could build something real. But right before it burned… it was something else. A time drain. A financial black hole. An endless list of fires to put out—even before the literal one.

I squeeze my eyes shut. Because the truth begins to form somewhere deep in my chest. Slow. Uncomfortable. Unavoidable. *What if the restaurant isn't the dream anymore?*

My eyes open as the thought startles me. Because once it appears, it refuses to disappear. What if the fire didn't just destroy a building? What if it gave me an exit?

My pulse quickens as the idea creeps in slowly, like a door cracking open in a dark room. What if I don't rebuild? What if I stop fighting so hard to hold on to something that's been slowly draining the life out of me? What if… I sell it? The thought settles into my chest. Heavy. Terrifying. But strangely… steady. Like a truth that's been waiting months for me to admit it.

I turn toward my brother. "Hey, Austin?"

He leans forward slightly. "Hmm?"

The question sits on the tip of my tongue, electric and fragile. "Can I sell Pier Ninety-two?"

The plane begins reversing from the gate just as Austin's eyes widen. "Come on," he scoffs. "Knock it off. You don't mean that."

But that's just it. I think I finally, actually might.

"I do, though," I say quietly. The words feel strange leaving my mouth, but something inside me settles the moment they do. Like a decision that's been waiting for permission finally got it.

"Is this because of everything that happened yesterday?" Casey asks.

The plane pauses on the runway and the intercom clicks again. "Flight attendants, please prepare for takeoff."

"Not entirely." I shake my head as the engines roar to life. "It's because of me, too."

The aircraft surges forward, pressing us back into our seats as it races down the runway. My heart pounds in the same rhythm. Because maybe this isn't about running away. Maybe it's about finally letting go…

The aircraft lifts into the sky, revealing the Los Angeles skyline glittering in the afternoon sun. Skyscrapers flash with familiar light. The shoreline curves along the horizon before the city begins to shrink beneath the clouds.

I squint past him, scanning the sprawling grid of streets below. Searching. For the place that defined the last several years of my life. The place that burned to the ground. Pier Ninety-two.

"But you love that restaurant, Lauren," Austin says slowly, still staring out the window. "Why would you want to sell it?"

I shrug, but my chest tightens. "I *did* love it." For years it was everything. My dream. My pride. Proof that I could build something real with my own two hands. But lately…

"But lately it's become…" I trail off, searching for the right words. Because what *has* it become? I close my eyes and sigh. "A time drain. A financial headache. An endless to-do list." My fingers twist together in my lap.

Austin and Casey both turn toward me now. Fully listening.

"I feel like my entire identity became Pier Ninety-two," I continue. "And when it burned down…" The words fade. Because maybe that fire didn't just destroy a building. Maybe it burned away the illusion, too. "Maybe it was a sign," I say quietly. "Like the universe gave me an out."

Casey's brows pull together.

"I didn't see it at first, but it hurt my marriage, too," I continue. "All the time I spent there—it hurt Mitch. He tried to tell me how much it consumed me." I swallow, the realization settling heavier in my chest. "I just didn't want to see it."

"But you just got the insurance check to rebuild," Casey says carefully. "Can you even sell it?"

I look at Austin. Because now we're right back to the question that started this. "Austin," I say again, steadier this time. "From a legal perspective, can I sell Pier Ninety-two? Just... cut my losses?"

The plane jolts slightly as it hits a pocket of turbulence.

Austin exhales and rubs the back of his neck. "Well... if you're really serious about it."

"I am." Because it's time to let it go. I see it now.

Austin studies me. "Then I guess you have two options." He kneads the back of his neck, a crease forming between his brows. "Damn, Lauren... are you sure?" He watches me like he's trying to X-ray my heart, searching for hesitation.

But before I can answer, Casey jabs him in the thigh. "Stop second-guessing her, you goon."

"I'm just surprised!" he says, nudging her back. "This feels like it's coming out of left field. I don't want her jumping into something this big because of what happened yesterday."

"I know." I sigh and glance between them. "I know it looks like a rash decision. But it isn't. Or at least... it doesn't feel like one."

Austin tilts his head. "And this isn't about Mitch?"

"No." I press my palm lightly against my chest. "This is about me." That part feels important to say out loud. But the truth nudges its way in anyway. "I mean... I won't pretend Mitch isn't part of it," I admit. "If there's even a tiny chance we can figure things out... this might help."

Austin nods slowly. "All right," he says. "Then here's the deal." The plane hums steadily as we climb higher into the sky. "You can take the insurance money, rebuild the restaurant, and then sell it. That'll take longer, but you'll make your money back. Probably turn a profit, too." He pauses. "Or you sell the land exactly as it is now. Burned lot and all. You'll take a financial hit, but the property changes hands a lot faster."

I swallow as pressure builds in my ears. "So… which one is better?"

Austin shrugs. "Depends what matters more to you," he says. "The money… or the time."

Casey sighs beside me and lowers the tray table just as the beverage cart rattles down the aisle. The flight attendant stops with a bright, practiced smile. "Can I offer you something to drink?"

"Water, please," I say.

She fills the plastic cup while Casey and Austin order their drinks.

I sink deeper into my seat, staring at the condensation sliding slowly down the side of the cup. *What's the better choice?* Mom and Dad helped me build Pier Ninety-two. I owe them that money back.

But then there's Mitch. Maybe the smartest thing to do is unload it as fast as possible and walk away. Give myself space to figure out who I am without it. Try to salvage what's left of my marriage.

And then there's Miguel. He gave years of his life to that place, too. He stood beside me through the late nights and broken equipment and staffing disasters. He kept the kitchen running when everything else felt like it was falling apart.

And what have I done since the night he kissed me? Avoided him. Dodged his calls. Pretended I'd "get back to him soon." Because talking to him meant admitting the truth. It meant addressing my feelings—and his. It meant admitting I might be walking away.

My stomach twists. Because he deserves a conversation. Hell… he deserves more than that.

For a fleeting second another thought flickers through my mind. *Would he want it?* Could Miguel take over the place? Run it himself? The idea sparks something strange in my chest—something that feels almost… right. I chew on a cube of ice until a shiver ripples through me.

"You, okay?" Casey asks.

"I will be," I say softly. Because the decision settles into place piece by piece. And the more we talk about it—the more it feels like the truth. "I just need a little time to think." A yawn sneaks up on me before I can stop it and exhaustion crashes over the adrenaline that's been carrying me all day.

"Sweet dreams then," Casey whispers. She shifts slightly, and I let my head tip against her shoulder, nestling into her soft blonde curls as sleep drags me under.

But my mind doesn't rest. It runs. Memories churn beneath the surface, twisting together until they blur into something darker. Mitch stands in front of me. His mouth moves, shouting something I can't hear. Because his voice is swallowed by the roar behind him.

Flames. Pier Ninety-two burns like a funeral pyre, the wooden beams cracking and collapsing as black smoke billows into the sky. Heat ripples through the air. Windows explode. The familiar neon sign flickers once before shattering into sparks.

Mitch reaches for me through the chaos. But I can't move. My feet are rooted to the pavement as the restaurant—the place I built, the place I sacrificed everything for—collapses inward. Then he points frantically toward the fire.

I squint through the smoke. And that's when I see it. A small wooden rocking horse. Handmade. The one Mitch sketched out on graph paper and stuffed in his wallet. Now it sits inside the burning restaurant. Flames crawl up its legs. The wood blackens. Splits. Crumbles. Then it collapses into glowing embers and something inside my chest shatters with it.

"Mitch!" I scream. But the fire swallows everything…

"Lauren."

A voice pulls me upward.

"Lauren, wake up."

My eyes snap open as the plane slows on the runway.

"You've been out for hours," Casey whispers. "I didn't want to wake you, but we just landed."

Sunlight floods through Austin's window, bright and blinding. I suck in a sharp breath and press a hand to my chest because my heart hammers. And sweat trickles down the back of my neck as another shiver tears through me. For a moment, the dream lingers—the flames, the smoke, the look on Mitch's face.

"Are you okay?" Casey touches my forehead and immediately recoils. "Lauren, you're burning! Do you feel sick?"

My pulse pounds wildly as I try to shake the nightmare loose. "No, I'm fine," I croak. "I just... had a really bad dream."

"You're pale," Austin mutters, leaning forward to study me. "You're not about to puke or anything, are you?"

My brain struggles to catch up with reality. Chicago. The plane. The dream dissolving like smoke. But the feeling it left behind doesn't fade as quickly. A hollow ache lingers in my chest, the kind that makes everything feel strangely distant—like I've been dropped into the world a few inches outside of my own life. The fire, Mitch's voice, the burning rocking horse... all of it still clings to me, leaving a quiet emptiness in its wake. For a moment, I feel oddly alone, like something important slipped away while I was sleeping.

I clear my throat and reach for my purse between my feet, grounding myself in the small movement. "No," I mumble. "I'm okay. Just a bad dream."

The plane rolls slowly toward the gate as the captain welcomes us to O'Hare. I pull my phone from my bag and power it on. And it immediately begins to ping.

Austin's and Casey's phones light up at the same time.

"What the hell?" Austin frowns. "Do you guys have a bunch of missed calls, too?"

"Oh my, God!" Casey gasps, shoving her phone toward him. "It's Mavis! She went into labor!"

I stare down at my screen. Missed calls. Texts. All from

Mitch. Then my stomach drops because there's also one voicemail. My thumb trembles as I tap it and lift the phone to my ear.

"Peaches… please answer me." His voice is frantic. "Mavs went into labor. Her water broke while we were at lunch. She's scared. I'm scared. And I don't know what to do."

Every word lands like a punch to my ribs. Because I picture him pacing the hospital hallway. Running his hands through his hair. Looking for me. The way he always has.

"I know you're mad at me and everything is a fucking mess right now… but can you please meet me at the hospital?" he continues. "We all need you right now." His voice breaks slightly. "*I* need you."

Something inside me cracks open. Because for the last twenty-four hours I've been convincing myself distance was the right choice. That leaving was responsible. That space would help. But hearing him like this—scared, vulnerable, asking for me… It hurts in a place so deep I can barely breathe. And then he says the words that undo me completely. "I love you."

Silence fills the line. The voicemail ends. And I slowly lower the phone from my ear. But my vision blurs. Because suddenly the dream makes sense. The fire. The rocking horse. Everything burning while I stood there doing nothing.

My chest rises and falls in sharp, shaky breaths as adrenaline floods my system. Then I look at Casey and Austin. "We have to turn around," I say. "We have to go home." I grab my bag and stand, my pulse racing as the truth slams into me with absolute clarity. "I have to go home."

Because suddenly nothing else matters. Not the restaurant. Not the distance. Not the pride that sent me running in the first place. But because Mitch needs me. And maybe—finally—I'm ready to admit I need him, too. I need *us*. No matter what that looks like anymore.

CHAPTER TWENTY-FIVE

Mitch

"Mitch, wake up." Josh's voice drags me up from sleep. My eyes crack open and the dim hospital waiting room swims into focus—fluorescent lights buzzing overhead, stiff vinyl chairs, the sharp scent of antiseptic clinging to the air. For a second, my brain can't place where I am. Then yesterday slams back into me.

Mavis doubled over in pain. My panicked call to Josh. The way we tore through traffic like every red light was a personal attack. The look on my sister's face as we burst through the ER doors.

My heart jolts violently as I sit up on the tiny couch, the panic rushing back before my mind can catch up. "Is she okay?" My voice is rough with sleep and fear. "Mavs? The baby?"

Josh's face splits into the widest smile I've ever seen. The kind that changes everything.

"They're both perfect," he says quietly, clapping a hand against my shoulder. His eyes are bloodshot, dark circles carved underneath them, but they're glowing with something bright and unbelievable. "Come on. Come meet your niece."

For a second I just stare at him. Because the word "niece" echoes in my chest like a bell. My lungs finally remember how to breathe. And relief crashes through me so fast my head spins. My sister is okay. The baby is okay. No bad news.

A laugh almost escapes me as I push to my feet, adrenaline flooding my system. "I'm an uncle?" I mutter under my breath.

Josh chuckles as we head out into the quiet hallway. "You are indeed."

My pulse pounds in my ears as we walk, the hospital strangely peaceful now compared to the chaos of yesterday. But after a few steps, the memory of the baby shower creeps back in. The fight. Josh's expression when he found out about Tess. The weight of the disappointment sitting between us like a third person in the room.

"Hey, Josh?"

He slows near the elevators and glances back. "Hmm?"

I shove my hands into my pockets, suddenly feeling sixteen-years old again. "About Tess…"

Josh exhales and shakes his head before I can finish. "She doesn't mean anything," he says simply. "To either of us. Right?" His eyes lock on mine—not angry. Just steady. "You're not pursuing her. And it was a one-time mistake. Agreed?"

Two-time mistake. But that part doesn't need to live here today. So, I nod slowly and pull in a breath. "Agreed."

He studies me for another second, like he's weighing whether to push further. Then he shrugs it off. "Good," he says. "Because today's not about that." His expression softens and he punches my arm lightly. "We've got way better things to focus on."

And the knot in my chest loosens a notch.

"Nice hair, by the way," he adds over his shoulder as we keep walking.

"Oh." I drag a hand through the shorter strands, still not

used to the feel of them. "Uh… thanks."

Josh's shoes squeak against the tile as he lifts a hand toward two women behind the nurses' station.

"Congratulations, Doctor Templeton!" they call out in unison.

Josh's ears turn pink as he mutters a "thank-you" and pushes open the next set of doors, holding it for me. "So, what prompted it?" He tips his chin up, gesturing to my head.

"Umm, Lauren, actually." The words land, and something in my chest settles into place. Because even as I say it, I know it's true in a way I didn't fully understand before. Tess might've been the one who suggested it—thrown it out like it was nothing—but she wasn't the reason I followed through.

Lauren was. She's the reason I stood in front of the mirror a little longer. The reason I let the scissors take more than just length. The reason it felt like more than a haircut—like a shift. Because my hair is only the beginning of the things I'm willing to change for her.

"Oh, hey, where is she?" Josh pauses outside room two-thirteen, brow creasing slightly. "I kind of thought she'd be with you."

My stomach drops. Because the last time Lauren and I spoke flashes through my mind—sharp words, wounded looks, the voicemail I left her afterward that she still hasn't returned.

I clear my throat and pull my phone from my pocket. "I don't know," I admit. "I texted her like thirty times and left a voicemail after we got here." I glance at the screen again like it might magically light up. "Nothing."

Josh studies me for a second. "She went to Chicago then."

I blink. "Chicago?"

"Yeah," he says. "She mentioned it to Austin at the bar last night. I didn't know if she was serious."

My stomach sinks straight through the floor. Because

she left L.A. and didn't tell me. For a moment disappointment claws through my chest, sharp and heavy. But I shove it aside and force a grin.

"Well," I say, pointing toward Mavis's room, "that just means I get to be the first one to meet the new addition."

Josh grins and knocks softly before cracking the door open. "Mavs?" he says. "I found Mitch. Can we come in?"

"Yes!" she calls immediately, bright and warm, like she's been waiting for this moment.

Josh steps aside and gestures for me to go first.

The steady beep of a monitor greets me as I step into the room. For a second my eyes sweep the space—Mavis in the bed, pale but smiling, hospital blankets tucked around her.

Then my gaze follows the sound of a tiny coo. And I see her. A tiny bundle of pink wrapped tightly in Mavis's arms. The blanket rises and falls with the smallest breaths I've ever seen in my life. A soft sound escapes the swaddle—barely more than a sigh—but it hits me square in the chest.

"Come meet your niece, Uncle Mitch," Mavis whispers.

The air leaves my lungs in a slow rush. I step closer, my entire body suddenly careful, like one wrong move might disturb something sacred. I lean down and press a kiss to the top of Mavis's head, my hand coming to rest against my chest like I need to physically hold my heart in place. "Mavs," I whisper.

She tilts her head against mine for a second, the same way she used to when we were kids and she needed reassurance after a bad dream.

Josh bumps my elbow beside me, grinning like he just won the lottery.

"You guys," I whisper, staring at the tiny face peeking out of the blanket. "She's perfect. Just look at her..."

Mavis smiles, her eyes soft as she glances down at the baby. "Meet Mirabel Marie Templeton."

My breath catches because the name hits me like a wave. "Mom," I whisper as my throat tightens, tears burning behind my eyes before I can stop them. "That's... perfect,

Mavs." I shake my head in awe. "She's perfect. Mom would be so proud of you."

Tears slip quietly down Mavis's cheeks as she looks down at her daughter. And something inside my chest cracks wide open.

Mirabel squirms beneath the blanket, her tiny fingers flexing, and just like that—just from existing—she steals my heart. The dollhouse I built flashes into my mind. The tiny painted rooms. The miniature furniture waiting to be played with. I picture her toddling around it someday, giggling as she drags dolls from room to room. And suddenly the future unfolds in my chest—bright and fragile and terrifyingly beautiful.

"Do you want to hold her?" Mavis asks softly.

My grin breaks free and I head straight for the sink. "Do I have to give her back if I do?"

Josh laughs. "We'll call you at three a.m. and take turns."

I scrub my hands with the hospital soap, the clean smell filling my nose as I rinse and dry them, suddenly hyperaware of every movement. When I turn back around, Josh drags the rocking chair closer to the bed.

"Have a seat, Uncle Mitch."

I sink into the chair while he drops a pillow across my lap. Mavis carefully lifts the baby toward him, her movements slow and protective.

Josh's smile grows as he lowers the tiny bundle into my arms. "Here you go," he whispers.

The moment she touches me, everything in my chest rearranges. Instinct takes over before I can even think about it. I pull her closer to my chest and begin rocking automatically, like my body already knows exactly what to do.

She's so small. Her head barely fills my palm.

"Well, look at you," I whisper, brushing a finger across the soft tuft of dark hair on her head. "You just couldn't wait to meet me, could you?"

Her little mouth opens in a sleepy stretch, and I swear

my heart doubles in size.

Mavis giggles from the bed and reaches for her water, draining half the glass in two long gulps. "I told her about the dollhouse you built."

Josh snorts and drops onto the end of the bed, rubbing the back of his neck. "Uncle Mitch," he says, shaking his head. "Provider of fun and fast car rides." He reaches under the blanket and squeezes Mavis's ankle. "I owe you one, man. That could've been really bad if you hadn't gotten her here so fast—"

A knock interrupts him. And a nurse pokes her head through the door. "Excuse me, Doctor Templeton? Can we borrow you for a moment? Tiny emergency next door and Dr. Emmet is twenty minutes out."

Josh groans quietly but pops to his feet. "Duty calls," he mutters, leaning down to kiss Mavis's forehead before slipping out with the nurse.

The room settles into a softer quiet. I glance down again at the tiny girl sleeping against my chest, then over at my sister. "How are you?" I ask gently. "You doing okay?"

Mavis rubs her eyes and lets out a tired laugh. "I don't think exhausted is even the right word." She shifts and winces. "And I hurt in places I didn't even know existed."

"I can't imagine," I say with a grin. Then I look back down at the baby. "But I'm just glad you're okay," I add quietly. "Both of you."

Mavis's expression softens. "Thirty-six weeks to the day," she says. "Josh said they'll monitor her lungs for a little bit, but so far she's doing great." She lifts her phone and snaps a quick picture of me holding Mirabel.

"She's a fighter already," I say softly. "Just like her mom."

Mavis smiles at that. Then she tilts her head. "Hey, Mitch?"

"Hmm?"

"Thank you for yesterday." Her voice is quiet now. "I don't really know what I would've done without you."

"Mavs." I wave it off immediately.

But she shakes her head. "No. I mean it. One minute I was eating cheese fries and the next..." She shivers. "Scariest moment of my life." Her eyes flick to the baby. "But I knew you were there," she says. "And if you were there, we'd be okay."

I look down at Mirabel again. "I'd never let anything happen to either of you."

"I know," she whispers, then reaches for the locket around her neck. Her fingers toy with the silver chain, rubbing it back and forth out of habit.

"Can I tell you a secret?" I ask quietly, adjusting the blanket around Mirabel.

"Always."

"I'm glad you came home."

Mavis laughs softly. "That's not a secret. You've told me that a million times."

"Okay, fair," I admit. "Maybe that's not the secret." She raises an eyebrow and I hesitate. Then the truth slips out before I can stop it. "I want one, too."

The words land heavy in the quiet room.

Mirabel sighs in her sleep, her tiny chest rising and falling against my arm. Every breath pulls on something deep inside me—something I've been trying not to look at for months.

"Mitch," Mavis says gently. "So does Lauren."

I nod slowly. "I know." My voice drops. "It's been really hard on her." Hard on both of us. "We tried for a while... but then everything else got in the way."

"Then change the stuff," Mavis says simply.

I glance up.

"Find Lauren and tell her everything you told me the other night. Show her the changes you're ready to make." She grips the bed rail and shifts as the blood pressure cuff tightens around her arm. She rolls her eyes at it before looking back at me. "Take it from me, Mitch Benson—you can have that second chance." She pauses. "You just have to be willing to work for it."

Her words settle deep in my chest. Because the last few months have felt like a compass spinning wildly—every direction wrong, every step taking us farther away from where we used to be. But as I look down at the tiny person in my arms, I smile.

You're my north star, aren't you? Did you show up early just to point me back in the right direction?

Mirabel squirms suddenly, her tiny tongue poking out as she wakes.

I laugh quietly and stand. "I think someone's hungry, Mom." I place her gently back into Mavis's arms and kiss the top of my sister's head again. "I'll give you some privacy."

She snorts. "Like I know what I'm doing anyway."

"Want me to grab a nurse? Or Josh?"

She shakes her head, staring down at her daughter with quiet wonder. "No," she says softly. "I'll figure it out."

I smile and reach for the door. Then I pause. "Hey, Mavs?"

She looks up. "Yeah?"

"You did good, kid."

Her face melts into a smile. "Love you," she says, blowing me a kiss.

I catch it automatically and tap my chest. "Love you, too." *More than you know.*

I push through the secure doors of the maternity ward and wander down the hospital hallway, feeling strangely uncontained—like my chest has been split open and someone forgot to close it again. Because I'm an uncle now. The thought keeps circling my brain like I'm trying it on for size. *Uncle Mitch.*

I almost laugh out loud. Mirabel's tiny face flashes in my mind, her little fingers curling in the blanket, the soft sigh she made when I brushed my hand over her head. Something inside me still feels rearranged from holding her.

I reach an intersection of identical hallways and spin

slowly in place, completely disoriented. "How the hell do I get out of here?" I mutter, scanning the walls for an exit sign. I pick a direction and start walking, but a few seconds later I realize I've wandered straight into the hospital gift shop.

Through the glass I notice a wall of flowers—pink lilies, yellow daisies, pastel balloons bobbing lazily above them. I'm about to turn around when something purple catches my eye. A fuzzy nose sticking out of a toy bin. I stop. Then do a double-take. "No way…" I whisper.

I head inside, reach into the bin, and pull out the stuffed animal. And the second those little beady eyes stare back at me, a wave of nostalgia crashes through my chest. I huff out a quiet laugh at the purple dolphin.

"Hey there, Finn," I whisper. "Well… Finn Jr."

Heat creeps into my cheeks as the memory returns—Pacific Park, the basketball game, the ridiculous shot I somehow made to win it. Lauren's face when I tossed her the dolphin. The way she hugged the thing like I'd just handed her the moon.

For a second I swear I can still see her standing there, wind blowing through her hair, smiling at me like I'd done something extraordinary.

"Can I help you with anything, sir?"

I glance up to find a sweet older woman behind the counter smiling at me. I walk over and set the dolphin down. "Nope," I say. "I think I've got everything I need."

She rings it up slowly, peering at the toy. "He looks like he'll make someone very happy."

Yeah. Me. He's going to save my marriage.

"I think so, too," I say quietly. Then I nod toward the flowers behind her. "Actually… could I also send some lilies and a balloon up to room two-thirteen? My niece was just born."

Her face lights up. "Oh, how wonderful! Congratulations." She slides a small baby-girl card toward me. "First-time uncle?"

I nod, grabbing the pen and scribbling a quick message while she rings everything up. And a minute later I tuck Finn Jr. into a small gift bag and step back into the hallway. But the second the door closes behind me, my stomach tightens.

He's going to save my marriage. The words echo in my head.

"Tess," I whisper. Because her strange text from two days ago flashes through my mind. The one I never responded to. I turn and follow the signs toward the emergency exit, pulling my phone from my pocket as I walk. A few taps later, her message reappears on the screen.

Tess: I gave your wife something to think about tonight, and it may have just saved your marriage. You're welcome.

"What does that even mean?" I mutter as I push through the doors and step outside. The parking lot stretches out in front of me, quiet except for a few cars drifting in and out. I drop onto a metal bench and set Finn Jr. beside me. Then I type.

Me: I have yet to see evidence of that. Pretty sure she left for Chicago without even telling me.

I barely have time to slide my phone back into my pocket before it rings. Her name lights up the screen and I glance around instinctively before answering. "Tess?"

She exhales softly into the phone. "You know, Mitch Benson," she says, "I think we could've been really good together."

I snort. "Our entire history says otherwise."

Her laugh crackles through the speaker. "Well," she says lightly, "we'll always have the lavender bush."

A laugh escapes me before I can stop it. The sound drifts out into the morning air as the sun finally breaks through the clouds. "We'll always have the lavender bush," I repeat, running a hand over my short hair. And it's funny. Because a few weeks ago, that moment felt reckless. Now it feels like... perspective.

There's a quiet pause. Then her voice softens. "Hey, Mitch?"

"Yeah?"

"I hope you make it work with Lauren."

I go still.

"I can see how much you still love her," she continues. "And after the other night... I know how much she loves you, too."

Her words settle somewhere deep in my chest. Because she's right. That's the thing that finally became clear. Not during the endless fights. Not during any stupid kiss. Not even when Lauren walked away from me after the baby shower. It became clear when I held Mirabel. When I pictured Lauren sitting beside me someday doing the same thing.

"Tess..." I swallow. "I never should've..." I shake my head. "It was wrong. I hurt Lauren. And... I think I hurt you, too." My chest tightens as the truth settles between us. "I'm sorry."

She snorts softly. "For what it's worth... I had fun."

I smile faintly. "Yeah," I admit. "Me, too."

But that's the thing. Fun isn't the same as love. And standing in that hospital room a few minutes ago made that painfully obvious.

"Tess?"

"Hmm?"

"Can I ask you something?"

She laughs quietly. "Shoot."

I lean back against the bench and watch a car glide slowly through the parking lot. "Did I see the real you?" I ask. There's a small intake of breath on the other end. "Or were you playing me the way you play everyone else?"

Silence stretches for a moment. Then she answers. "You saw the real me," she whispers. "And you're the only one who ever will."

Something in my chest settles. Because I don't know why I believe her. But I do. And strangely... I'm grateful.

Because she didn't just show me who she is. She showed me who I don't want to be.

"Go get Lauren back, Mitch," she says softly. "Don't end up like me."

Then the call ends.

I sit there for a moment, staring at the phone in my hand. Then I lean back and close my eyes. The sun warms my face as I inhale slowly. And that's when I smell it. Lavender.

I crack one eye open and turn my head. Sure enough, a lavender bush grows right behind the bench. I shake my head and laugh quietly. Then I glance down at the gift bag beside me. At Finn Jr. At the ridiculous stuffed purple dolphin. But somehow it feels like the start of fixing everything.

"Thanks for letting me see the real you, Tess," I say softly. "Now it's my turn to fix what matters."

CHAPTER TWENTY-SIX

Lauren

The Denver airport hums with the dull, restless energy of people who've been waiting too long. Rolling announcements echo overhead. Suitcases clatter across the tile. Somewhere behind me a baby cries, sharp and insistent, while a man argues quietly with an airline agent about missed connections.

I shift deeper into the plastic chair and glance up at the departure board for what feels like the hundredth time. Los Angeles — Delayed. Again.

I exhale and rub my temples. Chicago to Miami. Miami to Denver. And now Denver refuses to let me leave. The hours have stretched long enough that the adrenaline from the past two days has finally burned off, leaving only exhaustion and a strange, hollow clarity behind. Because when you sit in an airport long enough, you run out of ways to distract yourself. Eventually you're left alone with your thoughts. And mine keep circling back to the same place.

Pier Ninety-two. The source of so much contention and friction.

I stare out across the terminal for a moment, watching a

plane taxi slowly past the windows. Austin gave me two options. Rebuild it… then sell it. Or sell the land and the brand outright. On paper, both paths make sense. Smart business decisions. Clean exits. But the more I think about them, the more wrong they feel. Because neither option actually protects the thing that matters most to me. The thing I built with my own two hands.

The restaurant itself. The life inside it. The smell of garlic and butter drifting through the dining room. The clatter of plates during a dinner rush. The quiet pride on Miguel's face every time a table sent compliments back to the kitchen. That's the part I can't sell.

I glance down at my phone resting in my hands and exhale. I know I need to call him—not just Mitch. But Miguel, too. I've been avoiding him for weeks, terrified of the words waiting on the other side of a conversation we need to share. Terrified of the truth I need to say out loud.

A shiver slips down my spine as I stare at his name glowing on my screen. This conversation should happen in person. I know that. It deserves more than a rushed phone call in an airport terminal. But my flight supposedly leaves in forty minutes, and once I land in L.A., everything changes. Because the second my feet hit the ground, I have to go to the hospital. I have to see Mavis and Josh and meet my niece.

And more than anything, I have to figure out whether my marriage still has a future. But I can't walk into that moment with Mitch carrying Pier Ninety-two with me. I can't stand in front of him with this decision still hanging in the air. I need to settle this first. Only then can I face him.

So, I stand, grab my bag, and wander toward the far end of the terminal until the noise fades into a low murmur. I find a quiet corner near an empty gate and sit, staring at the phone for another second before I press his name.

The line rings just twice before, "Lauren?" Miguel's voice comes through the speaker, surprised—like he didn't actually expect to hear from me again.

"Hi, Miguel."

There's a pause on the other end. Then he exhales. "I thought you were avoiding me."

I lean back in the stiff airport chair and stare up at the high metal ceiling above the terminal. "That's… fair."

He lets out a quiet laugh. "So, I was right."

"Yeah," I admit. "You were."

The truth settles between us without resistance. And for a moment neither of us speaks. The airport noise swells around me—rolling suitcases, boarding announcements, the dull murmur of travelers drifting through the terminal.

"Things got complicated," I say finally. "And I didn't know what I wanted to do." My words come out steadier than I expect.

"But now you do?" he asks carefully.

I nod instinctively, even though he can't see me. "Yeah," I say softly. "Now I do." I glance out the massive window beside the gate. A plane slowly pushes back from the terminal, engines whining as it begins to taxi. "I've been thinking about you," I continue.

Miguel heaves out a heavy breath, but before he can respond, a loud chime echoes through the terminal speakers.

"Attention passengers traveling to Seattle on flight 482, now boarding at gate B32…"

The announcement spills through the gate area, followed by the low noise of people standing and gathering their bags.

Miguel pauses. "Are you at an airport?"

I shift in the chair and glance around the terminal. "Umm… yeah. Denver," I say.

Miguel pauses, waiting.

"I left L.A. with Casey and Austin yesterday," I explain. "We flew to Chicago." The memory feels strange now—like it happened weeks ago. "But when we landed," I continue, "Mitch called. Mavis went into labor. So, I turned right back around and started chasing flights home," I say with a tired laugh. "Chicago to Miami. Miami to Denver. And now

Denver to L.A." I rub my forehead and sigh. "Eventually."

Miguel chuckles softly. "That sounds miserable."

"It's been a long day." Another pause settles between us as I watch a plane outside begin its slow turn toward the runway. "But before I take off again," I add gently, "there's something I need to tell you."

Miguel exhales again, heavier this time. "Okay."

"I want you to take it," I say.

Silence. Then—"Take... what?" he asks cautiously.

"Pier Ninety-two," I answer, the words feeling surreal even as they leave my lips. "I want you to take it completely. The insurance money. The rebuild. All of it. Not just as the manager—but as the owner. I think it's time I let it go."

Silence fills the line. Not the comfortable kind. The stunned kind. Then Miguel exhales sharply. "Wait—what?" he says, confusion bleeding into his voice. "Lauren, that... that doesn't make any sense."

I close my eyes, bracing myself.

"I thought you wanted to rebuild," he continues. "Like, you were already working through the insurance numbers. You were talking about expanding the kitchen..." He lets out a small, incredulous laugh. "You were making plans, Lauren. Big ones."

I swallow. "I know."

"What changed?" he asks quietly. "Did something happen?"

A long pause stretches between us. "Yeah," I say softly. "Something did."

He waits. And I know what he's waiting for. The full explanation. The fire. Mitch. Vegas. The long, sleepless hours where everything in my life started rearranging itself whether I liked it or not. But the truth is simpler than that.

I stare out the airport window at the planes idling on the runway and let the words come. "I've spent the last day really thinking about what matters to me," I say quietly. "What I actually want my life to look like."

Miguel doesn't interrupt.

"And somewhere along the way," I continue. "I realized Pier Ninety-two just… doesn't have a place in that picture anymore." The admission lands softly, but it still tightens something in my chest. "That doesn't mean it wasn't important," I add quickly. "Or that it wasn't worth everything we put into it. It was. It always will be." I pause, choosing my words carefully. "But wanting something once doesn't mean it should belong in your life forever, right?"

There's a quiet rustle on the other end of the call.

"I'm just being honest with myself now," I say. "About what I have room for. What I want to fight for." I take a breath. "And the restaurant deserves someone who still feels that pull every day." My eyes close briefly. "Someone like you."

Another long silence settles over the line. When Miguel finally speaks again, his voice is different—sharper, unsteady with disbelief. "Lauren…" he says slowly. "You can't be serious."

I don't answer right away.

"You spent years building that place," he continues, the shock growing in his voice. "You fought the city for permits. You slept in your office for three nights before opening. And that night when you got the insurance payout, you told me you were going to rebuild it bigger and better after the fire." He exhales hard. "How can you say you're just… letting it go?"

The question hangs there, heavy with everything we both know that restaurant meant. Then he laughs softly—but it's strained, almost helpless. "Lauren, I don't even know what to say."

I hear him shift on the other end of the phone, like he's pacing.

"Even if I wanted to say yes to your crazy offer," he adds after a moment, his voice dropping, "I definitely do not have the money to buy your restaurant."

"You wouldn't buy it, Miguel."

Another pause.

"I'm serious," I say, sitting forward now. "You don't need to buy it from me."

He breathes out slowly. "And what, you're just… giving it to me?"

"Yes." And the second I say it, the certainty settles fully in my chest. Because for hours I've run through every version of Austin's advice. Rebuild it and sell. Sell the land. Sell the brand. Every path ends the same way—with Pier Ninety-two becoming something hollow and unrecognizable. A transaction. But the restaurant was never supposed to be that.

"I thought about every possible option," I tell him quietly. "Every exit strategy. Every 'smart' business decision." My fingers tighten around my phone. "And none of them felt right."

I close my eyes for a moment, remembering the dining room. The kitchen. The way the whole place came alive during a dinner rush. "The only thing that felt right was letting it live," I say.

Miguel waits silently.

"I don't want to watch someone strip it down and sell the pieces," I continue. "And I don't want to rebuild it just to walk away again." My voice softens. "But you wouldn't do that."

He exhales slowly into the phone. "Boss…"

"You're the only person I trust to carry it forward," I say. "You know that restaurant better than anyone. You love it the way I used to." The words settle gently in my chest, surprising me with how right they feel. "I just want to see it succeed," I finish quietly. "And you're the only one who can make sure that happens."

Silence fills the line. Not the stunned kind from earlier—something heavier now. Thoughtful. Miguel doesn't answer right away, and for a second I glance down at the phone to make sure the call didn't drop.

Finally, he exhales. "You really mean it, don't you?" he says softly.

"Yes."

Another pause. Then his voice shifts—rougher, like something he's been holding in for a while is finally pushing its way out.

"Lauren, I've been stressing over you for weeks," he admits. "Because I didn't know where we stood." He lets out a quiet breath. "I didn't know if you were mad. Or if you were going to fire me. Or if I should just… disappear. And now you want me to take your restaurant…" His words trail away.

And my stomach twists because it's my fault. I let him suffer in the silence.

"I started bartending at Food for Thought. Just to keep busy," he adds quickly. "Just until things… settled." He lets out a bitter laugh. "And I hate it."

But the confession catches me off guard.

"Every drink I make feels like I'm betraying you," he says quietly. "Like I'm pretending Pier Ninety-two never existed." The words land heavily between us. "You built something incredible there, Lauren," he continues. "I don't know if I can just… step into your place like that."

"You're not stepping into my place," I say softly. "You're saving it." And the words feel right the second they leave my mouth. "Pier Ninety-two was never supposed to belong to just one person," I continue. "It's supposed to belong to the people who believe in it."

Miguel always did. He believed in the restaurant when the kitchen flooded. When the city inspections nearly shut us down. He believed in it even when I stopped believing in myself. And maybe that's the part I keep coming back to. Because it's the right thing to do—hand it all over to him.

It'll take time for my parents to understand why I'm choosing this path. And it will probably take me the rest of my life to pay them back. But eventually, they'll get it. Because this isn't a failure. Not really. I didn't lose the restaurant. I just learned something along the way—about who I am, and who I'm not.

"There's also something else we should probably talk about," I say, the words coming out slower than I expect. But the moment they leave my mouth, Miguel groans softly.

"Lauren… I'm so sorry."

I blink, surprised by how quickly he jumped with me—like the thought has been sitting right at the front of his mind too, waiting for this exact moment.

He exhales hard into the phone, the sound heavy with embarrassment. "I've had a lot of time to think about it," he continues quickly, talking a little too fast now. "And I was completely out of line that night."

I stare down at the carpet beneath my shoes, suddenly very aware of the people walking past in the terminal. The awkwardness thickens between us.

"I shouldn't have asked you to stay. I should have listened to you when you said you needed to get home. And Lauren, I really shouldn't have kissed you," he adds after a beat. "You're *married*."

Another pause.

"You're my boss," he says, sounding like the realization still bothers him. "Or… you were. Are. I don't even know what we are right now."

Despite everything, a small laugh slips out of me. "Yeah," I say softly. "That part's a little unclear."

"Still… I shouldn't have put you in that position," he says quietly. "And I've been kicking myself about it ever since."

I stare out through the tall airport windows, watching a plane creep slowly across the runway. "It wasn't just you," I say after a moment.

Miguel doesn't interrupt, but I can hear him listening.

"I led you on," I admit. "And I shouldn't have." The truth feels steadier now that it's finally out in the open. "I let you believe there might be something more."

The silence between us stretches, but it's not as uncomfortable as it was a few minutes ago.

"And while I do feel something for you, Miguel… it's

friendship. It's appreciation. It's admiration." I swallow, forcing the rest out gently. "But I'm committed to Mitch," I continue softly. "I'm not exactly sure what that looks like right now," I admit. "But I know I have to figure it out."

Miguel exhales slowly on the other end of the line. "I know," he says quietly. "I've always known. I guess I just let hope get in the way."

Before I can respond, another boarding announcement rolls across the terminal. I glance up at the glowing departure board. Los Angeles — Boarding Soon.

"I think that's my cue," I say, shifting forward in the stiff plastic chair as the terminal begins to stir with movement.

"Yeah," Miguel replies. "You should probably get on that plane."

There's a brief pause. Then—"Lauren?"

"Yeah?"

"Congratulations on becoming an aunt," he says warmly. "That's... pretty incredible."

My chest softens. "Thanks."

"And we'll talk soon," he adds. "About the restaurant. The rebuild. All of it."

"We will," I promise.

Another quiet beat passes.

"Take care of yourself. Safe flight, okay?"

"Thank you, Miguel."

The line clicks softly as the call ends. I lower the phone slowly and lean back in the hard plastic airport chair. For the first time in weeks, the tight knot in my chest loosens. Not gone. But lighter.

Outside the window, a plane lifts into the pale Colorado sky, its wings cutting cleanly through the morning light. And as the boarding call for Los Angeles crackles through the terminal speakers, a small, unfamiliar feeling spreads quietly through my chest. Hope.

***

I drag my suitcase across the polished hospital floor and approach the nurses' station, the wheels rattling loudly in the quiet hallway. Every step feels heavier than the last. My eyes burn. My shoulders ache. And my entire body feels like it's been wrung dry. But I'm finally here.

"Can I help you, miss?" A nurse rounds the corner holding a clipboard and drops it onto the counter with a loud clank that makes me flinch.

"Oh—umm—yes, please." I rub my eyes, trying to wake up enough to sound coherent. "I'm here to visit my new niece."

The nurse glances at the clock behind her. "I'm sorry," she says gently. "Visiting hours ended at six." She points at the wall. It's 6:15. "But we'll welcome visitors back tomorrow morning at nine."

I straighten and grip the counter. "Please—can we make an exception?" I say quickly. "I just flew across the country to get here. Three flights. Two layovers. It's just fifteen minutes."

She shakes her head apologetically. "I'm sorry."

Panic flickers through my chest. "But my brother is Doctor Templeton," I rush out. "If you could just call him—"

"Oh! You're Doctor Templeton's sister?" Her entire demeanor brightens. "I'm Wendy," she says, extending her hand over the counter. "It's so nice to finally meet you! I've heard so much about you over the years."

Relief floods my chest as I shake her hand. "I'm Lauren," I say with a tired smile.

"I'll tell you what," she says, grabbing her badge. "Let's walk down to their room and see if they wouldn't mind a late visitor."

"You're amazing," I say. And for the first time in hours, I smile. "Thank you so much."

She leads me around the corner toward the secured doors and taps her badge against the reader. "Well," she says, pushing the door open, "I can't be the one who keeps you from your new niece. She's a sweet little peanut."

My heart lifts. "That's what I heard," I say quickly, tugging my suitcase behind me. "I can't wait to meet her."

We walk down the quiet hallway until she stops outside room two-thirteen. "Doctor Templeton?" she whispers, cracking the door open.

I slip in behind her. The room is dim and quiet, the soft squeak of a rocking chair drifting through the air in a slow, steady rhythm. And then I see them. Josh and Mavis are curled together in the hospital bed, both completely asleep. His arm is draped protectively across her shoulders, her head tucked beneath his chin, like even in sleep he's making sure she's still there. The sight of them settles over the room like a kind of peace.

"Lord knows they'll need all the rest they can get," Wendy whispers as she steps back into the hall.

But I barely hear her. Because Mitch sits in the rocking chair, gently rocking a tiny pink bundle in his arms. And he looks... different.

My breath catches when I notice his hair—or rather, the lack of it. The wild, dark mess he's hidden behind for years is gone, replaced with something shorter. Cleaner. His face looks more open somehow. Younger. Like I'm seeing him clearly for the first time in years.

But that's not what stops my heart. It's the look on his face. Soft. Careful. Completely captivated. He tucks the blanket more securely around the baby and murmurs something I can't quite hear, his voice low and warm.

My chest tightens. Because I can't take my eyes off him. The slow rhythm of the chair. The careful way he holds her. The way he studies her face like she's the most extraordinary thing he's ever seen.

For a moment, I just stare. Watching him. This man I've loved. This man I've fought with. This man I ran away from. My husband.

I step forward, the floor creaking softly beneath my shoe. Mitch glances up—and something in his eyes shifts.

First surprise. Then relief. And beneath it, something deeper flickers to life, warm and unmistakable.

"Come here, Peaches," he says quietly. "Come meet your new niece."

The nickname knocks the air out of my lungs. I move closer, my gaze glued to the tiny person in his arms.

"Aunt Lauren," he whispers, "meet Mirabel Marie Templeton." He gently pulls back the blanket. And the smallest little face I've ever seen looks up at me.

"Mirabel," I whisper, my hand gripping Mitch's elbow without thinking. His skin is warm beneath my fingers. "Oh, Mitch…"

The meaning hits me instantly. "Your mom," I say, emotion swelling in my chest. I lean forward and press a soft kiss to his cheek. Then I inhale—and that's when I smell it. Pine. The familiar scent wraps around me like a memory. Like home.

My eyes close for a moment as everything settles in my chest. The hospital. The baby. Mitch beside me. *Home.* I exhale slowly and rest my hand over his.

"Welcome back," he says softly. His eyes flick toward the suitcase sitting by the door. "I didn't know you left."

Guilt twists sharply in my stomach. Because I never should have gone. I search for something—anything—to say that isn't an apology I'm not ready to unravel yet. My gaze drifts back to him, really taking him in again.

"You cut your hair," I say. My fingers lift, brushing the short strands at the back of his neck, rubbing them between my thumb and forefinger. "I barely recognize you." I sink down beside the rocking chair and rest a hand lightly on the swaddle.

"Maybe that's a good thing," Mitch says quietly.

I glance up. "And why's that?"

He studies me for a moment before answering. "You ran away from the guy you did recognize."

The words land harder than they should. The fragile peace inside my chest flickers as the truth I tried to escape waits patiently between us. "I—I wasn't running," I say, the words tripping over themselves before I can steady them.

But Mitch doesn't even look surprised. "It's okay that you did."

Mirabel sneezes in his arms—the tiniest sound—and Mitch grins as he adjusts the blanket around her.

"After what I did... and the way I behaved," he says quietly, "you had every reason to run and never look back."

I watch him glance toward the bed where Mavis and Josh sleep, like he's making sure we don't wake them.

"I thought I needed time," I say softly. "Space to think."

He nods. "Yeah. I get that."

But the truth presses forward anyway. "Mitch, we had barely boarded the plane when I regretted it."

His head lifts slightly.

"I realized we can't fix anything between us if I'm not here with you," I add.

The rocking chair creaks softly as Mitch slows, the gentle rhythm fading into the quiet room. "So," he says carefully, studying my face, "you still want to fix things?"

I nod and push myself to my feet, moving toward the sink. The faucet hisses when I turn it on. Cool water rushes over my hands as I scrub them slowly, trying to steady the storm twisting inside my chest.

"I want a redo, Mitch Benson." My voice feels stronger now, steadier than I expect. "A real redo. Everything we talked about in Vegas. Everything we promised each other."

I dry my hands with a paper towel and toss it into the trash. Then I turn back to him and our eyes meet.

For a moment he just looks at me, his expression unreadable, the weight of everything hanging quietly between us. The rocking chair shifts once beneath him as he tightens his arm around Mirabel. Then he lifts his gaze back to mine.

"No," he says.

The word lands like a rock through glass. My entire body goes still. And suddenly the room feels too quiet. Too small.

The air rushes out of my lungs like someone popped a balloon inside my chest. And before I can even process it—

"Lauren?" Josh's voice breaks through the moment. He blinks awake in the dim light and pushes himself upright in the hospital bed, rubbing his face with one hand. "When did you get here?" he croaks.

I turn toward him, forcing a smile onto my face. "Five minutes ago," I whisper. "I'm so sorry. I didn't mean to wake you guys."

Mavis stirs beside him, her eyes fluttering open as she exhales a long, tired breath.

Josh presses a gentle kiss to her forehead before carefully climbing out of the bed, adjusting the pillows behind her so she can sit up more comfortably.

"What took you so long?" he asks with a tired grin. Then he pulls me into a tight hug, squeezing me against his chest. "It's not every day you get a new niece, you know."

I laugh, but it comes out weak and breathy. "Three connecting flights and two layovers," I say, shaking my head. "I can't believe I missed it." My eyes drift past him toward the bed. "Mavs, how are you doing?" I ask gently. "Are you okay, sweetie?"

Mavis drags her hair over one shoulder, beginning to braid it with slow, sleepy fingers. "I didn't know what tired meant before today," she says hoarsely.

My heart squeezes. "And here I am waking you up."

"No, no—it's okay," Josh says, glancing down at his phone to check the time. "Mirabel will need to eat soon anyway."

Almost as if she understands, the baby in Mitch's arms lets out a soft coo that quickly turns into a tiny protest. Mitch chuckles quietly and stands, carefully lifting the tiny bundle from his lap. He carries her over to the bed and places her gently into Mavis's arms.

"We'll give you guys some privacy," he says softly. "See you tomorrow, okay? Call if you need anything."

Mavis lets out a small, exhausted sob as Mirabel's cries

grow louder.

"I know you were kidding about that three a.m. shift," she sniffles, tugging clumsily at the ties of her hospital gown. "But I'm not."

Josh laughs under his breath and presses another kiss to the top of her head before adjusting the pillow across her lap. His eyes are red with exhaustion when he looks back at us. "They won't let you in at three," he says, "but they'll definitely let you in at nine."

"We'll be here," I promise. Then I grab my suitcase and follow Mitch into the hallway.

The exhaustion from the last twenty-four hours crashes into me all at once. My eyes burn. My shoulders ache from hours wedged into airplane seats. My chest feels too full—happy for them, overwhelmed by the tiny miracle we just witnessed... and painfully aware of the quiet, fragile mess waiting between Mitch and me. Joy and grief sit side-by-side inside my ribs. And I don't know which one I'm supposed to feel more.

"Come with me, Peaches." Mitch reaches for the handle of my suitcase. His other arm slides around my waist, guiding me down the quiet hospital hallway. "There's something I want to show you."

My tennis shoes squeak against the polished floor as we pass through the secured doors and head toward the main entrance. The hallway is quiet—too quiet for everything unraveling inside my chest.

I keep my eyes fixed straight ahead, like if I don't look at him I won't have to see whatever decision he's already made. But my stomach twists tighter with every step and I find my mouth opening. "What do you want to show me?" I ask, the words coming out thin with exhaustion and nerves. "A fresh stack of divorce papers?"

He stops so abruptly I nearly trip. "What?"

I turn back and find him frozen mid-step, staring at me like I just said something completely absurd.

"Why would you say that?" he asks.

Because you just told me no. You told me you didn't want what we agreed on in Vegas.

I lift my eyes to his face and see the confusion tightening his mouth. "Isn't that what you want?" I ask, shaking my head as I try to clear the haze. "You just told me you didn't want what we agreed on in Vegas."

For a moment he just looks at me. Then he inhales slowly—and the frown disappears, replaced by the faintest smile. "You're right," he says quietly. "I don't want that."

Before I can react, he steps closer and grips my waist, pulling me gently toward him. The overhead lights dim slightly as we stand in the empty hallway. Somewhere behind the walls, an elevator clanks as it descends. But all I can hear is my heartbeat.

Mitch's eyes lock onto mine as he leans closer, his hands tightening at my hips. Heat radiates through his fingertips, sending a slow burn through my entire body.

"Then what do you want?" I whisper.

He leans closer, his mouth hovering just inches from mine. His warm breath brushes my skin, and my eyes fall shut automatically, every ounce of anger I carried across three airplanes melting away as the man I love—the man who has always been my best friend—moves toward me.

My lips part, silently begging for him to kiss me. But he doesn't. The space between us stays exactly the same. And disappointment crashes through me just as his voice reaches my ear, low and rough.

"I need to show you what I want instead," he says, his thumbs brushing lightly against my sides as he slowly steps back. "Before this goes any further."

The sudden distance feels colder than the hallway air. I stare at him, searching his face for answers—for anything that might tell me where this is going. But Mitch only reaches for the handle of my suitcase again and starts walking.

After a second, I follow. Because whatever he's about to show me... I already know it's going to change everything.

CHAPTER TWENTY-SEVEN

Mitch

The truck rolls to a stop in front of the brick building, and my stomach flips like I've just stepped off a roller coaster.

Lauren squints into the dying sun and raises a hand to shield her eyes. "Where are we?" she asks, her voice lifting an octave.

Butterflies slam against my ribs as I unbuckle my seatbelt and turn toward her. The air-conditioning hums through the vents and I reach over, turning it down a notch even though I'm already warm.

"Can we talk before I answer that?" I ask.

Lauren releases her seatbelt and turns toward me, confusion tightening her brow. "Mitch... I'm really confused," she mutters. "What are we doing? Why are we here?"

Before I can lose my nerve, I reach forward and take both of her hands in mine. Her skin is warm. Familiar. Home. I slide my thumb along the back of her hand and gently pull it toward my chest, pressing her palm over my heart. It pounds beneath her fingers like it's trying to break through my ribs.

"Peaches," I whisper. "I love you." But the words feel too small for what I'm trying to say. The truth inside me is louder than that. Deeper. But it's the only place I know how to begin.

"I love you, too, Mitch. I always have." Her fingers press harder into my chest, nails biting through the fabric of my shirt. "What the hell happened to us?"

The setting sun pours through the windshield, painting her face in gold and amber. Tears glisten in her eyes, and the sight of them makes my throat tighten.

"I think I know," I say quietly. I release her hand and lift mine to her cheek, tipping her face up until she looks straight at me. "It was me."

Her head jerks back immediately. "No—"

"It was me," I repeat, more firmly this time. "And I wish I had realized it sooner. Before all of this happened." I draw in a slow breath and lean closer. "Lauren… I'm so sorry."

The apology sits between us, heavy and raw.

"I never should have given up on us the way I did. Everything that happened with Tess… that was the worst mistake of my life. And all the stuff I asked you to agree to in Vegas." I shake my head. "That was wrong, too. All of it." My voice softens. "I don't deserve it. But I'm asking anyway." My fingers tighten around hers. "Please, forgive me."

For a moment neither of us moves. Then I reach into the back seat and grab the little plastic bag from the hospital gift shop. It crinkles loudly in the quiet cab.

Lauren tilts her head, eyeing it. "What's that?"

"It's for you," I say, dragging a hand over my head.

Her eyes flick upward immediately, following the slow drag over my scalp.

"You know," she says softly, studying me, "I like it." Her fingers slide up and brush along the short hair at the back of my head. Her nails scrape lightly across my neck and a shiver runs down my spine. "What made you do it?" she asks, still tracing the new line of my hair.

"I needed a change," I admit. "I don't want to be the old Mitch anymore." Then I add quickly, "But I'll grow it back if you hate it."

She laughs under her breath and shakes her head. "I told you. I like it." Her smile softens. "You're like... a new you."

"I am," I say quietly. "Or at least I'm trying to be." I place the bag gently in her lap. "I've had a lot of time to think these last few days. And I realized some things that were holding me back."

"Like what?"

"Like the past," I say, nudging the bag.

She opens it. Then she gasps. "Oh, no way." She pulls the little purple dolphin from the plastic, her face lighting up. "Where did you find him? I thought my Finn was a Pacific Park original."

"Believe it or not, the hospital gift shop," I say with a small smile. I run my hand over the soft purple fur. "Turns out there's a Finn Jr."

"Finn Jr.," she repeats, hugging him to her chest. A tear slips down her cheek and disappears into the dolphin's fur.

"Lauren, I wouldn't trade our past for anything," I say quietly. "Not a single second." I pause. "But I think somewhere along the way... we stopped growing."

Her eyes lift slowly to mine.

"Mavis gave me some pretty incredible advice."

"She did?" Lauren asks through her tears.

I squeeze her knee and nod. "She told me the truth would be easy to follow once I admitted my faults." I let out a slow breath. "And she was right."

Lauren blinks at me, confusion flickering across her face. "I don't understand."

"Peaches," I say gently, running a hand over my hair again. "The promises we made in Vegas... they weren't fair. In fact, they were completely one-sided. Everything we agreed to affected *you*. Not me. And I have no idea how I didn't see that until now."

"That's not true," she protests. "We both made concessions."

I gesture toward the building in front of us. "Do you know what this place is?"

She turns toward the glass doors and studies them before shaking her head.

"It's a fertility clinic." The words settle into the quiet truck like a dropped stone. "And instead of agreeing to *maybe* visit it with you someday," I continue, my voice rougher now. "I should've been on the phone making an appointment the very next morning."

Her breath catches.

"No amount of embarrassment on my part should've stood in the way of our dream of becoming parents."

Tears spill down her cheeks as she presses Finn Jr. tighter to her chest.

I lean closer. "Holding Mirabel made everything crystal clear." My voice thickens. "You and I are meant to start a family together. And I'll be damned if that doesn't happen because of me."

Her shoulders shake.

"I promise you," I say softly, squeezing her knee, "the second they open tomorrow morning… I'm calling to make an appointment."

She nods slowly, wiping her nose with the back of her hand. Her cheeks flush pink, but a small smile breaks through the tears. "Well," she says softly, "while you're on the phone doing that… I have my own end of the deal to follow through on."

"Oh, yeah?" I ask. "What's that?"

She exhales like she's releasing something she's carried for years. "I'm handing Pier Ninety-two over to Miguel. For good. I'm done, Mitch. I'm not rebuilding."

I blink at her, stunned.

"I talked to him while I was stuck in Denver," she continues. "We're still working out the details, but he's going to rebuild it with the insurance money. And he'll love it the same way I once did." Her shoulders lift in a small shrug. "It's just not for me anymore."

For a moment I can't speak. The words I'd secretly hoped to hear for years just came out of her mouth. "Really?" I manage. "You're sure?"

She nods, her fingers tightening around the little purple dolphin. "It took too much out of me," she says quietly. "More than I realized." Her eyes drift toward the windshield, watching the last streaks of sunlight fade across the sky. "The restaurant wasn't the only thing that started consuming my life," she adds softly. "Somewhere along the way, the lines blurred. I got too close to it... and to everything that came with it."

A small breath leaves her chest as I fill in the blank for what she won't name—*Miguel.*

"I can see that now." Her gaze returns to mine, steady and certain. "And I'm not willing to let any of that take another piece of me." Her fingers slide over and squeeze my knee. "You said it yourself, Mitch. I don't have anything to prove." A smile spreads slowly across her face. "I can't keep running a restaurant that drains every part of me just to live in the shadow of my brothers and the Templeton name." Then she grins. "After all... I'm a Benson."

Something inside my chest loosens. Warmth floods through me as the sun sinks lower outside the windshield, bathing the truck in soft orange light.

I lean forward and kiss her. Really kiss her. And her lips move against mine—familiar and perfect and everything I've missed.

The woman from my past. The woman beside me now. The woman I want every tomorrow with.

When I pull back, I brush a kiss across her damp cheek. "It's a good thing you are," I say.

She raises an eyebrow. "Why?"

"Because Templetons might not fail," I say with a crooked grin, "but a Benson sure can."

Lauren laughs, the sound warm and bright as she wraps

her arms around my waist and pulls me as close as the truck's console allows. "The future's ours, Mr. Benson," she whispers. "Wherever it takes us."

I press my forehead against hers. "Just so we're clear," I whisper. "I've loved you every day of our life together." I tap Finn Jr. lightly on the nose. "And I'll love you tomorrow too."

Then I kiss her again, knowing when the sun rises tomorrow, it won't mark the end of our story. It'll be the beginning of our second chance.

THE END

EPILOGUE

Josh

Four Months Later

Mirabel flips from her belly to her back on the living room floor, and the entire room erupts. Cheers. Clapping. Laughter. She kicks her chubby little legs in the air, squealing with delight at the chaos she's caused, her tiny fists waving like she just won the Super Bowl.

"That's my little lady!" Mitch shouts from the floor. He rolls onto his back beside her, laughing like a kid himself. Mirabel squeals louder as he scoops her up and cradles her against his chest, pressing a loud kiss to the top of her head.

Her headband pops loose and Mitch catches the little strip of fabric before twirling it around his fingers and launching it across the room like a slingshot.

"Oh my, God, will you stop taking her headband off?" Mavis snatches it out of the air and wraps it around her wrist with an exaggerated eye roll.

"She doesn't like them," Mitch argues, bouncing Mirabel against his shoulder. "I can tell." Then he blows a raspberry against her belly and she explodes into giggles. The kind of giggles that make everyone in the room laugh whether they want to or not.

From my spot on the couch, I just sit back and watch. And grin like an idiot. Because my daughter just lit up the entire room. My chest feels light. Full. Like something inside me finally clicked into place the moment she showed up in this world.

Across the room, Casey scrolls through her phone, holding it up toward Mavis. "What size dress should I order Mira for the wedding?" She tilts the screen toward her, showing off a royal-blue flower girl dress with a sparkly neckline.

Mavis snorts. "Casey, I have no idea. Who knows how big she'll be a year from now!"

"I know! But take a guess!" Casey insists, already panicking. "I just don't want to forget anything." She presses a quick kiss to Austin's cheek and shoves the phone in his face. "Isn't it precious?"

Austin squints at it for half a second. "Cubbie blue."

Casey beams. "Cubbie blue," she repeats like it's gospel.

On the floor, Mitch pushes himself upright and climbs onto the couch beside Lauren. Mirabel rolls again on the rug, gnawing happily on a plastic frog. "Are you only ordering one?" Mitch asks casually.

Casey blinks at him. "Umm... yeah? Do we need more?"

Mitch slides his arm around Lauren's waist. Then he rests his hand gently over her stomach. And smiles. "We just might."

The room goes silent. Every single head turns. And then Mavis lets out a scream that could probably be heard three houses down. "Oh my, God!" she shouts, already crying. "You guys!"

Mirabel startles at the noise, but Mavis doesn't even notice. "Congratulations!"

I shake my head and grin. Because I've known for weeks. And it's been the hardest secret to hold onto.

Lauren's cheeks flush bright pink as the entire room

explodes into cheers and laughter and a whole lot of very loud Templeton energy.

Mitch jumps off the couch and disappears into the hallway. A second later he comes back carrying the rocking horse he built months ago. He sets it gently on the floor beside Mirabel.

And the look on his face… yeah. There's no question about it. He's going to be an incredible father.

I lean back into the couch cushions and take it all in. My wife—my soulmate since we were kids—sits on the rug bouncing our daughter in her lap. To my right, Austin wraps an arm around Casey while she cries happy tears into his shoulder. And across the room, Lauren presses a hand to her stomach, laughing through the early nausea she tries very hard not to show while Mitch kisses her like he still can't believe this is real.

Six people. Six lives tangled together. And somehow every one of us found the person who makes our world make sense. Because people grow. People change. But in the end, the person meant for you is the one who helps you find yourself again.

I look down at Mavis and brush a kiss across the top of her head.

"I loved you yesterday," I whisper so only she can hear. "I love you today. And I'll love you tomorrow, too."

ACKNOWLEGEMENTS

Thank you for reading *I'll Love You Tomorrow*, book three in the *Trading Heartbeats* trilogy! Releasing this trilogy has been simply incredible. I'm humbled. I'm fortunate. And I'm forever indebted to the kindness and support I've been shown.

Most notably, I owe my sincerest appreciation to Melissa Keir and Inkspell Publishing. Melissa, you continue to demonstrate professionalism, grace, and encouragement each and every day. You brought my dreams of becoming a published author to reality and I'm deeply grateful for your wisdom and belief in me!

Speaking of wisdom, I'd be remiss if I didn't shine a spotlight on my faithful writing partners and beta readers. Thank you, Marcia Bufalo Juarez, Shelby Holt, Elizabeth Chupp, and Kate Boutilier. Because of your insights and willingness to read endless drafts, the *Trading Heartbeats* trilogy is out in the world.

In addition, I stand in awe of both Emma O'Connell and Audrey Bobak, my two incredible editors. Emma, you take my first drafts and point out my nonsense and plot holes with such grace! And Audrey, surely you must be tired of correcting my inability to understand how characters must perform actions… not their body parts!

How gorgeous is this cover? It's unbelievably gorgeous thanks to Shel and Fantasia Frog Designs! Shel, you bring my vision to life every time I work with you. Thank you for your diligent work and creative mind.

My gratitude and appreciation also extend to my

marketing and PR masterminds! Claire Coffey and Daniel Almanza, what would I do without your strategic brains? Thank you for helping me brainstorm, create media lists, and draft press releases. And Silver Dagger Book Tours, Itsy Bitsy Book Bits, and Romance Me With Books, thank you for getting *I'll Love You Tomorrow* into romance readers worldwide!

Lastly, I'm forever thankful to my immediate support system. Mom, you have an eagle eye for proofreading and always have an encouraging word to share. Tommy, my dear husband, you are surely sick to death of my obsession with churning out books. I'm not sure how you tolerate me, but I'm thankful that you do. Lillian, Colton, and Brady, thank you for always going to bed at 7:30PM. You give me a healthy dose of "me time" to get my writing accomplished. I love you more than words can express!

Sneak Peek at TRUSTING LOVE

A New Trilogy by Julie Navickas

CHAPTER ONE

Tess

The paint flakes against my shoulder as I squeeze past the doorframe into Jerry's office, catching just enough to snag my sleeve. Because of course it does. Everything in this place is just broken enough to irritate me.

"Jerry, what's your timeline on the Rosewood Country Club gala piece?" I ask, wrinkling my nose. I can't even fake interest anymore. A charity gala for people who've never had to worry about anything in their lives? Perfect. Exactly the kind of story that reminds me how far off track I've drifted.

"I'm waiting on a call back from the gala's chair, Christina Cashmore," he says, not looking up, fingers tapping steadily across his keyboard. "Need a quote from her before I can finish."

"Think we can make Saturday's paper?" I lean against the frame, arms crossing. "Because right now, I've got absolutely nothing better for the front page."

He shrugs. "No quote, no feature. I left her a voicemail last week and sent two email follow-ups." He shrugs, tipping back in his chair before I see it click. Then his head snaps up. "Wait—don't you know her?"

My stomach knots, tight and sharp, like it's been pulled into a fist. Because yeah. I know her. How could I forget my ex-mother-in-law's best friend? She's just another thread in the tangled mess of my past, still somehow running straight through my present.

I swallow, forcing my face to stay neutral. "I think I can

get you that quote," I say, though the words come out thinner than I'd like.

Jerry's white hair stirs in the ceiling fan's breeze as he nods, like this was inevitable. Like this is exactly where I was always going to end up. "Thought you might."

"Let me make a call," I mutter, already turning away.

The hallway carpet catches the tip of my pink heel—the same snag it always does—and I stumble just enough to swear under my breath. My pulse picks up, a restless flutter building in my chest as I push into my office. I drop into my chair and roll toward the desk, the cheap plastic wheels squeaking in protest.

"Ugh. Susan," I mutter, dragging a hand down my face before grabbing my phone. My thumb hovers over her name.

This is what it's come to. Begging for favors from the woman who used to look at me like I was her daughter. Like I belonged. Before I ruined that, too.

I tap the screen and the ringing fills the room, too loud in the quiet.

One ring. I roll my shoulders, trying to shake off the tension settling in.

Two. I inhale slowly, like I can breathe my way out of the past.

Three. My stomach churns, unease rising fast and sour.

Because I can see her so clearly—perfect posture, sharp eyes, that tight, practiced smile. Judgment wrapped in pearls. Disappointment she never bothered to hide.

I press my lips together, ready to hang up, to pretend I tried, to add this to the long list of things I almost did right, but—

"Tess?"

The sound of her voice hits like a crack straight through my chest. Familiar. Unwelcome. Earned. I swallow hard. "Oh—um, Susan. Hi. Am I catching you at a good time?"

There's a pause. A shift. "Yes, but... forgive me. I'm a little surprised to be hearing from you."

I sink lower in my chair, like I can make myself smaller. "Yeah," I say softly. "I, uh…"

"Must be important."

Yeah. I'm desperate for a quote for a feature no one cares about in a paper that barely matters.

A job I never meant to still be doing. A life I never meant to still be living.

"I guess I'm in a bit of a bind," I say, the words catching on the way out.

"Please tell me this doesn't involve my sons. Or my son-in-law."

My breath catches on the mention of Mitch. Just hearing his name these days is enough to unravel me. I squeeze my eyes shut as the memory hits—his mouth on mine, steady and certain, like something I could've chosen. Like something I didn't deserve to touch.

Don't miss the first two books in the
TRADING HEARTBEATS TRILOGY

Book One
I LOVED YOU YESTERDAY

This new first-person rewrite dives deeper—more intimate, more raw, and a lot harder to look away from. You'll feel every twist in Mavis and Josh's story: the love, the fallout, the longing, and the moments that make you hope (even when you shouldn't). Don't miss your chance to read this second-chance story of love gone wrong—and two people fighting their way back to each other.

Secrets always have a way of coming out.

Mavis Benson made a huge mistake. Scratch that— *colossal* mistake. *Twice.* Sleeping with her high school sweetheart's twin brother definitely wasn't part of the plan... nor was falling in love with him.

But that wasn't the only complication Mavis faced. When an unplanned pregnancy upends her life at seventeen, Mavis skips town to spare her boyfriend, Josh Templeton, from the fallout. With only a letter of apology, she disappears, but not before confiding her secret to Josh's brother, Austin.

When Austin resurfaces in her life years later, he brings the past to Mavis's doorstep. Josh wants her back, Austin isn't willing to surrender, and the path to happiness isn't clear. Caught between both men, Mavis must choose between the brother for whom she broke her own heart, and the brother who picked up the pieces.

I LOVED YOU YESTERDAY is a heart-pounding reveal of best kept secrets. The truth is never easy, and neither is putting down this page turner. Fans of Nora Roberts and K.G. Fletcher will want to get a copy of I LOVED YOU YESTERDAY.

~Winner of a LITERARY GLOBAL BOOK AWARD, CLARION AWARD, 1st place recipient of the BOOKFEST AWARD in contemporary romance, and finalist in the AMERICAN WRITING AWARDS in romance.~

Book Two
I LOVE YOU TODAY

This new first-person rewrite pulls you closer than ever—sharper, more vulnerable, and impossible to put down. You'll feel every beat of Austin and Casey's story: the tension, the missteps, the undeniable pull, and the moments that make you believe in something more. Don't miss your chance to experience this friends-to-lovers romance where love isn't easy—but it just might be worth it.

Casey McDaniels never had a plan—until she met him.

After years of bartending, boyfriend hopping, and chasing her next night out, Casey's ambitions are little more than a blur. That is, until Austin Templeton—a charming, successful lawyer fresh from Los Angeles—moves to Chicago and turns her world upside down.

What begins as an unexpected spark quickly becomes something more. Austin's drive and determination awaken dreams Casey long buried, inspiring her to chase a future she never thought she deserved.

But when his career threatens to pull him back to California, Casey must confront a painful truth: the man who helped her find herself might be the one she has to let go. Because sometimes the hardest choice isn't between love and ambition—it's accepting that you may not be able to hold onto both.

I LOVE YOU TODAY is the enchanting sequel to award-winning I LOVED YOU YESTERDAY, and though it can be read as a standalone, you'll want to start at the beginning to feel every beat of this journey.

~Winner of the HIDDEN BOOKSHELF'S "2022 Book of the Year", 1st place recipient of the BOOKFEST AWARD in contemporary romance, and finalist in the AMERICAN WRITING AWARDS in romance.~

BOTH BOOKS ARE AVAILABLE IN EBOOK, PAPERBACK, AND HARDCOVER WHERE BOOKS ARE SOLD

ABOUT THE AUTHOR

Julie Navickas is a romance author represented by Chip Rice at WordLink, Inc. She is known for her keen ability to tell heart-wrenching, second-chance love stories through relatable characters with humility, humor, and heroism. Her Trading Heartbeats trilogy is the recipient of a Literary Global Book Award and five first-place wins with the BookFest in the contemporary romance category. Her debut trilogy has also earned three finalist designations with the American Writing Awards and a Clarion Award.

Julie is an award-winning university instructor in the School of Communication at Illinois State University and works in corporate communications at COUNTRY Financial. She has earned master's degrees in both organizational communication and English studies, as well as a bachelor's degree in public relations.

Website: https://authorjulienavickas.com/
Facebook:
https://www.facebook.com/AuthorJulieNavickas
Twitter: https://twitter.com/JulieNavickas
Instagram: https://www.instagram.com/julienavickas/
LinkedIn: https://www.linkedin.com/in/julienavickas/
Tik Tok: https://www.tiktok.com/@julienavickas
Threads: https://www.threads.net/@julienavickas
YouTube: https://www.youtube.com/@justwritejulie
Email: julienavickasauthor@gmail.com
Goodreads:
https://www.goodreads.com/user/show/134518278-julie-navickas

www.ingramcontent.com/pod-product-compliance
Lightning Source LLC
Chambersburg PA
CBHW030402180626
46812CB00005B/1894

* 9 7 8 1 9 5 8 1 3 6 4 6 1 *